HIGH ENERGY

OPPOSITES ATTRACT

Tyber had never experienced anything so...*intense*. At that
moment he wanted Zanita more than he had ever wanted
anything in his life.

For a man who was dedicated to explaining anything and
everything in his universe, this was a disconcerting
experience.

He pressed his thumb purposefully along her moist lower
lip, completely opening her for him.

No sense overanalyzing. Some things were better to accept
in life, he briefly thought before he seized her mouth in a
piercingly sweet invasion.

He might not know how to classify her, but he certainly
knew what to do with her.

"What are you doing, Tyber?" Zanita barely managed
to stutter as his arms locked her to him.

"I believe I am about to claim you, Ms. Masterson." The
heated, implacable words were breathed just against her lips.

"Oh, but I don't think—"

"Good. Don't think." His mouth closed firmly over her
own.

WHIRLWIND COURTSHIP

Jayne Ann Krentz

writing as Jayne Taylor

STRANGE BEDFELLOWS

Phoebe was at Harlan's mercy—at the mercy of the cold night and her own inner longing.

"Get in," he said almost tonelessly. "But first take off your jeans. They'll be too uncomfortable to wear inside the sleeping bag."

Phoebe's fingers went reluctantly to the button on her jeans and she stepped out of them under the shelter of the blanket. Harlan watched her, never taking his eyes from her face. A moment later she slid down beside him, reveling in the warmth and fearing the worst.

"This is much better than the floor, isn't it?" he asked.

"It's warmer," she agreed as she lay curled into the heat of his body.

"And more comfortable?" he suggested coolly.

"Yes," she responded stiffly.

"You're wondering what happens next, aren't you?" he persisted wickedly.

"Yes." The word was barely a whisper.

"You," he informed her with a soft, mocking smile, "are just going to have to trust me!"

JAYNE ANN KRENTZ

writing as Jayne Taylor

WHIRLWIND COURTSHIP

DARA JOY

HIGH ENERGY

LEISURE BOOKS **NEW YORK CITY**

To Josephine Mirisola—in physicist's terms, a
constant. This Tyber's for you.
—Dara Joy

A LEISURE BOOK®

March 1996

Published by

Dorchester Publishing Co., Inc.
276 Fifth Avenue
New York, NY 10001

DARA JOY
HIGH ENERGY

"And yes I said yes I will yes"
—James Joyce

Chapter One

"Men? Boil them in oil!"

"You don't mean that."

"Cut off their—"

"Zanita!"

Zanita grinned at her friend Mills. "—*lying tongues.*"

"Uh-huh."

"I *was* going to say lying tongues."

"Sure."

"Okay, so I wasn't. Anyhow, I am through, through, through!"

Mills sighed dramatically. "Haven't I heard this before?"

"I mean it this time, Mills." Zanita slammed her palms down on the kitchen table for emphasis. "I have had it!"

"Really. Was it any good?" Mills tried to hide her smile in her coffee cup.

"Will you be serious? I'm trying to have a discussion here."

Mills sat back in her chair. "Is that what this is? And here I thought you came all the way over here for a good old rant-and-rave session."

Zanita threw up her hands in disgust. "That too!" She looked dismally down into her mug. "It certainly wasn't for your coffee."

"Watch it. Everyone loves my coffee. Just because you happen to prefer brew a spoon can stand up in doesn't make you a reliable critic. And we are getting off the subject—something you are remarkably good at, Zanita."

"Well, what did you expect?"

Mills raised an eyebrow. "Lucidity? Rationality? Perhaps a modicum of believability?"

"All right." Zanita looked her square in the eye. "It wasn't."

"What wasn't?"

Zanita slumped in her chair. "It wasn't any good."

Mills peered at her friend as if she had just come off Mars. Since people often wore that expression around her, Zanita chose to ignore it.

"You didn't!"

"I did." She exhaled. "I don't want to talk about it."

"Then why did you bring it up?" Mills gave her a smug look.

"Okay, okay." Her friend knew her too well. No big surprise. "It was just so . . . *blah*."

Mills blinked several times. "Blah?"

"You're looking at me like that again."

"Like what?"

"Like I come from the mysterious face of Mars."

"Sorry." Mills leaned forward in her chair. "But we are talking about Rick, aren't we? Your current paramour?"

"My last, late paramour." Zanita ran a hand distractedly through her short black curls. "And why are you so shocked?"

Mills leveled her a look. "I shall count the reasons." She ticked her fingers off one by one. "First, as I recall, wasn't it you who said you would never get involved with anyone again after Steve left you with nothing to remember him by except a mountain of debt?"

Zanita closely examined the flowers on the wallpaper to her left. "I guess that was me," she mumbled.

"And wasn't it you who waited two years before going out again with anyone else?"

Zanita peered at the intricate pattern on the tile floor. "I guess that was me also."

Mills nodded to emphasize Zanita's admission. "And wasn't it you who's been dating Rick for three months, telling the poor guy, who happens to be crazy about you, that you want nothing more from him than a platonic friendship?"

Zanita drummed her fingers on the tabletop. "So what's your point?"

Mills zoomed in. "What made you suddenly sleep with the guy?" she bellowed. "And it's a little hard for me to believe a man like Rick would be 'blah' in bed."

Zanita hiked her shoulders. "I don't know why. Maybe I was curious."

"Curious? What kind of a reason is that?"

"I don't know!"

"I can understand passion, or a mad, wild fling, or even good old-fashioned horniness, but curiosity?"

"Get off my case, will you?"

Mills felt instantly contrite. "I'm sorry, Zani, it was just so unlike you. You weren't turned on in the least?"

Zanita grimaced. "No. And despite what you believe, 'blah' describes the experience perfectly. It was all over very quickly."

Mills lowered her voice to what she deemed a serious tone. "Did you . . . ?"

"No." Zanita ran her index finger around the rim of her cup; she was about to make a terrible confession. "Mills, I've—*I've never.*"

Mills eyebrows shot up. "Not ever?"

Zanita sunk further into her chair. "Nope."

"Not even with Steve?"

She sighed. "Not even with Steve."

Both women were silent for a few moments, the absolute

seriousness of the subject demanding the proper respect.

Zanita took a gulp of coffee. "Do you think it's me? I don't think it's me."

Mills was outraged. "Of course it isn't you!"

The two friends sat in silence pondering the dilemma.

Finally, Zanita broke the silence. "Well, what is it, then?"

As was Mills' habit when she was deep in thought, she took a large sip of coffee, then slowly lowered her mug to the table. Zanita knew she wouldn't speak until the sound of the cup hitting the table had faded away. At that precise moment, Zanita could count on Mills having an inspiration.

Here it comes, she thought; *the woman's a genius.*

Mills looked straight at her and pronounced, "It wasn't right."

Zanita's violet eyes blinked twice. "That's it? It wasn't right?" She dropped her head to the table. "Jeez, Mills, give me a break."

"Think about it."

"No." Came the muffled reply from the tabletop.

"Think about it. With Steve, subconsciously you never really trusted him—for good reason, I might add—so you couldn't . . . let your guard down, so to speak. There was always something missing. As for Rick—"

Zanita lifted her head slightly from the table. "Please, no more psychobabble, I beg you."

Mills continued unperturbed. "With Rick, there was *nothing*. No passion. No lust. Ergo *no fulfillment.*"

Zanita sat back up. "You really think so?"

"Yes. Zanita, I've known you practically all my life. When you're in doubt about something, you always hold back. You withdraw into yourself."

"I do?" She thought about it a moment. "You're right. I do. I never realized that before."

"On the other hand, when you feel strongly about something, you jump right into it, head first, no holds barred."

Zanita's tone became distinctly cool. "Are you saying I leap before I look?"

"Drop the affronted act. Face it, girlfriend, you are not by nature a person who is concerned about the end justifying the means."

"Meaning?"

Mills stretched her arms out. "Meaning, you act first, then live with the consequences later."

"So, Dr. Ruth, what does this all have to do with my problem?"

"Everything. When you meet a man who makes you leap before you look, you will be just fine."

"Well, I have nothing to worry about, do I?" she asked sarcastically. "We both know there isn't a man in existence who could befuddle me in that manner."

Mills started giggling, saw Zanita's expression, and quickly placed a hand over her mouth.

"What is so funny? You are supposed to be my friend."

"It's just that I suddenly got this mental picture of some man coming along, tricking you into playing the shell game, and when you don't guess correctly, throwing you over his shoulder and hauling you off to bed."

Their eyes met and they both burst out laughing.

"Talk about slight of hand . . ." This caused another round of laughter.

"Please—" Zanita gasped, holding her sides.

"The hand," Mills giggled, "is quicker than the eye!"

"Stop!"

"N-now you see it—" Mills couldn't finish, she was laughing so hard.

Zanita groaned. "That's terrible."

Mills wiped her eyes with the back of her hand. "Oh, I needed that. Didn't you say something about a seminar tonight?"

"Yes, thanks for reminding me—I need to get down to the student union at Hampshire to sign up for it." Zanita reached for a cookie on the table.

Mills automatically joined her. "I hate these damn things."

"Then why do you buy them?"

13

"Because they're so good." She took a big bite out of the cookie.

"They are good—give me another one."

"Here, take the whole bag—please." She pushed the bag to Zanita. Zanita pushed it back.

"No way. I couldn't stand to see them staring at me in the middle of the night."

"They never last to the middle of the night here." Mills sighed as she took another cookie. "So what's the seminar on?"

"Psychic development," she mumbled around a chocolate chip.

"I didn't know you were interested in stuff like that."

"I'm not—I want to do a piece on this guy who's been going around telling people he's a psychic healer. I've heard some disturbing things about him, but I haven't been able to substantiate anything yet. I thought if I went to a legitimate class on the subject, I could pick up some background information."

"The paper sent you on this story? They're finally letting you do some investigative reporting?"

"Not exactly. I'm doing this on my own."

"Is that wise?"

"I need to do this, Mills. I have to get off garden party assignments. All the Chief ever gives me to cover is fluff. How am I going to get at the good stories unless I take the initiative on my own?"

"Maybe he doesn't want you getting hurt. Stuff like that can be dangerous, Zanita. We both know Hank is a nice old relic from a prior century, but he's been around the block. Maybe he's looking out for you."

"Cripes, Mills, I'm twenty-seven years old! I don't need a curmudgeon of a boss who acts like my grandfather."

"The curmudgeon *is* your grandfather."

"That's beside the point. He used to be a great reporter. In his heyday, he exposed racketeers and gangsters. And a lot of political corruption. I cut my teeth on his stories."

"That was a long time ago. I think Hank is quite content with his small-town newspaper. And every now and then he does keep the selectmen on their toes."

Zanita drank the last of her coffee. "True, but I'm not content. If I can get a *story*, I can go to a major market."

"You mean you'll have a legitimate excuse for abandoning Hank. He's put blood, sweat, and tears into that paper. Sure, it doesn't have a large circulation, but the people around here like it. What's more, they buy it. And you know why."

Zanita closed her eyes. "Because they trust what they read in the *Patriot Sun*." She regarded Mills. "All the more reason for me to get this story. Old Mrs. Haverhill gave this man lots of money because he told her he could cure her stomach cancer with a healing. She died this morning."

"I don't mean this to sound cold, Zani, but the woman had an incurable illness. She would've died anyway."

"True, but she didn't deserve to be bilked and lied to. He took terrible advantage of her when she was in an extremely vulnerable position. It was contemptible."

"I agree. But not all psychic healing is bunk. I've read that many medical practitioners are incorporating the technique into their practices."

"Yes, which makes it even more important to expose the frauds. There are some people who could genuinely benefit from it. If these people end up with a charlatan, it's a tragedy."

"A double tragedy in most cases, I'm sure."

Zanita glanced at her watch. "I've got to run. Thanks for the tea and sympathy."

"You mean coffee and sympathy. Let me know how the class went."

Zanita nodded as she slung her enormous purse over her shoulder and headed out the door.

About an hour's drive west of the city of Boston, the picturesque town of Stockboro, Massachusetts, was surrounded by lovely rolling hills and green pastures. This peaceful, verdant land had once hosted a small but significant skirmish during the Revolutionary War, and the historical setting was the perfect backdrop for an Ivy League campus. In the mid-eighteen hundreds, the town leaders had planted the seed, and Hampshire University was duly harvested.

The community itself was an eclectic blend of intellectuals, jazz musicians, artists, a smattering of bluebloods, surviving sixties drop-outs, and farmers. All dyed-in-the-wool Yankees.

It was an interesting community, where locals tolerated all viewpoints, but were extremely vocal about their own. Everyone was always up in arms over something—a hold-over from Revolutionary days, no doubt.

Zanita loved Stockboro. It was a place where things always seemed to be happening. Alive, moving, and vibrant, its citizens were active in the community and cared about the town they lived in. In short, it was a perfect town for a newspaper.

Despite what Zanita had said to Mills, she did not want to leave the *Patriot Sun*; her greener pastures were right here at home. What she did want was for the Chief to give her some meatier assignments. She knew all too well that she was going to have to show the Chief she was ready in black-and-white.

The course she hoped to take tonight would provide good background information for her story. Zanita planned to do a series of articles on the subject of psychic healing. Knowing the opinionated citizens of Stockboro, she was pretty sure she could stir up a real hornet's nest with the piece.

Swinging her car into the lot by the student union, Zanita got directions from a young coed to the sign-up desk. There, she approached a middle-aged woman, who handed her a listing of the extension classes and special seminars being offered.

Quickly scanning the list, she checked off her choice and handed it back to the woman behind the desk, who was in the process of hanging up the phone.

''This is your lucky day.''

Zanita looked up from a circular a student had just handed her. ''What do you mean?''

''The class you marked has been filled up since the moment

it was announced. I just hung up the phone on a last-minute cancellation.''

"You're kidding!" She had no idea psychic healing classes were so popular. And if the classes were popular, her articles would really hit the—

The woman interrupted Zanita's thoughts. "Oh-oh."

"What 'oh-oh'?"

"I'm sorry, I should've guessed—there's a huge waiting list for this class."

She saw her article flying out the window. "Oh, but you can't!" The woman looked at her strangely. "I mean, I have to take this class. It's really important to me. Please?"

The woman seemed uncomfortable to be put in this position. Zanita decided to press her momentary advantage.

"You might not even be able to get in touch with any of those people on that list at this late time. The class is going to start in an hour. Here I am, ready and willing to attend. How will it look with an empty seat? Besides, you yourself said it was fate.''

The woman threw up her hands in surrender. "Okay, okay! You're in. Just don't tell anyone what I did." She stamped the form.

"My lips are sealed. Thanks a lot—I really appreciate this.''

"You should—I've dealt with some of these people on the waiting list, and they can get weird when they don't get what they want.''

Zanita's violet eyes opened wide. Perhaps she could get a tip-off here? She leaned toward the woman, whispering, "Weird how?"

"Oh, the usual. They throw an academic tantrum of some kind, and somebody gets rearranged. No one would dare mess with that department.''

"Why not?" Zanita took out her pen and pad.

The woman said seriously, "Because they know how to make your house glow in the dark." Then she winked. "Lecture hall 223. Have a nice day.''

17

Zanita was still gaping at the woman in horror as she turned away to help another student.

Do these psychics intimidate people with their so-called abilities? Was that how Xavier LaLeche was able to convince poor Mrs. Haverhill to hand over her bank books? She made a mental note to investigate this angle.

She had just enough time to get a hamburger at the cafeteria. By the time she got to the lecture hall, it was fairly filled. Spotting an empty chair in the third row, she made her way down the stairs, quickly taking the seat. It was strange, but she seemed to be the only woman there.

Her eyes flicked over the chairs in the hall. All men!

And a scruffy lot they were, too.

She briefly felt like tugging on the hem of her short skirt, only none of them seemed to be paying the slightest bit of attention to her legs.

Why not?

She purposely crossed them. Still no response. Very curious.

There was a buzz of excitement racing through the hall which had nothing to do with the shape of her legs. An odd little man sitting next to her confided to her how happy he was to be attending this seminar. His owlish eyes peered at her from behind Coke-bottle glasses as he extended a pudgy hand to her in greeting.

"Stan Mazurski."

She shook his hand. "Zanita Masterson."

"I can't wait to hear him, you know." The little man shook with enthusiasm. "He's quite a maverick—radical in a lot of his viewpoints, but so very brilliant. One of the greatest minds of our times."

So the lecturer had all the earmarks of a cult leader. She was supposed to be impressed with this? "I wouldn't know."

"You've never seen him before? I have—once when I was at Cern, I flew to The Hague to hear him give a talk."

Typical groupie. Poor man. She'd seen his type before. "I hope it was worth it." Her response was dry.

"Oh, yes! He was inspiring, I'll tell you. Turned my thinking around completely."

Damn! Here she thought she was attending a legitimate lecture—not about to hear some cult leader pontificate to his adoring masses. Well, she'd give the guy a chance; there was no sense judging him by one crazed fan. But if his talk even smacked of hoodoo chicanery, she was out of there.

"I hear they offered him a permanent chair at the Institute for Advanced Studies."

This was encouraging, although she had never heard of a psychic research center bearing that name. There was only one university she knew of that had done psychic research, and she had heard they closed the department down. Perhaps she had heard wrong. "Duke University?"

The round eyes blinked twice behind the thick lenses. "N-no, Princeton."

Well! More encouraging still. She would reserve judgment. "He turned it down."

Zanita was about to ask him why, when the double doors to the front of the lecture pit opened, and five men entered the room. Four of the men surrounded one man in the center, eagerly seeking his opinion on various subjects. Even though he was surrounded, Zanita had no trouble seeing him, for he stood head and shoulders above the other men.

He was sinfully handsome.

The second thing she noticed about him was his build. The man worked out—no question about it. It was the best body she had seen in years—maybe ever. He was wearing washed-out denims that hugged sleek thighs. His white tailored shirt was unbuttoned at the collar, the sleeves rolled back to the elbow, revealing muscular forearms.

He had very long chestnut hair, which was streaked golden. It was smoothed back from his face and hung down his back in a ponytail. His skin was a rich golden tan; it complemented his tawny hair color, evoking images of sultry tropical heat. . . .

Someone said something to him which made him smile,

19

causing him to reveal engaging, almost mischievous dimples. Then another person garnered his attention, probably not very interesting, because as this person continued to talk to him, he raised his sights and glanced around the lecture hall.

For a moment, his sharp gaze lit on Zanita before moving on.

She noticed that his eyes were clear, ice blue in contrast to his warm coloring, and seemed to spark with a keen intelligence. In his mid-thirties, his persona conveyed a man possessed of alluring, esoteric knowledge.

The man was captivating.

Zanita swallowed, reassessing her original impression. He wasn't just sinfully handsome; he was outrageously *sexy*.

"Who is he?" she whispered to Stan.

Stan looked up from a manual he was reading. "Who?"

Who? As if she would be asking about anyone else in the room! "The tall guy in the center!"

Stan pushed his glasses back on the bridge of his nose. "That's him!"

"Who?" Zanita gritted out.

"Tyberius Augustus Evans."

The name tickled the back of her mind, but she couldn't quite place it.

"Wait till you hear him speak!"

Zanita was surprised. So this was the psychic guru Stan had been gushing about. Her mouth parted slightly. Of course, charisma was an important part of his profession, so Zanita shouldn't have been so affected by his appearance. But she was. She hadn't been expecting someone that looked like . . . *him*.

This was going much better than she could have hoped for. Even if his talk was boring, she could wile away the time just staring at him. She relaxed in her chair.

Wait until she told Mills about this!

"So, who wants to define Chaos?" Appreciative laughter echoed across the room. Tyberius Augustus Evans rested against the desk in a casual pose, arms crossed over his chest.

His question was the first thing Zanita had understood in the fifteen minutes the man had been talking. He had begun giving her strange looks when he drew something on the board to illustrate a point he was making, and she crossed her eyes. Since then, his glance had strayed her way every now and then, his expression not unlike Mills' earlier in the day. The mysterious face of Mars look.

She had never realized that psychic healing was so . . . *obtuse*. At last something she could understand. Who would have thought the man would ask a trivia question? She tentatively raised her hand.

Tyber's eyebrows rose as the small hand went up. It had been a rhetorical question. He did not expect anyone to try an answer. More to the point, phrased that way, no one *could* answer it. He looked warily at the young woman with the remarkable violet eyes in the third row. "Yes?"

"KAOS were the bad guys who went against CONTROL on the TV show *Get Smart*."

Dead silence followed her comment.

A rich, deep laugh broke through the silence, echoing in a room which had gone as still as a tomb.

Tyber, still laughing, grinned up at her. "You're right, Ms.—?"

"Masterson, Zanita."

"Named after the manzanita tree, no doubt."

Zanita's mouth dropped open. "How did you—"

He turned back to the class. "Along with Ms. Masterson's definition, Chaos is also a behavior. This behavior has three properties: It is ergodic; it occurs in systems with a few degrees of freedom; and it displays sensitive dependence on initial conditions."

"*Excuse me*." Zanita spoke up. "But what does this have to do with healing?"

Tyber stared at her, speechless for a moment. He couldn't recall that ever happening to him before. "Nothing."

He was giving her that look again. "Oh." She thought

about it a moment. "Are you talking about crystals?" Psychics seemed to be enamored of crystals.

The man suddenly became very interested. "In what manner?"

"Well . . . I hear the vibrations . . ."

He jumped on her words. "You mean the resonance? I hadn't thought about that before. Go on," he urged her.

"I—I—" She threw up her hands, at a loss. "They transmit energy?"

He looked at her, astonished. "That's brilliant!"

Zanita scrunched her shoulders and warily glanced around the room. She had no idea what he had been talking about, and now she had no idea what *she* had been talking about. But he thought he knew what she was talking about.

The man was a kook.

She peeked at him. A gorgeous kook, but a kook. Time to leave.

She started to stand, adjusting the shoulder strap on her bag. "Look, I—"

He walked purposely towards her, his glance briefly flicking to her legs. At least *he* noticed; the thought danced at the back of her mind. At the forefront of her mind was getting away from this nutcake pronto.

"You realize that pendulum action is quite different, even when—why are you backing up the stairs?"

"I really, *really* have to go. You see, I didn't realize psychic healing was so intense, and I—"

"*Psychic healing*?" There it was again. That speechless sensation. He focused on her with interest now. "This is a physics seminar."

She looked totally confused, and, he had to admit, rather adorable.

"How did you—" His eyes twinkled in sudden amusement as he correctly assessed the situation. "Ahh. Not much of a speller, are you?"

Zanita blanched. "Physics?" she mouthed.

"Physics," he affirmed.

"Yuck!" She quickly looked at him. "I'm sorry, that just sort of—slipped out, Mr. Evans. I mean, Mr. Doctor—I mean, Dr. Evans." God, she sounded like a total jerk! Now the man was laughing at her!

He grinned, flashing her a dimple. "Tyber will do."

The whole class started laughing. Zanita wanted to crawl up the stairs and out the door. She started backing up the stairs again, feeling like a complete idiot. Tyber Evans just kept on advancing, totally enjoying the situation.

"You, Ms. Masterson, are unpredictable—what we physicists would call a random element. Very interesting . . ."

"Random element! Thanks a lot. You make me sound like some—some—"

Tyber raised an eyebrow as if daring her to complete the sentence accurately. *Arrogant* kook. She raised her chin in the air. "If you'll excuse me?"

"Not so fast." He folded his arms across his chest and leaned against the wall. "Not much on physics, are you?"

She stopped a moment to get her bearings. The sight of him leaning against the wall, smiling devilishly at her, had unnerved her. *Jeez, he was gorgeous.* She twisted a curl of her hair, a habit she had when nervous. "Well . . ."

"Hmm . . . as I suspected." He tapped his chin with a forefinger. "You know, I could open up a whole new universe for you. Why don't you stay for the course? I realize much of this won't mean anything to you, but you might pick up some intriguing ideas along the way. Much better than psychic healing classes. Of course, I'm prejudiced."

The man was asking her to stay in the class. Physics . . . *bor-r-ring.* How was she going to politely refuse this paragon in front of all these people? She decided to hedge and give him a way out. "I don't know. It's a little . . . dry."

His eyes sparkled. She knew right then he was not going to take the bait.

"*Dry*? Now you've challenged me, Zanita. I'm going to show you how *exciting* it can be."

He was talking about physics, wasn't he? By his expression,

Dara Joy

she wasn't so sure. Well, she had given him his out and he chose not to take it. "Thanks a lot, but—"

"No thanks necessary. The joy is in the teaching." His eyes danced as if they held secrets he would be more than willing to share with her. He came up on the same step and placed a warm hand at her back, gently but firmly urging her back to her seat.

"It's like this: you blundered in here, now we're going to keep you. Right, lads?" He addressed the class at large.

The class heartily concurred. Not that Zanita expected them to do anything else. It was obvious that the sun rose and set on this man as far as they were concerned.

Stan turned in his seat, grinning up at her. "You're stuck with us, Zanita."

She turned to look up at Tyber, who stood over her shoulder. He knew very well he had cornered her.

He winked! Who was he to . . .

She suddenly remembered where she had heard his name before.

Tyberius Augustus Evans was a brilliant, renowned eccentric, who held thousands of patents on various devices and was sought out by heads of state, scientists, business corporations, research facilities—in short, by anyone who thought they could get something from him. His explorations, which he conducted in the privacy of his walled estate, took him down various paths of endeavor. From what she remembered, some were sublime; some seemed to her sort of silly. But who was she to judge? The general consensus was that everything he produced displayed the rare genius he was known for.

What else could she recall? Ah, yes. He worked strictly by himself; in other words, he did not owe his soul to the company store. He guarded his privacy, and he never, *never*, gave an interview.

She smiled slowly at him. *Random element, indeed.*

The information she needed on psychic healing she could pick up elsewhere. She still fully intended to investigate Xavier LaLeche, but a class on psychic healing wasn't anywhere near as important as the possibility of gaining an interview with this man.

In a lightning display of deductive reasoning that would have fascinated Tyber had he been aware of it, Zanita calculated her chances. There was no real decision to make.

"I'll stay." The class applauded, but she barely noticed. Her sights were on Tyberius Augustus Evans.

Tyber narrowed his eyes slightly as he studied the woman in front of him. She had the look of his cat. Yes, when the cat was about to do something very cunning.

Tyber smiled to himself. He always loved a mystery.

He knew exactly what to do next.

The first step was to test the water. As she was taking her seat, he decided to shake her up a bit. Just to get it rolling.

"I'm going to follow up on that idea of yours."

She looked up at him in horror. Had he seen through her already? "What idea?" Her voice wavered.

"Vibration." He leaned down to whisper in her ear. "Energy." His warm breath tickled the side of her neck. "*Resonance . . .*"

She swallowed nervously, refusing to look at him. It was uncomfortably obvious to Zanita that for whatever reason, the man had taken up the challenge.

It was also obvious that he intended to enjoy it.

She sighed as her earlier conversation with Mills passed through her mind. Here was the perfect justification for her convictions. Damn, but he had a mischievous look on his handsome face.

Nothing was ever simple when a man was involved.

Boil them in oil.

Chapter Two

"That is why, in later years, Newton was responsible for sending several men to their death on the gallows. We physicists don't get mad; we get even."

The class laughed appreciatively at what Zanita suspected was in-house humor.

"Those of you who know me," Tyber went on, "know that I'm not much for a structured academic environment. What say we meet tomorrow night at Mickey D's on Route Nine?"

"The playground?" someone yelled out from the back of the room, making everyone laugh.

Tyber grinned. "Not a bad idea, but I'd hate to have to defend my place in line at the slide—some of those kids are meaner than I am. I think inside should be acceptable. How many of you can make it?" Almost the whole class raised their hands. Zanita was a noticeable exception.

"That many. I don't think we should have too much of a problem, as it's after the dinner hour. Okay, so tomorrow night—same time, different location." The class applauded the lecture as they vacated their seats.

Tyber's icy eyes lit on Zanita. "Ms. Masterson. I wonder if I might have a few words with you before you leave?"

Zanita, who had been slinging her bag over her shoulder, looked up in surprise and nodded.

Tyber, having got her consent, turned to a colleague who was asking him a question.

By the time Zanita made her way to the front, Dr. Evans was already surrounded by a group of sycophants who were panting around him like starving academic dogs—not that she wouldn't have liked to pant around him as well, but for entirely different reasons.

She waited patiently toward the back of the small crowd for the intellectual fallout to clear. After about fifteen minutes, Zanita started getting impatient, as the adoring masses did not seem to be thinning out. She was weighing the prospect of leaving against the slim chance of gaining an interview this evening when Tyber glanced her way and skillfully called a halt to the chit-chat, promising to continue the discussion tomorrow evening.

The room emptied so fast, you might have thought an air raid siren had gone off.

Of course, these guys would have gone *toward* ground zero, not away from it.

Zanita smiled to herself; it had certainly been an interesting evening.

Tyber folded his arms across his chest and leaned back against the desk. "You didn't like the class, did you?"

Zanita was surprised. "Why do you say that?" She thought she had managed to hide her confusion very well.

"You didn't raise your hand when I asked who could make it tomorrow evening. And there was that other thing . . ."

"What other thing?"

"The way you kept crossing your eyes whenever I drew an illustration on the board."

Zanita cleared her throat. "All right, I'll admit I wasn't overly enthused, but I did warn you." She threw her arms up. "Frankly, I had no idea what you were talking about."

27

"So, just because you were lost in a fog you're not coming tomorrow? Really, what kind of a reason is that? Most people go through their whole lives not understanding a damn thing. In that context, what's a few evenings spent in my lectures by comparison?"

His obtuse reasoning completely escaped her. She blinked. "What?"

"Tomorrow will be quite different—I promise. No mathematics of any kind. That's why I suggested the restaurant; not having blackboards will keep it honest." His smile was heart-stopping.

She decided then and there that nothing would keep her from going tomorrow night—interview or not. What sane woman would forego the pleasure of discreetly ogling him? Besides, whatever made him think she wouldn't come?

"I never said I wasn't coming. You assumed that because my hand didn't go up when you expected it to. I had every intention of going; I just wasn't in the mood to admit it."

Tyber stared at her, speechless. Again. When he did speak, his voice held a note of awe. "You are completely non-linear, Zanita."

She waved her hand. "I have no idea what that means, but I suspect it has something to do with the mysterious face of Mars looks I get—see? Like that one you're wearing now."

"Fascinating," he muttered. "So, you are coming?"

"Yeah. See ya tomorrow night, Doc." She waved goodbye as she headed quickly up the stairs, before Tyber had a chance to say another word.

It wasn't until she got to her car that she wondered why it mattered to him whether she showed up or not.

"Mills, he is to die for."

Zanita plowed her fork into the carton of Chinese take-out she had brought over to her friend's house.

"We are talking about the physicist, aren't we?" Mills asked around an eggroll. "Somehow I can't quite picture—"

"Trust me. To Die For. Of course I can't figure out what

he's talking about half the time. I mean, you'd have to be a rocket scientist to understand—''

"He *is* a rocket scientist." Mills pointed out.

"Oh, yeah." Zanita shrugged."At any rate, this is the best assignment I've ever had. If he would grant me an interview, just think—''

"He's not an assignment."

Zanita looked at her. "Well, no, not exactly . . ."

"What makes you think he'll give you an interview when he's turned down everyone else? No offense, Zanita, but you're not exactly Edward R. Murrow, or even Barbara Walters, or for that matter Yolanda Neade." Yolanda Neade was a ditsy local newscaster on a non-network-affiliated television station. Mills wasn't pulling any punches.

"This is true, but I have something they don't have."

Mills looked at her friend askance. "What, pray tell, is that?"

Zanita batted her eyelashes. "I am *non-linear*."

"Say what?"

"I have no idea, either, but Doc Evans seemed very interested in it."

Mills snorted. "Uh-huh. As Whoopi said, 'Girl, you in danger.' ''

Zanita grinned. "I wish. Believe me, the man is odd. Gorgeous, but odd. The most I can hope for is an interview with him. And I would be more than satisfied with that."

"Satisfied *is* the operative word here. Maybe he's the one."

Zanita swallowed a cashew. "The one what?"

"To *befuddle* you."

"Befuddle me as in make me crazy, roll around in the hay, knock my socks off, befuddle?" Mills nodded lecherously. "Tyber? I don't think so. I mean, he does have a body that won't quit, and he is sexy beyond words, but . . ."

"But?"

"He's . . . a kook."

Mills raised an eyebrow as if to say, When has this little aberration ever stopped a hot-blooded man?

"No. No, believe me, you have this all wrong. I'm sure he would never notice me in that way. He probably isn't interested in such base interactions, being so . . . so intellectually lofty."

"Right."

"Seriously. He might see me as interesting in some bizarre way known only to him." She thought of his expression and the tone of his voice when he had told her he was going to follow up on her idea, whatever *that* had been. "But only because he thinks he can teach me to understand what he's talking about."

Mills choked on her tea. "Zanita! I have no idea what you are saying! Do you?"

"Well, no. But don't blame me—it's Tyber's doing. No one could possibly understand a thing he says." She sighed. "This is not going to be a piece of cake."

As if her words were an omen, when she walked into the fast-food restaurant, Tyber was wolfing down a piece of cake a little girl had handed him. He looked up as she approached the tables where several men from the class, including Stan, were eating hamburgers and fries.

The past twenty-four hours had, if anything, enhanced his appeal. He was just as sexy as she remembered.

There was something about the man that invited touching.

His incredible pecs couched inside the soft cotton of his casual shirt, perhaps? His strong column of toasty warm throat? The boyishly intriguing dimples in his mischievous smile? The incredible intelligence behind his eyes?

It struck her anew how very different he was—not what one would expect at all.

"Hi. Want a sip?" He held out his chocolate shake to her. She eyed the drink dubiously, remembering the pasty taste from her high school years all too well.

"No, thank you. Who's the kid?"

Tyber shrugged. "It's her birthday. She gave us all a piece of her cake. Whether we wanted it or not." He winked at her.

"Fortunately, I'm a sucker for frosting." He licked a dollop off his finger.

It was an innocent gesture on his part, but for some reason Zanita couldn't take her eyes off that tongue slowly swirling around the edge of his long, beautifully tapered finger. The gesture so fascinated her that she stood riveted, watching him.

"I did promise you I'd be honest tonight."

"Wh-what?" Her face rose guiltily to his.

"The lecture." His eyes sparked expressively in his incredibly handsome face. "I think after tonight I'll have you hooked."

"Hooked?" She knew she sounded like a parroting idiot, but she couldn't get the sight of that sensuously swirling tongue out of her mind. Why did he have to look so sinfully delicious? What would that tongue feel like swirling against—

"Like peanut butter to jelly," he affirmed.

She swallowed convulsively, dispelling the image *that* provoked.

Tyber scooted over in the booth, making room for her to sit down.

Stan, having devoured his mountain of ground beef and grease; noticed her as she took her seat. "So you haven't given up on us, eh, Zanita? Good for you!"

Zanita glanced sideways at Tyber, who smiled softly at her. Even seated, he seemed to tower over her. "I didn't really have a choice, Stan."

Stan, completely misinterpreting her remark, replied, "I know what you mean. Doctor Evans is inspirational!" He grinned broadly at Tyber, who winced under the unexpurgated devotion.

Looking around the restaurant, he said, "We might as well start this."

He levered himself up on top of the back of the seat, straddling two booths with his long, jean-clad legs, and addressed the group. "I thought tonight we'd informally discuss artificial intelligence and some related topics . . ."

31

While Tyber spoke, the ultimate artificial life form, the restaurant clown, listened in, peering over Stan's shoulder intently, his orange hair glowing under the fluorescent lighting. Several stragglers from the class wandered in. Eventually they had to move out to the playground to make room for everybody. Even the clown followed them outside, his broom dragging on the ground behind him.

There in the playground, under the stars, with a gentle breeze in the night air, Tyber spoke of the mysteries of the universe from the top of a slide. Zanita thought him the most interesting and unconventional man she had ever seen.

Frogs croaked, shooting stars fell, owls hooted, and trees rustled in the wind as he discussed, in plain terms, bringing together seemingly dichotomous subjects such as absolutism underlying relativistic principles.

What fascinated Zanita most was his way of taking several divergent topics and bringing them together into a cohesive unit, pointing out similarities in subjects not often talked about synonymously. He was brilliant.

He was a man captivated by ideas, both the sublime and the ridiculous. His genuine curiosity about every aspect of the nature of the universe was contagious. The group was entranced by his enthusiasm as he delved into explorations of both the known and the unknown.

"Facts always remain absolute," he said. "It's everyone's point of view that is different, relativistic, although, paradoxically, everyone believes 'their' point of view is the correct or 'proper' one. As Einstein pointed out quite a while ago: 'I'm right and everything else is relative.' If one listens to two politicians in a political debate, one is observing the Theory of Relativity." Everyone laughed.

"And on that note, I believe we'll call it a night. I thought it might be interesting if we caught the new science fiction picture playing at the cinema at the mall in Stockboro tomorrow. I hear there are some intriguing ideas at work on the nature of space travel and xenobiology. We can have an open discussion afterwards if anyone's interested." Everyone was very much interested—including the clown, who asked if he could join in. He was assured he could.

Tyber caught up to Zanita in the parking lot as she was heading for her car.

"So—how was that? Did I keep my promise?"

Zanita smiled at him. "You did. In spite of myself, I was fascinated like everyone else."

"Hmm . . . not quite what I was aiming at, but it is a start."

She reached her car and unlocked the door. "As a friend told me recently, in certain matters I would do well to leap before I look." Of course, Mills had been referring to a totally different subject. "You have piqued my interest, Doc. I will be there tomorrow night."

He placed his hands against the door of her car, leaning down to speak to her through the open window. "It is you who has piqued my interest, Zanita. Did I tell you I have a cat? No? Well, I do. Good night."

Now what did he mean by that? she wondered.

The following evening, she waited for the group in the lobby of the movie theater, trying desperately to stay awake. She had gone to visit her grandparents at their farm last evening after the class. Her grandfather had been sitting out on the front porch, idly rocking on the swing, enjoying the unusually balmy October weather. The natives called it Indian summer, and every New Englander knew to enjoy the brief respite while it lasted, for it presaged the coming winter.

As usual, it didn't take long before they were heatedly "discussing" a current topic of town politics. Zanita always liked engaging Hank in such discussions, often playing devil's advocate just to rile the old man. Hank was something when he got going on a subject he cared about; and Hank really cared about everything that went on in Stockboro, and for that matter, the world at large. In her opinion, it was one of the traits that had made him a great reporter. No story was ever *just* a story to him.

Unfortunately, she had succeeded only too well in riling him up, for the discussion went on well past midnight, with neither one of them aware of the time. It wasn't until her grandmother came out onto the porch dressed in her robe to shoo them inside that they came to their senses.

Due to the hour, Zanita elected to spend the night in her old bedroom. When she made her decision, she hadn't counted on The Hogs hitting town.

It was around two in the morning when the pack squealed into the backyard, reminding her of a motorcycle gang storming into a town for the fun of causing mayhem. The "defiant ones" snorted and snuffled in glee, causing her to sit bolt upright in bed.

She cautiously lifted the shade on the window in time to see the little picket fence which surrounded her grandmother's rose garden crash over. Stomping pig feet echoed in the night.

Her grandmother's garden was trampled in a random display of violence before the herd inexplicably moved on.

Hank was fit to be tied.

The Hogs resided with their neighbor, Joe Sprit, who lived several miles down the road. Every now and then, for reasons known only to The Hogs, they escaped their pen to take a midnight foray through the town. It had been going on for years. Zanita referred to it in her goofier moments as "The Night of The Hogs."

Since no one was sure how to deal with the problem, they tended to live with it. Joe claimed he had reinforced the fencing several times, but somehow, when The Hogs wanted out; they got out. When a Hog had mayhem on its mind, there was little a human could do.

So now, she ruminated facetiously, she was just grist for the Hog mill. Deciding that some fresh air might revive her, she walked outside to the front of the theater. It wasn't long before she saw Tyber pulling into the lot on the back of a Harley-Davidson. Somehow she was not surprised.

He slung his helmet over the bars, spotting her at once. Smiling a greeting, he walked her way, looking altogether too sensuous and sinewy. He wore black, thigh-hugging jeans with

34

black boots. A gray shirt and cuffs turned back on his forearms completed the dangerous look. His long hair was tied back, once again, in a ponytail. She wondered what it would look like loose about his shoulders, silently thanking him for not putting her through that torture.

"Waiting for me?" He greeted her with a grin.

Unashamedly arrogant. "Getting some air. Everyone's waiting for you inside."

He nodded, steering her through the door. "I have a confession to make—I really wanted to see this picture, and I hate going to the movies alone."

"So you engineered it so the whole class would accompany you? Talk about abuse of power. . . ."

"Afraid so. I'll tell you what—to make it up to you, I'll buy your ticket. But you have to buy the popcorn."

"What kind of a deal is that? The popcorn in this place is more than my rent."

"I never said I was stupid." He winked at her, revealing that engaging dimple.

After greeting the class and telling them to meet after the movie in the mall court, he drew her determinedly over to the refreshment stand.

"A jumbo deluxe popcorn," he told the girl behind the counter.

"Thanks a lot! Why don't you get Stan to buy your popcorn for you? I'm sure he'd be more than willing."

He considered her question for a moment. "Because Stan doesn't have legs like yours."

That shut her up. He *had* noticed. "You shouldn't talk to your students like that."

He threw her a look. "You're not a student, and this is not a classroom. It's a seminar—for *colleagues*." He fished his wallet out of his back pocket to pay the girl.

"I am not a colleague of yours, and I said I would pay for that."

"I'm aware of that. As for the popcorn—I was joking."

"But—"

35

"Let's go see the movie."

As he led her to their seats, she got the uncomfortable feeling that she had somehow been maneuvered into a date without ever agreeing to one, or for that matter being asked to one. The sneaking suspicion crossed her mind that Tyber could have manipulated the entire class just for that purpose. But that was absurd. Why would he do such a thing?

She felt an elbow nudge her side.

"You're falling asleep again, Ms. Masterson. I don't mind, but the two rows behind us are complaining about your snores."

"I don't snore." She mumbled, falling into a doze again.

Jab.

"Will you quit it?"

"Why are you so tired?" he whispered low in her ear, sending a frisson down her bare neck. "Is my company that boring?" His heated breath teased against her.

"No, it's The Hogs," she murmured sleepily, turning unconsciously toward his warmth.

He was amused by both her response and her action; she was just short of snuggling into him. He casually put his arm around her, drawing her closer, pitching his voice low. "I beg your pardon?"

"The Hogs were on the prowl last night—God, you smell good." She promptly fell back asleep.

Hogs? What hogs? He looked askance at the sleeping bundle of woman in his arms. Curiouser and curiouser, he thought. And soft. Definitely soft.

He decided he liked the feel of her sleeping in his arms.

She awoke toward the end of the movie, mortified to find herself burrowed into Tyber's chest. Worse yet, she had managed to fit her head into the crook of his neck, her forehead flush against the warm skin of his throat. His chin was resting on the top of her head as he watched the movie; his arm was casually draped across her shoulders.

This was so unprofessional of her! Thank God the rest of the group were scattered throughout the darkened theater. Hopefully, they were too engaged in the movie to pay any attention to the two of them.

Damn! How could she ever expect the man to take her seriously now? He'd never give her the interview she wanted. And how did one extricate oneself from such a position gracefully?

Tyber's hand slowly rubbed her back, causing her to instantly stiffen.

"I know you're awake," he said into her hair.

"Can we pretend I didn't do this?" she asked in a small voice against his chest.

"Of course not." His husky tone held more than a hint of amusement.

Zanita quickly disengaged herself, affronted. "That's not very chivalrous of you."

Tyber did not seem particularly concerned about chivalry. "Do you often fall asleep in a public place in the arms of the person next to you?"

Before she could summon up a suitable retort, he grinned wickedly at her. "You talk in your sleep."

Zanita flushed, opened her mouth like a fish, then closed it. What had she said? Oh, God. Would he even tell her? Those damn Hogs!

She wisely stayed silent until the end of the picture, sitting ramrod straight in her chair, trying desperately not to look embarrassed.

When the movie ended Tyber took her hand as if he had every right to, leading her out to the mall court.

"Relax, Curls, you didn't say anything too revealing." He scratched his chin in thought. "Except for the part about the sexual aids hidden in a shoebox under your bed."

She stopped and stared at him, horrified.

He laughed out loud. "It was just a lucky guess, really."

She tried to tug her hand away from him; he held firm.

"I have no such thing! You're terrible—"

"That's not what you said in your sleep," he teased.

She blushed crimson. Considering her shameless thoughts about him, she might have said anything. Anything at all. She ran her fingers through her hair in a nervous gesture. Forget the interview; this was too embarrassing to be endured. What must the man think of her?

"L-Look,Tyber, I really have to get going; it's late."

"Oh, no you don't." He laced his fingers through hers. "You're not running away. You tried that once before with me, and it didn't work."

"Please, Doctor Evans . . . this is so embarrassing."

"You do seem to have a penchant for getting yourself into situations." He smiled remorselessly at her while maintaining his firm hold on her hand.

"I do not!" His disbelieving look compelled a modicum of honesty. "Okay; so sometimes I get myself into sticky—what did I say to you?" she demanded.

"You didn't say all that much in your sleep, Zanita." He thought it tactful to leave out her comment about how good he smelled. "Although I have to ask myself *why* you're so nervous about what you *think* you might have said."

"You rat!" She blurted out before thinking. "You let me think I—" She stopped abruptly, realizing what she had almost revealed.

"You were about to say?" He raised an eyebrow expectantly.

That you're gorgeous beyond words and I was wondering if you were as sexy in bed as you look. "You let me think that I might have revealed confidences entrusted to me by my friends," she prevaricated.

"Your nose is growing. However, I apologize if I've embarrassed you in any way." His voice was overly sincere. "Let me buy you an ice cream cone so we can be friends again."

"You may buy me an ice cream cone, but we are not exactly friends."

"Nonsense; you've slept in my arms, Curls. What flavor would you like?"

"Monkey crunch and stop calling me by that ridiculous name."

His gaze traveled assessingly over her short black hair. "Oh, I don't know—it seems to fit." He ordered their cones, his eyes twinkling at her as if he were just waiting for her to snap back at him.

Was he purposely irritating her just to irritate her?

She was about to let him have it with both barrels when the rest of the group caught up with him. "Saved by the cavalry." Her tongue swirled around the ice cream as if to punctuate her statement.

"Lucky me," he murmured. "Can I taste?" He didn't wait for her answer, leaning down to take a lick of her ice cream.

While his attention was focused on the cone in her hand, his head was on a level with hers. He slowly raised his eyelashes, meeting her eyes. Their lips were only a few inches apart.

He stared intently at her for several heart-stopping moments.

Zanita felt as if her stomach had fallen to the floor only to bounce back into her ribcage.

"Mmm—just what I like: not too sweet, varied texture, unusual flavor, with a creamy consistency." He licked the cone one more time, his eyes never leaving hers. "Want to try mine?"

He was shameless.

An unconventional, incredibly alluring, no-holds-barred kook!

Zanita *really* liked him.

He held his cone out to her. She tentatively licked his Coconut Brazilian Mud Rainbow Brownie Jubilee.

"Well?" He prompted her.

"It—it's *different*."

"Different good or different yuck?" He raised his brows in inquiry as if they were really talking about ice cream.

Zanita smiled secretively, not about to admit to anything. "I'm not sure yet."

Tonight, the last of the lecture series, he spoke about magnetic sails powering spaceships, hydrogen mining around Jupiter, and cryogenics. All the while licking an ice cream cone.

The clown, who turned out to be an undergrad philosophy student, surprised everyone by intelligently adding his twist to the topic. Soon everyone was debating ethics instead of theory.

Zanita dived into the discussion with both feet, loving nothing better than a rousing debate. She was not at all intimidated by the totally male group. Hank had raised her to voice her opinions, and voice them she did. Several times, as she touted her viewpoint, she noticed Tyber watching her intently, often unconsciously shaking his head in agreement with her comments.

The discussion was so lively, the group failed to notice that all the stores had closed and the lights were shutting off. Mall security ended up throwing them out.

Tyber thanked them all for coming to the class. Several of the members, including Stan, wondered if they might meet on a regular basis to continue the off-beat discussions. It was not what they had originally expected, but everyone had enjoyed it immensely.

Tyber, not without some amusement, said he would consider it. In truth, he had thrown away his original notes for the last two classes in the hope of keeping one small, violet-eyed woman interested in coming to hear him.

But then, he knew, better than most, that some of the best discoveries in science and life were accidental in nature.

Stan pulled out a pad of paper, handing it around for everyone's name and phone number, which he then dutifully handed to Tyber, leaving the decision in his court, since he was the motivating factor. Zanita bet it did not escape any of the men here that being in a regular discussion group with Tyberius Augustus Evans would grant them a certain professional elitism.

Tyber folded the paper, placing it in his shirt pocket, again

40

thanking everyone for coming. Zanita wondered if he would actually pursue the group. From what she knew of him, she tended to doubt it; he was a maverick and a loner by nature.

The crowd wandered off, leaving the two of them conspicuously standing there.

"Zanita, would you—"

"Tyber, can I—"

They spoke at the same time.

They both laughed. Tyber gestured. "You go first."

"Tyber, I was wondering if . . . well, I know you don't usually do this, I mean as far as I know, you've never done it, and I know you haven't known me long, but still, perhaps . . ."

He grinned at her. "Zanita, what are you talking about? It can't possibly be what it sounds like."

She swallowed, gathering her courage, knowing this was probably the only opportunity she'd have. "Would you give me an interview?"

He looked at her stunned. "*What*?"

"I'm a reporter for—"

His expression changed instantly. Gone was the smiling, approachable man. "I see. I should have known." He seemed terribly disappointed for some reason. "Was it all an act? Blundering into class and—"

"No! I had no idea who you were; I mean, not right away. I meant to take a psychic healing class for a story I hope to do and—"

"I see. Opportunity knocked." The sarcasm in his voice was evident. "No wonder you reminded me of my cat."

Her shoulders slumped. This wasn't going at all well. And what was that crack about his cat?

"What paper?" he demanded in disgust. "*The Globe*?"

"No."

"*Time*?"

"No."

"*People*?"

"No."

He looked at her inquiringly.

"The *Patriot Sun*."

He seemed surprised at first; then he visibly relaxed, breaking into a huge grin. "The Stockboro daily gazette?"

"You don't have to say it like that!"

"Like what?" He suddenly reached out, curling an arm around her neck to draw her close.

"Like you're—what are you doing?"

"Doing?" Despite his innocent gaze, he had a definite look of mischief about him. "Why, I'm answering your question. I'm relieved, Ms. Masterson. For a moment there, I thought you were a *real* reporter."

Her violet eyes went glacial. "I *am* a real reporter."

"Well, I'll try not to think of you as one."

"Thank you very much!"

He leaned forward, surprising her by kissing the tip of her nose. "You know what I mean." She pushed against his chest in a vain attempt to break his hold.

"No, I don't. And you are being presumptuous."

"Yes, you do," he countered. "And perhaps I am."

"You—" She wrinkled her nose, having lost the thread of the conversation.

He chuckled at her expression. "Forget it. Listen, I'm having an end-of-class, Indian summer pool party at my house on Saturday. Here's the address." He tore off a scrap of the paper Stan had given him, scribbling quickly on it. "You're invited to come—two o'clock. But *no interview*." He tapped her nose to emphasize the point. "Should I expect you?"

She looked down at the scrap of paper in her hand. She had heard vague stories about his house, something about it being very weird and very private. He was giving her the opportunity to view it. Perhaps she could change his mind about the interview, and if not, she could always write about his house. And who knew who else might be there at the party suitable for an interview?

Besides, she wanted to see him again. He was too fascinating not to want to see again. Of course she would come.

"I'll be there. Thank you Tyber; I look forward to it, but

I'm not promising that I won't try to change your mind.''

"Why would you want to change a perfectly good set of beliefs, Zanita?" His dry tone mocked her.

"On the interview only," she clarified.

"Whatever you think. Goodnight, Curls; see you Saturday."

Zanita never suspected that she had just been masterfully lured into playing the shell game.

Chapter Three

The sign on the high stone wall read, "My Father's Mansion."

Zanita stopped her car before the heavy wooden gate. *Looks like something out of the Middle Ages*, she thought. The high wall and copious trees and bushes beyond obscured whatever form My Father's Mansion took.

So how did one gain entrance through these imposing walls?

Spotting a grilled intercom at a level with the driver's side window, she reached over, pressing the red button.

It was obvious by the security measures she had already witnessed that no one could enter Tyber's lair unless he wanted them to. Since he conducted all of his research behind these stone walls, she supposed it was a wise precaution, although she suspected that he was the type of man who guarded his privacy as carefully as his work.

The sudden loud squawk of the intercom made her jump in her seat.

"Blast and damnation!" a strange raspy voice boomed. "Who be ye? Friend or foe?"

Zanita stared dumbfounded at the box. Who on earth was that?

"Speak up, I say, or I'll blast ye where ye stand!"

Good God! Was there a weapon trained on her? Zanita tensed and peered warily at the stone structure in search of a gun port.

"Well?" the impatient voice demanded.

"It—it's Zanita—Zanita Masterson. Dr. Evans invited me to the party. I'm from the class?" This last part ended in a tone which conveyed her doubt not only of being let in, but also of her sanity in wanting such a thing.

"Come aboard then, lass."

The solid wooden doors swung slowly open.

Zanita sat in her car, hands clutching the steering wheel as she cautiously surveyed the scene opening up in front of her.

A cobblestone drive surrounded by heavy foliage lay directly before her. She had a momentary sense of deja vu.

For an instant, she knew, just knew, that once she went down that road, her life would be forever altered. It was an eerie sensation.

Do I really want to do this?

She shook herself, dispelling the strange feeling. What was she thinking? Of course she wanted to do this. She needed this interview.

The car rolled forward to follow the road. As soon as she cleared the gate, the heavy doors swung shut behind her with a dull, final thud.

Zanita looked up into the face of a dragon.

The giant topiary beast stood guard by the right side of the road. It seemed to watch her in silent scrutiny as her car inched forward. *All ye who enter here abandon reality*, she mused. This definitely promised to be an interesting experience.

The cobblestone drive twisted and turned through the woods. All she could think of was "follow the grayish brick road, follow the grayish brick road," while keeping a wary eye out for techno-munchkins sleeping under fallen leaves.

The woods opened up onto a glade followed by a labyrinth

of mythological topiary creatures: gnomes, winged cats, dragons of all shapes and sizes, what appeared to be the Loch Ness monster, a three-headed beastie, and a giant wizard arrogantly presiding over all.

"This is incredible," she mumbled to herself.

Beyond the mazes were breathtaking gardens. From the distance of the road, she could see that each garden was separate in theme and mood. Many of the smaller gardens had beautiful fountains or little ponds.

Since it was fall, there weren't many plants still in bloom. She tried to imagine what the gardens would look like in full flower, knowing it must be a breathtaking vista. Perhaps sometime today, she would have the opportunity to walk through the hidden gardens, the little nooks and crannies that were so appealing.

She passed a large white gazebo with silken paisley curtains fluttering in the breeze.

When she rounded another bend in the road, a massive Victorian mansion came into view. Seven turrets jutted into the air.

In true Victorian opulence, the house was painted in multiple shades and colors. Gingerbread trim hung from every available edge. Several different styles of wood trimming and carvings adorned the intricate woodwork. Hand-carved flowers, ropes, and bows decorated doorways. Window boxes were filled with fresh pastel flowers. The wrap-around porch was designed with intricate fretwork banisters. Several stained-glass windows reflected the afternoon sun.

Zanita didn't know whether to label it a dream or a nightmare.

She parked her car in the circular driveway in front of the house. When she had closed the car door, she leaned back against it to gaze up at the facade of the painted lady in front of her. The house was a fabulous example of Victorian architecture, brilliantly restored and lovingly maintained. She decided it was definitely a dream and was now very eager to see the interior.

Climbing the few steps up to the wide veranda, skirting the hanging swing, she approached the wooden double front doors, wondering where on earth Tyber had found these beautiful stained-glass panels. She had no doubt that they were by Tiffany. The scenes depicted were celestial in nature, showing stars, comets, heavenly bodies, a few angels, and Cupids cavorting amongst the stars.

Before she could ring the bell, the door swung open to a smiling Tyber Evans. He was barefoot, in faded jeans and an old white tee shirt. His long gold-streaked hair swung free around his shoulders.

So that's what torture looks like.

As usual, his sexy appearence was licensed to kill.

"Hi—glad you could make it." He held the door open for her, gesturing to her to enter.

"You know, Tyber, you really should make an effort to break out of your introverted mold," Zanita quipped as she walked past him.

He rubbed his ear. "I take it you don't appreciate the nuances in my subtle foray into design?"

"*Subtle*? Tyber, next to you, an elephant wearing a pink pinstriped suit dancing on two legs down Wall Street is subtle. I love it."

He gave her an ear-to-ear grin. "Somehow I knew you would, Curls. Come on, let me give you a tour of the house." He casually draped his arm around her shoulders as he led her out of the foyer into the living room. She was soon to find out that it was one of the few rooms in the house that looked normal.

The room was a tastefully recreated late-1800s drawing room decorated with dark maroon carpets, heavy emerald-green upholstered chairs sporting antimacassars, tables in dark woods, a large pouf, lots of hanging fringe, and elaborate drapery composed of yards and yards of rich jacquard material. On the highly polished wooden mantel of a large fireplace was set an inlaid cabinet containing a collection of antique music boxes.

It was altogether lovely and she told him so.

"Did you design and decorate the entire house, Tyber?"

"Most of it. I love Victorian architecture—the flights of fancy, the imagination run amuck appeals to me. When I found this house several years ago, I was intrigued. My real estate agent tried to talk me out of it. You should've seen it then— it was a real mess, but I knew the house was structurally sound. When I saw that most of the original fixtures and detailing were still intact, I immediately put in an offer. The main house was restored, then I let my imagination loose on the twenty-five acres of grounds. After that, I decided to let my own flight of fancy take over. I added several wings decorated in what I call Neo-Victorian Evans." He smiled at her engagingly. "It was a lot of fun."

Tyber's own version of Victoriana turned out to be peculiarly fascinating. Rooms led into rooms, corridors took strange twists and turns, and stairways led into solid ceilings or around corners before going down or up.

Every room they passed in the wings had a different theme; there was a cave room with rock walls, a medieval room with a bed hanging from the ceiling on chains, an observation deck with a telescope on one part of the roof, a room done all in black except for the ceiling, which had tiny phosphorescent stars painted on it, and other rooms all unique in theme.

The feature he seemed most proud of was a doorway on the third floor that led to nowhere; it opened up to the outside with no supporting structures around it, like a window in space.

Zanita stared out the open door, careful not to lean over too far. "I don't get it."

"You'd have to be a physicist to understand—it has to do with the Uncertainty Principle."

She looked at him strangely. "Uh-huh."

There was an enormous English conservatory to the rear of the house, nicely decorated in white wicker. Zanita sank down into a cushioned chair, admiring the flowering plants around her.

"So, where do you work, in your laboratory in the dungeon?" she joked. Tyber nodded quite seriously. "You're not joking, are you?"

Tyber raised his eyebrows, shaking his head slowly back and forth.

"Whyever would you work in a musty old cellar?"

"I'm a traditionalist. All us mad scientists have a certain reputation to maintain." She laughed outright. The corner of his mouth lifted in a faint smile, then he held his hand out to her. "I want to introduce you to a few ... friends. Then, if you like, we can go sit out by the pool."

She placed her hand in his large palm; his skin was warm and dry, the strong fingers enclosing her hand, gentle.

"We are going to venture into forbidden territory, Ms. Masterson," he whispered. "We are about to enter into the outer limits known as Blooey's kitchen." He led her down several corridors.

"Do you ever get lost here?"

"No, but others have. Until I can get you a map, don't go anywhere without either me or Blooey leading you. I once lost a colleague for two whole days in the south wing. He hasn't visited us since." He grinned wickedly.

"You didn't by any chance engineer this occurrence, did you?"

"I'm surprised at you, Ms. Masterson. Just how unchivalrous do you think I am?" He mocked her with the term, recalling the moment she had awakened in his arms.

She flushed faintly. "As a guest in your home, I won't answer that question."

He pushed a swinging wooden door open with his bare foot, pulling her behind him into a very large, sunny kitchen.

An island with a malachite surface stood in the center of the cooking area. Copper pots dangled from rack above the island. The cabinets were rich cherry wood. All the appliances seemed to be restaurant-style equipment. Even the chrome gas stove, although designed to look like a turn of the century appliance, was completely modern. Several kinds of herbs grew along the base of the windows. The kitchen table was nestled in an alcove of floor-to-ceiling windows.

In the center of the floor stood a chubby little man and a very fat cat.

The man wore a red-and-white horizontally striped shirt, baggy brown pants, and old, scuffed hiking boots. Around his head was a red kerchief, which was tied in a knot behind his left ear—the ear that held a large gold hoop. He was whipping a batter to a frenzy in a stainless steel bowl.

The cat, an enormous orange tabby, watched the man cooking with a greedy gleam in his golden eye. He was a tough old customer, that cat. Zanita noted with some amusement that a piece of his right ear was chewed off. A black eyepatch covered his left eye. He looked like a rogue.

"Blooey!" Tyber's voice boomed in the kitchen, making Zanita jump. He leaned down to explain in a lower voice, "Blooey won't respond to me unless I speak to him in a certain—ah, tone."

The odd man spun around, squaring his shoulders. "Aye, Captain?"

Zanita immediately recognized the voice as the one she had heard on the intercom. *Captain*? He called Tyber Captain. Had Tyber been in the military? If so, this was a piece of information that could be useful in an interview. So far as she knew, no one had ever mentioned his being in the service. And just what were his government ties?

"I want to introduce you to someone. Zanita Masterson, this is Arthur Bloomberg, known to his friends as Blooey."

"Hi. Nice to meet you." Zanita put her hand out.

Blooey squinted, examining her through one eye. "She be yer lady, what ye mentioned, Captain?"

Tyber seemed distinctly uncomfortable. "Ah . . . she *is* a lady, Blooey."

Blooey nodded, then clasped her hand, giving her a quick, rough shake. "Fair enough, I say. Welcome aboard, Lady Masterson."

Zanita wasn't quite sure how to respond to the strange little man. "Um—thanks."

A loud, indignant meow came from the floor.

"I'm getting to you; keep your whiskers on."

Tyber was talking to his cat. And the cat seemed to understand; he sat back on his haunches, peering out of his one eye at Zanita expectantly.

"And this is Hambone." The cat raised a chubby paw.

Zanita knelt down to shake his paw. "Hi, Hambone, pleased to meet you." She swore the cat grinned at her.

Tyber clasped her shoulders, bringing her to her feet. "If you need us, we'll be out by the pool."

"Aye, aye, Captain. Supper will be at six bells."

As soon as they cleared the doorway, Zanita asked him as casually as she could, "When were you in the military?"

He looked puzzled. "The military?"

So, he was hiding something! "Yes, the military. Don't deny it, Tyber, it's too late. That man in there called you Captain."

A laugh line curved the left side of his mouth. "Oh, yes, I'd forgotten all about my illustrious military career."

She fumbled around in her bag, pulling out a bent reporter's notebook and a pencil. "Now this is interesting. Tell me all about it."

He crossed his arms and looked down at her. "Well, let me see. In those days, there was a lot of strife between . . . *you know*."

Zanita nodded eagerly. "The cold war. Go on." She scribbled in her book.

"I had commandeered my own ship, of course."

"Of course," she agreed, not looking up and therefore missing the grin that broke across his face.

"I sank and pillaged twenty ships—"

"*Pillaged*?" She looked up at him aghast. "The government condoned that sort of thing?"

"I had a letter of marque," he answered her seriously.

"A letter of—Tyber, what are you talking about?"

51

He gave her an innocent look. "What are you writing?"

She looked down guiltily at the notebook in her hand. "All right, so I forgot." He snorted at that statement. She quickly put the notebook away. "So, *were* you in the military?"

He laughed. "No."

"Then why does that man call you Captain?"

Tyber rubbed the back of his neck, seeking a way to explain this. "Blooey is an excellent cook." She stared at him expectantly. "He . . . thinks he's on a pirate ship and that I'm the captain."

As if that explained it. She continued to stare at him.

Tyber sighed. "Arthur Bloomberg used to be a brilliant mathematician. We worked together at one time. It was his work on imaginary numbers that drove him slightly over the edge—the paradox, you see. As Blooey says, 'What was the *point*?' Pun intended."

"I see. I think. He had sort of a nervous breakdown, and you took him in." She was beginning to see yet another side to Tyberius Augustus Evans. A side she liked very much. "Doesn't he have any relatives?"

"None that will claim him. Besides," he said by way of explanation, "Blooey's the best shipmate I've ever sailed with. Wait until you taste his cooking—I really think it's his true vocation, doctorate be dammed."

"That man has a doctorate?" Her expression was incredulous.

"Yes, but compared to his vegetable terrine, its meaningless."

Tyber led her through the conservatory onto the grounds behind the house. They passed more gardens, then passed through a high wrought-iron gate in yet another stone wall. This was the "pool area." The entire site was reminiscent of a secluded grotto, with boulders lining the pool itself, giving it a natural pond appearance. Several little waterfalls cascaded into the pool from the rock wall, which contained, of all things, an outdoor fireplace. A second iron gate led directly into the house.

It was a lovely spot.

It was devoid of guests.

Zanita looked around. "Where is everybody?"

"What do you mean?"

"You said you were having an end-of-class, Indian summer pool party."

Tyber threw himself onto a wicker lounge, crossing his hands behind his head. "And so I am."

Zanita's eyes narrowed. "There are no other guests, are there?"

"I don't recall mentioning other guests to you."

She tapped her foot. "I can see you have a tendency toward presumption, Dr. Evans."

"And how is that, Ms. Masterson? I issued an invitation; you accepted." He watched her from under half-lowered lids. "Now, why was that, I wonder?"

He was toying with her. He knew exactly why she had accepted!

Zanita kicked a pebble off the patio and into the pool. "You know why! I want an interview with you!"

Tyber's silvery blue eyes followed the pebble with some amusement as it skipped across the stones to plop into the water. Unfolding himself from the lounge chair, he walked behind her to cup his hands on her shoulders.

Zanita tried to move away; he pulled her back.

Bending low, he said firmly in her ear, "No interview. No more debris in my pool."

Zanita swallowed convulsively at the heat of him behind her. She suddenly wanted to rest her head back against his chest, feel those powerful arms come around her . . .

She blinked. Bad enough she behaved foolishly just now. No need to compound her error by throwing herself at the man.

What was wrong with her? She was usually a very cautious person when it came to relationships with men. Hadn't Mills told her so? Not that she wanted a relationship with him. He probably wouldn't be interested even if she did. And what if she had truly pissed him off just now? How stupid can one person be? After all, she was his guest.

His capable hands moved at her shoulders, massaging her tense muscles. The act did not relax her.

"Did you notice the topiary labyrinth when you came in?" His low voice sent shivers down her neck.

Still captured by his hands, she nodded her head warily.

"Good. I want you to know that the maze is extremely complex. To date, no one has successfully navigated through it. Do you know why I built it?"

She shook her head, sending her curls bouncing.

"I built it as a foil to anyone foolish enough to seek an interview. Those creatures eat little reporters like you for lunch."

Zanita gasped, her imagination running wild.

Tyber's answering chuckle was a strong, sexy laugh of male amusement. Was it her imagination or did his lips just brush her hair?

She broke out of his hold, turning to face him.

"Really, Tyber, I just want—"

"No." He tapped her nose. "Now, would you like something to drink, Curls?"

Tyber was being difficult. But not impossible. She would have to bide her time and try again in an hour or so. Smiling secretly, she accepted his offer of refreshment.

Tyber handed her a frosty glass of lemonade from the outdoor bar, thinking she had the look of his cat again. He knew the look well. She wasn't going to give up.

He sighed.

How was he going to get her mind off that damn interview? As long as she thought of him as a subject for her article, she wouldn't be seeing him as a person.

A person who was extremely attracted to her.

There was something about her that drew him like a magnetic force. From the moment he spotted her sitting in that third-row seat in the lecture hall, he had been captivated by her. He hadn't quite figured it out yet.

Despite his unorthodox persona, Tyber was not a man who leaped into idle indulgences with women. Because of his secluded lifestyle and his penchant for research, his experiences with women were usually based on a mutual interest in scientific matters, or were the natural result of a deepening friendship.

His liaisons followed a pattern.

He always knew the woman on a professional basis first before engaging in a friendly affair. These relationships had a tendency to last several months before being mutually set aside. There was tenderness, decent sex, and a certain camaraderie.

This one, however, was different.

For some reason, Zanita Masterson *incited* him.

She made him want her on a level he was unfamiliar with. There was an *urgency* in the air when he was near her.

The sight and scent of her aroused deep, mysterious passions in him—passions he ached to explore with the same thoroughness with which he explored his other endeavors.

And it wasn't just the passion—though Lord knew, that was enough.

What captivated him as much as the physical pull was that he couldn't seem to *anticipate* her. Zanita Masterson was a surprise in every way. He didn't understand it, but he wasn't particularly concerned about it. He was confident he would figure it out in time.

They sat in the sun slowly sipping their lemonades.

Zanita was careful to skirt the topic of the interview until she was ready to pounce.

Tyber was careful to skirt the issue of his raging desire lest he pounce.

In their quest to avoid certain topics, they found to their surprise a wealth of other subjects in which they shared similar viewpoints. They liked the same movies. They loved trying out new restaurants. They itched to travel and explore, knowing they had a nest at home, waiting. They were open to new ideas and situations. They shared a love of art and antiques.

And most important, they had a similar sense of humor.

Zanita wondered how it was possible for her to have so much in common with a man who was a genius.

Tyber calculated the odds of their being perfect together sexually as exponentially high.

Their thoughts were interrupted by Blooey yelling at the top of his lungs. "*Come 'ere, ye scalawag!*"

Tyber and Zanita stared at each other silently.

A second later, the gate banged open and a streak of orange fur whizzed by, a rack of lamb clamped firmly in its jaws.

Blooey followed hot on Hambone's tail, waving a kitchen cleaver. "He's got the dinner, Captain!"

The cat jumped on top of the barbecue, zealously guarding his prize.

Zanita's hand covered her mouth, but it did little to hide the giggles she could not suppress. Whoever heard of a cat making off with an entire rack of lamb? Being chased by a little pirate sporting a cleaver? She broke into peals of laughter.

Tyber turned to her, more than a glint of amusement in his eyes. "Never mind, Blooey. We'll pull into Port KFC tonight. My old friend the Colonel has invited us to dine."

Blooey beamed. "Ye think he'll be serving that fine chicken he does, sir?"

Tyber eyed the half-chewed rack of prime lamb wistfully. "There's a distinct possibility, sailor."

The three of them piled into the front seat of Tyber's 1955 cherry-red pick-up truck, affectionately known as "Big Red."

Zanita learned that he had restored the vehicle when he was still in high school. First the house, now the truck. It seemed the man had a penchant for bringing things back to life. Rather like Dr. Frankenstein, she mused.

When they stopped at a light, Tyber spoke low in her ear. "What are you laughing at now? Don't you realize I arranged all of this just to impress you? I had to promise Hambone a week's supply of filleted salmon. The cat's a tough negotiator." Tyber pressed on the gas when the light changed.

"I wouldn't doubt that for a minute. Actually, the reason I

was laughing was because I was thinking that you're rather like Frankenstein.''

''*Frankenstein*?'' Tyber hit the brakes.

''Oh, don't be offended; I mean the doctor, not the monster.''

He eyed her strangely. ''Gee, thanks,'' he said drily. ''For a minute there, I thought I was being insulted. I can't tell you what a relief it is to know you think of me as a deranged scientist with delusions of godhood instead of an ordinary old monster.''

Blooey let out a bark of laughter. ''T'weren't nowhere to go but down on that one, Captain!''

Tyber lifted one eyebrow. ''Indeed.''

''Have faith, Captain. Women are difficult creatures at best.''

''So I've been told, Blooey.'' Tyber peered down at Zanita menacingly, then he spoiled the effect by winking at her.

Zanita grinned back at him, thinking Blooey was right; he did resemble a pirate captain.

Big Red swung into the lot and up to the order window.

Tyber turned to his passengers. ''Okay, who wants what?''

Zanita licked her lips. ''I'll have Extra Crispy.''

''That spice is a fine blend, Captain.''

Zanita agreed. ''On the other hand I've been meaning to try the rotisserie style.''

''So you want me to get Rotisserie Gold?'' Tyber asked.

''No, fried is the Colonel's specialty, Captain.''

''Yes, that's right.'' Zanita agreed with Blooey. ''Original Recipe. Wait—''

''Don't forget the biscuits.''

''—white meat.''

''Ach, the dark is best, lass.''

Tyber dropped his forehead against the steering wheel.

''Potato wedges, too,'' Zanita added.

''Nay, the mashed potatoes!'' The car behind them honked. ''Don't forget Hambone loves the gravy, Captain. Though he's not deservin' it, is he?''

"That does it!" Tyber rolled down his window. "Give me the largest bucket you have and throw some of everything in it!"

Zanita and Blooey gave each other secret smiles on the drive back to the house. It seemed the two of them knew exactly how to get to Tyber. And did it right well together, too.

They ate outside on a wicker table by the pool, Hambone licking a little saucer of gravy at their feet. After they had cleaned up, Blooey decided to return to his "cabin" to finish a mystery he'd been reading. Zanita and Tyber elected to stay outside to enjoy the unseasonably warm weather. They plunked down on side-by-side lounge chairs, both of them kicking off their shoes.

Tyber absently watched the water rippling in the pool. "Do you want to go swimming?"

"I didn't bring a swimsuit."

A slow, wicked smile creased his handsome face as he continued to stare at the water.

"Forget what you're thinking, Dr. Evans."

His eyes flicked to her. "Would you go in if I told you I would give you an interview?"

"Certainly not!"

"Don't be offended; I'm just checking your moral fiber, Ms. Masterson." His gaze ran the length of her, from her sleeveless shirt to her shorts, lingering over her bare legs and feet. "It seems to be a tight weave."

Shameless. Absolutely shameless. Zanita shook her head and sighed. A small chair cushion sailed by Tyber's head. He grinned at her.

"You'll never make the majors, Ms. Masterson."

"Oh, I don't know." She flexed her fingers. "If I hang around you long enough, I'm sure I'll get in plenty of practice."

He turned on his side to face her. "I'll have to see to it then, won't I?"

The intimacy of the situation did not escape her. They were

lying side by side, practically touching each other. It wouldn't be so bad if Zanita didn't know for a fact that Tyber was purposely baiting her for a reason known only to him. That he might be seriously interested in her did not occur to her for one minute.

She ignored him to turn on her side away from him. So far, he had not budged an inch on the subject of the interview. It was time to face the fact that he was not a man to be easily swayed. She had given it her best shot. He was not going to relent.

Zanita lay on her back again, watching the sun sink in the western sky. She was not going to get the interview; Tyber was teasing her; and she had eaten way too much for dinner. She yawned sleepily as she stretched in the wide lounge chair.

"I really should be going soon, Tyber."

"You can't go yet, Zanita. Blooey's made a great dessert, and *The Curse Of The Mummy's Finger* is on TV later." Tyber stopped because she had fallen fast asleep. If it were anyone else but Zanita, he might have been insulted. This was the second time the woman had fallen asleep on him! Shaking his head, he padded into the house to get her a blanket. With the sun going down, it was getting chilly.

Chapter Four

Zanita opened her eyes to a full moon in the night sky.

"Good evening."

Tyber was sitting on the edge of her lounge chair, one corner of his sensuous mouth lifted in a faint smile. A light breeze caressed the free-flowing strands of his long chestnut hair, moonlight silvering the golden highlights.

What a sight to wake up to.

The dreamy thought flitted through her sleep-clogged brain. She smiled back, cuddling deeper into the lightweight blanket, still too hazy to wonder how she had come to be covered.

She bunched the blanket up under her chin with her fists, while her luminous eyes continued to drink in the sight of him leaning over her, barefoot and now shirtless in the night wind. Against the darkness of his skin, his washed-out denims looked white in the night light.

Realizing she must be staring, she hastily lowered her eyes, suddenly embarrassed. What was she thinking of—staring at the man like that?

"I fell asleep." Her voice came out a thin sound.

"Yes." His clear eyes wandered over her features, lingering for a moment on the baby-fine curls framing her face. Without thinking, he reached out, fingering a downy lock.

As he did, his scent tickled her senses; a tantalizing mixture of after-shave and something else that was uniquely Tyber—an elusive, heady, sizzling thing, which made her briefly close her eyes to delicately inhale more. The man could make a woman his captive with that scent.

She could feel the heat emanating from his bare skin as the cool night breeze washed over them both. For a moment, a strand of his silk hair feathered her cheek as the wind wafted through the evergreens surrounding the pool area. The scent of pine trailed behind like night incense.

A fire now crackled in the fireplace; warm lights danced across the rippling water.

His voice penetrated her hazy state, a low, mellow tone which was somehow both soothing and stimulating.

"I've been thinking about you. . . ."

The soft words echoed the gentle play of his fingers threading through her hair. She warily opened her eyes. She had never thought of herself as particularly thinkable.

"What's to think about?"

He tenderly smoothed the hair off her face, seemingly fascinated when the curls bounced right back.

"I can't seem to anticipate you."

She furrowed her brows. "What do you mean?"

"I can't quite figure out how your mind works. You're unpredictable." He flashed her an engaging look. "Not unlike Chaos."

She surprised him?

So, the great Tyberius Augustus Evans was stumped, was he? Would wonders never cease. *Good for me*!

She grinned impishly up at him. "You never will, you know."

It seemed she had confused him yet again. Better and better. By his expression, he hadn't a clue as to what she meant. "You'll never classify me," she clarified.

Smiling cryptically, he leaned forward, placing his hands on the flat surface of the chair on either side on her head. "I'm counting on it."

Before she could guess his intentions, his sexy mouth had already brushed across her own, taking a light skipping path across her face to nuzzle warmly at her neck.

The sudden, unexpected touch of his firm lips on the tender skin of her throat sent a frisson right down to her toes and back up again. The man was nibbling at her! Who ever thought Tyber would—

His teeth scraped a pulse point. A soft moan echoed in the night.

Was that me making that sound?

Her eyes opened wide in shock. She stared mutely up at him. Tyber's silvery blue eyes were glittering with . . . amusement? Interest? *Passion.*

He continued to gaze at her as he reached over to release the bunched-up blanket from her nerveless fingers. Taking her small hands in his, he skillfully brought them around his neck to engineer her embrace of him.

Their eyes met. Her breathing stopped.

He's going to kiss me.

The silky strands of his hair slid through her fingers as they glided forward with the slow descent of his head. Taking his time, he lowered himself to her, bringing his mouth over hers in a seamless move.

His lips were velvety slick and heated. So sensuous was the touch of his skillful mouth that this time she wasn't even aware of the little moans that escaped her throat.

Tyber was.

He kept his hands resting flat on the lounge chair beside her head as he deepened the kiss. He skimmed the tip of his tongue lightly along her slightly parted lips before gently suckling her bottom lip.

"Oh! That—"

"Do you like that?" he drawled, repeating the action.

An understatement. Her mouth opened for him.

Tyber had a sudden revelation; he wanted much more from her. Again he ran the tip of his tongue along her parted lips, inserting it just slightly into her mouth. Then he kissed her slowly, sweetly, as if he was content to go on whiling away his life forever kissing her.

Zanita had never been kissed like this; Tyber was . . . like a little taste of heaven. Enticing. Luscious. Damp.

A languid warmth spread through her.

He kept repeating his torturous routine—a touch of the tongue, the press of his lips, each repetition slightly more intense than the last.

Every time his dewy tongue touched her, she shivered and he entered her waiting mouth a little more.

Every time he kissed her, she moaned and he pressed a little harder.

The tempo of her breathing increased, but he did not increase his tempo.

He was deliberate and pulsating and utterly intoxicating.

Zanita quivered in his embrace. The obvious response Tyber was producing in her was making *him* tremble. Without warning, he felt raw and dangerous. He was more than just physically moved.

He wanted inside.

In every way.

But only his mouth touched her. Only his mouth captured her.

The next time he dipped into her, Zanita wasn't even aware of her fingers splaying through his long hair, pressing the back of his head closer, closer, hungry for the sensual pleasure of his creative lips and tongue.

At the feel of the insistent pressure to the back of his head, Tyber paused. His thick lashes flicked up as he examined her face. Her eyes were closed, her breathing ragged, her mouth still slightly parted for him. The gentle lips were moist and swollen from his kisses.

Something leaped in him and through him. A flash arcing through every pulse point. Searing. Pounding.

Suddenly he could not bear to be separated from the haven of those luscious lips. He had never experienced anything so . . . *intense*. At that moment he wanted her more than he had ever wanted anything in his life.

This woman did something to him he could not explain.

For a man who was dedicated to explaining anything and everything in his universe, this was a disconcerting experience.

He pressed his thumb purposefully along her moist lower lip, completely opening her for him.

No sense overanalyzing. Some things were better to accept in life, he briefly thought before he seized her mouth in a piercingly sweet invasion. His tongue swirled fully inside, gliding back and forth in a devastatingly thorough foray. In ardent ownership.

Zanita clung to him, overwhelmed by his sense of purpose. His taste was pure and sweet and as rich as cream. Unconsciously, Zanita's fingers clenched in his hair as he managed the firm, seductive onslaught of her senses. She felt dazed. And crazy for the feel of him.

He might not know how to classify her, but he certainly knew what to do with her.

Zanita was barely aware of him lifting the blanket that still covered her to get underneath it himself. Powerful arms surrounded her, drawing her close. She could feel him now all around her, enveloping her, his taut skin as smooth as velvet over rock-hard muscles. And hot. Very hot.

His fierce heat brought her temporarily to her senses.

She needed to slow down here. She needed to understand what was happening. Her palms brushed against his sleek chest hair; she placed them flat against his bare skin in an effort to stem the sensual onslaught. She looked up at him in confusion, meeting his scalding gaze.

"Wh-what are you doing, Tyber?" she barely managed to stutter as his arms locked her to him.

His eyes were definitely not clear ice now. They were smoky with desire. She had never seen a man's eyes look so . . . *smoldering*. He lowered his head to her, an intense, incredibly erotic look on his face.

"I believe I am about to claim you, Ms. Masterson." The heated, implacable words were breathed just against her lips.

"Oh, but I don't think—"

"Good. Don't think." His hot mouth closed firmly over her own.

Something happened when they came together.

Something beyond reason; something primitive and erotically wild. What started out as steady heat quickly escalated to an intense, untamable, unstoppable maelstrom of passion.

She didn't remember her shorts coming off. Or her top. Or her bra and panties, for that matter. She certainly couldn't recall Tyber slipping out of his jeans and underwear.

She was aware of the first time his powerful leg brushed against hers. And of his naked thigh inserting itself between her own. She remembered the feel of the hair on his leg gliding against the smooth skin of her inner thigh.

The touch of his hands, large and warm against the bare skin of her back.

The sultry caress of his long hair across her chest as his unyielding mouth took hers once again.

The commanding way he turned her to maximize the pleasure.

It seemed as if Tyber could not get enough of her. He massaged his palms ardently over her body as they lay facing each other, his untamed yet sensitive touch arousing nerve endings she didn't even know she had. He caressed and stroked as if she were his personal pagan sacrifice. His to do with as he wished. His to consume.

She would never forget the sultry, sizzling expression on his wildly handsome face as he lost himself in sensual pleasures the depth of which she had never experienced before.

Like hot, wet silk, his mouth fastened on the curve of her neck as he cupped her bottom to press her tight against him. He was throbbing. Incredibly hard.

Incredibly endowed.

In a feminine action as old as time, Zanita moved slightly away from him. *What am I doing?*

He firmly brought her back.

"I—I'm—" He never let her complete the sentence. Entwining his legs with hers, his large hands cupping her head, lacing through her curls, he held her still for his voracious, heart-stopping kisses. She dissolved totally, melting into his embrace.

Somewhere in the back of his mind, Tyber knew that a fever had him in its grip. Uncharacteristic or not, he had no intention of pulling free.

When he rolled the rosy turgid peak of her breast along the edge of his teeth, the choking sound issuing from low in her throat sizzled him.

When he drew the edge of her breast deep into his wet mouth and Zanita began to whimper, his body temperature soared.

Her little cries of passion made his rushing blood burn. His only coherent thought was—*more.*

Tyber's hands slid under her back, raising her to him, as he dropped his head between her full breasts to rub his face roughly against her skin, deeply inhaling her womanly scent. He was lost . . . *lost.*

Tyber's uninhibited sensuousness took Zanita's breath away.

He ignited her.

Zanita pressed her lips to his steaming throat, right over a throbbing vein. She could feel his pulse, his life force, beating strong beneath her mouth. Tyber turned his head to the side to give her better access; his ragged breath skittered across the top of her head as her mouth drew insistently on him. In response, his muscular arms fastened securely around her slim waist, an imprisoning web of masculine strength, as soft as silk, as strong as steel.

Each entangled the other. They clung together in passion like interwoven vines.

Zanita ran her kiss-swollen lips up the strong column of his throat, now craving him like her personal designer drug. She stopped to tug sharply on his earlobe, then ran the small point of her tongue around the rim of his ear, darting the tip just inside.

His quick intake of breath and slight tremor inflamed her.

Losing all reserve, her actions unconsciously mimicked his as she buried her face in his long, fragrant hair, breathing deeply of its clean masculine scent before writhing against him like a cat in heat.

Tyber went wild.

He rolled on top of her, pinning her beneath him. His mouth crashed down on hers, a searing brand of possession. His fingers laced with hers, pinning her to the cushion beneath them as he imprisoned her hands in a classic stance of male sexual domination. This enlightened Renaissance man had just shed his cloak of refinement; he became untamed, insatiable, and definitely ready for love.

He entered her in one sure stroke to the hilt.

They both cried out.

She wrapped her legs tightly around him. He wrapped his arms tightly around her. Then Tyber fused his mouth to hers and moved in her. And moved in her. And moved in her.

She felt the first tremors, not quite sure what was happening. She begged him to stop; Tyber ignored her.

He was relentless.

She began sobbing. She threatened him *if* he stopped. For the first time in her life, she lost her inhibitions; she screamed and hollered and had one hell of a time. When the exploding spasms rocked her, they were so intense, she took him with her right over the edge.

Tyber groaned from the depths of his soul and had the most powerful orgasm he had ever had in his life. Collapsing on top of her, he nestled his head in her shoulder, too shaken to move a muscle.

Zanita came down to earth, blinked her eyes at the moon, and grinned like the Cheshire cat against the sweat-slicked skin of Tyber's throat.

Good Lord . . . He had done it!

She had been well and truly *befuddled*.

After several minutes, Tyber raised his head, tossing back his mane of hair.

He had figured it out.

The knowledge that he wanted this woman now, again, tomorrow, became crystal clear to him. She had responded to him as she had to no other man, he was sure of that. His arms tightened around her as he bent forward to give her a sweet, lingering kiss.

His fingers massaged her scalp as he gazed thoughtfully into her eyes. "I'm the first one to make you feel that way."

"How did you know?" She seemed surprised at his level of perception.

Tyber raised a lordly eyebrow. "Well, let me think . . . I could say it's intuition or even my great psychic ability, but perhaps it was all the yelling—'Oh my God what's happening please don't stop you're killing me.' Yes, I definitely think—" She punched his shoulder.

He chuckled, planting a quick kiss on the tip of her chin.

"You're very proud of yourself, aren't you?"

"Mmm." His mouth trailed down to her collarbone where he lingered in possessive male afterplay.

"I'm thinking I really shouldn't have added to your arrogance level, Doc."

"The decision was, shall we say, taken out of your hands. Besides"—he nipped her chin—"I don't have an arrogance level."

"Ha! Oh, Tyber, don't do that . . ." She sucked in her breath as his open mouth drew strongly on her neck. She shivered.

He stopped to look at her. "Are you getting cold?"

Not hardly. But she nodded, discretion being the better part of valor. Now that she wasn't under the influence of her raging hormones, she was beginning to get slightly embarrassed. They were lying naked, outside in a lounge chair under the light of the full moon. True, the blanket covered them, but what if Blooey should decide to take a midnight stroll in the backyard?

More worrisome, she had never hopped into bed so fast with anyone in her life. She had known Steve for *two years* before taking the plunge, and Rick—even with that aberration, she had been dating him for several months. What was she to make of this? How was she supposed to behave? They weren't involved, yet she had been more intimate with Tyber than she had been with anyone in her life. He had seen her totally out of control.

She massaged the bridge of her nose with her thumb and forefinger. No, he had *caused* her to become totally out of control.

Tyber took command like a regular blood-and-guts general.

The man was dangerous. Positively lethal. Who knew what responses he could coax from her when she least expected it? She had absolutely no intentions of becoming involved again. At least not for the next millennium.

Tyber rolled off her, reaching down for his jeans. Suddenly shy, Zanita wrapped the blanket around her as she searched for her clothes. As soon as she had dressed, she tried to think of a graceful way to make a quick getaway. She needed some time to dwell on her wanton behavior. Looking and drooling was one thing. Touching and groping quite another.

"Look, Tyber, I'd better be going now. Thank you for inviting me, and good luck in your research—"

Tyber watched her knowingly as he pulled his jeans over his lean hips and zipped them up. She wasn't even looking at him when she spoke! He placed himself directly in front of her, removing that option.

"Oh, no you don't, Ms. Masterson. How many times do I have to tell you I won't let you run away? We just shared something, and I'm not just talking about the sex." He ran a hand through his hair as a vision of them entwined in a passionate embrace played in his mind. "Though it was incredible, wasn't it?"

Her chin came up defiantly. "I'm not running away. I'm leaving. There is a difference."

"No. You're not."

She sighed. "Tyber, I don't know what—*this* was." Her hand indicated the now vacant chaise with its rumpled blanket. "I don't know how I'm supposed to act in a situation like this—stop right where you are!" He had started to move closer to her. The last thing she needed right now was him *befuddling* her with his touch.

"Zanita . . ."

She would have to elaborate, so he would get the picture. For a genius, he could be awfully thick-headed. Surely he should have been able to figure out that a woman of her advanced years would have had enough encounters with his sex to swear off men entirely!

"I've had one and a half relationships in my life and—"

Tyber didn't hear the rest of her words; he was still stuck on the first part of her statement. "*A half of a relationship*? What the hell is that?"

She flushed. "I don't wish to discuss it."

He was looking at her as if she were some odd specimen he had just discovered under his microscope. Make that telescope, she amended. "And you can take that look off your face right now!"

"What look?" He still was viewing her strangely.

"You know what look! I am no different than anybody else—there is no need for you to peer at me like that."

He took a deep breath. "Zanita, you are so far removed from any other person I have ever met that the comparison defies description. Believe me, sweetheart, putting your name and the norm together is a contradiction in terms."

"And who are you to judge?" She tapped her foot, swinging her arm in an arc to encompass his bizarre home. "Need I say more?"

He narrowed his eyes. "So I'm eccentric."

"Eccentric!" She scoffed. "You, Tyberius Augustus Evans"—her index finger poked his chest—"are a kook!"

Tyber's mouth lifted at the corners. "*A kook*?" He placed his hands over his heart. "Zany, you wound me."

"That's Zani with an *i*."

A dimple popped into his cheek, and she was locked into a spontaneous embrace. "However can you tell?" he whispered laughingly while nuzzling her hair.

She looked up at him with a wounded expression. "It's the way you say it. I just know." His fingers idly toyed with the tiny curls at the base of her neck while he observed her earnest little face. He felt his heart jump.

"Zanita, I adore you." His lips pressed warmly against her forehead. "Stay with me tonight."

Stay with him? He adored her? She gazed at him in shock. Did that mean he wanted them to have a relationship or . . . Another horrible thought occurred to her.

"Tyber, you—did you use protection? You have to be so careful these days and—" Her hands covered her face. "Oh, God, what have I done?"

"Don't worry about it, baby; I took care of it."

Before she could think of an appropriate response to that, Tyber lifted her in his arms and carried her into the house. He didn't put her down until she was gently deposited in the center of his bed.

Which happened to be a giant oyster shell.

Zanita blinked up at him, nonplussed at his presumption. No other man of her acquaintance would have dreamed of acting so assertively. Then again, no other man of her acquaintance could have brought her so completely to satisfaction. Nonetheless, she was not about to let the man haul her around without her express consent. In triplicate.

She glared up at him. "Excuse me, I must have missed something. When did we leap back two centuries?" Tyber looked up at the ceiling as if he were seriously thinking about her question.

"Can't do that. At least according to Einstein. However, a wormhole—"

71

"Stop that doublespeak right now! You didn't even give me a chance to answer you!"

Tyber shrugged. "It was not a question."

"Tyber!"

He grinned down at her. "Technically speaking," he amended to sooth her ruffled feathers.

She threw him a pointed look and sat up. It appeared that she was in the middle of another one of Tyber's flights of fancy. Three walls were floor-to-ceiling aquariums. The fourth wall contained two doors which presumably led to a bathroom and dressing room.

"I'll admit the aquariums are relaxing, but an oyster shell bed?" Her eyes traveled above her, where the top half of the open shell loomed over her head. There were recessed colored lights embedded in it.

Tyber picked up a control box on a driftwood table beside the bed. He pressed a button and the lights dimmed romantically.

"What if you want to read in bed?" she asked sarcastically, still miffed at his overbearing behavior. Men! Boil them in oil! He pressed another button, and two bright reading lights came on, spotlighting her. "Now I feel like the Little Mermaid."

He snapped the reading lights off, leaving the soft pastel lights on. "You do look like a little pearl in there." She stuck her tongue out at him. He wagged his finger at her. "Obviously not a *cultured* pearl."

"People who live in glass aquariums shouldn't throw insults. You have a television in your bedroom. Talk about cultured . . ."

"Which reminds me, we missed *The Curse Of The Mummy's Finger*. I wonder how we could have forgotten?" He gave her a very male look.

"I wonder." She couldn't help it; her mouth curved in response. He was such an incredibly sexy man. And very sweet.

Despite his godawful arrogance.

To be fair, she supposed that just being Tyberius Augustus

Evans came with an arrogance factor. There was no one quite like him. The world knew it. And he probably knew it. She really did want to stay with him a little longer. So what could one night hurt?

Tyber sat on the edge of the bed. "Does that alluring little smile mean you are going to spend the night with me?"

"Is *that* a question?" He picked up her hand and brought it to his lips.

"Yes, Zanita mine, that is a question. Please stay; I want you to. How's that for humility?"

"I don't know. Somehow the Uriah Heap routine doesn't suit you. And, yes; I'll stay, but just for this one night. I've given up men."

Tyber raised an eyebrow. "You mean as in, I've given up red meat?"

"Something like that."

"Dare I enquire why?" She tugged her hand away.

"No, you may not."

"I see. So tonight you're going off the wagon, so to speak? I don't know that I like being compared to a behavioral slump." He walked his fingers up her arm.

"Be serious, Tyber. There's no insult intended. Consider it more like an . . . aberration."

"An aberration." He stared at her stonily.

"You're not upset, are you?"

"Of course not. I've always aspired to be someone's aberration. Now I'm yours. My life is complete." He flopped down sideways across the bed.

"Don't take it personally."

"So now I'm not even an *individual* aberration? I'm not even special, am I? I'm just an average run-of-the-mill aberration." He rolled toward her, grabbing both her hands in one of his. Her eyes widened.

"What are you going to do?" He loomed over her.

"I'm going to demonstrate something to you. This"—pushing up her shirt, he ran his fingers lightly across her belly—"is an ordinary aberration. While this"—he suddenly began ticking her midriff mercilessly—"is a special aberration." She began giggling mindlessly. "Now, would you care to rephrase your assessment of me?"

"Stop, Tyber, please!" He lifted his hand to let it hover menacingly a few inches above her belly button.

"I'm waiting." He flexed his fingers threateningly.

"Okay, you are a special aberration. There, satisfied?"

His lips brushed her stomach. "Not yet," he said against her skin. "But it's a start." Her hands were released as he sat back up on the bed.

"Do you know what's on TV even as we speak?" He had the expression of a man who had a bag full of diamonds behind him.

"No, what?" She asked eagerly, sitting up also.

"*Invasion of the Prehistoric Space Vampires.*" He raised and lowered his brows several times.

"No!" Zanita gasped. Tyber nodded with a glint in his eye. "My favorite movie!"

He retrieved the remote on the nightstand, snapping on the tube. A vampire in a silver spacesuit was chasing a caveman across the San Fernando Valley. "It just started. Stay right where you are; I'll be right back with something decadently rich. Let me know what I missed."

Zanita leaned back against the pillows, already absorbed in the movie, while Tyber headed off to ransack the kitchen.

He returned a few minutes later, holding a large serving tray. His bare foot pushed the door open, then closed it behind him. "What did I miss?"

"Nothing too much—the head vampire spaceman just spotted the cavegirl taking a bath by the stream and saved her from getting eaten by the sabre-toothed poodle. What is all that?" Tyber placed the tray on the nightstand and hopped on the bed beside her.

"This is Blooey's famous Toll House Pie." He handed her an enormous piece smothered in ice cream with a glass of milk.

"Is this cookie-dough ice cream?" He nodded. "This is

sinful." She tasted a piece of the pie. "Oh, God, Tyber, this is better than sex."

The fork stopped halfway to his mouth. "Watch it. You've already given me one complex tonight."

She licked some fudge off the corner of her fork. "I didn't mean sex with you, of course."

"I hope that's not the chocolate speaking."

"No, really, sex with you is much more delicious," she said impishly.

He turned to look at her, suddenly gone serious. "Zanita, do you—"

"Shh! The movie's coming back on."

They watched the movie companionably, making humorous comments about the implausible script and horrid acting. When the psychic shaman of the cavemen came on, they both started laughing.

During the commercial, Tyber turned to her. "That shaman reminds me—didn't you say you were doing a story about psychic healers?"

"Uh-huh. That's how I ended up in your class. You were right; I am a lousy speller."

A trait I am very grateful for. "What type of a story are you doing?" He crossed his hands behind his head, leaning back against the pillows.

"It's an investigative piece." She told him about Xavier LaLeche and poor Mrs. Haverhill.

"*The Patriot Sun* sent you on a story like this?"

She squirmed uncomfortably. "Well, not exactly. I'm sort of doing this on my own."

"Really. Are you an investigative reporter?"

"Um, sort of . . ."

"Sort of?"

"This is my first investigative piece, but I know—"

"I've heard that type of work can be dangerous."

"That's what Mills said, but I think she's overreacting."

"Who's Mills?"

"My best friend. The trouble is, my editor, Hank, only gives me fluff to cover. I want, *need* to do something . . . more. I'm determined to do this story—not just for the paper. I knew Mrs. Haverhill. She was a nice old woman who didn't deserve to be conned like that.''

"Why not complain to the head honcho about your assignments?"

"Hank *is* the head honcho. Believe me, he would never send me out on anything that was even remotely hazardous."

Good for Hank, Tyber thought. Although he was curious why. "Why not?"

"Because he's my grandfather," she mumbled into her chest. Tyber grinned above her bent head, quickly losing it when she looked up at him.

"Gee, that's a tough break, Zanita."

"Yeah. That's why I don't want him knowing anything about this."

Here was trouble waiting to happen, he thought. Xavier LaLeche—there was a phony name if he'd ever heard one. Who knew what she'd uncover? Put money, greed, and a shady con man together and the situation could get very dangerous. And with her penchant for getting into situations . . .

He rubbed his chin. "You know, Zanita, I find this fascinating."

"You do?"

"Yes. There is a definite parallel here. I can understand your desire to do this type of investigative writing. In a way it's similar to what I do."

"It is? How?"

"I consider my research to be a series of investigations." He snapped his fingers as if something important had just occurred to him. "I bet I could help you with this story."

She sat straight up, very interested. "Really?" She thought about it a minute. "I bet you could! It wouldn't take you long to get the jump on him, you knowing all that scientific stuff. Why, you'd be able to spot the fraud in a minute!"

"Well, maybe not that fast—but I probably could figure out his M.O. for you."

"This is great! I'm really excited! Will you help me, Tyber?"

There was no way in hell he was letting her go off by herself into what was sure to be trouble. "Yes, I think I will."

"Terrific! The first thing we ought to do is—You have some fudge on the corner of your mouth."

Tyber snaked his arm around her waist, pulling her to him. "Lick it off for me, baby."

Zanita hesitated for a fraction of a second, still surprised by Tyber's outrageously sensual nature. "Mmm, it tastes better on you."

"Did you know Newton said you cannot touch without being touched?" His quick tongue flicked the little indentation above her upper lip.

"I know someone who's 'touched.'"

"I'll ignore that because I understand your reluctance to learn physics. Newton also said that if I do this . . ." He bent his head, capturing her nipple right through the cotton material of her shirt. . . . "I should expect *this*." His fingers brushed against her opposite nipple which was now equally hard.

She sucked in her breath. "Newton said that, did he?"

"Mmm-hmm. He's very popular with the students." Tyber gently laid her on the bed, his hands going to the snaps on her shorts. "Want to know what else he said?"

She nodded enthusiastically.

His lips brushed enticingly against her stomach as he pulled off her shorts. Then he began dropping tiny kisses up her chest as he unbuttoned her shirt.

"In the absence of force, an object in motion will tend to stay in motion. What do you think about that?" He tossed her shirt away and unzipped his pants.

"I can hardly wait," she said breathlessly.

Tyber cradled Zanita against his chest, thinking that if he truly were the pirate Blooey thought him, he would lock her in his cabin and never let her go.

He nuzzled his chin against the springy curls on the top of her head.

Figuratively speaking, he had no intentions of letting her go. So, she thought she was giving up men, did she? Well, one could always reacquire the taste. For one man. The right man.

He would see to it *personally*.

Since he wasn't a pirate captain, his options weren't as clear cut. Although tying her to his bed was appealing, he would just have to come up with a better plan. . . .

Chapter Five

Seven pairs of bulging fish eyes were staring at her.

Zanita blinked, then stared back, dumbfounded.

An aquarium. She was lying on her side facing a tank. Odd how the little guys were lined up in a horizontal row, just watching her. . . .

Who would put an aquarium of nosy fish next to a bed?

Tyber.

Zanita came fully awake. It all rushed back to her: the pool party that wasn't a pool party, the elaborate dinner that ended up with take-out, the uninhibited seduction followed by a night of monster movies, cookie-dough ice cream, and wild, passionate lovemaking. All interspersed with physics lessons.

She knew of only one man who was capable of providing such an . . . *unusual* evening, and he was currently tightly wrapped around her, sound asleep.

His face was burrowed into her nape.

Gentle, even breaths pulsed against the hairline at the side of her neck. His arms clasped firmly around her middle; one long, muscular leg was thrown over hers. If Zanita had been more fanciful in her thinking, by the way he was holding her she would have suspected that the man was ensuring she would have to be there to greet him in the morning.

Not that she would have skulked out in the middle of the night.

Well . . . perhaps she might have, if she had awoken.

As it was, she had slept soundly—and very comfortably with him cozily warm right next to her—throughout the night. Not that she had a choice. Tyber had deliciously worn her out.

Where did he get his energy?

She winced, making a mental note not to ask him *that* question. Zanita could just imagine the show-and-tell he would require to "explain" all about the energy. She tried to stifle a giggle. Her original assessment of him had been correct—the man was a kook. But such an outrageously *wonderful* kook! She sighed, unconsciously leaning further back into him.

What time was it, anyway? It was impossible to tell here in Tyber's private grotto. The only lights in the darkened room came from the aquariums. She squinted her eyes, peering closely into the Atlantis aquarium in front of her. There was some kind of odd timepiece in there . . . 8:30 if she read the strange dial correctly.

Time to get up and maybe, just maybe, skulk away. It was not that she didn't want to *see* Tyber; it was just that she didn't want to *face* him. This had all the earmarks of being a very embarrassing morning-after scene. They both had been rash.

What if he regretted the evening? Wanted to forget it as soon as possible? What if he had already forgotten it? A man could have short-term memory loss when it suited him.

Besides, she was giving up men.

And mornings were the best time for that sort of thing.

Like starting a diet.

She took a deep breath and tentatively placed her hand on his to see if she could gently release his hold of her. His arms tightened around her stomach. Shoot!

She slowly tried to slide her leg out from under his. He

wouldn't budge. Why did men feel they had the right to sprawl unchecked in a bed?

Now that she realized escape was going to be impossible, Zanita fumed. You never saw women doing that—commandeering the bed and everything in it without an ounce of remorse. Pinning people to the bed and stopping them from leaving—it was reprehensible!

Zanita stiffened as a deep, sleep-hoarse voice murmured next to her ear, "Mmm. Much better than my teddy bear." His silky lips nuzzled her throat. They were hot.

Zanita swallowed. "Tyber, I don't think we should—" Her voice ended in a squeak as his mouth covered a spot of skin just below her ear and heartily drew on it.

"Have I explained resistance to you yet?" he whispered against her throat as his thumbs traced the underside curves of her breasts. "No? Resistance is a—"

"Tyber, I can't believe you're talking physics now! Besides, I need to get up and . . ." She never finished her sentence because he had neatly flipped her over onto her back and was now leaning over her. She was surprised as much by his action as by the look of him.

He was a sexy man in the morning.

His hair hung long and tousled over his shoulders. His blue eyes were half-closed, still drowsy; they had a slumberous appeal to them. His mouth was soft, the beautifully shaped lips still slightly swollen from her ardent kisses of the previous night.

Zanita was momentarily struck spellbound.

Which gave Tyber the opening he was looking for.

He wedged his leg between her thighs and dropped his head.

"Do you know the best way to overcome resistance?" he mouthed against her lips as he clasped her hands, threading his fingers through hers to pinion her to the mattress.

"Using a greater force to get one's way?" Zanita responded in a sugary-sweet tone, trying her best to irk him. She knew it hadn't worked when he chuckled low against her mouth.

"That is an option." His big toe skittered teasingly down

81

her instep. "But I think—*believe*—it is always preferable to introduce *another* force to overcome the resistant force." He stroked his leg against her inner thigh. Zanita sucked in her breath.

Desire. He was using her desire to overcome her resistance.

His leg moved higher and higher as he rubbed and stroked it against the inside of her legs. With each pass he came closer and closer to her juncture, never quite reaching it. The tricky devil! Whoever thought she would be waylaid by a scientific principle?

Challenging, passion-dilated eyes gazed directly into hers.

The anticipation was killing her. Would he? Won't he? *Please . . .*

Even though she bit her lip with his next teasing caress, Zanita could not stop the moan from escaping her lips. The small, sexy sound made Tyber's glazed focus shift to her mouth.

"Give over to me, baby," he groaned.

That was it. She was lost. Zanita raised her head slightly off the pillow, bringing her lips a hairsbreadth from his own. "Oh, Tyber, what am I going to do with you?"

"Any damn thing you want." His mouth crashed down on hers.

Zanita entered the kitchen, shocked to see that Blooey had prepared a huge Sunday brunch for them. Tyber was still in the shower, having played the gentleman by waiting for her to finish hers before taking his when she flatly refused to share it with him. How did he expect her to give up men when he continually made her fall off the wagon?

No. No more.

She'd be the first to admit that she had momentarily been swayed off her course by an incredible set of pecs and a boyishly charming, pouting lower lip and wickedly seductive eyes. But that was all over with.

The light of day had come, literally, when she opened the

bathroom drapes. With it had come reason. Sensibility. A sense of purpose.

Zanita shivered slightly in her shorts and sleeveless top. The weather had changed. The brief Indian summer had already gone. Swirling autumn leaves flew by the kitchen windows in a brisk breeze. Zanita wryly noted that Hambone was curled up next to the wood stove on a small braided rug. She would bet her next month's salary that the cat would wisely stay by the coveted spot until next spring.

Blooey walked into the room from the pantry, not seeming at all surprised by her appearance. She couldn't help but wonder how many other times he had witnessed a similar occurrence. Her glance took in the appetizing brunch laid out on the table. No, he wasn't surprised at all that she had spent the night.

Her shoulders sagged.

She supposed that anyone who looked like Tyber probably had guest brunches on a regular basis. There probably were a lot of women out there willing to overlook the fact that he was a physicist. She sighed.

"Good morrow, yer ladyship! Are ye hungry? I fixed a fair bit of food fer ye, thinkin' ye might be ravenous." He winked saucily at her. Zanita blushed.

"What's this now? Don't be shy, Lady Masterson. 'Tis a well-known fact the Captain be a vigorous man."

Zanita turned a brighter shade of red. The little pirate took some getting used to. "Do—do you do this often, Blooey?"

"Often enough; every Sunday, Lady Masterson." He noted her crestfallen expression. "But it's always been just me, the Captain, and that scalawag Hambone," he hastened to add. "It be more special with a lady such as yerself present."

"Oh. I thought . . ." Blooey looked at her knowingly, and for an instant Zanita saw the sharp intelligence behind his expression.

"The Captain's somewhat fierce about his privacy."

"Thank you, Blooey." Blooey nodded before going to pour her some coffee.

Tyber entered the kitchen, hair still slightly damp from his shower. He was carrying a red-plaid flannel bathrobe, which he held open for her.

"I thought you might be cold with those clothes. The weather's changed." She slipped her arms through the sleeves.

Tyber turned her around, perfunctorily fastening the tie belt with a firm tug. He kissed her nose, saying, "Sorry, baby, no more pool parties for us until the spring."

As if he had really had a pool party! The robe was ridiculously big on her. She felt like a child playing dress-up. Blooey handed her a cup of coffee just as she took a chair. Caffeine was needed quickly if she was going to deal effectively with Dr. Evans.

"Tyber, I want to thank you for a lovely . . ." her voice faltered slightly, "Time. I really have to be going."

He looked over the mound of scrambled eggs he was ladling onto her plate, a hurt expression crossing his face. "You're not going to stay for breakfast?"

"Well, I . . ."

"Blooey will be terribly disappointed, especially after he went to all this trouble. Won't you, Blooey?" He speared Blooey with a pointed look.

Blooey coughed. "Aye! It wouldn't be right of yer ladyship, would it?"

Zanita looked from one to the other of them, realizing she was neatly trapped. She slumped in the seat.

"We even have the Sunday paper for you." Tyber's eyes gleamed in triumph while he handed her the front section of the newspaper.

Hambone tested the air with an upturned nose, and sensing the serving of food, slowly lumbered to his feet to pad over to the table. He stopped at Tyber's chair, staring demandingly up at him.

Tyber unconsciously filled a small saucer with some eggs and bacon and placed it on the floor in front of the scruffy tabby.

Zanita gaped at him. Tyber caught her staring at him after

the third forkful of eggs. "What?"

"You forgot to give the cat some coffee."

"Huh? Oh, he likes his after he eats." He went back to his plate as if the earth was once again back on its axis, merrily spinning about the sun.

She was in a nut house.

Zanita wisely turned her attention to her newspaper.

They ate in companionable silence except for the occasional curses from the backyard where Blooey was trying to save his butternut squash from the predicted freeze that evening. Suddenly, Zanita sat straight up in her chair.

"Tyber, it says here that noted psychic Xavier LaLeche is giving a seminar and a demonstration on healing this evening!"

Tyber looked up from his *Analog* magazine with glazed eyes, taking a moment to readjust to this atmosphere. "Where?"

"At the Kingston function hall in Blaketon."

He rubbed his chin. "Hmm, two hours to get there and two hours back. What time?"

"Eight o'clock; think we can do it?"

"Yeah. It'll be a late night, though. Do you have to get up early in the morning?"

"Fairly, why?"

"If you promise you won't wake me, I'll drive."

Zanita flushed. "Tyber, we need to get something straight. I'm not going to spend another night here."

"Of course not."

Zanita nodded in agreement, pleased that he understood.

"I want you to move in."

Her cup clattered in the saucer. "*What*?"

Tyber left his seat, coming around the table to kneel in front of her on one knee. He took her chilled hands in his. "Don't get nervous, Curls. I know you've given up men and I respect that. It's just that I think it will be a lot easier to investigate this story of yours if we have ready access to each other. You know, sometimes the best ideas happen in the middle of the night." He smiled beseechingly at her.

"What—you never heard of a telephone?"

His thumb traced the top of her hand. "It's not the same. You can't brainstorm over the phone effectively. Didn't you ever hear of think tanks?"

She furrowed her eyes. "Yes, but do you really think it would help you?"

He trapped her hands inside his own. "Immeasurably."

"You mean, *temporarily*, just while we're working together on the story?"

"Think of all the time we'd save."

She scratched her neck. "I don't know . . ."

He leaned forward to give her succulent little kisses between his words. "Don't—you—think—it's—a—good—idea, baby?"

"But Tyber, I told you I don't want to get involved!"

He raised his eyebrows. "Involved? Who said anything about it getting involved?"

"No! I mean us! *Us* involved . . ."

"Mmm, we are, aren't we?" His tongue swirled inside her mouth in a devastating foray.

Blooey started to enter the kitchen carrying a basket of squash. Still kissing Zanita, Tyber motioned to Blooey behind his back. Without breaking his stride, the little pirate turned and left the room.

Tyber poured on the heat. "Yes?" he whispered into her mouth.

The man could kiss. Zanita tried to think. It wasn't easy under the circumstances. She needed his help, that she knew. With Tyber's background, his input would be invaluable in exposing the fraud. What's more, she would have more time to work on him for an interview, although she didn't hold out much hope for *that*. But move in with him?

Temporarily.

It wouldn't be as if she had to deal with a real relationship or anything.

It was a business arrangement. Sort of.

It would make it easier to work together; she could see that. And if they indulged in a side . . . *thing*, well . . . they were adults. Truth was, now that Tyber had given her a taste of the heretofore elusive fruit, she wouldn't mind taking a few more bites, so to speak. As long as he understood the ground rules.

She clutched his shoulders. "You—you wouldn't think of yourself as my—my boyfriend, would you?"

Tyber smiled against her cheek. "Hell, no."

Your man, baby. The one you're going to acquire an insatiable taste for. He kissed her without mercy.

"Yes?" he drawled once more against her mouth, the flat of his palms at her back, bringing her tight against him.

"Oh God, yes . . ." Her fingers filtered through the long locks of his hair as she kissed him back.

When Zanita was getting ready to leave, Blooey purposely walked by the kitchen door and discreetly gave Tyber the thumbs-up. Aye, the Captain was a pirate after his own heart. Blooey beamed. *Always sets his course and steers true to it.*

Blooey sauntered away singing a ribald sailor's ditty comparing the sleek lines of a clipper ship to those of the female form.

"I thought you said you were through with men?"

Mills picked up one of Zanita's paperbacks, read the title, and plopped it back onto the coffee table.

"I am. Kind of." Zanita scurried around the room throwing some clothes, books—whatever she happened to spot—into some cartons.

"Oh?" Mills looked unconvinced. She shook her head, muttered something under her breath, then plopped herself onto the coffee table.

"Really. Tyber is . . . *different.*"

"How so?"

Zanita blushed.

Mills sat up straighter. "You didn't!"

Zanita nonchalantly held one of her sweaters up to her in

front of the mirror, trying to decide whether to take it with her.

"*He did?*"

Zanita looked at her friend through the mirror and raised her eyebrows.

Mills grinned slyly. "When can *I* meet him?"

"Mills! Behave yourself."

"*That* good, huh?"

Zanita fell on the couch in a mock swoon, draping a hand across her forehead. "Incredible."

"Hmm. So, are you two going away for an intimate little trip?" She gestured to the cartons piled haphazardly over the living room.

"Oh. No, I'm moving in with him."

Mills started choking.

Zanita patted her on the back.

"Are you nuts? What do you mean, you're moving in with him?"

"It's not what you think. Tyber has agreed to work with me on the LaLeche story. We both thought it would be more . . . *expedient* this way. Believe me, Tyber understands how I feel about getting involved again. It's strictly temporary. We'll only be together for the duration of the investigation. Think of it as a professional relationship with personal overtones."

Mills gave Zanita The Look. "Is that what *he* said?"

Zanita thought a minute. Tyber hadn't exactly said it that way, but the general gist had been along those lines. "In a manner of speaking."

"*Whose* manner of speaking?"

"Will you lighten up? It's not as if he—" The doorbell rang. "That must be him; he said he was going to stop by to help me with this stuff."

Mills raised an eyebrow but wisely refrained from making any comments. She would reserve her judgment of this Dr. Evans until she met him.

Zanita opened the door to let Tyber in. He was wearing washed-out jeans, boots, and a brown leather bomber jacket.

His hair hung loose about his shoulders. "Hi, Tyber."

"Hi, baby." He wrapped his arm around her neck, bringing her to him for a quick kiss.

Flustered as usual by his touch, Zanita turned to Mills, performing a one-way introduction. "This is my friend, Mills."

Tyber smiled to himself before greeting her friend and completing the introduction. "Hi." He jerked his thumb in Zanita's direction. "I'm her special aberration."

Mills did something Zanita had never seen her composed friend do in all the years she had known her. She gaped, momentarily speechless. When she found her voice, it was slightly shaky. "Nice to meet you, Tyber. Zanita has said a lot of—" here she faltered—"*interesting* things about you."

Tyber's glance flicked to Zanita. His eyes sparkled in amusement. "Mmm, did she?"

Zanita rushed in to stop this line of conversation from going anywhere else. "Um . . . I'm taking all this stuff here, okay?"

Tyber eyed the collection of cartons piled pell-mell with God-knew-what inside. Anyone else would have packed a suitcase, but not his Zanita. He couldn't help the brief smile that crossed his face.

"Okay." He bent to retrieve the first carton.

Zanita eyed him with some trepidation. She knew she had overpiled the cartons. They must weigh a ton. He didn't seem to be having any trouble, though.

Mills went to stand next to her. They both silently eyed Tyber as he knelt down, jeans pulling taut against his muscular thighs.

Mills spoke softly so her voice wouldn't carry. "I could kill you."

A dimple popped into Zanita's cheek. "Meow."

"Unfortunately, I'm your friend, so I'll have to sheath my claws. You must have had one hell of a horoscope this month."

They smiled identical smiles at Tyber as he passed them effortlessly carrying the box.

* * *

"I think you turn right here."

"I think you said that an hour ago."

"Do you think we'll be late?"

"Only if the truck doesn't make warp 10," Tyber responded wryly.

"Damn! If we enter the seminar late, we'll stand out too much."

Tyber glanced over at the yellow-and-turquoise polka-dot pant suit she was wearing and wisely held his tongue.

"Maybe we'll sneak in." Zanita fished in her bag for a nail file.

"Maybe we won't." She stopped rummaging around in her purse to look at him, surprised. "I think that action is just as likely to cause suspicion as to alleviate it. What are you looking for, the directions?"

"No, my nail file—I'm hungry and I thought I'd have an apple."

He took his eyes off the road for an instant to stare speechlessly at her. *Non-linear.*

"Ah, here it is!" She proceeded to bisect an apple she produced from the depths of the same bag by spearing it with a metal file. "Here you go." She handed him the sawed-off half.

Tyber eyed the gritty edge dubiously. "Ah, no thanks— maybe later."

"Aren't you hungry?" She blithely crunched away at the fruit. "Blooey said he'd leave some sandwiches on the table for us before he goes to bed, or as he put it, 'before I hit me bunk fer the night.' "

"Zanita, do you have any idea where we're going?"

She paled, staring at him wide-eyed. "In—in what sense?"

He rolled his eyes. "In the sense of *do you know where Kingston Hall is*?"

"Oh." She fidgeted in her seat. "I do and I don't."

"It's a fixed point in space. I don't understand your statement."

"Well . . . I've been there once before, so I know where it

is; only right now I don't really know *where* it is."

Tyber shook his head. "Somehow, there was an interesting quantum aspect to your answer."

"If you say so."

"Wait a minute; here's that corner again. This time I'm turning left."

"There it is! To think we've been going right by it for the past hour and fifteen minutes because you've been turning *right* all this time."

Tyber narrowed his eyes at her.

Totally unaware of his searing look, Zanita leaned toward him, whispering last-minute instructions as if they were about to heist a bank.

"Remember—act nonchalant, try to blend in, and whatever you do, don't call attention to yourself. We'll just observe him tonight to see if there is anything odd we can pick up on."

Tyber watched her remove a pair of strapless polka-dot heels from her bottomless bag, raising a silent eyebrow when she slipped them on.

"Ah, Zanita, about your clothes . . ." Her head snapped up, a worried expression marring her sweet face.

"What is it? Is something wrong with them?" She nervously smoothed the crease in her pants, staring at him anxiously.

He swallowed. "No. No, baby; I just wanted to tell you that I think your outfit is . . . is rather . . ." She gazed at him expectantly, her large violet eyes widening. He rubbed his jaw. "It suits you."

She beamed. "Thank you, Tyber; that was very sweet of you." She linked her arm through his as they walked inside. "Remember—lay low."

"Uh-huh."

They found two seats to the rear of the hall. Zanita was relieved to see they hadn't missed too much; apparently there were a few "opening acts." In fact, Xavier LaLeche was just coming onto the stage now.

In black suit and turtleneck, LaLeche was in his early forties. He had perfectly coiffed black hair that was silvered around the edges just so. Zanita thought him picture-book handsome in a way that was much too slick. When he introduced himself, he displayed a compellingly suave voice that would have been at home on any pulpit. He was exactly what she had expected.

"Now *that's* more like it," she whispered to Tyber. "I can't believe that when I first entered your classroom I actually thought you were a guru. It's really sort of silly now that I think of it."

"Really. Would you like to see how fast I can mesmerize you?" He poked one of her polka-dots.

"Very funny. Shh—let's hear what he has to say like good little sycophants."

Xavier LaLeche faced his audience with a serene yet compelling demeanor. "Good evening and welcome to the Healing Heart Seminar. It gladdens my spirit to see so many new souls reaching for a higher attunement." He paused dramatically. "I hope tonight that each and every one of you, if only for a moment, will experience a finer perception, a lifting, if you will, of your consciousness, an embracing of your higher self, and you'll allow the miracle of healing into your being." A hearty round of applause followed.

Zanita leaned into Tyber. "What did he just say?"

He patted her knee. "Nothing to be concerned about, dear."

LaLeche continued, "In order to understand about healing we must first understand about energy."

Tyber leaned forward in his seat. Here was a subject he was an expert on.

"Ancient esoteric knowledge holds that the body is contained in a field of energy. But how is it contained?"

Tyber started to raise his hand, thought better of it, and lowered it.

"The energy in our bodies is, shall we say, controlled by our consciousness. Indeed, our very life force is an emanating energy coming from each and every one of our cells. That is why we are all so very different from one another."

"Huh?" Zanita scratched her head.

"Even Chinese philosophy subscribes to the belief in an energy system, preferring to think of it as an actual electric current which runs throughout the body. You may have heard of this in connection with the technique known as acupuncture. The Sanskrits believe in centers of energy within the body. They call these centers of energy *chakras*."

"I don't believe this." Tyber spoke low in her ear. "He's taking bits and pieces from different respected traditions, then he's tossing them together to form"—he pointed to the handout they had been given at the door—"*the LaLeche Method*," he mouthed, causing her to giggle.

"Energy vibrations!" LaLeche's voice boomed throughout the room. "All living things have energy vibrations. All living things vibrate with their own special frequency. All living things vibrate at their own levels."

"It's called a discrete frequency, but he got it completely skewed. This is what I mean about knowing your physics, Zanita. If the man had more background knowledge on the principles of—" A man behind them shushed Tyber.

LaLeche was on a roll now. "Our bodies are always vibrating!"

"I know mine is," Tyber drawled in her ear. Zanita elbowed him in the side.

". . . Our bodies are also instruments through which we experience spiritual as well as sexual ecstasy . . ."

"Ah, now we're getting to the good part." Tyber winked.

". . . sexual and spiritual ecstasy are both experienced through the chakras, specifically, the same chakra. This is why we so often mistake spiritual awakening with sexual arousal . . ."

"I can't say that's ever happened to me. How 'bout you, Curls?"

"Shh!"

"When I'm aroused, I'm definitely sure it's sexual in origin." He tickled her arm.

"Sexual energy is focused; it seeks a release through intense activity . . ."

"Is it getting hot in here to you?"

"Tyber!"

He grinned.

". . . whereas spiritual energy flows. It is everywhere, through you and me, rocks, trees, the stars—the body craves ecstasy . . ."

"Can't argue with that."

"Tyber, quit it! You're making me laugh."

"Allow me to demonstrate. I'll need a volunteer." Several hands went up in the audience. "You there"—he pointed in their direction—"the one with the polka-dot shirt."

"*Me*?" Zanita squeaked.

"Yes, you. Come on up! I want to demonstrate the difference between spiritual and sexual ecstasy."

Tyber immediately stood up. "Now just a minute—"

"I assure you, sir, it's perfectly *safe* ecstasy." He gave Tyber a smarmy smile. The audience laughed at the double entendre.

"It's okay, Tyber." Zanita stood next to him. "Don't worry, he's not going to do anything too weird on the stage. Try and remember, we're supposed to like this guy."

Tyber wasn't convinced. He clasped her shoulders. "I don't know if I want you going up there. Who knows what he might do? I don't want him putting his hands on you."

"Will you listen to yourself!" She leaned into his chest, speaking quietly. "You sound like a . . . *you know.*"

He looked perplexed. "A uno?"

"A boyfriend!" she gritted out.

Tyber dropped his hands from her shoulders. "Oh. Sorry." Zanita turned, walking jauntily up to the stage. *Regardless of what I sound like, if he puts his hands on you, baby, he's dead meat.*

"Hi, there." LaLeche held out his hand to her. "What's your name?"

"Zanita."

"Pretty name for a pretty lady. Tell me, Zanita, do you meditate often?"

"Um . . . every month."

Tyber winced at her response, but LaLeche seemed very understanding. Too understanding to Tyber's way of thinking.

"I know; sometimes it's hard to find the time in our busy days for the really important things. Now Zanita—have a seat—I want you to close your eyes and think of a white light. Do you see it?"

"Yes."

"It surrounds you. Embrace the white light."

"I thought you weren't supposed to do that."

"Whyever not, my dear?"

"In that movie, *Poltergeist*, they kept saying, 'Stay away from the light, Carol Ann. Stay away from the light.' " The audience laughed, thinking she was joking. LaLeche was caught off guard for a minute.

Tyber, recognizing the Zanita touch, smirked. *Just wait, buddy, it's only the beginning.*

"Yes, well, that was Hollywood and this is reality. You can trust me; let the light surround you."

"Okay; I'm surrounded."

"Er . . . good. Now I want you to meditate on scenes involving outer and inner self. When you breathe in, say inside; when you breathe out, say outside. This will help you to focus, to image."

"Okay. Inside. Outside . . ." Zanita performed the exercise, her breathing getting deeper, her voice breathy. ". . . inside . . . outside . . ."

Tyber looked around the audience, particularly at the male members, noticing that some of them were beginning to sweat. He crossed his arms and stared at the stage, watching LaLeche like a hawk.

"You see, sometimes an attunement can be as erotic as an actual sexual experience."

"Inside . . . outside . . ."

LaLeche put his hand on her shoulder. "That's fine, my

95

dear. You can go back to your seat now.''

When she reached Tyber's side, he noted that several men were watching her with speculative looks in their eyes. The pirate captain in him impaled them one by one with an appropriately icy glare. Their attentions skittered away like bilge rats.

''That was pretty impressive.'' He put his arm around her shoulders. ''Fine piece of acting up there, Curls.''

''Who was acting?'' She fanned herself. ''I feel like a cat on a hot tin roof!''

He grinned. ''You wanna go outside? Pick-up's got an eight-foot bed.''

''Cut it out. Next time you're the guinea pig. So what do you think so far? Genuine or not?''

''Not.''

''Because you don't think there's anything to this healing stuff?''

''No, actually I think there might be something to psychic healing. But not this guy.''

''Why?''

''He's too slimy.''

Chapter Six

"The audience seemed pretty impressed with him."

"He has an impressive stage presence; but then, most charlatans do."

They were once again in Big Red, making the long drive back to Tyber's house. Unfortunately, it was through dark back-country roads.

"I'm glad you're driving; I'm beat." Zanita yawned.

"Long day."

"Long night." She yawned again.

"If you noticed—his topics were very general in this seminar. On the handout they gave us, it says he'll be appearing next Friday at the South Town meeting center. Much smaller room. I have the feeling that performance won't be advertised."

"How come?"

"I think he filters through his audience until he gets the group he's looking for. On Friday, you'll see another gleaning."

"Looking for the most devoted?"

"That; and the most malleable."

"How'd you get to be so smart?" She playfully pulled a hank of his hair.

"I ate my vegetables when I was a little boy."

She peered disbelievingly at him in the dark confines of the truck's cab. "You were once a little boy?"

"Well, not really."

"I didn't think so."

"After he separates the next group out, you'll probably see something like an 'invitation only' demonstration."

"Think we'll make the break?"

"Yup."

"Why are you so sure?"

"Two reasons: first, he liked you." He threw her a slightly disgruntled look. "A *lot*."

"How do you know that?"

Tyber sighed deeply. "I know."

"What, is this like a *man thing*?" Zanita folded her arms across her chest, put out by the ridiculous assertion.

"Yes. Believe me; he liked you."

"Uh-huh. What's the second reason?"

"He recognized me."

Zanita sat forward in her seat. "How can you be sure?"

"I had my suspicions when his glance strayed my way once too often; I knew it for sure the instant he chose you from the audience."

She exhaled. "Does this blow our cover?"

"Not completely. He has no reason to be suspicious of you; as far as he's concerned you were just with me. He's probably as curious as hell as to why I was there."

"What are we going to say?"

"At the next meeting, when he contrives to meet with us, I'll tell him the truth—that I'm very interested in all aspects of psychic healing."

"What makes you think that will be enough to get an invitation to these inner circle meetings?"

"He won't be able to resist the bait. My name in any connection with his would instantly give him mainstream credibility. He will do everything in his power to lure me.''

"God, you make him sound like a vampire or something.''

"He is. But instead of blood, he sucks the hope, the money, and the spirit out of people who believe in him. People go to him with a pure desire to enhance their spirit; instead, he drains it away. I want to nail him, Zanita.''

She knew how Tyber felt; she had felt the same way when she found out about Mrs. Haverhill. She put her hand on his shoulder. "We will.''

"Are you cold, baby? Should I put the heat on?''

"A little.'' She yawned again, stretching her now bare feet to the heater under the dash. "Mmmm, that feels good.''

"Only another ninety minutes to go; we should be home about one-thirty. I wonder what kind of sandwiches Blooey left us. I'm hungry now—how about you?''

Somehow he wasn't surprised when he received no response. Zanita had, of course, already fallen asleep.

Blooey had left the porch light on for them.

Tyber made his way around the truck to Zanita's side, gently lifting her out of the cab.

"Mgphm . . .''

"Shh. It's okay.'' Tyber carried her up the stairs onto the porch.

When he inserted his key into the lock, she sleepily asked, "What is it? The Hogs?''

What was this with the hogs? "No, baby, go back to sleep.''

He grabbed a sandwich off the kitchen table with one hand, holding Zanita with the other. He devoured it as he climbed the stairs with her. Once in his bedroom, he quickly undressed them both, put her into bed, put himself into bed, took her in his arms . . . and immediately fell asleep.

He was already inside her when he woke up.

He didn't remember how it had happened, but he had a pretty good idea. Zanita had done *something* to him from the minute he laid eyes on her. He knew it; and his subconscious knew it, too. How would she react? He decided to tip the scales in his favor.

Zanita's eyelids were just fluttering open in confusion as Tyber lowered his head, joining their mouths as well.

"Good morning." His eyes sparkled slumberously down on hers as he readjusted his fit in her.

"*Tyber* . . ." Her violet eyes were heavy-lidded with sleep and rising passion; he thought her wildly sexy.

He lifted her hand from where it was resting on the bed, ardently pressing scorching lips to her palm before swirling his tongue across the sensitive center.

Zanita's breath caught.

His thumb and forefinger held her wrist up for the downward play of his open mouth across her inner arm. Slowly, he traversed the arm, caressing with velvet lips that gently blew across the moistened skin.

It was devoutly erotic.

And all this time, he remained embedded in her to the hilt.

Strange, but it seemed to him as though time had somehow slowed down just for Tyberius Augustus Evans, slowed down so he could savor each minute sensation, each quivering breath she took, each moment they were joined together.

Zanita watched him silently. On a strange level, coming from one dream into another, she felt as if she were two people: the awake Zanita, keenly feeling every point of indelible sensation from the pulsating touch of this man, and the other Zanita, the Zanita still caught in her dream, seeing, as if through a gauzy veil, a man so utterly beautiful, a man making deep-felt, torrid love to a woman while she was still sleep-warmed by him.

Tyber paused, quietly raising his lashes to meet her eyes.

Zanita held her breath. There was a seriousness about him.

He waited silently, staring into her with those light blue eyes of his . . . staring at her, not moving, as his pupils began slowly dilating to his arousal, staring at her while she felt the slightest trembling inside her from him.

"Kiss me. Kiss me now, Tyber." Her voice caught on his name.

He sealed his mouth over hers, blending them. A scalding heat poured from him into her; his lips teased, his tongue stroked, his teeth nipped. But he did not move.

He was driving her mad. She needed, wanted him to—

She tried to wiggle her hips.

His hands came down to hold her still.

She moaned against his mouth.

He twitched inside her, but stayed still.

"*Please*, Tyber, let me—"

He shook his head.

His tongue thrust inside her mouth. She whimpered, kissing him back, locking their mouths together.

"Just feel, baby."

He began to throb; she could feel him throb. Intensifying. Heat. It was beating along and through her. His pulsing or her pulsing? Something was happening. He was—she was—They. Became.

Her breaths were short, shallow, rapid; she was panting.

His breaths were deep, ragged, building . . .

When she began to cry into his mouth, he moaned into hers, squeezing his eyes shut. He did not move.

Impossibly, he was swelling more in her. Tight. He was in so tight.

She began to tremble.

He quickly clasped his arms around her and clutched her to him in a powerful grip. She screamed her release against him; he shouted his against her.

She felt a long, hot splash inside her.

"I'm sorry. It just happened. I wasn't going to. Is it okay, baby?"

She tenderly cupped his cheek. "Yes, it's okay." There was no need for him to be concerned in any way. "Don't worry, Tyber."

He smiled tenderly at her. "You too, baby." There wasn't

101

a doubt in his mind from that moment on that he was irrevocably hers.

When she came into the kitchen, Zanita skittishly viewed the orange muffin Tyber was popping into his mouth.

"What *is* that?"

"Butternut squash muffin." He placed one in front of her. "It's butternut-everything until next spring. I expect you to help me out here."

She eyed the muffin dubiously. "What does it taste like?"

"Like a mufffin made out of squash. Eat up." He saluted her with his half-eaten one.

Zanita sat down, tentatively taking a little bite out of the muffin. "Not bad."

"I'll remind you you said that come January."

"Can't Blooey freeze any of the crop?"

"Froze it; canned it; cold-stored it." Tyber looked at the plate of muffins in front of him with a resigned expression.

She reached across the table to pat his hand consolingly. "You'll survive, Doc."

Unfortunately, Blooey chose that exact moment to walk in the back door carrying yet another bushel. "Didn't get nearly as cold as what they feared last night. I managed to save these rascals—be looking forward to these beauties on a cold winter night, eh, Captain?" He whistled off to the pantry.

Tyber's head clunked against the tabletop.

Zanita giggled. "It's a good thing I love butternut squash."

He raised his head four inches off the table and showed a woebegone face. "Just wait until he starts on the soup." He shuddered, dropping his head again with a thunk.

"Well, at least you can look forward to your dessert every night."

"Squash *pie*," came the voice from the tabletop.

"I'm sure you're exaggerating . . . aren't you?"

He raised his head to give her a "you'll see" grin.

Zanita hesitated before taking a sip of her coffee, raised her eyebrow at him, then shrugged her shoulders.

Tyber drank his coffee slowly, watching her over the rim of his cup. "Do you have an unnatural fear of . . . hogs?" he asked conversationally, as if he were asking her to pass the butter.

"*What*?" Her cup clattered back into the saucer. "What are you talking about?"

"Well, several times when you've been disturbed in your sleep, you've mentioned . . . hogs."

"Oh, you mean *The* Hogs."

"*The* hogs?" He looked a little wary of her now.

"Yes; at night they sometimes come by my grandfather's farm causing mayhem."

He lowered his coffee cup. "You're kidding. In Stockboro?" He had never heard of any motorcycle gangs in the area.

She waved her hand. "All the time. And believe me, it's like they get some kind of demented pleasure out of ransacking the place."

"Is there no one to stop them? Where are the authorities?"

"Forget it. It's been tried before. It's hopeless, been going on for years. Why, I remember one night when I was still a teenager, I was coming home late from a party at my girlfriend's so I was trying to sneak in the back, when I was suddenly surrounded by them."

Tyber leaned forward in concern, taking her hand. "They didn't hurt you, did they, Curls?"

"Well, they snuffled me a little, but generally they're pretty harmless."

"*Snuffled you*?"

"Yeah, but they moved on quickly because they were really after my grandfather's corn."

"You're talking about *real* hogs, aren't you?"

"Of course. What else would I be talking about?"

Tyber leaned back in his chair, tapping his fingers against the side of his cup. "One can only surmise and hope for the best."

"Huh?"

"Never mind. Blooey wanted me to ask you if you like"—
he pulled a heavily scrawled piece of notepaper from his
pocket—"fritata."

"What is it?"

"It's a . . ." He paused. "It's got—it's sorta flat . . . I'll tell
him you like it."

"Okay." Tyber didn't see the corners of Zanita's mouth lift
in fond amusement as he absentmindedly returned the note to
his pocket. He was such a sweet man.

"Here." He pulled a little black box out of the same pocket,
sliding it across the table to her.

"What is it? A light sabre?"

He didn't even blink. "It's for the front gate, so you don't
have to call Blooey every time you come in. It's keyed with
a discrete frequency which I change on a regular basis for
security."

"What if I get locked out?" She took the box, placing it
in her purse.

He gave her a wickedly charming smile. "Not you, baby."

Throughout the following week, Tyber diligently "explained" to Zanita the Law of Gravity, the Law of Symmetry,
and Murphy's Law—the latter when he was interrupted by a
phone call during a vigorous explanation of Ohm's Law. Zanita knew that for the rest of her life, should anyone innocently
mention Sir Isaac Newton in passing, she would blush to the
roots of her hair.

She fell into a routine of sorts at My Father's Mansion.

Zanita left for work every morning at nine-thirty, after being
sent on her way with a hearty breakfast from Blooey and a
lingering kiss from Tyber.

Lately, Blooey had taken to giving her a brown bag for
lunch when he discovered she usually skipped the noon meal.
When she told him it wasn't necessary, he firmly closed the
subject by saying, "To keep the scoundrels out there from
devourin' ye whole." Zanita took the bag.

When Zanita returned in the late afternoon, Tyber was always on the veranda swing, sitting sideways with his back against the arm rest, his long legs bent at the knee, booted feet resting on the other arm rest, sipping a cup of something warm. Hambone was usually relaxing close by him, perched on the porch banister, obviously hanging out until the next meal.

After the first day, when Tyber drew her down to sit between his legs, resting her back against his chest as he shared his hot drink with her and giving her little nibble kisses on the back of her neck, it became something of a habit. Zanita never knew if it was Tyber's regular routine to sit on the porch swing at that hour, or if he stopped his work just to wait for her to come home so they could sit and unwind together after the day.

All she knew for sure was that she began looking forward to their quiet hour before dinner. Once she jokingly asked him what they were going to do when it got too cold to sit outside. He immediately replied, ''We move to the hammock in the conservatory—it's heated for the plants.''

Zanita was discovering that there wasn't anything about this man's life that she didn't like.

After a particularly trying day, she trudged tiredly up the veranda stairs. The porch had become her beacon that day. She just could not wait to sink onto that swing. Lie back between his legs. Let his warm strength surround her. Today, especially, she was immeasurably grateful for Tyberius Augustus Evans.

It had been raining on and off all day. She had been caught mostly in the ''on'' stage, chasing down a ridiculous story thirty miles outside of town involving a woman who claimed she had been abducted by aliens. All of these beings from outerspace, she said, looked *exactly* like Norm from *Cheers*.

Of course, Zanita didn't find out that last part until she had accompanied the bizarre woman across four miles of bog-infested fields in the pouring rain while she searched for the evidence the woman claimed she had hidden there.

The ''evidence'' turned out to be an empty six-pack of Bud.

Her head throbbed, her joints were aching, and she suspected the little scratchy feeling at the back of her throat was not going to just go away. She settled against Tyber with a heartfelt sigh.

He smiled against her hair as he handed her the hot drink. "Hard day?"

She held the warm mug up to her forehead. "I don't even want to talk about it."

"All right." He counted to three and waited.

"Can you believe the paper sent me out on this ridiculous lead about a woman abducted by aliens?"

Tyber grinned, gasping theatrically. "No! Not here in Stockboro!"

"I know—it's unbelievable! They had me trudging after this poor, misguided woman through *four* miles of bogs, looking for empty beer cartons."

"Empty beer cartons?"

"The aliens all looked like Norm."

"From *Cheers*," he supplied, wryly.

"Yes."

He nodded his head wisely. "Ah, yes, the transmissions."

She peered at him over her shoulder. "What transmissions?"

"The ones we've been sending into space for the past forty or fifty years. You lay people call it TV."

"I never thought of that! Maybe I shouldn't have dismissed her story so quickly."

"Zanita, I am sure you gave her credibility a more than generous hearing," he said dryly.

"Oh, but it was awful—look at my shoes!" She held up one small mud-encrusted foot.

"Poor baby."

"Why would she come up with such a—a *stupid* story?"

Tyber shrugged. "Too much joy juice in the sixties? We are an *interesting* community, aren't we? I know if I were an alien, I'd hightail here. Where else could I live undetected amongst the local flora and fauna?" He nipped her neck.

"Very funny."

"I missed you today." He kissed the top of her head.

"You say that every day." She sipped the mulled cider.

"I miss you every day."

"Don't be silly," were her words, but she scooted further back against him, letting his warmth enfold her.

He nuzzled her curls with his nose. "Don't you ever miss me?"

"Um . . . I guess."

His arms encircled her. "You know, it's okay; you *can* admit to missing me. I promise I won't tell anyone."

She laughed. "All right; I missed you too."

"I know you often drive into Stockboro just to use the word processor in your office. I thought it might be easier for you, especially when winter comes and the snow starts piling up, if you had a lap-top."

"I'd love a lap-top, but they're too expensive. I can't afford one on my salary. I have a confession to make: I'm not exactly a Rockerfeller."

"And here I thought I could woo you for your money."

She dug into her pocket, withdrawing thirty-five cents in change. "Will that suffice?"

"Yes. I can be had cheaply." He hugged her. "Seriously, let me buy you a lap-top."

"That's very sweet, Tyber, but far too grand a gesture. Besides, I'm sure we'll figure out LaLeche's scam way before then, so I'll be back in my cozy in-town apartment just a hairsbreadth from the office."

He stilled a moment.

"Christmas is only a few months away and it's our first case—it might take us longer than you think." *Might take years*, he thought.

She placed her hands on top of his, which were laced together resting on her stomach. "Oh, I couldn't let you do that, Tyber, really. It's so sweet of you, but please don't. Anyway, if I had a lap-top, I'd be tempted to do what I've always wanted to do."

"Which is?"

"You promise you won't laugh?"

"I'd never laugh at someone's dream. After all, I happen to live in one of my own." He gestured to the house.

"Yes, you do. Do you know how lucky you are, Tyber? To live your dream?"

"I do. But some dreams lend themselves to creation, Zanita. Take the atmosphere of this house, for instance. Atmosphere is not tangible, but can arise out of a collection of tangible things. I created the atmosphere, so in a sense, I created the dream."

"Tyberius Augustus Evans, dream-weaver extraordinaire." She cuddled into him.

He smiled faintly. "Then there are the other dreams, the ones that cannot be created. They're dreams of hope and desire. Should those dreams become reality, a person is indeed lucky." His arms tightened around her. "So what is your deep, dark secret?" He kissed her behind her ear.

"I would love to just . . . well, I've always wanted to investigate . . . the unusual and then write about it."

Tyber was not at all surprised. Somehow this was very Zanita. "Care to define unusual?"

"No, that's just it—whatever *I* think I should write about. I would take these unusual subjects, like the paranormal for instance, and write about them honestly. Seriously. No tabloid journalism. No slant on sensationalism. I mean real, serious exploration. If it wasn't so, I'd unveil it; if it was, I'd reveal it."

"Isn't it being done?"

"Not the way I would do it. Most articles out there are either not completely factual, or else the reader feels that the author left out a chunk of the story to support his or her particular slant. I want to do it in a totally unbiased way—report exactly what I found, whatever the subject. That's why I was so excited when the LaLeche story presented itself to me."

"Yes, but you did have an opinion about him before you met him," he pointed out.

"True, but one has to have a healthy dose of skepticism and that story is somewhat different. I still would have endeavored to write an unbiased article, regardless of my personal feelings at the outset. It's just that he's an eel and we both know it."

"So, what you're saying is, you want to explore paranormal topics, do your own investigation, and write about it." *My God, she's found the perfect mathematical formula for trouble*, he thought prosaically.

"Exactly! It's different when you observe someone doing the investigation and write about it. It's not the same as actually *doing* the investigation. Being there." She sighed contentedly. "I could *really* get into that."

Tyber gazed down at the top of her head, something close to horror crossing his features.

"But that's not my favorite dream."

Endless Zanita possibilities for danger rapidly traversed his mind.

She blithely continued, "If I had more time, I'd like to—" She stopped suddenly, aware that she was about to reveal another secret.

"Like to what? C'mon, you have to tell me now." *While I'm still numb.*

"Well, if I had a lap-top, I might like to give fiction writing a try; you know, using some of my stories as background. . . ." Now that sounded like an excellent idea to him.

She half-turned, gazing earnestly up at him. "So, what do you think?"

I think you're going to get a lap-top for Christmas. "Don't ever give up your dreams, Zanita." He placed his finger under her chin, gently lifting her face for the tender press of his pirate mouth. "I promise you; I won't ever give up on mine."

"This wasn't too bad a drive."

Tyber threw her a look. "How would you know? You slept most of the way."

She straightened her skirt, swallowing painfully. She had been right about the scratchy throat—it hadn't gone away. In fact, it felt distinctly worse. "Did I miss anything?"

"Just a perfectly good UFO sighting."

"Ha-ha."

"Red, cylindrical object, pulsating in the sky, seeming to appear from out of nowhere . . ."

Her violet eyes widened. "You *are* joking aren't you?"

"I'm not going to tell you. Maybe from now on you won't fall asleep on me." He glanced her way. "Although it does give you a lovely glow when you wake up."

It was probably the beginnings of a fever, but she wasn't about to tell him; he'd probably insist they return home and there was no way she was going to do that. They had a toehold on LaLeche; she wasn't about to lose it now.

The South Town meeting hall was about a quarter the size of Kingston Hall. As they took their seats, Zanita noted that Tyber had been right about the audience, too. It seemed only the most devout followers from the last seminar had chosen to come to this one.

She recognized a few of the faces, surprised when several of them remembered her by saying hello to her by name. Most of them were men.

"I can't believe they remembered me," she whispered to Tyber.

He stared at her stonily.

"What?"

"Nothing."

LaLeche entered the room, going behind the podium on the raised dais. "Good evening. Thank you for coming. This is much nicer, isn't it? Smaller, less formal—I prefer it, how about you?" Everyone applauded.

Except Tyber.

Zanita elbowed him in the side; he grudgingly clapped a few times.

LaLeche scanned the audience, noting the return faces. His eyes lit on Tyber and remained there. "Dr. Evans! Glad you could make it again. It's a real pleasure." Everyone turned to stare at Tyber, wondering why he deserved to be singled out by their great one.

"Thank you, Mr. LaLeche. I was intrigued by your seminar last time and made it a point to come to this one. I'm very interested in what you're doing."

Zanita inwardly winced at the double meaning behind his words. She only hoped LaLeche didn't pick up on it. Apparently he didn't, for his next words were full of chummy cheer.

"I was never one for the formalities; call me Xavier, please." He paused, waiting for Tyber to return the courtesy. He didn't. "Well . . . You must stick around after we're through here tonight. I'm very curious to hear your impressions of what I'm doing."

"I'm sure you would be," Tyber said under his breath, before saying in a louder voice, "I look forward to it." LaLeche glowed.

"Maybe it's *you* he likes," Zanita quipped.

"Only for the size of my . . . reputation," Tyber flashed back, causing Zanita to blush. He chuckled.

"Cut that out! Be serious or you'll blow everything!"

He had a very good comeback to that, but refrained from using it. "Okay, baby. But remember, serious is as serious does."

"What is that supposed to mean?"

"Look in the third row, fourth seat from the left—Isn't that Forrest Gump sitting there?"

"Tyber, don't start again." However, when she glanced in that direction, she discovered that the man in the audience *did* look like Forrest Gump. Despite herself, she giggled.

"And you didn't believe me about the red spaceship. Shame on you."

She started to shush him, but sneezed instead.

"That's the fourth time you've sneezed this evening."

"Maybe I'm becoming allergic to you." She blew her nose.

"Are you coming down with something?"

"No."

He examined her face closely, noting the flushed cheeks. "You are."

"I am not!"

He took her hand in his and made to rise. "Let's go."

"I'm not leaving!" This she said a little too loudly; several people turned to stare at her. She yanked her hand out of his. "Sit down this minute and stop making a spectacle of yourself!" she hissed.

"Why didn't you tell me you were sick?"

"Because I knew you would behave this way. And I was right! Storming over people's wishes like—"

The corner of his mouth quirked. "You're awfully cranky, aren't you? I mean, for someone who isn't sick."

"—like some bloody pirate captain!" She crossed her arms and refused to look at him for at least half an hour.

LaLeche was already warming up to his subject matter. "For instance, when you introduce an electric current into a wire, it generates a magnetic field. Isn't that right, Dr. Evans?"

"Ah, yes."

"Conversely, when one sends out a healing thought, one is sending out energy with it. The greater the strength or power of the thought, the greater the flow of energy. Now the more the flow of energy, the greater the field of energy. So you see how you create a magnetic field when you generate a strong thought."

Tyber shook his head several times as if to clear it from a punch.

"So, too, with strong healing thought. You see, my friends, the body is like a motor which needs energy fuel to keep running efficiently. Sometimes the motor breaks down and needs to be recharged. The power of healing can do this, especially—*especially*—when you have someone who can effectively generate this energy down the right pathways in the human body. Through my special talents, I can provide and direct the energy you need to heal yourself."

"Maybe he can cure you, Zanita." Tyber leaned over her.

"Then I won't have to be angry with you anymore for not telling me you were sick."

She gave him a disgusted look, saying, "You just earned another fifteen minutes of the cold shoulder." She promptly turned away from him.

"The flow of energy is a very important lesson you will need to learn if you wish to be effective in controlling your well-being. I will share an exercise with you on this technique." He looked into the audience. "Ah, Zanita!"

She jumped.

"I see you returned with our friend Dr. Evans. Since you did such a fine job on the last exercise, I know you won't mind helping me with this one."

"He presses his luck," Tyber muttered.

Zanita made a face at Tyber. "No, I don't mind." She went up to the podium.

Tyber sourly noted that several men leaned forward in their seats, eagerly awaiting the demonstration.

"Now this exercise is designed to make you aware of the flow of electrical energy throughout your body, so that you may begin to control the flow of your magnetic field. I want you to sit in the chair again and close your eyes."

"Okay."

"Surround yourself with the white light."

"Check."

"Check?"

"Surrounded."

"I want you to visualize the appropriate images for movement and stillness while you're doing the exercise. When you inhale, say '*movement*' and when you exhale, say '*stillness.*' All right?"

Zanita's eyes popped open; she stared directly at Tyber and swallowed. He returned her look, his lips twitching with suppressed laughter. They were both remembering a certain morning not too long ago when she had begged him for movement, and he had opted for stillness. It had been one of the most erotic experiences of her life.

There was no way she was going to go through with this exercise with Tyber staring so knowingly at her. She turned flushed cheeks to LaLeche. "Um . . . can we do something else, Mr. LaLeche?"

"Why, whatever for, my dear?"

Whatever for, indeed. Tyber grinned, lacing his hands behind his head. He leaned back in his seat.

Chapter Seven

"Movement." She inhaled.

"Stillness." She exhaled.

Tyber, not moving, eyes passion-drugged as he watched her ignite beneath him . . .

"Movement." She inhaled, deeply.

"Stillness."

The cords of his neck standing out as he threw back his head, struggling not to move in her . . .

"Movement." She inhaled, quicker now.

"Stillness."

The heated press of his mouth, his tongue, arms clasped around her, him inside her everywhere . . .

She exhaled on a moan. "Stillness," she panted.

"Very good, my dear. Do you feel the stillness within you?"

"*Oh, yes!*"

"Excellent. Now you have taken the first step in controlling the flow of energy within you. Do you feel the flow?"

"*I'm flowing.*"

A burst of coughing echoed in the dead silence of the room. Zanita snapped her eyes open and glared at Tyber.

He grinned back at her, a mischievous dimple popping into his cheek. "So sorry. Something got caught in my throat, baby."

He was just so-o contrite. As if he were sincerely apologizing to her! And calling her baby in front of the whole audience! She pierced him with a killing violet death glare.

His low chuckle just reached her on the dais.

She would kill him.

Later, when they were alone. When there weren't any witnesses to the crime.

"That's quite all right, Dr. Evans; we've finished the exercise anyway. I think everyone understands the concept. You may go back to your seat, dear."

When Zanita stood up, she got a healthy round of applause. In fact, on her way back to her seat, one man gave her the thumb's-up, saying, "Yeah!" as she walked by him. She had never been so embarrassed in her life.

When she took her seat, Tyber leaned over her, saying, "I have a much better exercise for you."

She murdered him with her look.

"For when you feel better, Curls."

"As far as I know, Massachusetts still does not have the death penalty," she gritted out. "It makes one contemplate the possibilities. If I were you, I wouldn't push it."

"I wish you'd make up your mind, Zanita. Push it—don't push it . . ." He let the tone of his voice imply that a man's work was never done.

She would ignore him again. It was the only thing to do with him when he got like this. Horrible, teasing wretch! God, her throat hurt.

The rest of the seminar went by at a snail's pace for Zanita, feeling as poorly as she did. LaLeche mostly jammered on, doing several "laying on of the hands," as he called it, to members of the audience. She was thankful he hadn't chosen her for that part of the demonstration. She didn't think she could bear those slimy hands on her.

This time they didn't receive any handouts. Instead, when the talk ended, LaLeche approached several of the participants individually while they were enjoying his largesse of free coffee and refreshments.

He hadn't approached them yet, but Tyber didn't seem particularly concerned. He drank his coffee, patiently waiting for LaLeche to make the rounds.

"Would you like a bite of my cruller?" he innocently offered Zanita.

"I will not talk to you while you are in this mood."

She spun away from him, engaging an elderly woman in conversation, and therefore missed his low snicker when he realized how she had interpreted his remark.

LaLeche circled his way around the room, closing in their direction. All that was missing was a dorsal fin, Zanita thought.

"So, Dr. Evans, what did you think of what you saw here tonight?"

Tyber slowly sipped his drink. "I was impressed." *By your showmanship.*

"Why, thank you. Coming from you, that is a compliment. I must say, it was nice to have a colleague in the audience—someone who completely understands the physical aspect of the universe."

"I can see where it would be." *Since you don't know jack about magnetic fields.*

"Although I was quite surprised to see you had an interest in such things." LaLeche scrutinized Tyber's face carefully, obviously looking for signs of a hidden agenda.

"If you know anything about me"—and Tyber would have bet that since their first meeting, LaLeche had made it his business to know *a lot* about him—"you know I am the type of person who lets his curiosity lead him down various paths. Some of them not very conventional."

"I have heard that about you. Although your particular style hasn't seemed to hurt you in your own community; to the con-

117

trary, it seems to have enhanced your reputation. But then, they say you are so very brilliant.''

''I wouldn't believe everything you hear,'' Zanita piped in.

''Zanita! Thank you so much for your help.'' LaLeche placed his hand companionably on her shoulder, causing her to shudder slightly. ''You have a natural talent, you know.''

Tyber's stare went from LaLeche's hand on her shoulder to his smarmy face. ''And what natural talent would that be?'' His dry tone was easily interpreted. LaLeche quickly disengaged himself.

''For healing, of course. Have you two heard about my retreat up in Vermont? No? Oh, I'll have to tell you about it— it's a small place, very rural, you know, no annoyances or interruptions from the outside world. I run a weekend empowerment session once a month.''

''What do you do up there?'' Tyber was trying to ignore the signal Zanita was giving his toe with the heel of her boot.

''I find that such an atmosphere is conducive to finding and illuminating the chakras. Through meditation and other techniques, we balance our light bodies to release the astral body.''

''All that, huh?''

Zanita ground her heel into his foot.

''And more! Often, in such surroundings of nurturing healing, entire sets of inhibitions are thrown away, allowing the participant to recapture his or her lost sexuality.''

''What does that mean?'' Tyber almost narrowed his eyes.

''It's a remarkable feeling of freedom! You and Zanita would enjoy it tremendously! In fact, I'm having the next workshop a week from today. Do you think you might be interested?''

Tyber was about to refuse; Zanita could sense it. LaLeche had crossed the line. Before he could respond, she jumped in to say, ''We'd love it!'' She ignored Tyber's arm, which had come around her waist, flattening her to him in a punishing grip.

''Wonderful! Here are the directions.'' He reached into his jacket pocket, retrieving a computer printout which he handed to Tyber. "We start around sundown. And remember—it's very rustic."

"Ah, I have a friend who owns an inn near there," Tyber quickly said. "I promised him that if I was ever up that way, I'd stay there. Is that going to be a problem?"

"No, of course not. Although some of the more *intimate* exchanges occur in the late evenings—it just seems to happen that way. You might miss out on those."

"You know how it is, Xavier. He's a professional acquaintance of mine. I thought I'd do some networking at the same time." Tyber spoke to him as if they were already old buddies.

"Absolutely! Don't worry about it! So, I'll see both of you next weekend? Good."

Tyber waited until they were in the truck driving back before he opened up his guns.

"Do you have any idea what you've gotten us into?"

"Of course I do! It's exactly what we wanted him to do."

Tyber counted to ten before he spoke. "Do you know what kind of a place he invited us to?"

"Yes—a retreat."

"A retreat," he repeated blandly.

"That's right. His place of operation, where we can be approached for—"

"Oh, we'll be approached, all right."

"What do you mean? And why on earth did you insist we'd stay at some inn? Do you really have a friend up there?"

"No, I do not have a friend up there! I simply told him that because there is no way in hell I'm going to stay overnight in that environment and neither are you!"

Zanita was affronted by his high-handed attitude. "I'll decide that for myself, *Captain*!"

"Didn't you hear him? All that talk about releasing one's lost sexuality was a euphemism for a weekend of partner exchanging and communal sex."

"Get out of here! I didn't think he meant it that way. He was talking about sexuality in the spiritual sense."

Tyber gave her the mysterious face of Mars look.

She swallowed. "Wasn't he?"

"No. And another thing—when he said rustic environment, you can interpret that to mean a broken-down shack with no amenities in the middle of the wilderness."

"Don't be ridiculous! He would never take prospective marks there. It would destroy his credibility. He would have to make it appear he was respectable."

"Oh really? Well, you're wrong about that, too. A man who might need to pick up and move quickly does not bury his roots deep."

She lifted her chin in the air. "Meaning?"

"Meaning he would invest as little as possible of his own capital in the venture. I bet the place doesn't even have indoor plumbing. And if you're about to ask me how he would get away with it with marks, don't bother—I'll tell you. He'll simply explain it away as part of the 'experience' of getting in touch with your inner self."

Zanita's side of the truck was suspiciously silent.

"What—no comeback?"

Her shoulders sagged. "No, you're right. I didn't think of any of those angles. I'm really not very good at this, am I?"

She looked so dejected, he instantly felt remorse. "You would have, baby, if you were feeling better."

"I suppose so," she sighed.

"How are you feeling?"

"There is nothing wrong with me!" A sneeze punctuated her adamant statement.

"I'll tell you what—why don't you take one of your instant Zanita naps, and if another UFO comes along, I promise I'll wake you up."

She smiled faintly. "Thanks, but I don't think I could fall asleep now."

"This is Zanita talking, isn't it? The woman who has developed the habit of snoozing to a fine art?"

The corners of her mouth twitched. "Well, I suppose I could *try*."

"I have complete confidence in your abilities in this area.

In fact, I can give you a recommendation, should you ever need one.''

"That's a real comforting thought, Doc.'' She sneezed again.

"You're sure you're not sick?'' he asked in a dry tone.

"I told you, I'm fine.''

"Don't you dare even think of rubbing that vile stuff on my chest!''

Tyber had entered the bedroom carrying a tray of various sickroom paraphernalia. Thermometer. Flashlight. Tongue depressor. *Tongue depressor*? Tissues. Aspirin. And a jar of disgusting ointment.

"C'mon, baby, Blooey concocted it just for you. He says it has fresh herbs in it.''

"Like what?''

"Sassafras, comfrey, horehound . . .''

She crossed her arms stubbornly over her chest. "It stinks!''

"Okay.'' He put the jar of salve on the night table. "Guess I'll have to go to Vermont without you.''

"You will not! *Achoo*!''

"You'll never be better by next Friday if you don't take care of yourself.''

"I am taking care of myself!''

"Vermont is so pretty this time of year—peak foliage season. Too bad I'll have to enjoy it all by myself.'' He sat on the bed, patiently waiting for her to come around. It didn't take long.

"My head hurts.'' Her lower lip pouted.

"I know,'' he commiserated sadly.

"My throat feels scratchy,'' she explained, as if he didn't know.

"Poor thing.'' He dipped into the jar.

"And my joints ache, too.''

"This will help.'' He rubbed the ointment on her chest. "Feel better?''

"A little,'' she grudgingly conceded.

"Let me take your temperature.'' He popped the thermometer into her mouth, thinking she really looked quite adorable with her mutinous expression and flannel granny gown buttoned up to her chin. Not that he would mention it to her. God knew how she would interpret it. By comparison, men preferred to have their fingernails ripped out.

When he removed the thermometer, Zanita tried to stare over his shoulder at the reading, but he turned to the side to scrutinize it privately, as if it were a top secret formula of some kind.

"Well, what does it say?" she demanded.

"It says you have a temperature. Say ahh. . . ." He stuck the tongue depressor in her mouth and peered down her throat with the flashlight.

"I hate to break this to you, Doc, but you're a Ph.D, not an M.D."

He arrogantly raised his eyebrow at her.

"You know what you're doing?"

He nodded.

"So, what's the verdict?"

"Mild case of flu."

"*Mild*? I'm dying!"

"Not for another sixty years—if you eat your vegetables."

"You just want to get rid of all that squash." She stuck her tongue out at him.

He clicked his tongue. "You are a terrible patient."

"So what?" She glared mutinously at him.

"My, my, my. We are cranky, aren't we?"

"I hate being sick!"

"Really? What a revelation! Excuse me while I call the *Enquirer*." Her mouth quirked at that. "Haven't completely lost our sense of humor, I see. Would you like me to sleep in one of the other bedrooms tonight?"

"No!" She belatedly flushed at the vehemence of her response. "I—I sort of . . . well . . ." She picked at the bedcovers.

Tyber yawned. "Feel free to finish anytime."

"I like the feel of you next to me at night, all right?" she snapped.

Tyber smiled broadly. "All right." He quickly shed his clothes and got under the covers. "You don't have to be so touchy. Jeez, *women*!" He took her in his arms.

Zanita cuddled against his broad, warm chest, snuggling in to go to sleep.

"Comfy?"

"Mmm-hmmm." She rubbed her face against his chest.

"Good, but you better not sneeze on me."

"I wouldn't do tha—ah . . . ah . . . *achoo*!"

"*Zanita!*"

She was dying.

Her head throbbed. Her joints throbbed. Her throat was on fire.

Worse than that, she was paralyzed from the knees down. She could not move her legs!

Blearily, she opened her eyes and managed to lift her head a few inches off the pillow to see an orange ball of fur lying contentedly across her feet. Hambone! She dropped her head to the pillow and groaned.

The door opened and Tyber strolled in, all chipper with morning cheer. "Hey, how are you doing this morning?" He placed some orange juice on the bedside table.

"Get the cat off my legs," she croaked. Hambone opened his eyes, and seeming slightly insulted, lumbered off to lie next to her.

"Shame on you; he only wanted to see how you were feeling. I brought you some oatmeal."

"Oatmeal? I *never* eat oatmeal!"

"Well, you do now." Tyber leveled a no-nonsense look at her, causing her to cave in immediately.

"Oh, all right." She viewed the bowl sullenly until she happened to lock eyes with the cat. A silent communication seemed to occur in that moment. They both smiled at each other. "Just leave it there; I'll try to eat some later."

Tyber placed his hand across her forehead. "You still have a fever."

"I feel worse," she said petulantly.

"Today will be the worst day; you'll feel better tomorrow. Anyway, Blooey's making you some chicken soup for lunch, and Hambone's here to keep you company. Do you want to watch TV?"

Her nose arched in the air. "I don't watch daytime television."

"I have satellite. I hear there's a monsterthon on Channel 132 today." He raised and lowered his eyebrows as if to say, how could you not?

"You have satellite? I never noticed a dish."

"I didn't say *which* satellite, did I?" Her mouth gaped. "Here's the remote. By the way, I called your office and told them you wouldn't be in for a few days."

"Tyber! I was going to go in later! You shouldn't have—" She broke off, coughing.

"Uh-huh. I'm going down to do some work in the lab; if you need anything, Blooey's in the kitchen. Don't forget that oatmeal."

As soon as he was gone, Zanita looked at the cat. The cat looked at her. And the oatmeal was history.

"Prepare yourself." Tyber strode purposefully into the room a few hours later to glare down at her from the foot of the bed.

"What is it—more oatmeal?"

"No. I don't think Hambone is up to anymore just yet. He's still trying to digest the last batch."

She didn't quite meet his eyes. "How did you know?"

"He's lying in the sun like a snake that just swallowed a gopher. Besides that, he had oatmeal all over his whiskers. Blooey had to chase him all over the house with a wet rag to clean it off him."

"So that's what all that racket was. Then if it's not oatmeal, what is it?"

"Grandfather Hank just called and he's hopping mad. He wants to know who I am and what the hell I'm doing with you." He leveled a searing look at her.

"Oh," she said in a small voice.

"You didn't tell him you were moving in here, did you?" She winced. "No."

He leaned over the bed, trapping her between his arms, which came down on either side of her. His voice was deceptively calm. "What did you think would happen when he could not reach you at home?"

She gulped. "That wouldn't have happened."

He pinned her to the pillow with a look. "I'm waiting."

"Call forwarding," she said in a small voice.

He just stared at her, a little muscle ticking in his jaw.

"You—you don't understand. You just don't tell Hank stuff like this. He's—he's like from another century. And since this is only a temporary situation, why upset the old guy?"

"The *old guy* is on his way here even as we speak."

Her eyes widened. She clutched his hand off the mattress. "Tyber, don't let him take me to my grandmother! She's a Valkyrie with sick people."

"You're not going anywhere. I'll deal with Hank, but I think it was very irresponsible of you to worry him like this."

"Irresponsible! He wouldn't have known anything about it if you hadn't taken it upon yourself to call my office. And did you have to tell them who you were?"

He threw her a seething look and exited the room.

She never knew what Tyber said to her grandfather, but by the time Hank entered her room, he was all smiles and solicitousness. He inquired after her health, petted the cat, admired the house, spoke highly of Tyber, and told her to call her grandmother when she felt up to it. Then he insisted that she take the week off.

She watched her grandfather leave with an odd, sinking feeling in her chest. Hank, who had gone through wars, seen presidents murdered, and was once almost shot by a gangster, had unwittingly been Tybercised.

125

Zanita sighed philosophically. She would have to watch the captain like a hawk from now on. He was definitely starting to act like a boyfriend.

Tyber stood at the foot of his once-pristine shell bed watching Zanita sleep while propped up against four pillows.

The bed was littered with empty candy wrappers, various magazines, paperback books, tissues, cracker crumbs, a writing tablet, and Hambone. A half-eaten Oreo cookie floated in the aquarium next to the bed. His extremely rare, extremely expensive tropical fish were in the process of committing suicide by nibbling on it.

Theme music from a 1950s science fiction movie blared from the television set, signifying the approach of the beast from the planet Gilgamesh.

This is one definition of Chaos, he thought, smiling fondly down at her.

He got a net to retrieve the cookie before the fish did serious damage to themselves. Only Zanita would wonder if fish might like to share a chocolate cookie with her.

"Hmm? Oh, Tyber, it you . . ." She sleepily opened her eyes.

"Feeling better?"

"Yes, much better." She took his hand, bringing it to her cheek. "Tyber, you've been so sweet."

"I have, haven't I?" He kissed her forehead before sitting on the bed next to her to watch the monster being electrocuted by the high tension wires. He chuckled. "Gets 'em every time."

"Hey, look at this—I almost finished *The New York Times* crossword puzzle. If I only knew the name of a three dimensional rectangular cube in twenty-seven letters . . ." She looked at him expectantly.

"A rectangular parallelepipedon," he supplied dryly.

"That's right! It fits!" Zanita had a great idea. "You know, you should go on *Jeopardy*."

"You're still feverish, aren't you?"

"No, I'm serious. We could make a bundle."

"*We?*" He arched a brow at her.

She sat up on her knees, putting her arms around his neck. "You have such a gorgeous . . . mind."

His arm came around her waist to secure her. "You *are* feeling better." He gazed down at her through half-closed eyes.

"Mmm, much." She rubbed his nose with her own.

"I have something for you," he drawled, low and sexy.

Her eyes flashed at him in a come-hither way. "What?" She whispered seductively.

"This." He handed her a sheaf of papers from behind his back.

"Oh." She glanced down at the papers, then back up at him. "*Oh*. Where on Earth did you get this?" It was a complete dossier on one Xavier LaLeche.

"You might say a friend of mine gave it to me."

"Tyber, these look like . . . *are these F.B.I. files?*"

He looked affronted. "Zanita! That would be illegal. I'd never do anything illegal."

The next day, three dark sedans rolled down the driveway and came to a stop in front of the house. Six men in suits came out of them. They all had identical "don't screw around with me" faces.

Tyber went out on the porch to greet them. Zanita warily hung back behind him, peering around his shoulder to see what was going to happen.

One man, obviously the one in charge, stepped forward and pointed an accusing finger at Tyber. "You son of a bitch!"

Tyber did not seemed fazed in the least. "Hello, Sean."

The irritated man turned to his men, barking out a command. "Don't huddle around—fan out!"

Tyber leaned against the porch balustrade, arms crossed. He immediately countermanded the order. "No, *don't* fan out."

The man named Sean glanced at Zanita, then spoke to Tyber. "Let's go for a walk, shall we?"

"Be right back, baby."

Zanita apprehensively watched them walk down the footpath to one of the far gardens. Then she turned her eyes to the other "visitors." Five double-barreled sets of steely eyes had her directly in their sights. She smiled rather sickly at them.

"I'll just stay right here," she offered magnanimously.

"Dammit, Tyber; you did it again!"

"You know what I told you."

"Yeah, if you could do it, someone else could. But I'm not so sure I buy that anymore. There's no one quite like *you*." Sean ran a hand distractedly through his short hair, causing it to spike.

"Don't delude yourself."

"All right," he grumbled. "We'll go over the system again. But dammit, Tyber, it's embarrassing! Your little breach occurred at a most inopportune time."

"Visiting dignitary and you just had to break away from the function when they called you?"

Sean flushed. "Not quite."

Tyber nodded sagely. "Ah, different type of function."

Sean rubbed his jaw. "Yeah. Say, who's the dish with the terrific gams?" He raised his hands. "Wait, don't tell me—she's some egghead from one of your highbrow institutions and you're diligently working together in your sterile laboratory for the good of all."

Tyber stared at him, not responding.

Sean scratched his ear. "Well, I suppose in some odd way, I should thank you for that little stunt."

"You're welcome."

"That grin is nothing less than evil. And I more than suspect you didn't have just the Department's best interests at heart. Especially by what was taken." He looked at Tyber sharply. "What *are* you doing, Tyber?"

Tyber put his hands in the back pockets of his jeans. "I couldn't say."

"Yeah. Right."

They walked back to the front porch.

"Let's go," Sean said to his men. "Good day, Ms. Masterson." He opened his car door, saying to Tyber, "I'll be in touch."

Tyber gave him a sharklike grin. "Not if I am first."

The man's eyes widened. "Christ," he muttered, slamming the door shut. They exited in the same formation they had entered.

"How did he know my name? Did you tell him my name?"

"No. Want to go get some lunch, baby?" He put his arm around her shoulders, steering her back into the house.

"But Tyber—"

"Mmmm, smells good—squash casserole."

"*Oh, no*! Blooey told me he was making a chef salad for lunch."

"Smells like squash casserole to me."

"Cripes! Ah . . . you know, I just remembered something I need to get at the store. I'll be back before dinner—"

He grabbed her by her shirt collar. "Oh, no you don't."

"You're taking the motorcycle?"

"To Vermont? Are you kidding, baby?"

"It won't fall off there, will it?" Zanita watched Tyber secure the bike to the bed of the pick-up.

He chuckled. "No. I would've liked for us to ride up in it, but with you just getting over that flu, I don't think it's a good idea."

Thank God. Zanita was not overly fond of motorcycles. The idea of riding on the back of one for five hours in a brisk fall wind at seventy miles an hour with bugs squashing into her teeth held little appeal.

Tyber opened the driver's side door, squeezing their suitcase into the well behind the seats. Zanita had originally packed a carton. Tyber gave it one disdainful look and dumped her stuff into his bag. When Zanita objected, he simply stated, "I am not walking into the Marble Manor Inn carrying that carton."

"Hpmh! Cartons make much more sense than suitcases. You just throw them away when you're done."

"Zanita, you are an extremely strange woman. And I admire that in you. But I am still not taking that carton." And that was that.

"It shouldn't take us more than five hours if we don't make too many pitstops." He started the truck. "Did you bring the directions?"

"I didn't have too; I memorized them."

Tyber groaned. "Make that a seven-hour trip."

"That's not funny. You know, I don't think the paper's going to reimburse you for staying at a place rich enough to be called the Marble Manor."

He viewed her obliquely. "I wasn't aware that I was on their payroll."

"You aren't. Well, at least not formally. I mean, you are helping me with this story, and even though it wasn't exactly an assignment, once the article gets published, the paper generally reimburses for out-of-pocket expenses. But not unreasonable expenses, and this inn sounds very expensive."

The corners of his mouth crooked. Zanita would do anything to avoid the appearance of having a relationship. He couldn't wait to see how she was going to rationalize this. "Don't worry, the paper is off the hook."

"No, I couldn't do that! After all, we're working together. It's not fair for you to—to—"

"Treat you?" he more than helpfully supplied.

"Um, yes. It's not that I don't—"

"Take you out for some really sumptuous dinners?"

"No, I don't think—"

"Ply you with fine wine over a candlelit table for two?"

"Candles? I mean, that wouldn't be—"

"Dine on cold raspberry soup and medallions of veal in cognac cream?"

"I . . . I'm not sure. . . ."

"Make love to you in a hundred-and-twenty-year-old brass

bed in front of a fireplace in a room completely made of golden marble?''

"Well . . . maybe just this once.''

"How about just this twice?'' He threw her a wicked smile.

"Tyber!'' She blushed.

"Or just this *thrice*?''

She crossed her arms over her chest. "You're starting up again.''

"Probably.''

Tyber had elected to take back country roads instead of the highway so they could enjoy the spectacular New England foliage at a leisurely pace.

His schedule of a five-hour trip was totally optimistic since they had already stopped twice—once at a picturesque farm to buy a huge pumpkin to take back with them for Halloween and another time at a roadside stand to buy a bushel of apples and a zucchini bread.

"We have to leave room back there for a couple of jugs of maple syrup. I promised Blooey we'd bring him back some.''

Zanita kneeled on the seat to peer through the back window. "There's plenty of room back there. We can even bring Hambone some Vermont mice.''

"He'd love that.''

Zanita reached down to her purse and withdrew the dossier on LaLeche.

Tyber glanced over and when he saw what she had in her hands, he briefly closed his eyes. "Tell me you didn't bring that with you.''

"Of course I did. We need to study it so we know what we're dealing with.''

"We know what we're dealing with—a scam artist.''

"Yes, but there's nothing concrete in here to nail him with.''

"Do you suppose that could be the reason he isn't in jail?'' He asked facetiously.

"Why do you think *they* had this on him?'' Zanita had not discussed with Tyber how he had gotten the documents. She

131

really didn't want to know, and she more than suspected he really didn't want her to know.

"Apparently, according to the report, he's been under investigation for some time by the bunko unit, as well as being under suspicion for a number of other Federal crimes."

"I don't see that here."

"I must have forgotten to give you those sheets."

As if Tyber ever would make such a mistake! So he had chosen to hide some of the more sensitive documents from her. Okay. She could live with that. As long as he came clean with her concerning any other information.

"If there are any other . . . sheets you've forgotten to give me, perhaps you can just fill me in."

He pulled the truck to the side of the road and shut the engine.

"What are you doing? Why did you sto—"

He took her in his arms and kissed her. Deeply. Passionately.

Then he started the truck and got on the road again, leaving her completely stunned.

"What on earth did you do that for?"

"I like your style, baby. Always have." He gave her a roguish grin.

Well, I'll have to do that again sometime, she thought. *That is, once I figure out exactly what it is he thinks I did.*

Chapter Eight

"Dimitri Ziest, Marvin Broconol, Damon Green, Xavier LaLeche—all aliases at one time or another." Zanita flipped through the dossier. "Born Steven Liss, 1948, in Buffalo, New York. Only son of Marguerite Liss. Father unknown."

"This sounds like we're entering the Twilight Zone." Tyber swung the truck onto a side road.

"Submitted for your speculation . . ." Zanita hummed the theme song.

Tyber laughed. "What else does it say?"

She gave him a look that said, *you know very well what it says*. "He lived under many different names in many states: Massachusetts, California, Ohio—"

"Where did he stay the longest?"

"Um—" She scanned the form. "California. Why?"

"I don't know yet. What about the other places—is there a pattern for length of stay?"

"Actually, yes, now that you mention it. About four months in each city. Why do you suppose that is?"

"He left before things got hot for him, always one step

ahead of implication and the law. I suspect that's how he's managed to elude full-scale investigation by local authorities. How long was he in California?''

''Two years. What do you make of that?''

''I think there was a definite reason he needed to be in California for that length of time. From his profile, he's not the type of man who just goes with the flow like flotsam and jetsam, buffeted about by the currents. No, this man controls his life—every aspect. He was there for a purpose.''

''Any ideas?''

''Not yet. Where did he live when he resided in California?''

''Let's see . . . San Francisco, briefly; then L.A.''

''I seem to remember something about an electronics plant there.''

She nodded. ''It almost seems as if he went legit for a couple of years; he worked for a company called Space Age Systems. An investigator noted in the margin that it was a respectable company. They manufacture shuttle components. I don't see any connection there, do you?''

''No. It had to be something he was doing on the side. Anything else?'' He entered a private drive leading up to a breathtaking mansion.

''Nothing definitive. I wonder if—what are we doing here?'' Zanita looked up at the palatial house and manicured grounds.

''Welcome to the Marble Manor Inn.'' He stopped the truck in front of the portico.

''Tyber, you're kidding! This is beautiful.''

''It is.'' Tyber scrutinized the interesting architectural details fondly. ''Beautiful. It was built in the mid-1800s from locally quarried golden marble. The original carriage house is still standing. See?'' He pointed to the rear of the house.

''Wow! I can't wait to see the inside. Will we really have a room made out of marble?''

Tyber swung their suitcase out of the truck, resting it on the driveway. He lifted her chin with the edge of his hand, brushing her lips with his own. "Of course we will."

She threw her arms around his neck, bringing his head down for a deeper kiss. "This is wonderful, Doc. Really wonderful."

"It's just the beginning," he promised, kissing her once more before he released her, leading her into the inn.

The inn was a splendid example of Tyber's preferred Victorian charm, and Zanita wasn't really surprised he had chosen it for their stay. They eagerly explored the downstairs before checking into their room.

Fresh flowers, exquisitely arranged in vases, graced every chamber. The ceilings were all thirteen feet high, with carved moldings and crystal chandeliers brilliantly suspended from rosette medallions.

There were several parlors, each furnished in opulent Victoriana. One room had been turned into a cozy library with a huge marble fireplace fronted by couches and chairs. The remains of late afternoon tea were still evident on the sideboard. A half-finished chess game waited patiently for completion on a low table by the window.

When they checked in, the friendly innkeeper gave them a brief history of the house, informing them that all the rooms were named after famous people. When Zanita learned that Tyber had requested the Errol Flynn room, she looked at him askance. He just put his arm around her as he led her up the stairs, saying, "How could I resist?"

Zanita sighed as she viewed the sumptuous room.

It was utterly beautiful.

Gabled windows were open to fresh air and rolling Vermont hills, displaying the vibrant colors of fall. The center of the room sported a massive brass bed, which was indeed one-hundred-and-twenty years old. It was covered with an antique, hand-crocheted spread.

The promised fireplace of gold marble faced the bed. Two overlarge Queen Anne chairs flanked the raised hearth of the fireplace. A large red oriental rug graced the floor.

The walls, floors, and ceilings were all of golden marble.

Zanita eyed the sunken marble tub in the bathroom. "Now I know why they call it the Errol Flynn room." Tyber came up behind her to peer over her head.

"It does give the imagination healthy exercise, doesn't it?" he murmured, bending down to nip her shoulder.

She glanced up at him, grinning impishly. "What time do we have to be at LaLeche's digs, Captain Blood?"

"Bring me to a hotel room and that's the first thing you think of." A dimple curved his cheek. "And you women wonder why men are so skittish about these things." His hands rested on her shoulders as he turned her to him. "Unfortunately, we don't have time."

The back of Tyber's hand smoothed the hair from the side of her face; he bent toward her, placing a sizzling kiss in the hollow at the base of her throat.

"No?" She ran her fingers through the tawny strands of his hair, massaging his scalp, bringing him a little closer to her.

"No," he affirmed as his tongue lazily traced the line of her collarbone in slow, languorous strokes.

She sucked in her breath. "You're sure?"

"I'm sure," he whispered, right before his mouth pressed heatedly against her own. His fingers began to nimbly unbutton her blouse.

"I see."

He emphatically stated, "We need to stop this right now, Zanita." At the same time his hand closed firmly over her breast.

"Okay." She went up on tiptoe to delicately suckle on his enticing lower lip.

He made a low sound, somewhere between ecstasy and agony, deep in his throat. Unconsciously, he returned the favor by rotating his palm around her hardened nipple. His action incited Zanita to lean into him, rubbing against his arousal, which was now straining the seams of his jeans.

"I mean it; we don't have time!" he growled. So saying, he immediately fell to his knees in front of her, his hands seeking the waistband of her pants.

Zanita couldn't help but smile. "I get the message, Tyber. It's definitely no."

"Now that we've got that straightened out—" He quickly unzipped her jeans, his lips scalding the trail in a burning, fiery tasting. Zanita felt his scorching breath right through the silk of her underpants. Her knees immediately buckled.

Tyber's strong hands caught her about the thighs to support her, taking the opportunity dip his hot, roving tongue into her belly button. Her fingers clutched the top of his head. "*Tyber*."

Tyber's arms flinched, but remained in an unyielding grip around her thighs. He rested his damp forehead against her bare midriff while he tried valiantly to regain some measure of control. Great gulps of air shuddered through his heaving chest. Several seconds ticked by.

He failed.

And knew it.

He groaned in needless explanation against the flat of her stomach, "This is what is called a core meltdown, baby." Suddenly he yanked her jeans and panties down and off with one decisive stroke of his hands.

Without waiting, he unzipped his jeans and brought her down right on top of him while he was still kneeling on the bathroom floor.

He slid into her like a steel pylon through molten ore.

It was the first time since she had gotten over her flu; they were both primed and ready. Zanita threw her head back, clutching his broad shoulders under the red flannel of his shirt, which now hung open to his waist.

"God, Tyber, you feel . . . oh, God, Tyber!"

It was all Tyber had to hear in his present condition.

He went nova.

The flat of his hands drew her closer to him as he surged up inside her. "So good, baby . . . you're so good, so good," he croaked.

"I want to feel your tongue inside my mouth." He cupped her head, bringing her face up to his.

Zanita buried her tongue inside him.

Tyber drew on it voraciously, letting her taste him as well.

Relentlessly, he was moving ever stronger and faster inside her. He began kissing her all over her face, wildly, desperately. She did the same to him. They writhed against each other, clutching, kissing, cleaving to one another in an increasing conflagration. It was pagan, reckless passion.

They were out of control.

Zanita cried out. Tyber cried out. They rocketed.

Still gasping for breath, Tyber clasped his arms around Zanita and fell backwards onto the marble floor of the bathroom. Zanita lay draped over his chest, completely undone.

"I don't know how you do that to me, Curls." His hand still shook in aftermath as he ran it caressingly over her short, springy hair.

Zanita braced her palms against his chest, slowly levering herself up to look him in the eye. "How *I* do that to you? You're the one who said we didn't have the time, and the next thing I know it's nuclear winter."

He chuckled. "I did sort of go up in flames, didn't I?"

"Yes, you did." Smiling, she grazed his cleft chin. "I liked it."

He smiled back. "I did, too." He kissed her very sweetly.

Unfortunately, because of their bathroom romp, they had to have an abbreviated version of dinner, which upset the innkeeper, who had a very talented, very touchy chef. His feelings were somewhat mollified when they explained to him that they had an engagement to attend—it was not a reflection on the wine-poached shrimp and peach brandy tart.

After driving for half an hour in the dark through wooded country back roads, they finally found the turn-off to La-Leche's so-called retreat. Once again, Tyber had been correct: the retreat was nothing more than a tumble-down shack in the middle of the wilderness.

Since they were late in arriving, several cars were already parked haphazardly in the clearing. Tyber laughed when he noted one BMW sinking into four inches of Vermont mud.

"All part of the experience, my dear." He imitated Xavier's affected speech perfectly.

Zanita knocked on the crude wooden door to the cabin. Several voices rang out, bidding them enter. She tentatively opened the door.

Eight people were huddled around a huge fireplace. An old, scarred wooden table rested against the right wall. It was generously overflowing with refreshments, presumably brought by the guests.

And that was it.

Nothing else in the room. No furniture. No appliances.

Zanita quickly scanned the one-room cabin. No amenities.

Several blankets and sleeping bags lined the walls. In one corner, a tape player was issuing forth New Age meditation music—lots of Celtic harps and chimes.

"Dr. Evans! Zanita!" LaLeche stood up to greet them. "I was beginning to think you couldn't make it this weekend."

You mean you were getting concerned that a good mark was getting away from you. Tyber looked him directly in the eye, saying, "We got a little sidetracked, but we're here now."

Zanita threw him a killing look.

LaLeche smirked knowingly, his slimy gaze falling on Zanita. "Yes, well, that does happen. Glad you could make it." He gestured to the sideboard. "Would you like some refreshment before we start, perhaps something to drink?"

"Ah, sure." LaLeche wandered away while they approached the table. Zanita was already filling a cup with punch when Tyber stayed her hand.

"What are you doing? And did you have to make that crack about being sidetracked? It was embarrassing; he knew exactly what you were implying," she fumed.

"Yes, I did. We don't want him getting suspicious about us. He's less likely to do that if he thinks we can't keep our hands off each other." He grinned rather slowly at her. "And it's true, isn't it?"

139

Zanita flushed. "Never mind that. I want some punch; I'm thirsty from the shrimp."

"Here, try this cola." He opened up a bottle, pouring her some. She looked at him quizzically. "Just a precaution. I don't think we should eat or drink anything here that isn't in its original packaging or factory-sealed."

She almost choked on her Coke. "You think he might drug us?"

"Not really; but it doesn't hurt to be cautious."

LaLeche's voice interrupted their low conversation. "Why don't we all sit in a circle in front of the fire? Dr. Evans, you sit here." He pointed to a spot two spaces away from him. "And Zanita can sit between us, here."

They took their spots on the floor, Tyber not seeming very happy that Zanita was sitting next to LaLeche.

"John, can you lower those kerosene lamps? Good. Now let's all join hands. First, why don't we introduce ourselves by going around the circle? Xavier."

"Kim," the next woman supplied. Zanita noticed that she had yet to take her eyes off Tyber. Zanita surreptitiously glanced his way again, noting the sensual, masculine planes of his profile outlined in the flickering light. He had tied back his hair before they left their room, reminding her of the first time she had met him and the effect he had on her then. Still had on her. Probably would always have on her. She grudgingly admitted that he was gorgeous even in firelight. *Especially in the firelight.*

"John," the young man next to Kim said. He was staring avidly at Zanita.

"Elizabeth." A wan-looking elderly woman with gray hair was next.

"Marcie." This woman seemed totally belligerent. Zanita wondered why she had bothered to come.

"Eric." He spoke in a low voice, seeming very shy and withdrawn.

"Stacy."

"Ralph."

"Bob."

"Tyberius Augustus."

"You're kidding!" Kim giggled.

Tyber grinned back at her, shaking his head. The grip on his Zanita side threatened to break every bone in his hand.

"Zanita," she mumbled through her teeth. *Why was Tyber smiling at Kim like that?*

"Weren't you at the seminar last Friday?" John asked her, breaking into her thoughts.

"Yes. You remember me? I can't believe it!" Tyber just shook his head.

"Now that we all know each other, let's try to break some of the psychic walls around us by going around the circle again; only this time I want each of you to address someone in the circle that you either know or have just met, and tell them something about them that you noticed or intuitively felt about them. For instance, I feel a certain hostility coming from Marcie. Am I right, dear?"

"Yes. I guess I'm still agitated about my job. I had a fight with my boss before I left. She's such a jerk. I haven't been able to let it go. It's amazing you picked that up, Xavier." Everyone concurred, marveling over LaLeche's gift.

Tyber's finger discreetly tickled the underside of Zanita's hand. She tried not to smile.

"You must let it go, Marcie. After all, one of the reasons you are here this weekend is to release your anxieties. To free the astral body, you must be at peace—balanced. Kim, let's continue with you."

Kim didn't waste any time. She looked directly at Tyber and said, "You're a very handsome man. I was wondering if you're as beautiful on the inside as you are on the outside."

For some reason, Zanita hated this woman. Intensely.

Tyber looked at Kim without blinking an eye. "Thank you; I don't know what to say. I'm not used to that kind of flattery." A snort of disbelief came from his left side.

"That was honest, Kim." LaLeche seemed pleased. "John?"

"Yeah, I, ah, I like Zanita's eyes—they have a compassionate look about them. Real pretty. Violet eyes. Makes me think I can open up to her."

Zanita felt suddenly uncomfortable. Was this guy serious? Tyber tugged on her hand, prompting her. "That's . . . uh, nice of you, John."

And so it went around the circle. Zanita realized LaLeche was trying to get them to feel at ease with themselves and him. The sooner the barriers broke down, the sooner everyone would have good feelings toward their leader. LaLeche undoubtedly hoped those wonderful feelings would translate into hefty donations. Both the cars in the drive and the apparel of these people indicated to her that they were well chosen for that purpose.

The cycle came around to Tyber.

"I would like to tell Zanita that her—"he paused, smiling boyishly—"her shirt is mis-buttoned."

Zanita's head snapped toward him, her eyes widening, before she looked down. Sure enough, her third and fourth buttons were out of line.

"How did you do that, baby?"

Zanita closed her eyes in acute embarrassment. He knew very well how—*he* had buttoned her back up!

She started to release LaLeche's hand to fix it when he said, "Oh, no! Don't do that—you can't break the circle now. It's not important; you can fix it later. Who knows? In a couple of hours, it may be of no importance to you whatsoever."

Tyber leaned forward and threw LaLeche a chilling glance. Fortunately, he missed it.

Kim smiled seductively at Tyber. "Maybe we'll all take off our shirts, so we don't have to worry about buttons."

"Great idea." John winked at her.

Zanita swallowed. Tyber had been right. These people were looking to release all inhibitions. "Tyber?" Her voice squeaked in an aside to him.

He bent over her, as if he were affectionately nuzzling her nape. "Don't worry, baby. They won't start getting frisky for a couple of hours yet. I'll have you safely out of here by then,'' he whispered against her.

It wasn't long after that that Tyber went out to the truck, coming back with a blanket. He scooted Zanita in front of him, between his thighs, and draped the blanket around them. ''It's getting chilly, and you did just get over that flu. No sense taking any chances.'' Zanita thought he was incredibly sweet.

LaLeche took them through several more exercises involving deep breathing and meditation techniques before he brought them back once again to the subject of healing.

''We must align our energy fields. I'm sure our friend, Dr. Evans, agrees with this, at least in principle.''

Tyber surprised Zanita by saying, ''I do. In principle, anyway.'' He adjusted his arms around her under the blanket. Only Zanita's head poked through the top opening, under his chin. She was feeling nice and toasty from his body heat.

''I have always believed there must be order within the body as there is in the universe,'' LaLeche addressed the group at large, though his comments were directed to Tyber, ''in order for there to be a smooth and constant flow of energy.''

''Mmm, yes . . . but the universe is not as ordered as you might think.''

''How so, Tyber? I always thought the universe is an increasingly structured place,'' John said.

''You're forgetting about a little thing called entropy.'' He rested his chin on top of Zanita's head.

''Entropy? What's that—a new type of meditation?'' Kim asked.

Zanita could feel Tyber smile against her hair. ''No, Kim. Entropy is the measurement, or as we physicists say, the property, of disorder. I'm afraid, contrary to your beliefs, John, *disorder* is the natural order of things in the universe.''

Marcie scoffed. ''I don't believe that!''

Tyber shrugged. ''Second Law of Thermodynamics.''

''Wait just a second—isn't energy always, like, the same? I mean, you can't create more energy, only change it from one form to another.''

"You're talking about conservation of energy. Yes, energy is always conserved; in other words, you can't get more out of a system than you put into it. Entropy is something else. With entropy, you get more than you started with. We all know there are many more ways to screw up something than to get it right. Disorder continually increases, for there is so much more opportunity for disorder to occur rather than order. Zanita is a perfect example of this principle."

She hunched her shoulders. "*What*?"

Everyone laughed.

Except Zanita, who pinched his thigh under the blanket. He captured her wayward hand, clasping it by the wrist.

Tyber gazed down at Zanita affectionately. "Like going into the wrong class instead of the right one. What's more, the process is not reversible. I'm afraid the trip to disorder is, alas, a one-way, non-refundable ticket." Several people chuckled, but Zanita fumed at him, squirming ineffectively under the blanket.

"But then energy is not conserved." Marcie gloated over the brilliance of her statement.

"Yes, it is." Tyber valiantly subdued Zanita's thrashing as he continued, "*Usable* energy is not. Feynman, a great physicist, liked to say that energy is never lost, but *opportunity* is. For example, once a cannon has been fired, its usable or potential energy is lost."

"Like in sex," Kim purred.

Tyber cleared his throat. "Yeah."

"So, you're saying the universe isn't increasingly ordered?" John came back to his original statement. "Then how do you explain the emergence of galaxies, stars, and planets out of the initial Big Bang? That seems like an increase in order to me, rather than disorder."

"It appears to be something of a paradox, doesn't it?" Tyber grinned. "The answer is that you have to *pay* for order, or structure, with energy."

"How do you do that?" Eric shyly asked.

"You do the civilized thing." Tyber chuckled. "You borrow it."

"Like a credit card?" Kim asked.

"In a sense. Except you borrow it from a different part of the universe."

John scratched his head. "But eventually you couldn't borrow anymore, and I should know—I've maxed out more credit cards than I care to remember."

"Not really," Tyber said, "this is a bottomless pit of borrowing since increase in entropy simply dissipates in the infinity of space. The debt is spreading out forever through the vastness of space."

"Sounds like the rationale for government spending to me," Zanita grumbled into the blanket. Tyber heard her, though, because he leaned forward to nip the nape of her neck.

"Too weird." Kim winked at John.

Zanita had been paying close attention to LaLeche during the discussion; she noted that he seemed very interested in the way the group was responding to Tyber's words. She was sure Tyber had noticed it as well.

LaLeche sipped his punch, watching Tyber over the rim of his paper cup. "So, Dr. Evans, how would you relate this to energy fields in the body? Are we doomed to fall apart in disorder? Or, in your view, is there hope for healing methods?"

"We are ultimately doomed to disorder, or death; but there's no sense in being morbid. Your question is very interesting, Xavier, as the obvious exception to entropy is life. Life is the ultimate order. Purpose is the essence of being. In fact, life is in a constant struggle with the Second Law of Thermodynamics. And life often wins out. Curious, isn't it?"

"Not to a mystic," LaLeche responded shrewdly. "Energy is the essence of life."

"Yes, and it takes a profound amount of energy to create a new life." He gazed down at the top of Zanita's head. "I suppose that's what makes the existence of life so very precious." Zanita turned to look up at him and their eyes met in

145

a moment of pure understanding.

"So healing has a place in all this?" LaLeche smiled.

"I believe so," Tyber replied. *Although not your brand of healing.*

"Excellent!" LaLeche rubbed his hands together. "This has really been a most enlightening evening." Everyone concurred. Zanita privately thought it was Tyber who had been enlightening.

"But it's far from over." Kim stretched her long legs out. "What was it you were saying about energy and sex and all, Tyber?"

A dimple popped into his cheek. "Well . . ." Zanita elbowed him in the gut. "*Umph.* It, ah, it's getting kind of late. Zanita and I really have to get going. . . ."

"You're leaving?" Kim pouted.

"Yes," Zanita answered for them. "We're visiting some friends and really have to get back." She impaled Kim with a frosty glare. "So sorry."

"We'll be back tomorrow," Tyber added helpfully. Zanita threw him a disgusted look.

John stood up with them. "Too bad you have to leave, though. Zanita, maybe you and I can take a walk tomorrow through the woods. I'd like to show you a perfect place for meditating I found this afternoon."

"We'll see," Tyber responded, placing his hands on her shoulders.

LaLeche walked them to the door, gushing fondly over them. "I'm so glad you both came. We'll resume the sessions tomorrow around two in the afternoon. See you then."

As soon as they were in the truck driving to the inn, Tyber issued a proclamation straight from the quarter deck. "You're not going walking with him through the woods tomorrow."

Zanita faced him, surprised by his attitude. He seemed so nonchalant in the cabin when John had suggested it. "What if he has some information for the article—"

"No."

Zanita sighed. There was that pirate streak again. "Tyber,

146

you can be very unreasonable when you want to be.''

He did a double take. "What does that mean?"

"It means, sometimes you are unreasonably reasonable, and other times you are reasonably unreasonable, but right now you're unreasonably unreasonable.''

Tyber muttered something under his breath that sounded suspiciously like "doomed to disorder" and that he was an "entropic victim.''

Moonlight filtered across the bed through the open curtains.

Tyber leaned over Zanita, letting the tip of his finger trace the center line of little ribbons and bows on her thin cotton nightgown.

He sighed. "What is it?"

"What do you mean?"

"As much as I think this nightgown is pretty and sexy and downright irresistible, I have to ask myself why you're wearing it.''

"Don't be ridiculous.'' She pushed his hand away.

Tyber raised his eyebrows.

"Something I said?'' She remained silent. "Ahh. Something I did.''

She turned her face to the window.

He turned it back.

"What did I do, baby?'' His open mouth brushed tenderly along her jaw. She stiffened under him.

"You know very well what you did!''

The corners of his mouth curved slightly. "Why don't you refresh my memory?''

She shoved at his chest, pushing him away from her. "Did you have to smile like that?''

Tyber peered at her, cautiously bewildered. "I beg your pardon?''

"And well you should!''

"What are you talking about?''

"As if you didn't know!''

Tyber looked up at the ceiling and counted to ten. "Let's start over, okay?"

She stuck her chin in the air. "You'd like that, wouldn't you?"

"No."

Zanita gasped in horror.

"Yes!"

This time she threw her pillow at him.

"I mean . . ." Tyber put his hands up beseechingly. "I don't know? Dammit, what answer am I suppose to give here?"

"You're so smart, you figure it out." She gave him her shoulder, turning on the bed.

He put his hand on her arm, turning her back. "What is the matter with you?"

She glared at him. "Do I have to spell it out for you?"

"Humor me."

"All right." She sat up, crossing her arms over her chest, unwittingly pushing her breasts up against the scooped neckline of her nightgown.

Tyber's sights fell to those breasts and remained there a second too long. "I'm listening."

"I am not talking to the top of your head. This is just what I'm talking about!"

Tyber locked eyes with her. "I'm glad one of us knows what it is."

"That look!"

"*What* look?"

"The one you just gave my . . . chest."

His brow furrowed. "You don't like me looking at you?"

"Don't be ridiculous!"

Tyber rubbed his ear. "Does that mean, don't be ridiculous you do like my looking at you, or don't be ridiculous you don't like me looking at you?"

"Are you being obtuse on purpose?"

Tyber let out a bark of laughter.

Zanita continued unabated. "Because if you are, I don't

appreciate it.'' She lifted her nose in the air.

He clasped her shoulders. ''Baby . . .'' He took a deep breath and bravely forged ahead. ''Do you like me looking at you?''

''Of course I do!''

''Good.'' Tyber nodded. ''Then there's no problem.'' He bent toward her, ready to creatively press his mouth against those luscious full lips of hers.

''I—wasn't—talking—about—me.'' She spaced her words with deadly accuracy.

Tyber froze on the downshift. *This* had all the earmarks of trouble. He raised his lashes slowly to look into her eyes. ''Something bothering you, baby?''

She narrowed her eyes at him until all he could see was little violet slits. He released her, flopping onto his back. He knew that look: he was in for it. Although, he still had no clue—but then again, this was his Zanita.

Tyber decided in a lightning-quick calculation that his best chance of survival lay in doing nothing. So he patiently waited for her to throw the next volley. He didn't have to wait long. One small, deadly word rent the air.

''Kim.''

His focus shifted from the intricate marble ceiling to Zanita lying beside him. ''What about her?''

''Don't be coy.''

''*Coy*?'' He choked. ''I have no idea what you're talking about.''

''You looked at her.'' Her lower lip pouted.

Light was beginning to dawn. His blue eyes twinkled with understanding. Tyber was careful to make his tone a combination of surprise mixed with a light dash of horror. ''I did?''

''Yes! And you smiled at her, as well.''

''I didn't!'' Tyber tried not to grin as he gasped.

She nodded emphatically. ''Your come-hither smile, too.''

''Aw, baby, I'm sorry.'' He put his arms around her. ''I didn't realize I was doing it.'' That was the truth. He couldn't even remember what Kim looked like.

"You . . . you didn't?" She gazed up at him earnestly, tugging at his heartstrings.

"Of course not." He brushed her lips with his several times. "Why would I give anyone else my—what did you call it? My come-hither smile?—when you're the only one I want to come hither? Or is it thither?"

Relieved, Zanita snuggled against him, putting her arms around his neck. "It doesn't matter, Doc; it's really not important." Now that she was mollified, Zanita saw the wisdom in dropping the subject immediately. If not sooner.

Tyber was not so easily sidetracked. His blue eyes glittered down on her, amusement evident in their crystalline depths. "You know, Zanita, you almost sound jealous." She stilled in his arms at once.

"Don't be silly."

"One could almost say that you sound like . . ."—he paused to shudder slightly—". . . a *girlfriend.*" Then he laughed deeply, rubbing his nose teasingly against hers.

"I do not!"

"No?" His open mouth possessively slipped down the column of her throat, stopping midway to lave a particularly enticing spot. "If it looks like a girlfriend and acts like a girlfriend . . ." He sharply bit the rounded curve of her breast.

"Tyber!" She walloped the back of his head with her pillow.

Unfazed, he nuzzled between her breasts, chuckling low against her heart. "Then it must be a . . ."

"Don't you dare even think it."

He raised himself to look down at her. A laugh line curved the side of his cheek as he lifted one imperious eyebrow. "Have I taught you about resonance yet?"

Zanita groaned. Tyber looked intent on delivering one of his "special" lessons.

As he lowered himself onto her, his seductive whisper echoed provocatively against the marble walls. "Let me tell you all about pairs and harmony and synchronous vibration. . . ."

Chapter Nine

"Throw your leg over and climb on. It's not going to bite you, baby."

Zanita eyed the motorcycle warily. "I don't know, Tyber, it doesn't look all that friendly to me."

"It's not supposed to look friendly—it's a Harley. Now, c'mon—hop on."

"I—I'm not sure. Why don't we take the truck instead of—*eee*!" Patience at an end, Tyber had simply reached around with one arm and hauled her up behind him on the motorcycle. With a brief "hold on tight" thrown over his shoulder, he gunned the bike and took off down the drive of the mansion to the main road heading toward the small village the innkeeper had told them about that morning.

"I don't think I like this, Tyber." Zanita buried her head in the broad plane of his back, her arms clasping his waist in a death grip.

"If you opened your eyes, you might like it better, Curls." Tyber threw her an amused glance over his shoulder. "C'mon now, you're missing some beautiful scenery. Look; we're coming up on a pond."

Zanita wasn't sure she actually wanted to see scenery whizzing by her without the protection of at least a half a ton of metal between her and it, but she stalwartly opened her eyes to check it out.

They were approaching a small pond on the right side of the road. The glass surface of the pond reflected the autumn leaves on the surrounding trees. A few geese drifted by, honking sporadically. It was a picture-perfect New England fall scene. Zanita marginally relaxed her grip on Tyber.

"It's different on the back of a bike, isn't it?" Tyber yelled back to her. Zanita eyed his shoulder blades, wondering if he was starting up again.

"Is it?" She tickled his hard stomach with two fingers, feeling his muscles tense. He didn't respond, but she caught his slow smile in the side mirror. A flash of white teeth and a dimple.

The scenery proved magnificent as they sped along the winding road under a canopy of red and gold leaves, the crisp fall air invigorating in the late morning. Zanita was just beginning to think she might be able to endure riding a motorcycle every now and then when Tyber began weaving the bike in and out just to tease her. She walloped him on the head to let him know how much she appreciated it. His low chuckle reached her on the wind, but he smoothed the ride out.

The village was a quintessential small New England town. Most of the houses were white clapboard with black shutters. The center of the village sported a single street of interesting little shops that probably depended on the ski crowd for most of their trade. At this time of year, they were blessedly empty of tourists. Tyber swung the bike into the curb.

"Brunch or browsing?" he asked as he helped her remove her helmet. They had elected not to eat breakfast that morning in lieu of trying out one of the local restaurants.

"Browsing sounds good; I can wait until lunch. How about you?" Zanita was already eagerly eying the shops.

"That's fine—the innkeeper recommended the Hungry Kitten for lunch. That must be it." He pointed to a small wooden sign shaped like a cat swinging from the portico of a large-columned house on the corner of the street.

Zanita's voice trailed after her as she headed into the first shop. "Looks good—hey, look at these!"

Tyber smiled indulgently as he strolled into the shop after her. "Remember, we have to be back at LaLeche's by two and—those are great!" They both were entranced by delicate crystal figurines of winged dragons hanging in front of a display window.

"He's cute." Zanita fingered a little tubby one with a goofy look on its face.

Tyber eyed a swooping dragon that had a very cunning expression. "I rather like this one."

Zanita viewed his choice, thinking it somehow appropriate for him. All the dragon was missing was an eye patch and a little sword. "Where would you hang it?"

"Over the bed." He winked at her.

She wagged her finger at him.

"I know I'm going to regret this, but—" She reached up, unhooking the swooping dragon from its display.

"For me? Baby, that's awful sweet of you." His arm curled around her shoulders, giving her a small squeeze. He bent down to kiss the tip of her nose. "Let me respond in kind." His free arm reached up to retrieve the chubby dragon.

"No, Tyber, please don't," she protested, placing her hand on his arm. "You've already spent so much money on this weekend—"

He held Tubby up in front of her. "Look at this face; you wouldn't leave him here all by himself, would you?"

Zanita frowned; Tyber knew exactly which button to push. "Well . . ."

He turned the dragon to face him. "I told you not to worry, Tubbs," he said, sotto voce. "Piece of cake."

After they had made their purchases and left the store, Tyber asked her where she was going to hang her dragon. "In the kitchen window, I think."

"Perfect place—Blooey will love him."

153

Zanita glanced over at him. She had meant her kitchen window at *her* apartment, not his. Perhaps he hadn't realized what he'd just said. After all, she was only in his home temporarily, until they finished this LaLeche business.

She shrugged her shoulders, deciding to let the remark pass. But later she thought about it again when he insisted on buying her an antique shawl. It was an old-fashioned violet crochet with tiny pink rosettes.

"The parlor can get drafty in the winter," he said by way of an explanation, "even with the fireplace going. For all I've renovated it, the house is still over a hundred years old. And much as I'd like to, I can't cuddle you *all* the time, Curls."

She was not going to let that comment go.

"Tyber." She gritted her teeth. "Let's get one thing straight—you are not my boy—"

"You don't like it?" He seemed vaguely hurt.

"It's beautiful, but I am not—"

"It's perfect for you; I can picture you wearing it, curled up in the big Queen Anne chair in front of the fireplace, reading a favorite book while Hambone nestles at your feet."

Her fists clenched. "I do not belong in that picture! It sounds like something out of *Little Women*. Besides which, I don't think the story is going to take that long."

"It might. And why should you suffer a drafty house because of it?"

She blinked. He was doing it again—confusing her with his obtuse way of making a point. "What does that have to do with—why should—it doesn't . . ."

He regarded her from under half-lowered lashes. "It has; you should; and it does." Her mouth gaped. "Now say thank you and let's go into this fascinating but incomprehensible art gallery."

Before she could think of a response, he had ushered her into the shop.

By the time they stopped for lunch, they were pretty much shopped out. Tyber had purchased two large jugs of maple syrup for Blooey and a piece of Vermont cheddar for Hambone. When the store owner found out they had driven a motorcycle to town, he graciously offered to drop off the jugs at their inn on his way home from work.

The Hungry Kitten revealed itself to be a very elegant restaurant. Zanita had misgivings about entering the linen-draped dining room in her jeans and boots, but Tyber just clutched her hand in his, half dragging her to their Limoges and crystal-set table.

"Isn't this rather fancy for lunch?" She looked around at the other diners, who seemed to be dressed for the occasion and speaking in very hush-hush murmurs.

"Better enjoy it while we can; I don't think we'll make dinner this evening at the inn. I suspect LaLeche expects us to stay the entire day and well into the evening. And from what I remember of the offerings of food laid out on that rickety table last night—"

"I get your point." Zanita eagerly opened her menu. "Jeez Louise! Look at these prices!" She gaped at the menu in awe.

"*Zanita*," Tyber said dryly.

"I was going to treat you to lunch." She raised her violet eyes to his. They were suspiciously moist. "But I—I can't afford this, Tyber."

He put his menu down and covered her hand with his. "It's nice of you to want to take me out, sweetheart, but it's not necessary. There's absolutely no reason for us not to completely enjoy this weekend as long as we're here."

"But Tyber—"

His eyes locked implacably with hers. "Don't worry about it." He picked up his menu again. "Now let's see what looks good here—How about the lobster pie?"

While Zanita viewed her menu, Tyber thoughtfully gazed down at her bent head. She had absolutely no idea how wealthy he was, he mused. Imagine becoming overwrought about what he considered a simple, although elegant, lunch.

As a reporter bent on getting an interview with him, she had to know he held literally hundreds of patents. Not to mention the income from his teaching seminars and the books he had written. Somehow Zanita had blocked this all off from her consciousness, choosing instead to see him for the most part as just an interesting, albeit eccentric physicist.

And he knew why.

As long as she could view him in that manner, he wasn't so threatening to her.

He understood how she would see him as threatening in terms of a relationship. On one hand, he wanted her to feel threatened by him. It meant she recognized that he was shaking up her nice, safe world. On the other hand, what good was having anything in life if you didn't allow yourself the pleasure of it?

Tyber wasn't about to let her fear of commitment color their time together. In the broadest sense, it had nothing to do with money; it had everything to do with his philosophy of life.

He was an unconventional man who believed in enjoying all aspects of life to the fullest. Whether it was traveling first class on the Orient Express, the joy in creating a masterpiece, or the sheer beauty of discovery. It was about excellence. It was about being alive.

And he wanted Zanita to share those life experiences with him.

Now and in the future.

Because of her background, he realized she hadn't had the opportunity to experience the kind of life he lived, but he was in the process of changing that. Tyber knew Zanita possessed not only the capacity for it, but also the zest.

To make his point, he ordered an extraordinary chilled wine to accompany their main course.

"Lobster pie sounds good," Zanita said to the waiter in a small voice, not looking up from her menu. *Twenty-eight-fifty for lobster pie a la carte.* She swallowed a sip of water from a crystal goblet. *For lunch.* Tyber needed to get a handle on reality, she thought.

The Doc lived a secluded life, enclosed behind the walls of his mansion, his mind wrapped up in arcane subjects; she really didn't think he had a clue. The poor, sweet, misguided man.

Well, now that she was with him, she'd make every effort to open his eyes to people reality as opposed to physicist reality, whatever that was. Over a hundred dollars for lunch! No wonder this entropy thing kept growing! It was being fueled by the very physicists who discovered it.

The waiter brought some croissants and their wine, pouring a small amount out for Tyber, who tasted it and nodded. After he finished pouring their wine, the waiter left them to their conversation. Zanita picked up her glass and relaxed back in her chair.

"Do you think we'll survive all those hours of intense healing today?" Zanita smiled at Tyber, at ease once again now that they were back onto a subject she was comfortable with.

"We can only hope. Remind me to bring an extra blanket in the truck tonight—it's going to be cold in that shack in the woods, and probably damp as well. I heard the weather report earlier and they're forecasting a cold rain tonight, with frost in some low-lying areas. I don't want you getting sick again."

Just the thought of the cold made Zanita shiver. Until she remembered how well he had kept her warm last night at the cabin. "Will you promise to keep me warm like you did last night?"

The corners of his mouth twitched. "As long as you promise not to pinch my thigh again under the blankets. You almost got me in a relevant area."

"Don't be silly; I pinched you just above your knee."

He raised his eyebrow arrogantly.

"You wish," she scoffed.

He grinned back at her.

"Do we have a plan for this evening?" she asked. "Do you know what we're looking for?" The waiter brought their meal.

Tyber tasted his lobster pie, pausing to answer her. "Yes, we do. I think he'll take us through some more of those exercises of his during the day, getting us all to open up some more—although I suspect that our happy fellow campers at the cabin have already done just that.''

Zanita's eyes opened wide; she leaned forward in her seat. ''Do you really think so? Like who?'' She unconsciously sipped her wine. ''You know, this wine is really good,'' she murmured distractedly, her mind more on the lurid details of partner exchanging than the bouquet of the drink.

A dimple popped into his cheek. He regarded her for a moment as if she were the answer to an equation he had just written. ''You'll see when we get there. I have a feeling that tonight will be the night he does something—what I don't know yet—to cinch the hefty donations he's trying to get for this weekend.''

''Donations?'' Zanita slapped her forehead. She hadn't thought about donations. ''Do you think we can get out of that by snowing him—you know, sound like we offer him the chance of more money in the future, etc.?''

''I doubt it. Never kid a kidder and all that. That's not a problem; don't worry about it. I have to admit I'm curious to see just what he comes up with. After all, neither the FBI nor local authorities have been able to get anything on this guy that will stick.''

''You think it will be tonight, huh? Not tomorrow?''

''No. Definitely tonight. In the darkness of night, when people have a tendency to suspend some of their hard and fast beliefs.''

When they arrived at the cabin, everyone was eager to start the day's session. Zanita was fascinated by the sudden closeness between Kim and John. Apparently, not having succeeded with her and Tyber, they had consoled each other during the night. She turned to catch Tyber's eye, trying very hard not to stick her tongue out at him when he gave her a look that indicated he was not in the least surprised.

LaLeche began the session, adopting the mien of a man who has a great deal of serious knowledge to impart. Once again, Tyber was right. He led them quickly through exercise after exercise, breaking down the barriers between them as he coaxed them to reveal their innermost thoughts and fears. It was not an easy thing to participate in the session while still maintaining a separateness.

Zanita tried to temper her responses, hoping she wasn't revealing too much of herself, while at the same time making it appear as if she were totally engaged in the experience. It seemed Tyber was more successful at it than she was; it was difficult for her to tell when he was being honest and when he was baffling the group with B.S. At one point, during a brief break, he leaned over to whisper a warning in her ear.

"Be careful what you reveal to him of yourself; he will use it against you at a later time. You don't want to give him any power over you."

"I know, I already thought of that; I'll try to be more careful. Did you really read *The Importance Of Being Earnest* when you were three years old?" She whispered back.

Tyber contemplated her from beneath lowered lids, choosing not to respond. It was one of the traits that both infuriated and fascinated her about him; he knew exactly how to yank her chain. She unconsciously hunched her shoulders in annoyance, missing the flash of roguish amusement which lit his eyes.

"Now, I want everyone to sit in a circle again." LaLeche sat down Indian style in the middle of the ring they were forming. A cold drizzle was already falling in the dreary late afternoon.

LaLeche instructed Eric and Ralph to cover the two small windows with some blankets to block out what was left of waning daylight. Well, Zanita marveled, Tyber had foreseen that tactic as well; it seemed LaLeche wanted to get them into inhibition-freeing darkness as quickly as possible.

When everyone was settled, LaLeche inserted a cassette into the tape player. Chirping birds and gurgling water issued forth amidst the tuneless meditation music. Zanita instantly relaxed to the point of drowsiness. She felt Tyber's elbow jab her in the side.

"No snoozing on the job," he mouthed in her ear.

"Everyone join hands; we're going to have a meditation circle. I want you all to take a deep breath just like I taught you this morning. Breathe into your stomach, to your center of power. Hold . . . feel your breath . . . release. Again. Now close your eyes and relax each muscle of your body starting with the top of your head and working down to your toes. Take all the time you need. Relax . . ."

LaLeche's deep, carefully modulated tone was having the desired effect, especially on Zanita, who jokingly sagged against Tyber. He nudged her upright with his shoulder, taking the opportunity to plant a quick kiss on her neck.

"I want you to envision yourself in a place of perfect calm and serenity. Can you see it? You're in a garden. . . . It is a beautiful, sunny place, free from care and woe. . . . Listen to the singing birds, the sweet sound of water flowing over rocks, wind chimes tinkling in the soft breeze . . . You lie down on a cushion of springy grass, letting the serenity of this special place, this sanctuary, steal over you . . . letting it take you to your inner place of joy and peace. . . ."

He let the music carry them for a few minutes.

"As you drift in contentment in this world of harmony, you see before you a mirror. The edges of this mirror are hand-etched with intricate flowering vines, and as you look into it, you realize this is a very special mirror, for you see not yourself in it, but the reflections of your desires. . . . What you want to do . . . what you are ready to do now . . ."

Zanita was letting her mind drift along with the vision when she felt a long, tapered finger languidly stroke down between her index and middle finger.

Tyber was letting her know *exactly* what desires he saw in his personal mirror.

When he massaged his finger suggestively back and forth against the tender skin between her fingers, each pass a silken caress, she began to see a very interesting reflection in her own mirror. *The two of them, naked, intertwined, making slow, passionate love in the flowing meadow.*

Her breath caught in her throat.

In acknowledgment of her reaction to his touch, the tip of Tyber's finger etched tiny circles in the sensitive center of her palm. His action formed a private link between them in the darkness that went beyond proximity.

". . . as you confront your desires, you realize that you can now cast aside your groundless fear and embrace your secret self. Let yourself be free! Explore the hidden realms which make up all that is you. Don't be afraid to share yourself with others. . . . Let us all share with each other. Dr. Evans, are you exploring?"

"Ah . . . yes." At that moment his fingers were inching across her palm to glide over the tender skin of her inner wrist. Zanita tried to tangle her fingers with his to put an end to his dangerous playfulness, but he deftly avoided her ploy, lightly scraping his nails over her bare skin in a highly erotic manner.

"Very good! And what are you exploring?"

"*I'm spelunking.*"

Zanita almost choked. It seemed that Tyber's inner child was an imp. She gripped his hand and yanked. Hard.

"Exploring caves. You know, that's very spiritual, Tyber. It signifies that you are willing to cast off your mantle of protectiveness and reach below the surface to search for your true being. I believe you are on the precipice of a breakthrough."

"I certainly hope so," he responded sincerely. Zanita wanted to kick him.

"Let's explore this a little further then—you're not frightened, are you?"

"Nope."

"Good. What do you see; will you share it?"

"I'm in a tunnel. A long, dark tunnel . . ."

I don't believe he's doing this. Zanita hissed his name under her breath. She knew he heard her because he pulled her trapped hand closer to him, resting it on his rock-hard thigh. At least, she hoped it was his thigh.

"Can you tell us anything about the tunnel? Is there any light at all?"

"No. No light . . . but it seems to be . . . *moist* in here; the walls seem almost *wet*."

"Water is a very common mystical symbol."

"It seems thicker than water, Xavier, more viscous, sort of like . . ." Zanita held her breath. ". . . like *syrup*."

"I see. Does this liquid essence disturb you?"

"On the contrary. I embrace it."

Zanita pushed her face against his ear and gritted out, "Stop it! He's going to see through you in a minute." He didn't answer her except to quickly turn his head in the dark and capture her lower lip between his teeth, letting it slide ever so slowly from his grip.

"Yes, very good. What else can you tell us? Is it cool so far underground?"

"No, it's warm—almost hot, in fact. I can see now that the heat is making the walls look like they're quivering."

"Are you hot?"

"Yes, but not too hot. I'm . . . good."

"What happens as you keep walking along this tunnel?"

"I keep going deeper and deeper . . . I sense that the end is just ahead of me."

"So you speed up?"

"No, I slow down."

"You're reluctant to leave the cavern?"

"You might say that."

"So you feel comfortable in this place?"

"Yes, I want to stay . . . forever." Even though she had promised, Zanita pinched him anyway. When he flinched, she wondered if she had missed his thigh after all.

"But you realize you can't; you realize you must go on with your journey."

Tyber sighed deeply. "I suppose so."

"Where are you now?" LaLeche almost seemed to be getting into this himself. If Zanita didn't know him for the self-serving slime he was, she might have believed him herself.

"I suddenly burst through to a room of light. Everything is peaceful here, yet I feel spent and exhilarated at the same time.

I feel great." He bent forward, toward LaLeche. "I mean *really* great, Xavier, you know?"

Even though the room was dark, Zanita could sense La-Leche's self-satisfied smirk. "I know exactly what you are feeling. You feel renewed."

"Yes. That's it exactly. Renewed."

"Can you think of something in your real life which gives you this same feeling of newness? This feeling of being reborn? Joyfully alive?"

Tyber gently squeezed Zanita's hand. "Yes, I can."

Surprised, Zanita swung her head toward him. What a beautiful thing for Tyber to imply, even if he was acting. Before she could stop herself, she lifted their joined hands to her lips to place a gentle kiss on the back of his hand. His threaded fingers tightened on hers, sending his warmth to her.

"Now you have found an attunement from within yourself to your outer being. You have had an important revelation here, Dr. Evans. How do you feel? Everyone may open their eyes."

The first thing Zanita saw when she opened her eyes was their joined hands resting on his lap. It struck her in an odd way: his hand, large, capable, strong, enfolding her much smaller one, confidently, protectively. For a moment, the sight of it almost made her panic—until she took a deep breath, came down to planet Earth, and quietly disengaged herself from his grip.

Tyber watched LaLeche carefully as he replied, "I'm grateful, Xavier, and somewhat in awe. I never expected to receive this kind of insight this weekend. Thank you for leading me to it."

He was playing LaLeche like a master, Zanita reflected. Tyber really was very good. If only he could resist his penchant for teasing, he might have a second career calling in the wings. Not that he wanted a second career. She wondered if he had ever figured out exactly what his first career was.

"No thanks are necessary, Dr. Evans; it's my pleasure to help people along the path to inner peace. Why don't we take a break for an hour and have some dinner? I know I'm hungry, and those tofu burgers Marcie brought look delicious." Zanita tried not to visibly gag.

"I don't believe I'm going to say this," Tyber murmured in her ear, "and don't you dare tell Blooey I ever admitted to it, but I think I'd actually prefer one of his squash surprises to tofu burgers."

"Mmm, I know. I'm not really that hungry anyway, after our lunch."

"That's good, baby." He helped her up. "Because I don't want you to eat anything except the popcorn, potato chips, and soda, and those only if the containers are new."

"Okay. Did you notice how happy LaLeche seemed when you had your 'breakthrough'? I could almost see him mentally adding up his donations. Speaking of which, how are we going to deal with that? I have a twenty in my pocket; do you think that's too much?"

Tyber caught his lower lip between his white teeth. She really had no idea what was expected here. "Let me deal with it, okay? If a donation has to be made, we might as well get some mileage out of it."

She furrowed her brows. "What do you mean?"

"You'll see. I would suggest going for a walk, but it's starting to rain in earnest out there. I think I'll go out to the truck and get those blankets; it's beginning to get uncomfortable in here."

"All right. I think I'll make use of the elegant facilities." The "elegant facilities" was an ancient outhouse at the rear of the cabin.

"Brave soul." He gave her a thumbs-up.

"By the way, Tyber, you did a great acting job back there. You almost had me convinced, even if you were ticking me off. If you didn't kid around so much, you wouldn't be half-bad at this."

"Uh-huh. And who said I was acting?" He ducked out the door into the night before she could respond.

Everyone settled down on the floor to have a relaxed dinner.

Since there were no other seating arrangements, there wasn't really a choice in the matter. During dinner, LaLeche lit the fire in the fireplace, which made Zanita immensely happy. Both she and Tyber managed to get through the meal by munching on a few chips, explaining truthfully that they had had a large lunch and were not very hungry.

Afterwards, Elizabeth, the elderly woman, showed everyone how to make popcorn over the fire. Although she had been quiet throughout most of the seminar, Zanita liked her. She seemed very nice, yet removed in some indefinable way.

Then it hit her.

Elizabeth acted much the way Mrs. Haverhill had, when she was trying to deal with the ramifications of her illness. Zanita studied the older woman carefully. She had noted the first night that the woman had seemed rather wan-looking. Now, she realized, the woman looked downright pale and sickly.

The hackles on the back of her neck rose.

LaLeche was probably bleeding this unfortunate woman dry just as he had Mrs. Haverhill. Who knew what promises he had made to her? Her experiences garnered as a reporter told her that desperate people would often try anything, believe anything, sometimes even do anything, as long as a glimmer of hope was held out to them. She watched Elizabeth with a new sadness in her eyes and a growing concern.

"What is it?" Tyber put his arm around her, drawing her close to him. It always amazed her how observant Tyber was. From the moment she met him, little had escaped his acuity. While the trait made him very attractive to her, the downside was that a girl couldn't ever hope to get away with much around a man like him.

"Elizabeth. Have you noticed—"

"That she's very ill? Yes, I noticed it last night. I hope I'm wrong, but I think she may be his main mark."

"Oh, Tyber, what can we do? We can't just stand by and let such a nice old woman be flimflammed. Perhaps if I talk to her in private—"

"No." His hand stayed her. "You'll completely blow our

165

cover as well as this story, and she won't believe you. Remember, she *wants* to believe him.''

''We can't just do nothing!''

''We'll do something.''

''What?''

''We'll shift his focus by giving him a better mark.''

She transferred her sights from Elizabeth to stare up at Tyber. ''Who?''

''Me.''

''You've got to be kidding! He isn't going to easily trust you, Tyber. He knows how smart you are; he'll be very leery of you suddenly falling over him, begging to ply him with money.''

Tyber pushed an errant curl off her forehead. ''And who says I'm going to be begging him to take my money? I'll be very careful with him, lead him just so. Believe me, his greed will overcome his misgivings soon enough.''

Zanita seemed concerned. ''I don't know, Tyber; I didn't count on this when I asked you to help me. You could get in over your head here.''

I'm already in over my head, he mused as he gazed down at her. ''I can handle myself. Elizabeth is vulnerable to him in ways I could never be. I have no concerns at all, Zanita. After you've faced Field Theory not much *phases* you anymore.''

''Huh?''

His mouth curved in a smile. ''A little physicist humor. And we'd better change the subject and mingle before we invite unwanted attention. Speaking of unwanted attention, I wonder what Kim thought of my breakthrough? Think I'll go ask her.'' He made to move away, but Zanita clutched his arm.

''Don't you dare. All right; we'll play it your way, but the paper can't allow you to take any unnecessary financial risks. In other words, we can't afford to reimburse you if you goof up. In which case, you don't have to worry because my grandfather will have my head on a platter and I'll never speak to you again.''

"Thanks for taking the pressure off, baby. Now I can lie back and enjoy it.''

"*Tyber!*''

Chapter Ten

It was late in the evening when LaLeche finally made what Tyber later referred to as his "move."

Once again, they were seated in a circular pattern in the center of the cabin floor. The temperature had dropped considerably with nightfall, turning the damp, raw day into a chilly, dank evening. A heavy, steady rain fell against the rotted windowsills of the shack. Even the light of the fire did not dispel the cold darkness in the room.

It was almost eerie.

And certainly not the best atmosphere for conveying a "spiritual" warmth.

A scientist not just by title, but by nature, Tyber observed the room and the man, collecting the facts which presented themselves to him. The room was uncomfortably cold. No doubt this would be the last session held here until spring. Even those on the path to inner truth would not expect to travel through these temperatures on the journey.

LaLeche would probably have to content himself with living off donations garnered from seminars, or else find a new location to conduct his weekend retreats.

In either case, Tyber figured the man was going to have to make this one count. Xavier was going to have to impress them into some heavy donations to tide him over the winter in the lifestyle he was obviously accustomed to.

Perhaps, Tyber speculated, there was something in that angle he could use later?

He thought about it as he snuggled Zanita closer to him under the blanket.

"It's freezing," Zanita croaked out of the side of her mouth. Even though Tyber had placed one of the blankets on the rough floor planking beneath them, it wasn't doing much to prevent the cold from seeping up through the floorboards. She tried to stop her shivering; it was only making her colder.

"I know," he spoke low, close to her. "Do you want to sit up on my lap?"

She nodded gratefully. "Just for a few minutes. Do you mind? I'm so cold." Levering herself, Zanita scooted from between his legs onto his lap. Tyber's body heat enveloped her immediately. "Ahhh . . . Thank God you're a warm-blooded type, Doc."

"If you keep squirming like that, you're going to find out just how warm-blooded." His hands clamped down on her hips, holding her still.

"John," LaLeche called over, "could you turn up those kerosene lamps? Thanks." He turned to the group at large, his oh-so-sincere gaze focusing on each of them in turn. "Well, my friends, we have been through a lot with each other this weekend. I know I don't only speak for myself when I say that I feel I know each of you now so very well. I think we all feel close to each other after this special time we've shared."

Several heads nodded in agreement.

"I couldn't help but sense, however, that there is someone among us who has—shall we say, held back." For an instant his gaze seemed to rivet directly on Zanita.

Zanita tensed. Was he on to them? She felt Tyber's hand

stroke her thigh, warning her to relax.

"Elizabeth." LaLeche broke his gaze on her, turning to the older woman. "I have sensed that you are not completely with us this weekend. Am I correct, my dear?"

Elizabeth looked down at her hands, which were tightly clasped in her lap. "Well, I've tried—"

"I understand. You have much on your mind which weighs heavily upon you, don't you?" Still looking down, the older woman nodded.

"I have seen a disturbance in your energy flow. There is an angry color swirling about you in the vicinity of your torso."

"That narrows it down." Tyber's low sarcastic words floated to her. He was right, of course. The torso could mean just about anywhere on the body. It was a pretty safe guess, although judging from the rapt faces surrounding them, no one seemed to realize that.

When Elizabeth nodded, LaLeche continued. "There is an illness within. A dis-ease." He said it as if it were two words.

"Yes." The woman's voice was a faint sound.

LaLeche leaned to her, taking her hands in his. "Where is it, Elizabeth?"

"My abdomen." Several people in the room murmured in sympathy for her.

Tyber took the opportunity to whisper in Zanita's ear, "Did you notice, he came right out and *asked* her where her illness is?"

Zanita patted his leg under the blanket.

LaLeche humbly regarded Elizabeth with the utmost sympathy. "I want to give you a healing, Elizabeth. Will you let me?"

"Yes, but I don't know if—"

LaLeche spoke gently to her. "This will be a special healing, Elizabeth. I don't do this often as it is very draining on me, both emotionally and physically, but I am moved to help you, my dear."

"Thank you." There were tears in the older woman's eyes.

Zanita clenched her fists under the blanket; she couldn't stand to see this poor woman being so taken advantage of.

"Hang in there, baby." Tyber tried to calm her down. "I believe we are about to be entertained on a grand scale."

And entertained they were.

LaLeche asked Elizabeth if she would lie on her back on the floor in the middle of the circle.

Tyber, feeling concern for the older woman, immediately offered her the use of the blanket beneath him. Elizabeth smiled her thanks, and Tyber spread it out on the floor for her, once again resuming his seat with Zanita on his lap.

As soon as Tyber had rewrapped them in the blanket, Zanita turned to kiss him on the cheek. "That was awfully sweet of you, Doc. Forget what I said in the past about you not being chivalrous."

He cocked an eyebrow as he looked down at her, his tone suspiciously dry. "Really?" He opened his legs and she fell through to the cold, hard floor.

"Ow!"

"I wouldn't want you to get the wrong impression of me, Curls." Her only warning was a dangerous grin; his palms came up under the blanket and settled right over her breasts.

"Tyber," she choked, "Cut it out! You'll cause a scene."

Resting his chin on the top of her head, he chuckled low against her. "*I* won't." He slowly rotated his hands on her just to punctuate his statement.

Zanita squirmed and turned red. Quickly glancing around the room, she noted with relief that no one seemed to be paying any attention to them. Everyone's eyes were focused on Xavier and Elizabeth.

"Please, Tyber," she breathed as she desperately clutched his roving hands, trying unsuccessfully to still his movements.

"Uh-uh."

He caught a strand of her hair between his lips.

The pirate! She was starting to get turned on! Well, two could play at his game. She reached low behind her, between their bodies, and rubbed. Hard.

171

Tyber stopped his play immediately.

"I—ah, suddenly see the wisdom of your words."

"I thought you might." She smirked. "What's he doing?" She wiggled her rump on the cold floor beneath Tyber's thighs.

LaLeche had rolled up the sleeves of his shirt past his elbows, revealing surprisingly well-shaped forearms with a smattering of dark hair.

"Looks like he's preparing for surgery. Up you go now." Tyber's hands settled at her waist, effortlessly lifting her back onto his lap.

LaLeche leaned over the supine woman. "Are you comfortable, Elizabeth?"

"Yes."

"Good." He flipped on the cassette player and chirping bird sounds filled the room. "Now I want you to relax. I'm going to start now."

He closed his eyes briefly, then began running his hands down the length of her body, never actually touching it. "Concentrate with me, my dear, on the flow of energy through your body."

Elizabeth seemed a little nervous.

"Relax. Stretch your muscles. Breathe deeply. In. Out. Everyone join in."

"Don't you dare take a deep breath while I'm sitting on your lap, Tyber," Zanita muttered, causing him to let out a bark of laughter which he tried to disguise as a cough.

"Now, Elizabeth, I want you to see yourself, your body, your energy. Picture the energy flowing through you, unimpeded, unobstructed in any way. You feel the strength of your energy flow through you and around you. Good . . ." As he spoke, LaLeche moved his hands on a parallel course with her body, up and down, then in strange circular motions.

"Do you feel the heat of healing energy yet?" he asked Elizabeth.

"A—a little."

"Good. That's good. Keep concentrating as I am—concentrating on feeling you well, seeing you well. . . ."

Zanita halfheartedly watched the healing until her attention was suddenly brought up short by a strange glow that seemed to be coming from LaLeche's hands.

She blinked to clear her vision. Her vision did not change.

Her body jerked upright.

She felt Tyber's hands lightly squeeze her shoulders, a gesture which told her that while he was acknowledging what they were seeing, he was, at the same time, encouraging her to relax.

Zanita could sense the others in the room shifting their positions, all watching the strange phenomenon, each afraid to speak lest they break the spell.

The glow was all around his hands now.

Little arcs of light played around his fingers as he continued to pass his hands in the air just above her body. LaLeche seemed to be in deep concentration; a bead of sweat rolled down his forehead.

It was an unnerving experience.

It seemed absolutely genuine.

It scared the bejesus out of her.

"Tyber," Zanita croaked in a whisper, "could we have been wrong?"

Tyber didn't respond except to give her the strength of his gentle hug. It was a welcome ground in a situation that seemed . . . unearthly.

"Do you feel it, Elizabeth?" LaLeche almost seemed to be speaking out of a trance.

"Yes—oh, yes! I feel a—heat. It feels—" The experience proved too much for the woman. She burst into tears. LaLeche sat back on his haunches and wiped the sweat off his brow.

There was dead silence for several moments, then everyone started to whisper at once.

Elizabeth clutched LaLeche's hands. "Did it work, do you think?" There was a poignant desperation in her voice.

"Yes, I know it did." He gave her a small, benevolent hug.

Zanita turned to Tyber, her violet eyes huge in her face.

173

"Tyber, what did we just see?"

Tyber looked perplexed. He didn't answer her for several minutes. When he did, it was not the reassurance she was looking for.

"I don't know."

Zanita clutched his arm and he gazed down at her.

"Whatever it was, baby, I can guarantee it wasn't what you think it was."

"Are you sure?"

She looks really worried, he thought, surprised. Her face had gone pale, her eyes wide. He lifted a finger to run it encouragingly down the side of her smooth cheek.

"Yes. I'm sure, baby. I just need time to figure it out. It's late; why don't we make our excuses and head back to the warmth of our room? I think the show's over for now."

Wise words from a man who was proving himself to be a rock of strength for her. "I agree." She stood up, stretching her creaking, frozen joints. "We need to go back and mull this over."

Tyber stood. "The only thing I want mulled tonight is some hot cider, quickly followed by a hot bath."

They made their way through the throng to LaLeche, acting suitably awed by what they had seen.

"I'm so glad you got to partake in this particular session." He almost sounded giddy. "I must tell you, this doesn't happen often."

No, only when you need to drum up some hefty donations. Tyber listened to him with a bland expression on his face.

"Tomorrow we'll have a brief farewell blessing at noon. I try to keep the Sunday sessions short because most of us have a rather long trip home." It was amazing how considerate he sounded. "You will be here tomorrow, won't you, Dr. Evans?"

The man seemed rather overeager to him. Tyber thought quickly. "Actually, we won't be able to make it tomorrow. I've promised my friend we'd have lunch with him."

Zanita's head whipped toward him in surprise, but Tyber

ignored her, reaching into his inside jacket pocket to extract his checkbook. He took out his pen, opened the cover, and stopped, as if something had just occurred to him.

"You know, Xavier, I'm having a few friends of like mind down next weekend. Would you care to join us for the weekend at my home? That is, if you don't already have other plans? I'm really very interested in what you've done and I have to tell you, I'm very impressed."

A glint, somewhere between avarice and exultation, came into LaLeche's eyes. "Why, thank you, Dr. Evans! Coming from you that is a compliment, indeed. I'm flattered. Of course I'll accept your invitation!"

It was obvious to Zanita that the man could barely contain his excitement. Tyber clicked his pen and began writing out a check. *A very large check.* Zanita's eyes widened.

Before Tyber could cross the T in his name, LaLeche's hand stopped him.

"No need for that now, Doctor. I appreciate the gesture, but, after all, you've just invited me to your home. Why don't we wait and see what develops?"

Tyber glanced down at him through veiled eyes. "Yes. Why don't we?" He tore off the left-hand corner of the check with a secret smile, handing just the little piece to LaLeche. "Here's the address. We'll expect you around seven—for dinner."

"Thank you. I look forward to it!" He stuck out his hand. Tyber shook it briefly before quickly ushering Zanita out into the rainy night.

They made a mad dash through the mud to the truck.

"*Heeeeat!*" Zanita wailed as soon as Tyber started the engine.

Tyber slammed a couple of levers to the far right and a blast of warm air began filling the cab. They both moaned in ecstasy.

"We're getting right into a hot tub as soon as we get back to the room." Tyber negotiated the truck onto the road heading back to the inn.

Zanita tried to talk between the chattering of her teeth. "It

175

was nice of you to leave those blankets behind.''

"How could I not? I hope those poor bastards don't get pneumonia tonight.'' A street light illuminated the set of his jaw and the disgust on his face.

"They're adults, Tyber. No one is holding them there; they can leave if they want to.''

Her words visibly relaxed him. "I suppose you're right. Although I'm not sure that's altogether true in Elizabeth's case. She's looking for a miracle and perhaps she thinks she's found one. In that case, wild horses wouldn't drag the woman away from there.'' The palm of his hand slammed against the steering wheel. "It's the worst sort of manipulation!''

Zanita put her hand on his thigh.

He turned briefly to meet her eyes. "Now I know why it was so important to you to go after this guy; I imagine Mrs. Haverhill was much like Elizabeth.''

She nodded. "Yes. A very nice woman in a horrible situation. I think she probably was reaching out for help, for contact with another human being. It was her last chance to trust someone, and along comes someone like Xavier. . . .''

"It's disgusting,'' he bit out.

"Tyber . . . why did you write out such a large check to him? What if he had taken it?''

"It was a calculated risk. First, I told him we couldn't attend tomorrow, letting him think this was his last shot at us. Then I took out my checkbook to confirm his supposition. I thought if I casually invited him to the mansion as I wrote out a check, he would see the possibilities in a future, even larger donation.'' The corners of his mouth lifted slightly in private amusement. "Something to tide him over the long winter.''

"Is that why you invited him next weekend?''

"Yes. We need more time with him. Seeing him at seminars occasionally over the winter isn't going to cut it. We need to develop a more intimate relationship with him. Don't forget, we don't know what we're going after to entrap him.''

"Smart. But what if he had taken the check anyway? That was an awfully large check, Tyber.''

He shrugged unconcerned. "As I said—a calculated risk."

"So . . . what *did* we see?"

Tyber exhaled a long breath. "I'm not sure yet. But I promise you—I will figure out exactly what scam he's pulling."

"You don't think he has some genuine ability and is using it to manipulate people, do you?" Silly as it seemed, she was almost afraid to ask this question.

"Absolutely not. What we saw in there was impressive, but it was showmanship. He did something. . . ."

"But how? You saw yourself—his shirt was rolled up way above his elbows. He wasn't concealing anything in his sleeves. I watched his hands closely—he didn't palm anything. Everyone was surrounding him. There was no sleight of hand."

"I know. I observed that as well. . . ." His words trailed off. Deep in thought, brow furrowed, Tyber drove the rest of the way to the inn in silence.

True to his word, when Zanita came out of the tub dressed in one of the terrycloth robes the inn provided, she spotted Tyber sitting in the large chair in front of the fireplace, sipping a hot mulled cider.

He was wrapped in the other robe, his bare feet resting on the mantel, toes wiggling as he tried to warm his feet. He gestured to the other mug on the tray, then patted his lap.

Zanita gratefully took a sip of the hot drink as she curled up on his lap. "Mmm, this is good. I wondered why you left the tub so fast."

He ran his hand lazily down her back. "Someone had to wait for the drinks. I think I'm actually starting to feel my toes again."

"It was horrid, wasn't it? I hope my next investigation leads me someplace warm—like the Caribbean."

Tyber gave her an indulgent look. "Uh-huh. You ought to put that imagination of yours to work writing fiction. The Caribbean!"

Zanita sighed. "I know; more than likely my next piece

will take me back into the wet bogs of cranberry country, sloshing through a quagmire of mud in search of beer-swilling aliens.''

Not if I have anything to say about it. There was no way he was slogging through swamps with her In Search Of. He rubbed his freshly shaven jaw. ''You know, baby, I'm serious. Why don't you think about it?''

''Maybe.'' She snuggled into him, yawning.

He smiled above her curly head. *Here we have three factors in the Zanita Equation: a warm drink, a warm lap, and a toasty fire. These three factors combined could only add up to . . .*

His blue eyes twinkled as he looked down at the woman fast asleep in his arms.

A sharp knock on the door to their room woke Zanita up the next morning. She heard Tyber mumble something incoherent next to her ear while she tried unsuccessfully to untangle their naked limbs.

The knock came again.

''Just a minute,'' she called out. ''Tyber, move your leg!''

Tyber sleepily raised his head off the pillow. ''Huh? Oh, the door—I'll get it.'' His head flopped back down onto the pillow. ''Just give me a minute.'' He burrowed his arms back under the pillow, closing his eyes.

A disembodied chipper voice called through the door, ''Room service!''

''Did you order room service?'' She shook his shoulder. He blearily opened his eyes. Glass-blue orbs tried to focus on her.

''What?'' His vision cleared. He smiled. ''Oh, yeah! I ordered breakfast in bed for us last night.'' He threw back the covers, grabbing the terry robe on his way to the door.

Zanita eyed his backside appreciatively from the bed. Pity he had to cover those gorgeous buns, she thought.

Round. Smooth. Tight. Hard.

Just the way she liked them.

A real handful.

Tyber returned to the bed carrying a large wicker tray. His hair, as usual in the morning, was in sexy disarray around his shoulders.

"What d'ya got?" she asked, eyeing the tray with interest and thinking it was a very nice gesture on his part.

He placed the tray carefully on the bed, shucked his robe, and crawled back inside beside her. His body was still sleep-warmed. "Let's see . . ." He brought the tray across his lap.

"A little bottle of champagne, apple pancakes and maple syrup, some orange juice"—he took a sip—"fresh-squeezed, a basket of cinnamon rolls, and what appears to be homemade jam."

"Champagne for breakfast?"

"Of course." He uncorked the bottle with a pop. "Try it; it will do wonderful things for you in the morning." He poured her out a flute.

She tasted it appreciatively. "It does! I think the bubbles are actually invigorating!" She took another sip. "I think this could replace caffeine."

Tyber put a finger to his lips. "Shh. It'll be our secret." Zanita giggled. Smiling, he leaned over to place a quick kiss on her lips.

"Here you go." He handed her a plate of pancakes.

"Thanks; they look delicious."

"Mmm." His long lashes lifted slowly, revealing a devilish twinkle in his eyes. "*Syrup?*" The corner of his mouth quirked ever so slightly.

Tyber was teasing her with his "tunnel" allusion, reminding her of his "syrupy" quivering walls. Zanita blushed to the roots of her hair.

"You are outrageous!"

A dimple curved his cheek. When he spoke, his voice was a husky drawl. "I do my best for you, baby." He poured some syrup on her pancakes, ignoring her gape-mouthed expression.

Zanita decided it was wise to ignore Tyber when he got into one of these moods of his. She dug into her pancakes.

They were delicious, light and fluffy with chunks of fresh

179

native apples. There were worse things in this world than having a champagne breakfast in bed, she decided. She leaned back against the pillows, closed her eyes, stretched her toes under the blanket, and sighed.

"More?"

"I don't think I could." She patted her stomach.

"I'm not talking about the breakfast." The sultry purr came from somewhere to her left. Her eyes snapped open.

He had removed the tray, placing it on the bedside table. And those ice eyes of his were regarding her with a sharp heat, focusing strictly on her mouth.

Under his intense scrutiny, her lips tingled, parting slightly. His pupils darkened and dilated.

It was difficult to form a cogent thought with him watching her like that. Her breath caught in her throat. The man was sizzling! Without a doubt, he was the sexiest male she had ever seen.

She attempted speech. "You're—you're not?"

"Well, I could be."

It took Zanita a moment to realize that he wasn't agreeing with her steamy assessment of him, but answering her question. In any case, she didn't have time to wonder about it because he lifted his hand, threading his fingers slowly through the curls on the side of her face, immediately capturing her attention.

With his other hand, he idly reached over to the tray to dip his index finger in a little pool of syrup left on one of the plates. His eyes never leaving her full mouth, he diligently traced her lips with the syrupy finger, leaving the sticky residue behind.

"Wh—what are you doing?"

This time he didn't answer her.

He just lowered his head to carefully lick the sticky syrup off her parted lips with the tip of his swirling tongue. It was a sultry dalliance of playfulness and demand.

"*Tyber . . .*" Zanita whispered his name against the brush of his velvet lips as they feathered across hers.

Very lightly, in the barest of caresses, he skimmed the backs of his fingers down the sides of her breasts, her waist, her hips. His flitting touch ignited sparks of yearning as he seemed to barely dance over her satiny skin.

All the while, his fluid tongue teased at the corners of her mouth. He gently probed her lower lip, laving across the seam.

Zanita lifted her mouth for his kiss, for the savory press of his mouth. When it came, she nimbly caught the tip of his tongue between her lips and gently suckled on him. He tasted deliciously of syrup and Tyber.

A thick sound issued low in his throat.

His uninhibited moan of desire resonated through her. There was a physics term he had taught her . . . what had Tyber called it?

Synchronous vibration.

Yes, now she understood it very well as a matching pulse of longing throbbed through her.

Tyber's beautiful mouth moved across her face, slowly, languorously. Passionately. His hot kisses swept across her in a fiery burst of controlled heat. A chaotic contradiction of the senses, he was somewhere between ambling and deliberate.

He took her breath away.

He reached for the syrup dispenser.

While Zanita watched him, eyes passion-glazed, his thumb pressed back on the spring mechanism, releasing a thin stream of the amber syrup. It slowly cascaded down the center of her breasts in a meandering pattern, pooling in her navel and, following the course of Tyber's direction, flowed down thick into the nest of curls between her legs.

Before she had the presence of mind to wonder what he was doing, he came over her.

His open mouth leisurely followed the trail of rich sap, consuming as he went with sensual sweeps of his tongue.

Zanita lay back against the pillows and gave herself over to this mind-drugging experience.

He scraped his tongue across the peak of one breast, letting her feel every tiny bump on its syrup-coated surface as he slid across her extended nipple. Then he caught just the tip between his teeth and tugged. She clutched his shouders, moaning at the sheer erotic pleasure of it.

Strong, well-shaped hands came up to cup her breasts as he went about licking and sucking the syrup from her chest. The flat plane of her stomach. The little pool in her navel. And lower still . . .

Was he going to . . . ?

Zanita clamped her legs shut. She wasn't altogether sure about this.

Tyber hesitated, looking up at her. "What is it, baby?"

"I—I'm not sure . . ."

But I am. He rubbed his chin against the delicate skin of her lower belly. The faint stubble of his morning beard rasped against her, eliciting an acute response from myriad nerve endings. She shivered.

Tyber noted her response, felt her response. He softly blew against the nest of curls, watching the slick, glistening thatch part under his breath.

Zanita stopped breathing.

He lowered his head.

"*Tyber*—" She could feel his lips almost against her; his breath warm against her.

"Shh. I want to see if I can tell the difference between maple syrup and honey."

His raw words, so quietly yet so inexorably spoken, made her heart stop.

Then he was there.

Tasting her. Kissing her. Parting her and licking her in long, hot, relishing strokes of his tongue.

Zanita threw back her head, shuddering under the onslaught, her fingers clenching in the pillow above her. The pleasure so exquisite that it was almost painful. So intense that it was almost unbearable. When he found her hidden, now ultra-sensitive, throbbing nub, she bucked off the bed calling out his name in a choked sob.

Tyber smiled against her, loving her feel, her taste. Especially her taste . . .

His hands slid under her, cupping her bottom, imprisoning her right against his face. He inserted his tongue inside her.

She came instantly against his mouth in powerful spasms, her body convulsing in great wracking tremors. And he felt every one of them.

When her body stopped shaking and had subsided into small quivers of sensation, he still stayed with her, reluctant to stop the tongue-loving he was giving her.

"I think I'm dead," she squeaked.

His low laugh carried up to her. Kissing her one last time, he raised himself above her, hugging her tight to him. He caught her bottom lip between his teeth, then covered her mouth with his own. He tasted of her and maple syrup. And Tyber.

She felt the hard, pulsing length of him pressed to her thigh. Hot for her. He was always hot for her.

He buried his face in the curve of her neck, cuddling his cheek against her.

"Did you?" she mouthed against his ear.

Husky breath feathered the side of her face. "Did I what?"

"Tell the difference?"

"Yes. *I like the honey better, baby.*" His teeth pulled on her earlobe as he thrust sharply into her.

Chapter Eleven

On the drive back to My Father's Mansion, Zanita could not keep her sights from straying again and again in Tyber's direction.

She stared at his beautiful hands on the steering wheel, so competent and in control, and she couldn't help but recall how they had felt stroking her body just a few short hours ago.

She watched the quirk of his lips in a smile, the way he bit his bottom lip when she asked him a question he needed to think about, and she could not stop herself from remembering the way those velvet-soft lips had taken such firm control of her, had her begging for more. *Another touch, another tender press, another sweet caress.*

And it occurred to her how very dangerous this man was to her.

How important he could become.

Had already become.

She was afraid she was acquiring an insatiable desire for him. Shakily, she brushed a strand of hair out of her eyes and stared worriedly out of her window.

Tyber's glance flicked her way. A slow smile curved his outlaw lips.

Blooey was ecstatic with the arrival of two jugs of maple syrup and a bushel of apples, immediately declaring his intention to bake a squash-apple cake with the new ingredients. Tyber gritted his teeth.

Even Hambone seemed happy to see them; the fat cat purred and twirled his bulk through Tyber's legs as he brought in their bags, almost tripping him several times. As soon as the front door closed behind them, Hambone sat down in front of Tyber to let loose a huge, screeching wail.

"I brought you something; just a minute, Hambone!"

Tyber quickly found the cheese, cutting off a good-sized chunk for the demanding tabby from hell. In the trusting way of cats, Hambone cautiously sniffed it first to make sure his beloved human wasn't trying to pull a fast one on him. Once properly assured that the offering was not laced with arsenic, Hambone let out a short purr before attacking the cheese.

Zanita watched this scene play out, amazed. Who had ever heard of a cat with a penchant for Vermont cheddar? She smiled to herself. *Yes, she was back in the nut house again.* But it felt good to be home.

Home.

Funny how she was starting to think of this place in that way. When Tyber drove through the gates after dark and Zanita caught her first view of the house lit up in welcome for them, all crazy turrets and impossible features, she had felt a rush of warmth inside her. Then Blooey and Hambone had come out onto the porch to greet them.

It was really a very nice feeling.

Much better than coming home to her empty, sterile apartment.

The enticing aromas of Blooey's cooking wafted from the kitchen. Zanita sighed; yes, this was a very nice feeling.

She smiled while observing Tyber. He had quickly shed his jacket and was now kicking off his boots. In stocking feet, well-worn jeans, and a soft, red flannel shirt, he looked very much at home.

"Mmm, something smells good; I wonder what Blooey cooked up for dinner?"

"Don't know—but whatever it is, I'm sure it's elaborate. Blooey always thinks my palate suffers when I walk out that door," Tyber answered her distractedly while riffling through the mail Blooey had piled onto a sideboard in the foyer.

He suddenly grinned at a postcard in his hand, eagerly flipping it over to read the back. "It's from my parents."

"Your *parents*?"

Somehow she had never pictured him as having a mother and a father. Parents. That made him sort of . . . normal. Zanita was not sure she was ready to embrace a normal Tyber. A Tyber who had regular family. A Tyber who was not so outside the realm of normal relationships.

Tyber leaned back against the door frame, crossing his arms over his chest. He stared at her with an expression of combined disbelief and amusement. "Did you think I sprang from the forehead of Galileo fully grown?" he asked dryly.

"Well no, of course not. I just never pictured you with—" He quirked an eyebrow at her. "All right, so maybe I did think that! So, are they traveling?"

"Yes, my father is on sabbatical; they're in Greece."

"He's a teacher?"

"Professor of Antiquities at Harvard."

Zanita digested this piece of information, fidgeting slightly. Then she suddenly smiled as something dawned on her.

"Of course." She snapped her fingers. "That's how you ended up with Tyberius Augustus." The father must be just as much of a kook as the son. Who named their kid Tyberius Augustus?

"What are your brothers and sisters named—Claudius Aurelius and Hera Athena?" She giggled.

Tyber frowned at her. "I am an only child, and what's wrong with my name?"

"Nothing; its a beautiful name. Very unconventional—suits you to a tee."

"My mother thought so. She's always said that as soon as Dad suggested it, she knew it was perfect for me."

This woman was either very much in love with her husband or Zanita was involved with the Addams Family. Probably both. She cleared her throat. "Is your mother a professor too?"

Tyber grinned. "Hell, no. She's an artist. She paints trash."

"That bad?"

He laughed. "No, I mean she actually paints trash. You know—flea market stuff; she uses it in her work. She's really quite good."

Another kook. Yep. The Addams Family.

As if to lend credence to her thoughts, at that moment Blooey bustled into the foyer, squawking, "Are ye gonna stand there all night diddlin' away with the lass while me supper goes to the squabs, Captain?"

Probably chastised, Tyber followed behind Zanita into the kitchen, bending down once to murmur in her ear, "*Diddlin*'?"

Zanita, who knew exactly what the word meant, just shrugged her shoulders, thankful that he was behind her and couldn't see her blush.

Catching her expression in the hall mirror they passed, Tyber grinned wickedly. Blooey was a crusty old tar. He liked that in a man.

The following days seemed to fall into the regular Evans pattern, if anything having to do with Tyber could be called either regular or a pattern.

Zanita worked on her usual array of articles; Tyber worked on . . . well, whatever it was Tyber worked on. One evening he uncharacteristically went back down to his lab, saying he had an idea he needed to "get down" right away. He was back upstairs in less than thirty minutes.

Zanita, who had been watching an old movie, looked up in alarm at the sharklike grin on his face as he began walking—no, stalking—toward her, proclaiming that he had a sudden uncontrollable urge to teach her quantum mechanics.

She shrieked and fell right in with his plans by bolting up the stairs and into their bedroom, a pursuing Tyber right on her heels.

It had been an in-depth lesson.

The next night, he corraled her in the parlor. His eyes had a wild gleam.

"You're in a dungeon."

"What?"

"Go with this for a minute, Zanita. You're in a dungeon—"

"What are you talking about?"

"I'm working on a computer game and—"

"*A computer game*? Here, all this time, I thought you were *this close* to the cure for the common cold. I can't believe it!" One of the greatest minds of the day, and he was working on games!

Tyber seemed affronted. "Games are wonderful things, Zanita. They can teach all sorts of things if presented in an engaging format—reasoning ability, a sense of accomplishment, not to mention exercise for the imagination."

His eyes twinkled down at her, forcing her to recall the imaginative, engaging format he used last evening to teach her . . .

She felt the peaks of her breasts harden with the memory.

"Well, I suppose . . ."

He knelt before her chair, taking her hands in his. "You're in a dungeon. In order to escape, you have to negotiate a maze of logic—"

"I'm doomed."

"Hmm. I can see I'm going to have to wait until I can test the prototype on you."

Zanita waved her hand. "No way. I'm lousy at those kinds of things. I can't even shoot a straight line; one of those weird ninja things would have my head before the game even started.''

A dimple curved into his cheek. ''It's not that kind of game; it's an adventure game.''

''I'd still be lousy.''

He rubbed his chin back and forth against her knee, his clear, flashing eyes engaging hers. ''No. You're very good at adventures, baby.''

The man could stop a heart from beating.

She mentally shook herself. ''Well, no adventures for me right now. I told Hank I'd get this extra article done for him in time for Halloween which, in case you don't realize it, is tomorrow. I haven't even started it yet.''

''What's it about?'' He leaned further over her lap, trying to read her hieroglyphics upside down.

''You know the old cemetery down by the mill?''

He furrowed his brow. ''The one from the seventeen-hundreds with all the interesting sayings on the gravestones?''

''Yeah. Well, there's this legend that on midnight on All Hallow's Eve a ghostly carriage rides through the cemetery over the headstones.''

''Ye Olde Federal Express?''

She laughed, then dropped her voice to an enticing whisper. ''Supposedly it rides amongst the graves looking for someone or some *thing*. Rumor has it that two hundred years ago, on the eve of Halloween, at the stroke of midnight, a beautiful young woman—''

''*Cherchez la femme.*''

Zanita whacked his shoulder before continuing with the lurid tale, ''—goes to an assignation with her lover. Unfortunately, her husband has found out about the tryst, gets there before she does, and whacks off the head of her paramour.''

''And rightly so, the poor cuckolded fellow.'' Zanita stuck her tongue out at him. ''Go on, baby, I'm breathless with curiosity.''

Zanita ignored his sarcasm, leaning closer to him. ''When the lady arrives, who greets her but—''

"Let me take a wild guess: the headless man about town?"

She nodded. "The woman sees her hunk sans head and instantly dies of fright. The coachman runs off, and the coach with the dead woman is forever doomed to wander the graveyard looking for her love, who can't find her either because he has no head." Zanita made the appropriate scary sound, "*Oooo . . .*"

"That is lame."

"Easy for you to say. I don't see you running down to the cemetery to see if—" A light came into Tyber's eyes. An unholy light.

"All right."

"What do you mean, all right?"

"Let's go down there tonight—at midnight. Check it out."

Zanita swallowed nervously. She always got the willies over ghost stories. "We don't have to—I have to get this article done and—"

"So, write your article now. I need to finish up something myself," he said mysteriously. Then, "You're not afraid, are you?"

"Don't be silly! Okay, you're on."

"Fine. We'll rendezvous in the foyer at eleven."

"Fine." Her voice quavered slightly.

Tyber stood to leave, stopping to point a finger at her. "If you don't show up, Curls, I'll know you're chicken."

Zanita snorted disdainfully, turning back to her article as if to dismiss him.

It was just as well she didn't see the expression of ungodly glee on his roguish face.

Hollywood couldn't have done it better.

A dense fog wafted around the decrepit headstones, several of which had fallen over and settled thickly around the cab of the truck. The light of a full moon filtered eerily through the thick, soupy haze, barely illuminating the road they were parked on. *The only road out.*

An owl hooted atmosphere into the night. A cold, biting

damp permeated the interior of the truck, seeping into her bones even with the stadium blanket Tyber had thrown over them.

She could hear Boris Karloff assuring her that this was a thriller.

She expected to see Michael Jackson and his moonwalking zombies any time now.

Zanita peered at the small digital clock Tyber had hung on the dash. 11:40. Twenty minutes to go.

"Do you want to tell ghost stories?" Zanita could hear the mocking laughter in his voice.

"No." It was the last thing she wanted to do. *This is creepy.* How had he maneuvered her into this display of idiocy?

Tyber leaned back in the seat, vainly trying to stretch his long legs out. He laced his hands behind his neck, cracking a few cold, stiff joints in the process, then draped his arm across the back of her seat.

He stared straight ahead. "Want to neck?"

"No."

"Have you thought about who you're going to invite for the weekend?"

She turned to him. "What do you mean?"

"I told LaLeche we were having some friends down for the weekend; it seemed a convenient excuse to invite him. Don't you think he'll be suspicious if there's nobody there but him?"

"Why didn't you mention this before! What are we going to do?"

"We?"

"It was your plan!"

"Yes, but it's *your* story." Zanita folded her arms over her chest and glared at him. "Okay, okay. Think of some people. Fast. What about your girlfriend Mills?"

"Mmm. She might; especially if she's not doing anything this weekend. I've already told her about your house, and she's dying to see if it's as kooky . . ." Her voice trailed off as she realized what she was saying.

Tyber's brows slanted down, making him look rather like a

191

disgruntled Viking. "Who else?"

"I don't know."

"How about Hank and your grandmother?"

"No! I don't want Hank getting a clue about this. What about some of your friends and colleagues?"

"No way. Forget it. Get that idea right out of your head."

"Why not?"

"Why not, she says. Other than irrevocably destroying my credibility amongst my colleagues and friends by setting them up to get bilked by a con man, I can't think of a single reason."

Zanita snorted. "Oh, Tyber, no one expects *you* to be normal."

He threw her a look. "I am a well-respected eccentric. At least I was until I met you."

"What about Stan Mazurski?"

"Stan?" He said the word as if it had just been coined. "Okay, he seems stolid enough not to fall under LaLeche's spell. I'll invite him and his wife for dinner on Friday night."

"Not for the weekend?"

"Don't push it. Who else?"

Zanita tapped her chin. "I suppose there's always Auntie." She said it like a true New Englander: *ahn-tee*.

"Why does that statement make me uncomfortable? Who is Auntie?"

"Hank's sister, my great-aunt. Oh, you'll love her, Tyber; she's wonderful."

"Why would you place a sweet, elderly aunt in the sphere of a piranha like LaLeche? I don't think it's a good idea. Why are you giggling?"

"Auntie eats piranhas."

Tyber's eyes widened. He sank down in the seat as he got the picture. Great. *Aunt From The Planet Attitude*. Just great. "All right, invite her down for the weekend, but I want you to clue her in just the same."

"I won't have to. You'll see. She loves hats—always wears three of them."

He was afraid of that.

"I'll ask My—Maggy in to help Blooey with the serving."

"Who's your Maggy?" Zanita's tone held just a faint trace of jealousy, but not so faint that Tyber didn't pick up on it. He immediately decided to play on it by acting chagrined.

"I, ah—an old friend. I like her a lot. My—Maggy's a hell of a woman." Zanita pursed her lips. *Interesting*, he thought. First Kim, now My Maggy. Zanita was definitely showing potential.

"Will she be staying the weekend?" Her voice was flat.

"If I'm lucky. I really need her." He counted to three. Zanita lit off right on time. He stretched his arm back behind her seat.

"What do you mean, you need her!" She walloped him in the stomach with her enormous purse. "I won't—"

"Shh! What was that? Did you hear something?"

"W-what?"

"I thought I heard something—listen!"

Zanita went instantly still. "I don't hear anything."

"Look, it's midnight," he whispered, pointing at the clock.

Then she heard it. Faintly at first, getting slightly louder as if it were coming toward them. A clip-clop of horses. Harnesses tinkling in the night. The roll of wooden wheels over . . . *gravestones*?

Zanita was paralyzed in terror. Any moment she fully expected to see a ghostly carriage loom out of the fog, the visage of a decaying corpse peering out the window at her as it rolled by. She sucked in her breath.

A hand trailed its way down her neck.

Zanita let out a blood-curdling scream.

Tyber doubled over, laughing his head off. A small tape recorder rested in the palm of his hand. She turned to him with the light of murder in her eyes.

"Trick or treat?" He blinked ingenuously at her.

"Evans, you are dead meat!"

The truck had not even come to a complete stop before

Tyber jumped out and raced up the stairs, a furious Zanita on his tail.

"Now, Zanita—" He was still laughing, which ignited her further. She chased him into the parlor.

"Don't Zanita me; I'm going to kill you!"

He scooted around an oak tea table, feinting left when she lunged right. "Baby, it was just a joke."

"You scared me half to death!" She just missed his arm that time.

Tyber gave up the table tag, racing back into the foyer. Zanita ran right after him. He suddenly stopped and turned to her, arms open, and her momentum plowed her right into him.

"*Oof*!"

Tyber grinned wickedly, then tossed her over his shoulder.

"What are you doing? Put me down this minute!" She tried to lever her way up his back.

"Is it a call to arms, Captain? Are we under attack?"

The commotion must've woken Blooey up. He was standing in the hallway wearing a red nightshirt and sleep cap. He rubbed his eyes sleepily. Hambone sat on the floor next to him; the groggy cat leaned against Blooey's leg as if by doing so he could pretend they were still cozy in bed.

"Nay, Blooey, just a hot-blooded wench what needs to be taught a lesson in the Captain's cabin." He heartily slapped her rear end.

"Ow!"

"What lesson might that be, Captain?" Blooey grinned.

Tyber regarded the wiggling rump next to his face. "The Laws of Motion, I think. Especially *oscillation*." He leaned over and nipped her buttock.

"Cut it out!"

"And you being the perfect one to be teachin' her such a lesson," Blooey chuckled. "Good night, Captain; good night, Lady Masterson." He yawned and headed back to bed, Hambone trailing behind him.

"Blooey, don't leave me with this madman!"

Tyber clicked his teeth. "Tsk-tsk. Listen to you, asking a

man who believes himself on a pirate ship to commit mutiny. I'm worried about you, baby. Truly, I am.'' His hand stroked down the back of her thigh as he climbed the stairs with her.

"Oh!" She clenched her fists. "You are a—a—*rogue*!"

Tyber threw back his head and laughed. "Why, thank you, baby."

She was late. She was a mess.

It was after five and she had promised Tyber she would be back around three to help with the arrangements for the weekend. And she would've been if it wasn't for the flat tire on Rural Route 23. Now their guests—no, *her* guests—would be arriving within the hour. Tyber would have a right to be put out with her.

She trudged up the stairs, quietly closing the door behind her. Maybe she could sneak upstairs—

"*Where have you been*? I've called your office a hundred times—Good God! What happened to you?" Her clothes were streaked with dirt, her jacket ripped at the shoulder. A smudge of grease slashed across her forehead.

She didn't answer him right away; she was too stunned at the sight of him. He was wearing black dress slacks with a white pin-striped shirt. As was his habit, he had rolled the cuffs back, revealing those sinewy forearms of his. His long hair was sleekly tied back from his masculine face, accenting the strong column of his throat.

All she had ever seen him in were very casual clothes, mostly jeans. He looked positively gorgeous. He looked positively furious.

"I—I had a flat tire on 23. I tried to change it, but the stupid jack wouldn't stay put. I crawled underneath to see what the problem was—" He paled.

"Are you telling me you were under the car when the jack slipped?"

"Not quite, but—"

He ran a hand through his hair, mussing it up slightly. "My God. Why didn't you call me?"

"I didn't have to; a nice truck driver stopped to help me. He was really very sweet."

"You let a stranger help you on a deserted road? What the hell is the matter with you! Don't you read the newspapers—what am I saying? You're a reporter, for christsakes!" Zanita winced. He was really working himself into a full-blown tirade.

"Really, Tyber, you're overreacting—"

"*Why didn't you call me*?"

"I didn't want to bother you." Wrong answer. She could tell by the way his pupils glazed over. She quickly added, "Besides, there was no way I could call you; it was a country road, nothing around for miles."

That stopped him. He considered her words for a few moments.

"All right. Only next time, *call me*."

Zanita knew men always said stuff like this in situations such as this, completely ignoring logistics. As if the next time something similar happened, they would somehow miraculously appear out of the ether to take care of it!

She never understood it.

Her grandfather Hank acted the same way. Zanita also knew that once you agreed to what they said, regardless of how farfetched it might be, their feathers immediately unruffled and they forgot about it. Tyber apparently was no exception to this peculiar male trait.

"Okay."

"Mills called; she said she'd be here in about half an hour." Feathers sleek again.

"I better hurry and clean up—"

There was a crash from the kitchen, followed by a roar from Blooey. Zanita jumped, throwing a questioning glance at Tyber.

"My-Maggy's here." Another crash was followed by more yelling, Blooey cursing, and a raspy bellow from a distinctly Irish-accented voice.

Tyber winced. "Don't worry—they love each other." At

Zanita's disbelieving look, he added, "Sort of, Zanita, why are you staring at me?"

She still couldn't stop looking at him. "You're *dressed*."

Tyber wondered if her recent experience with the flat had shaken her brains. He slowly approached her and carefully lifted her chin with his index finger. "Yes, but don't worry, baby; it comes off."

He brushed her lips, standing well away from her dusty clothes. "Better hurry; they'll be here soon."

As he watched her walk up the stairs, he made a mental note to add a cellular phone to his shopping list.

Zanita whispered to her friend. "So, what do you think, Mills? Did I exaggerate or what?"

"No, it's just like you said. This place is incredible." Her sights strayed to Tyber, who was sipping a drink while watching the sunset through the large sitting room window. "And so is he. I still hate you."

"Thank you, Mills. You don't know how much it means to me to hear you say that." And she meant it. Mills had given her the supreme compliment between girlfriends: she was pea-green and woman enough to admit it.

They both giggled.

Tyber was thinking how beautiful Zanita looked when she came down the stairs a little while ago in a long, dark blue dress. An amethyst choker circled her slender throat, bringing out the color of her incredible eyes.

The corner of his mouth lifted as he smiled distractedly. He had noticed she had chosen to bring her curls over her forehead. He just bet that grease mark had been a bitch to get off; he should know, he'd worked on enough cars in his—

A screech of wheels drew his attention to the front of the house where an old Mercedes, going much too fast, was turning the curve of the drive on two wheels. What kind of a knuckleheaded dimwit drove down a private drive like the flames of hell licked at their heels?

His eyes widened as he realized what was in the direct path

of the erratic automobile. He clutched the edge of the window sill, his knuckles turning white.

"The Harley—not the Harley!" he gritted out.

There was a *crash crunch*, a sound of gears grinding, the squeal of the tires again, then the thump of a heavy door being slammed shut.

Tyber dropped his forehead to the window glass, closing his eyes in acute pain.

A second later, a decisive rapping issued from the front door knocker.

Zanita threw a wary glance at Tyber, wondering what had happened. Since he wasn't moving to answer the door, she gingerly went to do it.

"Zanita!" A loud, nasal voice filled the foyer. "How *marvelous* to see you at last! I can't tell you how happy I am to be with you."

"Auntie!" Zanita threw herself into the woman's arms.

"Let me see you!" The flamboyant woman held Zanita at arm's length as if checking her for damage. "You wouldn't believe it, but some idiot left a motorbike right in the middle of the road."

A choking sound came from the direction of the windows.

Auntie waved her hand, immediately dismissing the subject as if it were of no importance. Her piercing brown eyes fell on Mills. "Look what we have here—it's Marvelous Mills!"

"Auntie." Mills plastered a smile on her face, embracing the older woman.

Auntie, in her usual forthright manner, marched into the parlor, throwing her enormous handbag onto the pouf. Tyber briefly wondered if enormous handbags were a genetic trait passed on to the women in Zanita's family.

"Why didn't you tell me she was coming?" Mills hissed at Zanita.

"Because I wanted you here. Now hush up. You know Auntie loves you."

"She has a strange way of showing it; she always makes me feel like a kid whose hand got caught in the cookie jar."

"It's not personal; Auntie makes everybody feel that way."

"And who is this *marvelously* handsome young man?"

Auntie turned to Tyber, who was valiantly trying to throw off his internal pain by straightening his shoulders. And if the woman said *mahh . . . velous* one more time he was going to spontaneously combust. *His motorcycle!*

"I'm the idiot," he responded curtly.

Auntie's eyes narrowed. Zanita quickly stepped in. "Auntie, this is Tyber. Did you—did you have a nice trip down?"

"Oh, horrors! I thought it would never end." She reached into her purse, withdrawing a card. "I'm sorry I tapped your bike, Tyber. Do send me the bill." She handed him the card before peeling off her faux leopard coat and collapsing onto the couch with a whoosh. "I am so parched."

Tyber stared at the card for a moment, thinking, *tapped*? The woman had crushed his bike.

Zanita cleared her throat pointedly.

Tyber's head snapped up. "Uh . . . can I get you something to drink, Auntie?"

Zanita could tell he was having trouble with the name.

He thought of an acceptable drink to offer an elderly great aunt who murdered motorcycles without an ounce of remorse, blithely going on her merry way as if the remains of the crime weren't lying belly-up in his driveway! *Hemlock.* "Some mineral water or ice tea?"

"Bourbon."

He paused just for a moment. "Bourbon it is." He tossed the card into a small wastebasket he passed on the way to the liquor cabinet. He had no intention of contacting this woman. Ever. "Some water or ice?"

"Heavens, no!" She answered in the voice that sounded as if it had escaped from locked jaws. "Just bring me an empty glass and that bottle of Wild Turkey." She tapped the coffee table to show him exactly where she wanted it.

Tyber did as he was told. Although an idiot, he was no fool.

Auntie took a healthy swallow of her drink. "Ahh, now I feel like a human being again."

Tyber raised his eyebrow. A human being? From what planet? The woman was wearing three hats.

Zanita picked up the faux leopard. "Let me hang up your coat for you, Auntie. Would you like me to take your hats?"

"Just these two." She removed them from her head. "I always leave one on; my trademark, you know." She focused on Tyber. "Be a dear, young man; could you get my luggage out of the car for me?"

"Of course, Auntie." He quickly turned to leave, glad for any reason to be free of that room. Of that woman.

Auntie scrutinized his departure with interest. "*Marvelous* buns."

Tyber's step faltered for a second, then seemed to speed up.

"So, Mills, what have you been up to?"

"Oh, the usual." Mills swore she wouldn't give this woman any ammunition. None. She reached for a stuffed mushroom from the tray Blooey had left earlier. Zanita returned to the room.

"You know, Mills, I was in Bloomingdale's the other day, and I saw the most perfect sweater for your coloring." She focused pointedly on Mills' statuesque frame. "Although I'm not sure they had your size."

Mills' mouth closed. Slam-dunked, she lowered the mushroom back to the tray.

"Excuse me . . ." Tyber's voice sounded from the doorway. "There are seven suitcases in your car; which one did you need, Auntie?"

"Why, you silly boy—all of them, of course."

Tyber went back out. Zanita winced when she heard him bellow "*Blooey*!" in his best pirate captain voice.

He came back in just when Auntie said, "So where's the fish? Is he here yet?"

Tyber took a deep breath. "Zanita, can I talk to you for a minute?"

His voice was low. Too low. Zanita wet her lips, nervously following him out to the foyer. He reached around her, sliding the parlor doors shut with a commanding snap of his wrist.

"Yes, Tyber?" She tried for a sweet, innocent expression. It didn't work. He looked about ready to fire all cannons. Tyber was in a rant.

"She has seven rock-stuffed pullmans with her! She's drinking straight bourbon in there. Her mouth doesn't move when she talks. She ran over my motorcycle!" This last was said with spleen.

"Well . . ." She opted to answer for the least of Auntie's offenses in an attempt to sidetrack him. "Auntie talks that way because she went to Wellesley."

"What the hell does that have to do with it?"

"They sort of trained them to talk that way in those days." She bit her lips, waiting to see if he was appeased. No way. Not even close.

"Zanita, she commented on the shape of my—" He stopped, feeling too foolish to say it out loud.

"The shape of your what?" she asked curiously.

"My buns," he spat out.

Zanita put a hand to her mouth and giggled. He frowned down at her.

"Well, they *are* worth commenting on." She winked at him.

Tyber knew when he had been outmaneuvered. The outrageousness of the past half hour hit him. Against his will, his left eye twinkled; the corner of his mouth lifted. She was defusing him. He wasn't sure he wanted to be defused, dammit!

He tried to regain his righteous indignation. "You did just invite her for the weekend, didn't you?"

"By tomorrow you'll love her."

He crossed his arms over his chest, staring straight down at her, the imprint of doubt.

"I suppose it's a relative concept." Zanita suddenly beamed proudly up at him as she realized something. "That's a physics joke, Tyber!"

His expression softened. "C'mere."

His arms went around her. He bent to her lips.

The parlor door rolled open, and Mills stuck her head out.

"If you leave me alone in there with her for another minute, I'm going to kill both of you! Now stop smooching; get back in here and do your time."

Tyber exhaled in resignation. They each took one of his hands and dragged him back into the room.

Auntie's no-nonsense lock-jaw greeted them. "What were you two naughty children doing out there? Come sit by me, you thoroughly *marvelous* man. I want to know everything about you."

Tyber groaned.

Chapter Twelve

LaLeche arrived exactly on time at the stroke of seven.

He entered the parlor all smarmy charm, immediately sizing up the occupants as Zanita hoped he would, making a beeline for Auntie. This, of course, was only after he had gushed on and on about the charming grace of Tyber's Victorian mansion while undressing her with his eyes.

Zanita sank back into the thick cushions of the green velvet chair, thankful LaLeche had just missed the tragicomic altercation that had started in the kitchen and ended up in the sitting room. She winced as she remembered it.

There had been another loud crash from the kitchen and a lot of furious yelling before Blooey came charging into the room, a dripping wooden spoon held aloft in his hand like a righteous weapon of indignation.

"She's done it this time, Captain! The harpy has done it this time, I tell ye."

Tyber, grateful for any reason to be released from the grueling clutches of Auntie's third degree, courageously stepped into the fracas.

"What is it, Blooey?"

He pointed a condemning finger at the stout woman standing behind him. "She put salt in me vichyssoise!" All eyes turned in fascinated horror to the culprit, who stood there implacably at anchor.

She was a battleship of a woman.

A white cook's hat sat low on her forehead, allowing only a few stray steel wisps of hair to escape around her ears. Her visage was stern, uncompromising, and would likely put a stop to a cattle stampede. A starched white apron covered a flower-splashed shift that might be called a dress in kinder circles.

She looked like countless cafeteria cooks Zanita had seen in her school years—those stalwart ladies of institutional kitchens everywhere who, from substandard ingredients, loads of grease, salt, and mystery meat, whipped up cast-iron fare for the beleaguered masses of the student body. *Les Femmes du Gastro Morte.*

Arms akimbo, My-Maggy threw her pointed chin in the air, proclaiming, "The man has a cork fer a brain."

Dead silence followed her pronouncement.

Zanita guessed half of the guests were too flabbergasted to respond, while the other half agreed with the Battleship but were too polite to say so. Taking into account the self-preservation rule of dining—one never insults a host's cook and expects to get a choice piece of roast served to them by said cook—the silence was perfectly understandable. Normal under the circumstances. Normal. Right.

Tyber strolled over to the pair, throwing his arms around both their shoulders. It was clear to Zanita that he was going to use the "we're all good ol' boys—what's the fuss" method of calming them down.

"Now, Blooey, I'm sure she meant nothing personal by it. She probably didn't think about what she was doing, did you, My-Maggy?" Wisely, he didn't give her a chance to answer. "And Blooey, you know how much store I put by crew members getting along. These are dangerous times; we need to be able to depend on one another. We never can tell when those bloody Lobsterbacks are going to attack us again, can we?''

Blooey dropped his head in shame.

My-Maggy stared stonily at Tyber, muttering, "Sure and I'm liking you, Mr. Tyber, but I'm thinkin' you've got a bigger cork fer a brain than he does.''

Tyber patted her back in commiseration, steering them back toward the kitchen. "See now? All settled.''

"Just so she keeps her dockside cooking away from me own.'' Blooey's voice trailed off as they turned into the hall.

Auntie was the first to recover. "I have always loved a man who takes charge in these situations.'' As if *these* situations were a commonplace occurrence. Zanita tried to hide behind her iced tea.

"He's *marvelous*! Zanita, where did you find him?''

She couldn't even remember what she had told her aunt. Shortly after that, the doorbell had rung. Coming from different directions, both she and Tyber arrived at the door at the same time. Their eyes met in mutually exasperated humor.

"Have courage,'' he whispered before he opened the door.

Stan Mazurski, the physicist, was standing there, but his wife was not beside him. Next to him stood one of the most beautiful little boys Zanita had ever seen. With coal-black hair and emerald-green eyes, he was destined to grow up a lady-killer.

Zanita looked over at the balding little physicist with the coke-bottle glasses. How had this man ever produced such a remarkable child? His wife must be stunning.

"Hi, Stan,'' Tyber said. He threw a questioning glance at the child.

"Hello, Doctor Evans.''

"Tyber, please.'' He smiled at Stan, thinking he really was a very old-fashioned man. Perhaps his European heritage factored into it.

"Thank you, Tyber. I hope you don't mind my bringing the child; my wife regrets she could not come tonight. Willa had the most awful headache.'' Stan looked pointedly down upon the boy's head, leaving no doubt as to what had caused said headache. "She needed to lie down with some medicine so I had no choice, other than canceling, which I didn't want to do at such a late date, after your kind invitation."

"Don't worry about it, Stan. Your son is welcome here."

"Oh, no! He's not my son!" Zanita was amused at the rapidity of his denial. She just bet this boy with the angelic face was a little devil. "We don't have any children. This is my brother Gregor's child, my nephew, Cody."

Tyber sat down on his haunches. "Hello, Cody." He put his hand out. The little boy responded at once. No shy child this.

"How ya doing?" He shook Tyber's hand. "Hey, whose motorcycle is crunched up in the driveway? Greg used to have one, but I don't remember 'cause I wasn't borned yet. He used to race 'em back then. That was before he went to live like a bo—bohemy—"

"Bohemian," Stan supplied quietly.

"Yeah. Bohemian. In the south of France."

Tyber grinned; he liked frisky kids and this one was a pistol.

Zanita was still trying to follow Cody's rapid shift of topic. "Your father raced motorcycles in the south of France?"

"Nah. What's for dinner?"

Stan looked mortified. "Cody, that isn't polite."

Tyber chuckled. "It's okay, Stan. I'm not sure—but maybe we can get Blooey to make you something special. You like fried chicken?"

Cody's face lit up. "Yeah!"

Tyber acknowledged the pure, simple truth that most children knew nothing about, and liked even less, haute cuisine. A child's idea of gourmet was Spaghetti Os. He thought Blooey was preparing Chicken Veronique for their main course this evening. The crusty swabbee would be more than happy to pan-fry some chicken for Cody because Tyber knew Arthur Bloomberg was a sucker where children were concerned.

Tyber wouldn't be surprised if a chocolate cake was hastily added to the dessert selections.

"So, what does your father do, young man?" Auntie's inherent nosiness effortlessly came to the fore.

They were all seated around the table in the formal dining room. It was such a lovely room, Zanita thought. An arrangement of fresh flowers graced the center of the walnut table, which was elegantly set. She supposed Tyber had taken care of these small details while she had been detained with the flat tire. She made a mental note to thank him.

Zanita was also pleased to note that since Tyber's little lecture, all had been relatively smooth in the kitchen. My-Maggy had served the infamous vichy. The boy had surprised everyone by lapping his up.

In response to Auntie's question, Cody's face screwed up with a puzzled expression, clearing when he thought he figured out what he was being asked. He shrugged his small shoulders, while shoving a heavily buttered pecan roll into his mouth.

He replied innocently, "He does women."

"*Cody*," Stan hissed.

"Well he does, Uncle Stan. When we're watching TV, Greg always says, 'I'd love to *do* her, Cody.'"

Zanita coughed.

Auntie's smile froze on her face.

Stan turned beet red.

Mills blinked several times.

Tyber chuckled.

"Children have such an aura of naturalness about them. It is so refreshing." LaLeche patted his mouth with his linen napkin.

It was the first time Zanita had wanted to thank Xavier LaLeche. He had stepped into an embarrassing moment and with his oily charm had eased the awkwardness.

"How so, Mr. LaLeche?" Auntie, who was sitting on LaLeche's right turned to him.

"Xavier, please. Children do not carry years of inner pain, hurt, and degradation with them. They are honest. Fresh."

This one is fresh, Mills thought to herself.

"Often the thrust of my work, as our host knows, is to find the inner child, release him from bondage—set him free."

Cody perked up. "There's another kid here?"

Everyone laughed.

"Sorry, pal." Tyber said. "You're it."

My-Maggy came into the dining room to serve the main course, Blooey right behind her bearing a dish piled high with fried chicken. He placed the plate in front of Cody with a flourish.

"Here you go, lil' mite. I cooked it up special fer ya." Cody's eyes rounded; he licked his lips, ready to dig in. His uncle stopped him.

"Wait until everyone is served, Cody."

Mills thought Stan was a very good uncle, indeed. She told him so.

"Why, thank you, Mills. I wish my brother could hear that; we have many disagreements on a certain topic." He was purposely being circumspect for Cody's benefit.

"Well, yer a good lad in my book. I heard ye liked me soup, too."

"Yeah, it was awesome."

"Did ye ever think of becomin' a cabin boy?"

"What's that?"

Tyber cleared his throat. "Blooey, I think—"

"A cabin boy assists the captain. On a pirate ship such as this—"

Cody's green eyes grew huge. "You were on a pirate ship?" Blooey had been instantly elevated to hero.

"Aye. I'll tell ye all about it when ye have your dessert—it's chocolate cake, you know." The corners of Tyber's mouth twitched with a secret smile.

"Wow! This place is neat; we'll have to come here again, Uncle Stan."

Stan smiled fondly at his nephew. "We'll see."

"Does your father do the same work as your uncle?" Auntie was nothing if not persistent. There was always an answer to any question, if one tried hard enough.

"Nah, Greg don't work. He's a noncon—a noncon—"

"A nonconformist," Stan supplied drily, while catching the napkin on his nephew's lap before it slid to the floor.

"He sounds a very interesting man," LaLeche put in.

This creep of a father sounded like a deadbeat to Mills. "Does your mother work?" Mills asked in spite of herself.

"Well . . ." Cody thought a minute. "She used to ride the rodeo." He took a huge bite out of his chicken. "Greg says I'm named after some dude called Buffalo Bill."

Mills almost choked on her wine. "Your brother's wife is a rodeo rider?" She turned to Stan with all the horror of eight generations of Yankee forebears for any activity which didn't require a coat and tie.

Cody snorted. "My ma wasn't his wife. I figure Greg's never gonna get married." The audacious boy winked broadly at her. "Got too many girlfriends."

Stan's face reddened.

"Zanita tells me you're an absolute marvel, Xavier." Auntie's interest in the child having been satisfied, she quickly moved on to her next victim. In this case, the prime victim.

"Oh, I wouldn't quite put it that strongly."

False modesty had its moments, Zanita reflected. Too bad this wasn't one of them.

Auntie leaned toward him in her chair. "Do you really perform healing ceremonies? I can't tell you how fascinating this subject is to me."

"My dear lady, fascination barely describes it." LaLeche pointedly gazed into Auntie's eyes as if fascinated to death. But not, Zanita noted, before he gazed down at the emerald-and-ruby ring gracing her index finger.

Stan's fork clattered against his plate. "You aren't talking about physic healing, are you?"

"Yes, yes, yes." Auntie waved her hand impatiently. "Get with the program, Stan."

"Surely you don't subscribe to this quackery, Dr. Evans?" Everyone turned to stare at Tyber.

Talk about being put on the spot . . . Zanita grimaced. If

Tyber denied it, LaLeche would become suspicious. If Tyber admitted to it, Dr. Mazurski would rapidly lose respect for his Physicist King. And might spread the word among Tyber's colleagues. There could be professional ramifications. Zanita bit her lip, sorry she had placed him in this situation.

If Zanita had been in Tyber's mind at that moment, she would have seen that she was worrying needlessly. Tyber could care less what his colleagues surmised about him personally. His work spoke for itself.

However, he sipped his wine slowly before responding, taking the time to come up with an answer acceptable to everyone. "Surely by now, Stan, you know I always keep an open mind—to everything."

"Yes, but psychic—"

"Greg says the same thing," Cody piped in. "He says never rule anything out 'cause life is full of possibilities." Tyber could've kissed him.

"Greg appears to be a fountain of wisdom," Mills murmured sarcastically under her breath. Zanita kicked her under the table.

After dinner, everyone returned to the parlor.

Mills had to make a phone call and had just hung up when Cody found, or rather, cornered her in the hallway. She looked down at the little boy in surprise.

Cody surveyed her up and down, joining his thumb and forefinger together in the "okay" sign. "Lady, you are *stacked.*"

Mills' mouth dropped open. "How old did you say you were?"

Cody puffed up his chest proudly. "Six."

"Do you live mostly with your uncle Stan?" Mills asked hopefully.

"Nah, I live with Greg. Me and him is like that." He crossed his little fingers to demonstrate.

"Hmm." She took his hand, leading him firmly back into the sitting room.

* * *

Tyber reached up to the bookcase, handing Stan the book on quantum theory he had been telling him about.

"Isn't that Arthur Bloomberg working for you?" Stan thumbed distractedly through the book.

"Yes."

"What happened to him? He was a brilliant mathematician."

Tyber rubbed his ear. "Um, he had a real problem with convergences."

"Oh." Stan watched Mills with a speculative gleam as she entered the room holding Cody's hand. "Mills seems very nice. Is she married?"

"No, but you are," Tyber responded dryly.

Stan colored. "Oh, no! Not me! I was thinking about my brother. . . . She seems such a down-to-earth person—just what he needs."

"And why is that?"

"Don't ask! My brother, Gregor, is . . . is, well, he's something of a serendipidist."

Tyber pictured a "wild and crazy" Stan Mazurski in his mind, instantly negating the image. He said diplomatically, "I don't know, Stan, ah—I think sometimes it's best to leave these things alone."

Stan stroked his chin in thought. "I suppose you're right. Pity, though. Tyber, are you really serious about this psychic stuff?"

"Between the two of us?" Stan nodded. "Well, who knows? There could be something to it. But not this guy. Keep it to yourself, will you?"

"Of course I will. I find myself agreeing with you. I wouldn't rule it out completely—but it doesn't have much to do with what we do."

Tyber just smiled.

"A cat! You got a cat!"

Cody's voice held the awe usually reserved by six-year-old boys for such things as toy laser guns and interstellar battleships. He jumped off the chair, racing toward Hambone. The tabby's singular eye momentarily widened, but the pirate cat held his ground.

Zanita guessed the steady flow of tidbits the cat had been getting all day from the kitchen had just run dry. Knowing this cat as well as she did, she figured Hambone had probably come in to see if there was anything on the floor to vacuum. He would tolerate Cody only until he discovered the child was not carrying any food.

Hambone, being a cat, did exactly the opposite of what she thought.

When Cody put his arms around the great bulk, shoving his face right into the soft fur, Hambone closed his eye in ecstasy, emitting a strange low sound. One could easily interpret this odd sound to be a purr. Zanita threw an astonished look at Tyber.

"In case you haven't guessed, Cody loves cats." Stan addressed the group, a fond smile gracing his kind face as he watched his nephew hug the animal.

"You can't have one where you live?" There was a sad note in Mills' voice; she loved cats herself and empathized with Cody. Pets were against the rules in her apartment house as well.

"It's not 'cause of that." Cody petted Hambone's broad head. "Me and Greg gotta be free and not tied down to anything. We gotta be able to move where the mood takes us."

The Creep just dropped another notch in Mills' book.

"What about school?" She turned to Stan. "Surely your brother—" She stopped when she realized that she was overstepping the bounds of polite inquiry.

Stan just looked at Mills, shaking his head. "Another topic of dissension," he said quietly to her.

A few moments later, Blooey caught Tyber's attention from the doorway. "There's a bloke what wants to come aboard, Captain. Says his name is Gregor Mazurski; should I lower the plank?"

"Gregor? I wonder what my brother's doing here? He told

me he would be gone for the weekend.''

Tyber nodded to Blooey. "Open the gate, Blooey."

A short time later Gregor Mazurski entered the room.

He was a surprise to everyone, for Gregor Mazurski was the complete antithesis of his brother Stan.

Gregor stood about six-foot-three and had a thick head of raven-black hair and glittering green eyes. He was dressed in black boots, black jeans, and a black leather jacket. Only a maroon sweater worn under the jacket broke the stark effect.

Zanita's eyes met Mills'. Mills' eyes met Zanita's. Both conveyed the age-old secret message among girlfriends everywhere: *Hunk*.

Upon seeing his father, Cody released Hambone, racing pell-mell across the room to throw himself into his father's arms. Gregor lifted the boy up, holding him under the seat of his pants with one broad palm.

Mills had no way of knowing that Gregor had left his son only three hours before. From what she observed of the reunion, Mills came to the erroneous conclusion that the man hadn't seen his son in a very long time.

It was obvious the boy idolized him. Hunk or no, he was still the Creep.

"Greg!" Cody hugged his father.

"Hey there, Spike, how these people treating you, huh?" He ruffled his son's hair. "In case you people don't know it— there's a Harley smashed up in the front drive."

Tyber rubbed his forehead. Perhaps he needed Mrs. Mazurski's headache medicine. If one more person mentioned his dead bike, he was going to bring the damn carcass in here and hold a wake.

"Have a seat, Greg—I'm Tyber Evans." He gestured to a chair.

Gregor had heard about Tyber Evans, had even admired his maverick attitude. A similar attitude was a part of his nature. Therefore, he was a little surprised to find his staid brother, Stan, in the home of such a man. By all outward appearances, they had little in common.

"Thanks, but we really should be going. Spike's probably tired—"

"I am not!"

"I thought you were going to Bermuda for the weekend, Gregor. What happened?"

"I got a new plan, Stan." He flashed his brother a smile of pearly whites. Cody giggled, recognizing the song lyrics.

"You're welcome to stay for dessert." Tyber graciously extended the invitation.

"Come on, Greg, they're having chocolate cake." Cody's small hand turned his father's face so he could whisper loudly in his ear, "*Chocolate cake.*" Everyone laughed.

Greg grinned at his son. "I guess I can't fight chocolate cake."

He released Cody, who went to sit on the rug next to Hambone. Gregor took a seat and was soon introduced to everyone. His sights lingered for more than a few moments on Mills.

Blooey wheeled in a dessert cart loaded with goodies. Cody was personally handed a huge piece of cake.

LaLeche continued on his topic of spiritual quests. Tyber caught Zanita stifling a yawn and immediately substituted her decaf for regular. Zanita yawning was a warning sign not to be overlooked.

"Now the Tantric viewpoint is somewhat different—by the way, the Tibetans are a remarkable people. Over one hundred thousand of them are in exile."

"I heard the Chinese government has been systematically destroying Tibet." As a removed observer, Tyber reflected on the entropic aspects of the situation.

"I recognize that speculative look, Doctor," Stan joked. "Care to share with us what you're thinking?"

"I'm thinking about entropy, the Tibetan people, and quantum theory."

"There's a lighthearted mixture," Greg quipped.

"How very *marvelously* interesting." Auntie probably didn't have a clue, but Zanita knew she doted on "ponderous" men. "Tell us more, Tyber."

"Here is a spiritually advanced culture taken over by a political regime which to them represents disorder. Their way of life is being systematically destroyed—entropy rears its ugly head. Now, in quantum mechanics, the observer, by the very nature of his existence, cannot help but affect the outcome of the experiment or observation; indeed, he becomes part of it simply by his inherent presence.

"So, here we all are, the quantum observers, if you will, in a closed field of experimentation. How do we effect what is happening in Tibet, and how is what's happening in Tibet affecting us?"

Stan jumped in, "But Doctor, you are drawing parallels between quantum aspects and the macroscopic world. As you know, quantum deals with the micro-universe, and such theory does not necessarily apply outside the parameters of this microcosm."

Tyber decided to play devil's advocate. "Don't they? We're talking about the spiritual realm here, Stan—which is presumably neither micro- nor macroscopic. What quantum aspects would apply, do you suppose?"

"None. You see, that is the very point, Tyber. It is a different *realm*; therefore, these aspects *cannot* apply. Contemporary physics does not prove, disprove, agree, or disagree with a mystical belief system."

"I'm inclined to disagree. If laws apply throughout the universe and the spiritual realm is inclusive of this universe, such laws *must* apply. Otherwise, you could argue that there is a breakdown in the belief system and the laws are useless."

"No. Scientific theory has nothing to do with a spiritual worldview. Spiritualists examine the universe directly, while we physicists examine the universe through the abstraction known as mathematica—which is just the language of the reality, not the reality itself."

"Interesting switch, Stan," Tyber complimented him, then set about to negate the viewpoint. "So now science is abstraction and religion is reality? Isn't that contrary to Planck's—"

Gregor interrupted the two men, who had lost the rest of

the room and were oblivious to it. "Physicists love to engage in these esoteric discussions. I think they're trying to fool us into thinking they're open-minded."

Everyone laughed, relieved that someone had stepped in to stop them.

Whew. Zanita took a breath of air. *Madmen across the water.*

Mills wondered if Greg was subtly insulting his brother's conventionality.

"I was in Nepal once." Gregor took a sip of his coffee.

Cody bragged from the floor, "Greg met with the Dolly Parton." His lower lip was rimmed in chocolate, his upper in milk.

"The Dalai Lama," his father corrected.

"Wonderful!" LaLeche's tone conveyed that he somehow had a hand in it. "You went on an inner quest."

Gregor's green eyes glittered jovially. "You might say that."

Cody licked his fork while enlightening everyone. "A chick he knows took him there. She told him they had all kinds of kinky ways of doing *it*. Right, Greg?"

Mills and Zanita looked at each other.

Stan, as usual, turned red.

Tyber burst out laughing.

"C'mere, Spike." Greg wrapped Cody in a bear embrace, teasingly covering his son's mouth with his hand. Cody squirmed and giggled behind his palm.

Greg's dancing green eyes met Tyber's over his son's head.

There was a silent meeting of the minds; in that instant the beginning of a friendship was forged between the two men.

Then, for a reason he couldn't name, Greg's focus shifted to Mills.

Mills was lifting her coffee cup to her lips. At the sight of two pairs of identically glittering green eyes focusing on her, she froze. A chill skittered down her back. *Someone's walking on my grave.* She mentally shook herself, intentionally breaking the moment by sipping from her cup.

Gregor released Cody and stood up. "Thanks for the hospitality, but we really gotta run. If you want some help with that bike, Tyber, give me a call. I'm good at bringing things to life. I have a lot of background experience." He was speaking to Tyber, but his focus was on Mills.

Mills pointedly ignored his look and his double-entendres. While the son was adorable, she wanted nothing to do with the errant father. Even if his hair curled ever so slightly over his collar and he had the greenest eyes she had ever seen.

Cody said good night to everybody very sweetly. After saying good night to Mills, he beamed up at Greg while jerking his thumb in her direction and raising his eyebrows up and down a la Groucho.

Out in the hallway, Gregor helped Cody put on his jacket. Glancing back one more time at Mills, he put his hands on his son's shoulders. Leaning down, he whispered into the little ear, "*Stacked.*"

They left the house trying to whistle a song together.

"Do you think Auntie is safe in the same wing as La-Leche?"

Tyber watched Zanita remove her robe from under heavy-lidded eyes. "The question is: Is LaLeche safe from Auntie?" Zanita stuck her tongue out at him.

He grinned, closing his eyes. "Are you ever getting into bed tonight?"

She had washed her hair, dried her hair, took a bath, redried her hair, slathered on lotion, made faces at herself in the mirror to see if she had developed any new lines since this morning, and sprayed perfume on. Through all of this, Tyber waited patiently.

"In a minute . . ."

"Are you expecting company this evening?"

Her head whipped around. "What do you mean?"

"Well, the way you're primping yourself, I don't know who you're expecting, but it sure as hell isn't me. I'm already right here in bed. See? All by myself." He yawned loudly.

"I'm thinking. I always walk around doing stuff when I'm thinking."

"You mean you can walk and think at the same time? Baby, I'm impressed."

Zanita made a running tackle for the bed.

She dived on top of him, laughing when he rolled across the bed with her.

"This is why I have to put guests in another wing, my Zanita. You are a savage in the bedroom."

"Don't you want to know what I was thinking?"

He lowered his head to hers.

"No."

"I was wondering if this was all worth it."

He stilled. His voice became very quiet. "What do you mean?"

"I don't see how we are going to trip him up. You went to all this trouble and—"

Tyber released the breath he was holding. She had almost given him a heart attack. "We don't have to trip him up, baby. I thought you understood that—we just need to observe him, talk to him, draw him out. Like any problem, it'll solve itself when least expected. Trust me, there'll be something that will stay in our minds—"

"You know, you scare me when you talk like that."

Tyber let out a bark of laughter. He lowered his head to her again.

"I wanted to thank you for taking care of the stuff I should have; it was very nice of you, Doc."

"Then thank me." His lips were a hairsbreadth from hers.

"Are you very upset about your motorcycle?"

He retreated, looking down at her with a frown. "Are you purposely trying to kill my mood?"

"Auntie's awfully sorry about it; she feels terrible."

"She hides her grief well. Forget the motorcycle—it's one of those things in life that can be repaired."

Her lower lip pouted. "You haven't forgotten it."

He caught her pouting lip between his teeth and gently suckled on it. "Make me forget it. . . ." He settled against her, embracing her gently.

"Tyber?"

"*What*?" he roared.

"I just think you should talk to Auntie."

"What is it, Zanita, are you just not in the mood tonight?"

"Whatever are you talking about?" She pushed against his broad shoulders. "Have you lost your mind? We're talking about you apologizing to Auntie—"

"*What*?" he roared for the second time in as many minutes.

Zanita totally ignored his outraged expression. "She feels so terrible about the bike; I thought if you apologized to her for leaving it in the middle of the road, she might realize it wasn't her fault and feel better."

"First of all, the Harley was not in the middle of the road; it was parked in the driveway. *My driveway*. Second, it *was* her fault. She came barreling down the drive going at least fifty miles an hour. Third, I don't want her feeling better about it, but you don't have to worry because the woman forgot about the incident before her car door slammed shut. And lastly, I am not—I repeat, I am *not* going to apologize to her."

Tears filled her violet eyes. "Do you mean it?"

Tyber's shoulders sagged. He sighed. It was the tears that did him in. Zanita was obviously the one who felt bad about it. His lady was very tender-hearted. "All right, I'll apologize to her."

"Thank you, Tyber. I knew you would, once you thought it over."

He rubbed his nose against hers, "Are you sucker-punching me?"

"I don't know . . . what do I have to do?" She smiled seductively at him.

Tyber grinned. "It's very kinky."

"Kinky as in Nepal kinky?"

Tyber chuckled, remembering Greg's expression over his son's head. "I don't know; I've never been to Nepal. But I sure as hell am putting it on my travel wish list."

Zanita ran the sole of her foot down the inside of his leg. "What else is on your wish list?"

"This." His mouth fastened on the curve of her shoulder as his hands reached underneath her to cup her buttocks.

"And this." His bare leg wedged between hers, rubbing against the cleft between her legs. She was already moist for him. He groaned.

"Your skin's getting hot." She stroked his back.

"Heat's a motion of expansion." He replaced his leg with his hard member, running it along the outside of the wet crevice.

"I do declare."

"But it's not a uniform expansion throughout the body. . . ."

"No?"

"Uh-uh." He took her nipple into his damp mouth, laving the bud with tender care. "In the smaller parts of it." He blew against her breast.

She sucked in her breath. "I see."

"The body requires a motion alternative." He entered her swiftly, causing her to moan against him. "Perpetually quivering." He withdrew to thrust deep within her again. "Striving . . ."

She gasped. "Tyber, what are you talking about?"

"I don't know." He gave up all pretense of the physics lesson, clutching her tightly to him. His hot mouth fastened on hers. He plundered her sweet mouth, mirroring his erotic movements below.

Yes, he was expanding with the heat.

Sometimes demonstration was the finer art of teaching.

Chapter Thirteen

Zanita gazed out of the upstairs bedroom window, trying to focus on the two figures walking slowly across the far acreage of Tyber's land, near where it bordered the woods.

Even from this distance, she could discern Tyber's tall form, his distinctive stride: one part smooth, hip-rolling gait, three parts conquering presence. The shorter man gesturing expansively at his side would be LaLeche.

After lunch, Tyber had decided to take LaLeche on a personally escorted, carefully edited tour of his property. He wanted to see if LaLeche would be relaxed enough to inadvertently drop his guard in some way.

When he had approached Zanita with the idea, she shrugged her shoulders, thinking, what could it hurt? So far, to her way of thinking, the self-proclaimed psychic had been annoyingly in "character" and as far as she could tell, had revealed nothing to either of them of any import.

Zanita had sensed that Tyber hadn't felt completely comfortable opening his entire home to LaLeche. Right from the beginning she knew that Tyber was a very private man—his

221

personal life was just that. She had a strong feeling that invitations to his walled domain were carefully given.

So what happens to the poor man once he hooks up with her?

He had an invasion force in his house, his sanctuary. It had to go against his grain, yet he was being the most gracious of hosts. A nagging question surfaced.

Is Tyber doing all this just for me?

Zanita knew she could gloss over the implications of such a gesture by telling herself that he was just as involved as she was in the investigation. She could even try to make herself believe he hadn't minded his life being turned upside down this weekend, but she would be lying to herself.

The simple truth was, Tyber was doing this for her sake alone.

The flowers. The gracious, sumptuous meals. The dress slacks. *Auntie.*

It was all for her.

Was the Captain proclaiming himself?

She bit her lip. If so, what should she do? How should she handle this? Somehow the word *handle* and Tyber didn't go together in the same sentence.

While she watched, a gust of wind lifted a long strand of Tyber's gold-streaked chestnut hair. Zanita sighed. He really was the most stunning man. She leaned her elbows on the windowsill, resting her chin in the palm of her hand, her thoughts brooding on her partner cum lover.

In her past, the only real relationship she had had was with Steve. The experimental disaster with Rick she dismissed as a momentary insanity.

The truth was, she had never experienced anything like what she had with Tyber. Aside from his wonderful kookiness and heady individuality, when Tyber made love, he put his whole self into the act. His entire being became present tense. Reactive. Pro-active. He was *there*.

Zanita dropped her forehead against the windowpane, rubbing her heated skin against the cool glass. She had warned him about this, repeatedly. Told him straight out she was not getting involved in any relationships. Had he paid any attention to her?

No.

He had gone about his merry way—buying her little gifts, taking her out for dinners, watching over her like a mother hen when she was sick, and physically loving her to the point of exhaustion.

The pirate.

He had laid siege to her! Not with the traditional tools of his craft—no, not with cannon and cutlass, but with honeyed lips and heated caresses. With the scorching press of his body. With the masterful command of her pliant response to his overwhelming sensuality.

She had been broadsided.

Zanita winced and took a deep breath, valiantly trying to salvage the wreck. She was still afloat. The grappling hooks had been thrown, but she wasn't boarded yet.

Her eyes narrowed while she observed him through the window.

The two men had stopped walking and were facing each other, deep in conversation. Tyber's long legs were spread in a familiar stance, his hands planted firmly on his hips. *Convince me*, the arrogant pose said. She had seen this invincible stance before. Many times. The overbearing rogue!

Well, she would convince him! Later, when she could be sure they wouldn't be interrupted. This time she was going to pierce through his vigorous hide to impress upon him exactly what was what.

No more lavish displays of affection.

No more *just one more time, baby* heatedly whispered in the middle of the night into her ear.

No more!

They were working together for a common cause. Co-workers and . . . friends. It was time Tyber was reminded of just where they stood.

Zanita swallowed the lump of agitation and something else

which didn't bear examining but which had suddenly lodged in her throat. Her shoulders squared, resolutely quelling the irksome feeling. She recognized this feeling as one which could get her into deep trouble. *Had* gotten her into deep trouble in the past.

Tyber was an adult. He would see reason, would listen to her when she told him he needed an attitude adjustment.

If Zanita had her druthers, remodeling Tyberius Augustus Evans was not a task she would have voluntarily taken on, but a girl had to do what a girl had to do. After all, it was up to her to get them back on track. Left to his own devices, Tyber would lead them down a very dangerous road.

She had no intention of being derailed from her course of self-preservation.

A realignment was definitely in order.

"Tyber, you have created an oasis of tranquility in this jungle of stress called modern life. No wonder you choose to spend your working day right here in the peaceful beauty of your gracious estate."

Tyber listened to LaLeche, dark lashes veiling light blue eyes clouded by disgust. He'd seen Rocky Mountain oysters with less bull. He inclined his head slightly, as if thanking and agreeing with LaLeche at the same time.

"You know, I believe most people, given a choice, would prefer just such an environment in their daily lives."

Tyber wondered where LaLeche was leading with this. "Oh, I don't know, Xavier, different strokes for different folks. I'm sure many people couldn't bear this type of isolated work and living environment. Some people thrive on the excitement of rubbing up against the mass of humanity on a daily basis. Just look at New York City."

"No, you look at it," LaLeche quipped.

Tyber smiled in spite of himself. "People do choose to live there—strange as it may seem to you or me. Sometimes even I enjoy an occasional foray into the Big Apple. The theater, restaurants, shopping, nightlife . . ."

"Yes, there is something to say for the culture and choices available there." The man was smooth, Tyber gave him that. He knew just how to oil a conversation so no offense could possibly be taken, no real opinion given.

"This has all got me thinking. . . ." LaLeche rubbed his chin, trying to convey the impression of a man on the verge of a great idea. Tyber waited patiently; he was positive he would soon find out where LaLeche was going with this "fresh" idea of his which had probably been bubbling around in the man's head for ages.

"What's that?" Tyber played along.

"What you're saying is very true—even if people do live in the city, they need to get away on occasion to untangle the spirit, to renew their sense of perspective."

I said that? I must've stepped out of this dimension for a minute and missed my brilliant observation. Silly me. Tyber gave himself a mental shake of the head. LaLeche enthusiastically continued on his preordained pathway. He vaguely reminded Tyber of Venus in retrograde.

"I've often thought how very wonderful it would be to have a retreat like this for people to come to when they feel a need to seek inner harmony."

Tyber stopped walking. LaLeche was looking to fleece his sheep in better surroundings. He better not be coveting *his* surroundings. He turned to the shorter man, hands on hips. "Are you saying you want me to open my home to your—"

"Oh, heavens no, Tyber! I would never suggest invading your personal space in such a manner."

"Then what are you suggesting?"

"Look around you, Dr. Evans." His arm swung in an arc indicating the gently rolling landscape. "Think about what such an environment would do to open minds, enlighten beings!"

He wanted money. Lots of it, if Tyber was on to his little game plan. Tyber rocked back on his boot heels, quelling the distaste he had for this charlatan. "You're talking about a retreat?"

"More than just a retreat! A center for personal growth and study! A research facility for psychic endeavors! A place for spiritual peace and harmony for everyone."

A place where workshops for the individual ran into the hundreds of dollars. A place where LaLeche could sell videos and tapes of himself being wonderful. A big business New Age kinda happening sort of thing. Tyber got the picture.

"I don't know, Xavier, won't that be kind of expensive?"

"Think of it as an investment, Tyber."

Here we go. "An investment? What do you mean?"

"If you would like to get in on the ground floor of this, I can pretty much guarantee you a fine return on your money."

"Are you saying you'd *profit* from this, Xavier?" Tyber couldn't help throwing that in.

"Everyone would profit from it in all ways, spiritually and monetarily. There's absolutely nothing wrong with making money, Tyber. It's one of the very topics I plan to have a seminar on."

For fifty-nine ninety-five. "How do you incorporate a . . . zest for making money into spiritual practices? Aren't the two mutually exclusive?"

LaLeche sighed deeply, shaking his head sadly as if to convey that such a wise teacher as he often had to deal with the ignorance of his pupils. It irritated Tyber no end. "Unfortunately, a widely held misconception. Negative attitudes regarding success run deep. It is this type of unhealthy conviction toward abundance in our personal lives which needs to be healed."

"Healed? How can the attitude of money being an end to a goal be healed?"

"Think of money as you would sunshine." LaLeche seemed extremely proud of this idiotic comparison.

Tyber's voice was bland. "How so?"

"Sunshine brings light into our lives; its rays shed warmth and enlightenment on us. It brings us happiness; it brings us life. By the same token, sunshine is also responsible for drought, sunburn, unbearable heat, burnt crops."

"I don't know that I follow your train of thought." Especially since the tracks of those thoughts are following a Möbius strip of convoluted logic.

"I'm saying that the effects of sunshine can be good for us or bad for us, depending on how careful we are in our relationship to it. You see, the sunshine is neither good nor evil in and of itself. It is simply an energy. Money, a materialization of energy, is the same way—it can be good for us or not good for us, depending on how we choose to utilize it."

Tyber stared back at him, dumbstruck. The man had just whipped together a seemingly palatable omelet from chalk and cheese.

The fact of the matter was that sunshine had nothing whatsoever to do with money. One was radiant energy, the other a medium of exchange. With carefully chosen words, tangled mystical principles, and a dash of spiritual superiority, the man had made a sweeping conclusion.

And why not, Tyber asked himself facetiously; after all, nature abhors a vacuum.

Would some people actually buy this ridiculous analogy under the guise of self-fulfilling enlightenment?

Yes. Definitely.

"I hadn't thought of it in those terms before. I can see what you're saying now. So tell me, Xavier, how much of an investment would we be talking about here?"

"Not much, considering the size of the project. We'll need some raw acreage, of course. Although it would be nice to find a site that already has a suitable building, I don't think that will occur. After all, we have certain special needs for the buildings. A dormitory. A cafeteria. Grounds . . ."

Uh-huh. LaLecheville. "So what were you thinking?"

"I figure if I could get together two more investors, each of us would have to throw in about three hundred grand."

Tyber tried not to cough. He rubbed the back of his neck. "Three hundred, huh?"

"If it's too steep for you—"

"No. Of course not, but just what kind of a return can I expect on my money?"

"How does five hundred percent sound?" LaLeche's mouth wiggled with a smirky grin.

"Sounds like you might have an investor." Tyber returned his smirk with a mysterious little grin of his own.

"Wonderful!"

"Of course, I have to shuffle some funds around, free up some cash—you understand. Come to think of it, I have some extra bonds coming due in a couple of months—-why don't you start scouting out a location in the meantime?"

"I'll do that!"

"Oh, one other thing, Xavier, I'd appreciate it if you didn't mention my name in connection with this project. I prefer to be a silent investor." The last thing Tyber wanted was LaLeche using his name to hoodwink other investors into this scam.

"I understand, Doctor." LaLeche winked at him, interpreting Tyber's remark in his own way. Which was just as well, as long as it achieved his objective of keeping LaLeche silent.

So now he could string LaLeche on a little longer. This "business" venture was just the legitimate cover Zanita and he needed to stay in constant touch with the man. Hopefully they wouldn't need to be in touch with him for too much longer.

As Tyber made his way back to the house, he realized that if worse came to worst, he could try to set up a sting operation with the phony investment scam, although that could be a tricky business and he hated the idea of exposing Zanita to the kind of danger it might entail. On the other hand, he wanted the scum out of their lives A.S.A.P.

He wondered just how risky it would be, thinking he might eventually be forced to call Sean in.

Zanita had come straight upstairs after dinner. She had one hell of a headache. She immediately threw off her clothes, donning her thick flannel nightgown. Proper clothes for the proper job.

Moistening a washcloth with ice-cold water, she draped it across her forehead and flung herself prostrate onto Tyber's oyster bed. *Zanita on the half-shell.* She grimaced.

Dinner had been a complete fiasco.

Blooey got into another fight with My-Maggy. This time they fought over the sequence of the layered salad.

Auntie had proclaimed the escarole quiche marvelous but terribly rich, this last said while pointedly staring at Mills.

Mills threatened to use her fork as a catapult for said quiche, aiming it directly at Auntie when Auntie wasn't looking.

LaLeche, lapping up Blooey's cooking and casting the occasional lecherous glance at her chest, continued dropping pearls of spiritual wisdom, somehow managing to look like the cat who had swallowed the Tyber canary.

Hambone took turns wailing piteously during the meal at the lack of tidbits forthcoming and growling at LaLeche's ankles. At least the cat was a good judge of character.

Throughout it all, Tyber sat in stony silence while being mercilessly grilled by Auntie on aspects of his virile physique.

No wonder her head was splitting.

She supposed she should feel bad at deserting Tyber to their guests, but her head was pounding too loudly for her to care. Besides, she needed to get rid of this headache to make room for another one. She was going to confront Tyber tonight with his attitude adjustment.

The door to the bedroom flew open—and slammed shut.

Zanita twitched, then moaned as the reverberations hit her skull. Tyber's words sliced across her brow.

"Thank you very much for leaving me with that barracuda, Zanita."

"LaLeche?" came the muffled voice from under the washcloth.

"No. Your aunt."

She could hear him stomping across the floor toward the bed. Zanita lifted one corner of the cloth to peer surreptitiously at him. He was unbuttoning his shirt with short, angry movements of his fingers. When he finished, he dragged it off, wadded it into a ball, throwing it in the general direction of the closet hamper. It bounced off the lid, puddling on the floor. Tyber, who normally was the neatest of men, uncharacteristically ignored it.

He turned back to her; she quickly lowered the cloth to play dead again.

"Are you sure that woman is a relative of—what the hell is that draped across your head?"

"A cloth."

"Yes, but why?"

"I have a headache, Einstein."

She felt the bed dip with his weight. "Do you feel sick?"

His tone had instantly gone from irritation to concern. It was precisely this—this *caring* behavior that was at the root of her headache in the first place!

Not receiving a response, Tyber lifted the washcloth from her face only to be confronted with a glaring visage.

"Put that back!"

"I just wanted to see if you were all right."

He was caring about her again! She began to smolder. In her mind's eye, she could see smoke fuming all around her. "I told you I have a headache!"

"Then why don't you take some aspirin like most people do?"

"Because I prefer the medicine cloth. Now give me that." She tried to rip the cloth out of his hands; he wouldn't let go.

"I've never heard a doctor say take two cloths and call me in the morning. You are the crankiest person when you don't feel well. I'll get you some aspirin."

He started to get up; Zanita clamped her hand on his arm like a vise. "You get off this bed, mister, and it'll be the last aspirin you ever get."

The idea of this petite woman physically threatening him over a wet rag had its humorous side. Tyber really wanted to laugh, but relationship survival being foremost in his mind, he settled for a confused, hurt expression. "I'm sorry, baby." He handed her back the cloth.

Zanita felt instantly contrite. "Forget about it, Tyber." She flung the cloth over the aquarium.

"You think the fish have a headache now?" A dimple popped into his cheek.

"Very funny."

"Here, let me massage your headache away." He scooted back against the pillows, placing her head on his lap. His two forefingers began massaging her temples on either side. It felt good. Real good.

Zanita tried to talk herself out of turning her head into the silky warmth of his bare chest. Or rubbing the curve of her cheek against his heated velvet skin. The plane of his upper torso was lightly fuzzed with gold-tipped hair and rock hard.

The man was built like a brick! He could probably take a punch. Oh, well. She relaxed against his lap. That left trying to reason with him.

Before she had a chance, Tyber broached his own subject.

"I had a little talk with LaLeche during our tour this afternoon."

Zanita closed her eyes under his soothing ministrations. "Did you find out anything we can use?"

"Not exactly. He wants to open up a center for—for—" Tyber realized LaLeche had never said specifically *what* research the center would be geared to. The man had spoken in sweeping, generalized terms, quickly offering him a return on his money that was too good to be true. LaLeche was smooth; he'd give him that.

"For what?"

Tyber shrugged his broad shoulders. "LaLechisms." Zanita giggled.

"Why did he discuss it with you? Did he want your advice?"

"No, he wanted my money."

Zanita opened her eyes. "What do you mean?"

"I was told that for a nominal investment in his project, I

could see a tidy return on my money.''

Zanita gave him a speculative look. "How nominal?"

"Three-hundred-thousand dollars."

Zanita sat up. "Outrageous! Even if you were suckered into his scam, who has that kind of money to throw around?"

Tyber raised a regal eyebrow, watching the emotions play across her face. It was just as he suspected; Zanita refused to have a clue as to how wealthy he was. It was her way of not having to deal with the reality of the situation. Her way of not having to deal with the reality of him.

Zanita blinked at his expression. His implication stopped her for a minute. "You do?"

She never realized Tyber had that kind of . . . She shrugged her shoulders. It was not important right now. She would think about that some other time, if at all. "Even if you could, Tyber, you wouldn't."

"No." *Nice job of suppression, baby.* "But I'll let him think I will."

Zanita sagged against the pillow. "None of this is what we're looking for, though. We already know he inveigles money from people. It's not illegal to get a business partner."

Tyber laced his fingers behind his head, stretching stiff torso muscles by twisting sinuously left, then right. "I keep thinking it's much simpler than we suspect."

"Simplify, simplify." Her grin was gamine.

"You think I should go meditate by Walden Pond?" He leaned over to tug one of her curls.

Here was her opportunity. "Actually, I was thinking you should go jump in the pond." He released her hair to watch her with an apprehensive expression.

"I don't know whether to ask you to elaborate on that or not."

"You don't need to ask me." She patted his shoulder. "I'm going to tell you anyway."

Tyber gave her a guarded look. Women had the inalienable right to toss men into the dog house at a moment's notice.

Now why, he wondered, was he making this trip to the back-yard?

She crossed her arms over her chest. Zanita meant business. "Tyber, you have overstepped the terms of our agreement."

Tyber stared at her, his thought processes skittering off in a hundred different directions at once. He wasn't sure what she was talking about, but he had to tread very carefully here lest he inadvertently give her ammunition in a whole new area. Any man past the age of puberty knew that the only way to respond in this scenario was with a question. A brief, non-informative question.

"Our agreement?" There. That should be reasonably safe.

"Yes. If you will recall, when we began this partnership, we entered into an agreement."

"I don't recall any written agreement between us."

"It was not a written agreement; it was a verbal agreement, which I will remind you is binding in the State of Massachusetts." He gave her the mysterious face of Mars look.

"I don't recall any verbal agreement, either. Zanita, what—"

"I will refresh your memory. Do you recall asking me to move in here with you?"

"Of course I do, but—"

"Do you recall telling me it would be easier for us to work together on this if we were . . . together?"

He knew where this was headed now. A one-way ticket to Doghouse Land. "Yes," he answered her cautiously.

"Do you recall my telling you I didn't want to get involved in a relationship?"

He started to respond; Zanita cut him off.

"Do you recall telling me you wouldn't act *like my boy-friend*?" She raised her chin defiantly at him, demanding an answer to the unanswerable.

Tyber swallowed. "Baby, I—"

"Frankly, Tyber, I'm not sure what to do about this. It is quite obvious to me now that you are acting like my boyfriend and you've been doing it right from the beginning." She pointed a stern finger at him. "What do you have to say for yourself?"

"I—"

"There's nothing you can say!" She ticked off his sins one by one. "The pretty gifts. The attentiveness. The numerous little kindnesses." She shook her head sadly as if to indicate there was nothing else to be said. "I suppose I could move back to my apartment as soon as LaLeche leaves—"

"No!"

Zanita jumped at the vehemence of his response.

Tyber racked his brain for some bizarre explanation which would make sense to her. He couldn't let her move out now; they needed more time. He stalled. "You can't move out now—we're so close to nailing him."

"How do you know?" She didn't seem to be buying it.

He threw his hands up in the air in exasperation. "I just do!" As an explanation, it made no sense. Zanita seemed to be mulling it over, though. She tapped her chin.

"I suppose I could move into one of the spare bedrooms."

He ran his hand through his hair. *Stall her.* "Why would you want to do that?"

"To remove the temptation from you; it's obvious to me, Tyber, you can't help yourself from acting like a boyfriend."

Think. *Think.* "You've got this all wrong, baby."

"I do?"

"Yes. I'm not acting like your boyfriend. I—" *Think!* "I'm conducting an experiment."

"An experiment?" Her brows furrowed as she mulled this over. "What kind of an experiment?"

What kind of an experiment! *I'm testing my sanity.* "It's . . . it's an experiment on . . . High Energy."

"High Energy? What's that?"

"It's a branch of physics—particle physics, actually. You've heard of particle accelerators, right? Like the one in Stanford? Well, another name for an accelerator is an atom smasher, but that term is not politically correct, so we don't use it anymore."

"What does any of this have to do with us?" She was looking at him as if he had a gear loose.

"Um, I'm getting to that. You see, physicists love to make things collide just so they can see what happens. Especially atomic particles." He rubbed his hands together. "Lots of fun."

"You are really strange, you know that?"

"No, I'm *charmed*."

"Huh?"

"A little physics humor; strange and charmed are two kinds of particles—"

"Really, Tyber, this is not solving—"

"You didn't let me finish. To a physicist, an excited particle is an interesting particle."

"Why do I care?"

"Because excited particles do all kinds of intriguing things, especially when high energy is involved. May I demonstrate?"

Zanita nodded warily. What was the kook up to now? Her eyes widened as he slipped off his slacks and underwear. "What are you doing?"

"Exactly what you told me to—I'm demonstrating." He folded his legs, sitting in a lotus position on the bed.

"This is your experiment?" Her tone was skeptical.

"Uh-huh. I'm testing the effects of high-energy transfer among humans in regard to excitation of the body." Right. It was the hokiest thing he had ever heard, and it had come from his own mouth. Any second now, she was going to toss him out on his ear and vacate the bedroom.

Zanita, being Zanita, did neither. She peered at him with a face alight with interest. "You mean you really *are* doing an experiment?" That would make everything okay, she thought. There would be a scientific reason for his behavior.

Tyber didn't bat an eye. "Yes. I'll show you."

It was time to engage the opposition. He reached for the hem of her nightgown, pulling it up over her head. Without delay, he lifted her onto his lap facing him. His hands clasped her ankles, bringing her legs securely around his waist. Then he lifted her chin with his forefinger, locking their sights together.

"What's this for?" she whispered, so as not to interfere with the procedure.

"I'm getting myself into a state of excitement for you. Feel this?" He rubbed his hardening member against her stomach.

Her eyes widened in affirmation.

"See; it's working."

He draped her arms around his neck, bringing his head down to hers. The flat of his palms splayed against her bare back.

"Now I want to see if it's possible for me to convey to you my sense of excitement. . . ."

His lips immediately took hers in a deep, soul-robbing kiss. Strong, white teeth gently captured her upper lip, which he delicately suckled.

A tingling line of excitement quivered from the top of her head to the tips of her toes.

His low voice feathered against her mouth. "I do believe I'm on the right track here."

A small sound issued from Zanita's throat. Maybe he *was* on to something here. To help him out, she ran her tongue across his bottom lip, convinced Tyber was on the verge of a great scientific breakthrough. She told him so.

He agreed.

His palms massaged their way up her back, the strong fingers invigorating and soothing. Competent hands stroked her neck, relaxing the stiff muscles just enough to allow anticipation to seep in.

Their skin, where she sat on him, radiated scorching heat. A teasing fire kindled through both their bodies. Zanita felt she was going to melt in his lap.

Tyber's hands continued working in languid circular motions up her back, her shoulders, her neck, until they cupped the back of her head. His long fingers tangled in her curls.

Growling low in his throat, he held her head immobile for the thorough, rich invasion of his mouth.

Beguiling masculine lips trailed across her face, her forehead, her eyelids, the tip of her nose, the underside of her jaw. His breath was hot on her.

He scraped his cheek against hers, back and forth, in a totally sensuous, catlike gesture which left her reeling. Then his lips nibbled lightly on her collarbone, a soft tasting. She shivered in response.

"Am I exciting you, baby?"

His breathy words tickled the sensitive vee at the base of her throat, raising goosebumps. Before she could think to respond, he dragged his moist tongue diagonally down her chest to the peak of her breast, where he captured the taut, pebbly nub in liquid loving. His palms braced firmly against her back to hold her steady against his mouth, the position giving him complete command of her flesh to play and suckle to his liking.

Her hands threading his hair, clutching him intimately to her, let him know that he was, indeed, exciting her. The tiny sounds she made confirmed it.

This time, when Tyber rubbed his shaft against her lower stomach, he was diamond-hard.

Zanita reached down, clasping his manhood.

Her fingers stroked down the stiff shaft, lightly tracing the throbbing vein. In a duplicating action, she simultaneously ran her open mouth down the strong column of his throat.

Tyber sucked in his breath.

Her thumb and index finger encircled him at the base of his erection, gently squeezing. A husky moan rolled low in his throat.

He buried his face in her hair, groaning, "Baby . . . baby . . . baby . . ."

She rolled the broad head of his manhood around the palm of her hand, feeling a small droplet of liquid escape the tip. The dewy, slightly sticky droplet was lovingly massaged back into his secret, petal-soft skin.

Tyber trembled. His whole body shook while he battled between control and the ecstasy of the moment. Her beautiful, uninhibited lovemaking was driving him crazy. He wanted more of her—had to have more of her—*right now*.

Tyber's hands came under Zanita's arms, suddenly lifting her onto him with a power she had only seen glimpses of in the past. He slid fast into her. Deep. Tight. Potent.

Zanita cried out from the fullness, the exquisite sensation of him so deep inside her, so close inside her. Her arms went around his chest, tightly drawing him to her. Then she placed the flat of her hand over her lower stomach.

He was throbbing inside her.

She could feel it beneath her fingertips! A vibrancy that was uniquely Tyberius Augustus Evans. Her breath caught. Everything that was this man hit her in that one instant of intimacy. *Tyber.*

Her eyes lifted to his, full of wonder and . . .

Tyber saw the look on her face, recognizing it for what it was. Moved, he clutched her to him in a fierce grip; his lips scattered kisses over the top of her head. "Zanita, I—"

But whatever he had been about to say was lost when she began moving on him.

He closed his eyes, letting the sensations flood him. And when he thought he would drown in it, he clutched her buttocks, rocking her back and forth on him, augmenting her oh-so-sweet movements with his own. He took her with him, reveling in the exquisite feel of her, the spicy taste of her, the passionate scent of her. He was lost in his Curls.

The only sounds in the room were the gentle bubbling of the aquariums and their ragged, strained breathing. Then her catchy, mewling sounds, begging him for . . . something, anything . . .

Followed by her whimpering sob. His throaty growl. Their sighs.

They collapsed together back on the bed, Tyber still holding her close to him, his open mouth clinging to the damp skin of her neck. Leisurely, he swept the vulnerable spot with a slow lick of his hot tongue. Zanita still shivered beneath his touch.

"So, you see"—he nuzzled her just below her ear—"what I mean by High Energy."

"Mmm." She curled up around him. "Not a relationship; an experiment." Her face was smiling as she drifted off into a sated slumber.

The corner of Tyber's mouth twitched in a roguish grin as he gazed down at her sleeping in his arms. The battle was won. His satiated purr, the victor against her dreaming lips. "A rose by any other name, my Zanita."

He lowered the Jolly Roger.

Chapter Fourteen

"*People of Earth, do not be frightened—we are your friends.*"

Uh-huh. Whenever an alien said that in a nineteen-fifties sci-fi movie, all the armed forces on the planet were immediately mobilized in a rapid montage of black-and-white stock-footage clips. Yep. There go the Brits, the Russians, the Chinese, what looked suspiciously like a German U-boat, and for some inexplicable reason, the U.S. Navy—just in case the aliens were sub-mariners.

Then came the spinning newspaper headlines: *Aliens among us!; U.N. Meets to Discuss Alien Menace!; Who Goes There?;* and the ever-popular call to salvation, *There's Still Time, Brother!*

Zanita lay back down on the couch in the den, shoveling popcorn into her mouth. Half her attention was on the TV screen in front of her; the other half was mulling over recent events.

Almost a week had passed since LaLeche's visit—or extortion attempt—and they still were not any closer to exposing him. Tyber didn't seem particularly concerned with their lack of progress, but it was starting to worry her. How long should she give it?

It wasn't that she was in any hurry to leave Tyber's home—just the opposite if the truth be told.

And therein lay the problem.

She loved living here: Blooey's fussing over them, the scent of his wonderful cooking filling the house; Hambone's cozy company; Tyber's sweet albeit commanding nature; the house itself—an enchanting haven so utterly a home.

She had adored the fall season in this house—the change of leaves, Blooey's late harvest and squash everywhere, after-work hot drinks on the porch or sun room with Tyber wrapped warmly around her, fireplaces lit in the evening to ward off the brisk chill, the cat curled up on the rug.

It was easy to look forward to the winter at My Father's Mansion.

Zanita imagined Tyber's private, walled world blanketed in white—evenings by the fire, wrapped in her Victorian shawl, reading, cold nights cuddling together under the soft quilts in his shell bed, cozy as clams. . . .

It wasn't good.

In fact, it was going to be incredibly hard to leave here. And the longer she stayed, the harder it was going to get. There was only one thing she could do; she was going to have to set a deadline and stick by it. Story accomplished or not, when the deadline came, she was going to have to leave.

The thought was depressing.

So how long did she wait? At least until after Thanksgiving. Before Auntie had left, she had given Zanita her customary Thanksgiving dinner invitation to her home in Wellesley. Of course, Hank and her grandmother would be there; it was a family tradition, and there was no way she could get out of it. Auntie had extended the invitation to Tyber and Blooey as well. Which meant they would all be going as a unit. Zanita thought it would just be too awkward if she moved out around that time.

Before Christmas?

Hmm. Blooey had seemed depressed that he wasn't going to be making Thanksgiving dinner, so Tyber had cheered him up by promising him he could make a big Christmas feast. He had already mentioned to her inviting her grandparents and Mills, since Mills didn't have any close family and she usually spent the holidays with Zanita's family. Tyber had even graciously included Auntie.

How could she mess up everyone's holiday?

This was getting increasingly tangled. She sighed. Here was prime reinforcement of her new tenet: Nothing was ever simple when a man was involved.

"Colonel, the aliens are demanding a meeting with the King of Rock and Roll."

Zanita gaped at the set, a popcorn kernel balanced on her lips.

Tyber stood in the doorway, chuckling. "What are you watching?" He leaned against the door frame, crossing his arms over his chest.

"Aliens Über Alles."

Another man would have scoffed at her choice of entertainment. But then, other men weren't Doc Evans. "And you didn't call me?" He seemed miffed that he had missed the beginning of the movie.

"I thought you were helping Blooey give Hambone a bath."

Tyber didn't respond verbally, just held up both forearms, which now sported two long scratches.

"That's terrible! Shame on Hambone."

"He gets me every time, the scalawag." He sauntered into the room, sprawling down on the carpet in front of the couch. Zanita held out the bowl of popcorn.

They watched the movie in companionable silence, occasionally making their usual comments. Tyber rested back against the couch, the top of his head brushing against her thigh. Every now and then his hand came up over his shoulder in a blind search for the popcorn bowl. A couple of times he playfully missed, tweaking her leg instead.

From her vantage point draped across the sofa, Zanita had an excellent view of his long, muscular, jean-clad legs. Personal experience told her his thighs really were as powerful as they appeared encased in those hugging pants. He looked as sexy to her now as he had the first moment she had seen him.

The effect he had on her would never change.

Tyber was that rare type of man whose masculinity was always apparent, no matter what he was doing. He was the only man she had ever known who could turn her on simply by being there. Zanita was constantly crazy for the feel of him.

She exhaled, briefly debating whether or not to lean over, lift his thick fall of hair, and nibble-kiss the back of his neck. Reluctantly, she decided against it; such an action would undoubtedly lead to them missing the rest of the movie.

The other-worldly music suddenly increased in volume, letting the audience know that either the aliens, or something to do with the aliens, or something the aliens had done, was about to be seen. Zanita turned her focus from Tyber's silky hair back to the screen.

The camera panned a stock shot of Carlsbad Caverns.

Something was moving inside the cavern, coming out. Several stalklike tentacles were waving in the opening to the cave now. The music reached a deafening crescendo.

A large carrot with giant eyeballs showed itself to the Earthlings, who ran screaming for cover.

Zanita and Tyber burst out laughing.

Of course, the military was there to open up machine guns, cannons, and dynamite onto the terrifying nemesis from outer space. Predictably, none of our superior weapons worked.

"There's got to be some high-tension wires around there somewhere," Tyber quipped, naming his favorite choice of monster death.

Zanita crunched on her popcorn. "Nope, I say it's the ever popular Torch Method of Alien Decimation." As soon as the words were out of her mouth, a flame thrower appeared stage left, turning the unfortunate invader into a fireball. "Alien succotash. Now they'll be a two-minute voice-over rife with dire warnings and schlock philosophy.''

''. . . *And so, they came from out there, eager for new worlds to conquer . . .*''

''What did I tell you?'' Zanita grinned.

Tyber chuckled. ''Whoever said nature abhors a vacuum has never seen one of these movies.'' The grin suddenly died on his face.

Zanita sat up, concerned. ''Tyber, what is it?''

Nature abhors a vacuum. He had been thinking that very thing when he had his private little chat with LaLeche last week. There was something here which connected the two. . . .

''I've been an idiot!'' He stood up.

Zanita, kneeling on the couch, gazed up at him with a dimpled grin. ''Yes, but what specifically are you referring to?''

''What time is it?''

''About a quarter to eight—why?''

He was already headed to the phone. ''If we're lucky, we can still catch them on the West Coast.''

''Catch who?'' She went to stand beside him.

Tyber called Los Angeles information, asking for the number of Space Age Systems, Inc. He met Zanita's eyes over the handset. ''Bear with me.'' He dialed the number, handing her the phone. ''Ask them if they do anything else besides manufacturing shuttle components.''

She gave him a strange look over her shoulder, but did as he asked. Her eyes widened as the woman on the other end responded. ''Special effects in cinema.'' She hung up the phone.

Tyber immediately picked it up again, redialing the number. ''Not just shuttle components as we thought.'' Someone answered the phone on the other end, presumably the same woman. Tyber asked to speak to an engineer.

When he got through to the engineer, Tyber told the man who he was, launching into a hokey explanation of some information he needed for a VR project he was working on.

Zanita knew VR stood for virtual reality. She wondered if

Tyber really was working on such a project. At any rate, the man on the other end didn't seem to hesitate, giving him all the information he needed. She guessed Tyber's name had been enough of an introduction, especially since nothing he asked in any way connected to virtual reality.

He hung up the phone, a huge smile breaking across his face. "We got him, baby."

"Tell me! Tell me!" She clutched his hands, just as excited as he was.

"That little healing demonstration he put on for us in Vermont—I know just how he did it."

"*How*?" Her violet eyes got huge with anticipation. Tyber thought she looked totally delectable. Without thinking, he lowered his head to give her a heated kiss. She pushed against his shoulders.

"Not now, Doc! Tell me how he did it!"

"That's just it; he didn't. It was all a fake; he's a fake. Have you ever seen those nylon filament lamps—they look like multicolored hedgehogs or sea anemones? They were very popular back in the early eighties."

"You mean the stuff that sprouted on people's coffee tables in black box bases and lit up at the tips in different colors?"

"That's the stuff. Our friend LaLeche was wearing them or something like them. You see, light travels through those clear filaments from an end source. In this case, LaLeche probably used a small circuit board with some light bulbs, like the little ones they use in Christmas tree lights, connected to the filaments."

Her eyebrows rose. "That would explain the light-show we witnessed, but how could he conceal the filament wires? You saw yourself—his sleeves were rolled up way past his elbows. There was nothing there but bare arms."

"Not quite; there was nothing there to *see* but bare arms. That's the beauty of it—he was wearing prosthetic skin."

"Prosthetic skin? Are you sure? It looked so real; his arms even had hair on them."

"According to this engineer I spoke to, they use this stuff

all the time in motion pictures. It does look real—human hairs are individually inserted into the skin to augment the effect.''

''You don't think we would have seen something odd about it?''

''No. Don't forget, it wasn't all that bright in the cabin; LaLeche only brought those kerosene lanterns for lighting. And he made sure he did the trick at night.''

Zanita thought about it a minute. ''You shook hands with him when we left. Wouldn't you have felt anything strange?''

''Not necessarily. Remember, it was late; it was cold as hell; the handshake was brief; and, most importantly, I wasn't *expecting* to feel anything unusual. Besides, the engineer told me the stuff feels very close to human skin in texture.''

''If memory serves me,'' Zanita said, ''LaLeche worked at Space Age Systems for two years, the longest he had ever stayed in one place. We even remarked on it, remember?''

Tyber shook his head. ''I bet he was learning all kinds of new tricks there. He probably doctored up a fake resume to go along with his fake name. It also explains why he only did the trick once. I imagine it's not a simple thing to set up.''

''So, the filaments were under the prosthetic skin?''

''Exactly. He must have had the on-off switch within easy reach. The circuit board would have been concealed somewhere on him. My guess is inside his pants. One flick and viola! You light up my life.''

Zanita blew the curls off her forehead. ''Tyber, how did you ever figure this out? Where was the connection?''

''When I saw the veggie alien and I commented on nature abhorring a vacuum, it reminded me that I was thinking the very same thought when I was talking to LaLeche. I knew there had to be some intuitive connection between the two, which my subconscious brain had already figured out. I got to thinking about the hokey alien make-up in the movie, and that thought led to special effects, which led to Hollywood, which is in L.A. I remembered Xavier spent two years in L.A. at Space Age Systems. Alien—*Space Age*—LaLeche. It hit me; Space Age Systems might not have been just a shuttle component manufacturer as we had originally thought, but an F/X studio. Simple linear reasoning.'' He looked at her expectantly.

Zanita rolled her eyes exactly as she had done the first time he met her and he was explaining Chaos at the seminar.

Simple reasoning? Only Tyber and, perhaps, Sherlock Holmes, could've made those brilliant deductive leaps. "Whew! Doc, you are amazing.''

Tyber grinned, winking at her. "It's all part of the service. Go write your article, baby.''

Zanita frowned. "But we don't have anything to put him in jail with.''

He put his arm around her shoulders, hugging her to him. "All we have to do is *expose* him. You write your piece; they'll come out of the woodwork to nail him.''

The article was published in the Sunday edition of the *Patriot Sun*.

Hank wasn't in when Zanita dropped off the piece, but she didn't have to wait too long to find out his reaction.

He called her at Tyber's house after dinner and chewed her out for putting herself at potential risk. Then he demanded to speak to Tyber. Tyber gingerly took the phone from her, not getting much in by way of conversation except a lot of "yes, sirs'' and "I know, sirs'' and "I will, sirs.'' Then he handed the phone back to her with an apologetic shrug.

Once Hank calmed down, the newsman in him came to the fore. He told her the piece would run Sunday and that he had sent a photographer out to a seminar LaLeche was doing so they could run a picture with the article. "Damn fine article. Don't do it again,'' he said just before he slammed down the phone.

Zanita made a face at the receiver. "You curmudgeon!''

The article with the photo was picked up by the wire services and was reprinted across the country in numerous papers. Zanita had a *name*. Not a big name, but a name.

Tyber had congratulated her by sending three dozen long-stem roses to her office that morning with a note promising her a special dinner from Blooey and him.

Theoretically, it should be her farewell dinner, only she hadn't been able to broach the subject with Tyber yet. Since the story had wrapped up faster than she anticipated, she wasn't sure what to do now. Should she move out before Thanksgiving? What about Auntie's invitation? They could all still go, but it would be awkward. After all, they had no real reason to continue their relationship other than as friends.

She rubbed the bridge of her nose, trying to relieve the sudden tension.

Perhaps I should take a page out of Scarlett's book and worry about this tomorrow? Why ruin the celebration with upsetting thoughts that could just as easily be faced in the morning? She deserved this day, and so did Tyber.

Feeling somewhat better, she straightened her shoulders and hit the keyboard. Hank had put her on a story about a successful new day-care center in Stockboro—for dogs—Hank's retaliation for taking on the LaLeche story without the paper's permission. She had spent the entire morning being licked to death. Hambone wouldn't come near her for a week.

Tyber poured himself a cup of coffee.

In the fall and winter, Blooey always had coffee and hot water for tea on the stove. As far as Tyber was concerned, that service alone made the man invaluable.

He sat down on the stool next to the counter, cradling the warm cup in his hands. Blooey was hard at work chopping nuts for some brownies he was making.

Tyber didn't speak for several minutes.

Blooey, sensing that the Captain was pondering something of great import, waited for the him to gather his thoughts.

Aye, the Captain always seeks out my opinion on matters weighing on him. Sometimes, Blooey knew, the Captain came to him like a younger brother seeking an older, wiser ear. Truth was, neither one of them spent much time off the sea. Because of what they did and the way they lived, men such as they didn't have much experience in port, as it were.

So, when they found themselves on dry dock, they needed to stick together.

Tyber took a deep breath, then took the plunge.

"I think Lady Masterson should become a permanent member of this crew; what do you think, Blooey?"

So, there's the way of it. Blooey smiled inwardly.

Carefully maintaining a serious expression, he stopped chopping walnuts for a minute as if he were pondering the question. He slowly shook his head, "Aye, Captain; she's copper-bottomed, clipper-built, sir, and that's a fact."

The set of Tyber's shoulders relaxed. He gave Blooey a huge grin. "What say you, we think of something really special for dinner tonight? Something to let her see how much we like her being here with us?"

"Well now," Blooey said, stroking his chin, "once when I was working the Far East trade, iffen you get my drift, Captain—"

"You were ransacking the East Indies trade routes."

"Aye, just so. I learned of an exotic cuisine which stimulates the passionate soul to near recklessness. Met a sheik there once what swore no woman could resist him after she partook of the delights of such a feast." He closed one eye and gleamed at Tyber with the other.

"You've convinced me." He set his empty cup on the tile counter. "Carry on, sailor!"

Dinner that evening was absolutely exquisite.

Blooey had gone all out, preparing a gourmet feast fit for a queen. There was a compote of fresh melon and passion fruit sorbet, spinach salad with raspberry vinaigrette followed by breast of chicken in a vermouth and ginger cream sauce, and an exotic rice pilaf containing little bits of dried fruits and pistachio nuts.

Tyber opened a bottle of Crystal to accompany their meal. The dining room table, with the leaves taken out for more intimate dining, was beautifully set with candlesticks and a centerpiece of white camellias.

Where the men had found the camellias this time of year, Zanita could only wonder, but she was touched that Tyber had remembered they were one of her favorite flowers.

The table was so elegant, she almost felt silly sitting there in her knock-about jeans and sweater.

She was just about to take a sip of Crystal when an uncomfortable thought hit her.

What was Tyber up to?

This was very extravagant for a congratulatory dinner. She sneaked a peak at him over the rim of her glass. The man looked totally innocent, which meant he was definitely up to something.

Tyber also drank his champagne, wondering if he had timed this right. It wasn't that he hadn't given it a great deal of thought. Left to her own devices, Zanita would never make the commitment he was seeking from her. Their collaboration on the LaLeche story was over; it was time to start a new one.

He wanted her to stay here.

Frankly, he was surprised that she hadn't broached the subject of moving back to her apartment yet.

Tyber did not delude himself; she just hadn't gotten around to it. He knew his Zanita. As soon as it occurred to her, as soon as her circumstances smacked of his being her significant other, she would definitely be *Gone With The Wind*.

But Tyber had no intention of letting her go. He was not something to be given up, like red meat. Or an aberration. He was hers, and he knew that deep down inside, she knew it. If he could only get her to admit it . . .

"Zanita." He reached across the table to take her hand in his. "I was wondering if you would like to—"

"There's a bloke on the telephone for ye, Captain," Blooey called him from the doorway. "He says he's the engineer from Space Age Systems what ye spoke to the other day."

Tyber raised his eyebrow, shrugging his shoulders at Zanita's questioning look. "Excuse me."

While he went to answer the phone, Zanita took the chicken's way out by telling Blooey she was finished, complimenting him for the lovely meal. She quickly escaped to the bedroom, where she decided to take a nice long hot bath.

What had he been about to ask her?

Whatever it was, it had "relationship" written over it. She broke out into a cold sweat even with the hot bath water surrounding her. She squeezed her eyes shut, not wanting to deal with this, but knowing she was going to have to.

Okay, so he wasn't Steve or Rick or even remotely like any other man she had met, but after her experiences with the opposite sex, just the thought of a relationship with his kind gave her the dry heaves. Men didn't mean to be . . . *men*, they just were. They couldn't help it.

They were bad for your health.

Men should come with a warning label: Caution. Prolonged use is dangerous to your peace of mind.

Leave. She was going to have to leave. Soon. Tomorrow, at lunch time, she'd go air out her apartment, get it ready for her imminent return.

The decision was made.

She would tell Tyber when he came upstairs.

When she came out of the bathroom, he was lying on his side, fully clothed on top of the bed quilts. Elbow bent, the side of his face nestled in the palm of his hand, he regarded her from under hooded lids.

Zanita tightened the sash on her robe, marching resolutely to the bed. She didn't like that look on his face.

Somewhere, she was sure she had read it was always best to throw your opponent off by speaking first, on a totally different subject than the one you really wanted to speak about. Loosen him up. Get his hackles nice and smooth. Then, *whamo*! He's agreeing with whatever you say before he realizes it.

"What did the engineer want? Was it something to do with LaLeche?"

"No." His free arm came up around her shoulders, dragging her down beside him on the bed. "He wanted to know if I'd be interested in doing some consulting work on a project they're doing for a movie which revolves around VR."

"Oh. Did you take the job?"

"Uh-uh." His index finger traced along the opening of her robe. The slow action unnerved her.

"Why not?"

"It would mean being out in California for extended stretches. I didn't want to leave you for so long." His eyes met hers. "You might get lonely rattling around this big house by yourself."

Why did she always get the feeling that he knew what she was up to? Courage. She sucked in a deep breath. "Tyber, we need to talk about this—"

"Hey, look," he interrupted her, "one of the tropical fish is staring straight at you with a strange glint in its eye."

"Where?" She peered over her shoulder at the tank. He swooped across her.

"Zanita, really, how could a fish affect a strange glint?" His eyes danced with mirth. And something else. Something suspiciously close to the quarter deck.

"If they're *your* fish, they could. Get off!"

"Know how fish kiss? Like this." His open mouth covered her own. He raised his head, strands of his hair brushing across the peaks of her breasts.

"They look like this, don't they?"

Pressing his lips together, he sucked in his cheeks, causing his lips to bow out like a fish's mouth. Leaving his mouth tightly closed, he moved his pursed lips up and down while crossing his eyes. It was the funniest thing she had ever seen.

Peals of laughter caused her to clutch her stomach.

Tyber untied the sash on her robe, bending over to nibble her midriff with his undulating fish lips. Zanita couldn't stop laughing. It tickled and every time he raised his head to stare at her with those crossed eyes and moving lips, she was gone.

It wasn't until much later, after they had made love—Zanita was still laughing—that she realized he had used the same technique on her that she was going to use on him.

He had expertly shifted her focus.

The apartment looked so small.

So empty.

So cold.

Zanita stood in the doorway observing her digs with the eyes of a stranger. What had seemed so adequate before now seemed barren. Bleak. It was bleak.

She walked into the musty living-cum-bedroom. One room and a kitchenette. That's what it was. Not a home. A place for singles, students, and transients.

It was depressing.

The fold-away couch lay open, as she usually left it, being too lazy to close it every day. A few books were scattered across the bed table. Her one cactus plant, the only living thing in the apartment besides herself, sat forlornly on the window sill, the meager late fall sunlight barely sustaining the poor thing. A chair. Her compact disc player. Her twelve-inch portable television. A few wall hangings.

That was it.

The sum total of her life.

Did she really want to come back here? Leave the warmth of Tyber's home? Come here instead of being in a place she felt nurtured and cared for and . . . *cherished*?

She must be mad to even consider—

The door behind her closed with a click.

She swung around. LaLeche was standing there inside her apartment.

He was wearing a ski jacket and—her eyes trailed down to his hands—leather gloves. The first thought that filtered through her shocked brain was, *Why is he wearing gloves? It isn't that cold out.*

Then several thoughts ran at her mind at once, the foremost being: *Get yourself out of here.*

"What are you doing here?"

He didn't answer her; he just reached behind him, turning

the deadbolt to lock. Zanita backed up a few steps.

"What do you want?" She forced her voice to sound coldly clipped. Fear was not something you wanted to show in a situation like this. Even if you were terrified.

His gaze raked her contemptuously. "I think that should be obvious."

"I'm busy; I don't have time for this. I'll have to ask you to leave." Yeah. Right. Like he hadn't locked her in here with him.

"That's too bad, Zanita. I have plenty of time for you." He started walking toward her. She began backing up, although there really wasn't too far to go in the small apartment.

Stall him, her panicked mind screamed. "All this just for a little article?"

He stopped stalking her to give her a sickeningly evil grin. "You flatter yourself, my dear. It's not the article I care about. It was the picture you ran with it. Now that was irresponsible."

Picture? What picture? It took her a few moments to realize that he was talking about the photo Hank had run with the piece. How ironic! Here Hank was worried about her being in danger when it was his actions that had placed her there. Not that Hank was in any way responsible for this; he had done the right thing.

"You see, names can always be changed, but once you're exposed by a photo, well—plastic surgery is expensive, and I so hate the pain."

She lifted her chin, trying to be brave. "What are you going to do about it?"

LaLeche shook his finger at her. "Now there's the question. You've caused me a lot of trouble. The kind of trouble that calls for . . . a certain revenge. What should it be, do you think?"

"Leave me alone," she whispered, genuinely frightened.

He ignored her. "Accidents can happen so easily. That idiot retainer of his, for instance . . ."

Blooey! Sweet, kind Blooey. What would he do to him?

"Blooey is no threat to you. He had nothing to do with this—leave him out of it."

"A little gardening accident, perhaps? I've heard of people being careless with gardening tools. All kinds of nasty things can happen should one trip over one and fall on, say, some shears."

"Stop it. I won't let you hurt—"

"Then there is that god-awful beast of his. Cats are such easy victims, aren't they? And this one should have been put out of its misery years ago. It so likes its food . . . it seems to eat just about anything." He leveled a hateful look at her.

He was toying with her now, she knew. Threatening to poison Hambone. Even though she knew what his sick game was, she still couldn't stop the trickle of fear down her spine. She couldn't take it if anything happened to Hambone because of her. She had grown quite fond of the idiosyncratic tabby.

"I don't know how much you care for the wretched beast, but *he* does, I'm sure."

Tyber. "What do you have against Tyber? I was the one who wrote the article."

"Yes, but he provided the material. I'm not stupid—I know all about Tyberius Augustus Evans. I know his reputation, and I know what motivates him. He figured it all out for you, didn't he? Not his usual type of pastime. I had to ask myself why he bothered; the answer was immediately apparent. *You.* He wanted you, so he gave you what you wanted."

Zanita stared at him. Was it true what LaLeche said? Did Tyber only help her because he wanted her? She had always assumed it was the other way around; he was helping her because it intrigued him, just as his research did. She kind of came along with the deal.

Had she been blind or was LaLeche just confusing her for his own demented thrill?

Chapter Fifteen

"Then there is the other—that perfect revenge against both of you."

She angled her chin at him, refusing to be pulled into the sick game. He seemed to be waiting for her to ask him what he intended and seeming put out when she didn't.

"I could take you, you know." His lecherous observation made her skin crawl. She forced herself to remain calm.

"I don't think so, Mr. LaLeche. I'll scream the house down." She infused his name with all the contempt she felt for him.

He rubbed his jaw, contemplating her words as if they were merely having an existential discussion on the topic and he wasn't threatening her with real violence.

"I disagree. I could do it and get away with it. There are no other tenants here this time of day; I checked. Scream all you like. No one will hear you."

Zanita's heart sank to her toes; apparently she and Tyber had been blinded by his traits of greed, dishonesty, and lack of human decency. They had never once considered that when cornered, he would aggressively seek revenge. She was in real trouble here.

"Someone will see you." It was worth a shot.

"No." He shook his head. "No one saw me come in; I'll make sure no one sees me leave. I'll simply slip away into the ether as I always do. No one will be any the wiser. Except you and Doctor Evans. After this, I imagine I'll stay with you for the rest of your lives. Always between you, as it were." He chuckled maniacally at his twisted pun.

Zanita had never faced the prospect of violence before. Somewhat in shock, her thoughts seemed icy clear and removed at the same time. This was about subjugation, control, and revenge. The malignancy of the crime was brought home to her.

What he was threatening would be beyond horrible for her, and it would torment Tyber for the rest of his life. She knew him; he would feel responsible for not protecting her. It was an illogical male attitude, but she was positive Tyber would blame himself.

LaLeche was right—it was a chilling revenge, for if he succeeded in carrying out his threat, it surely would destroy them both.

She had to think of something to put a stop to his line of thinking. There was only one thing her fear-numbed brain could come up with. "There will be evidence. . . ."

"I have a condom right here in my back pocket—what evidence?" He started approaching her again, this time with deadly intent.

She moved around the sofa. Did he think she was going to go down without a struggle? "I'll fight you; I'll make sure there will be bruises, scratch marks, trace evidence—"

"I'll do my best to prevent that, you understand. I'm quite strong; it won't be too difficult for me to subdue a tiny thing like you. And if you should manage a few black-and-blue marks—" He shrugged. "Trace evidence—not much to convict a man on. If you happen to have some bruises—*and you will*—well, it will look like your boyfriend just got carried away. Everyone knows he's something of a wild man.''

He thought for a minute. "Even if you do decide to press charges, there will always be that doubt in everyone's mind: Maybe the illustrious Tyberius Evans abuses women and she's protecting him. Should do wonders for his career, don't you think? He'll have you to thank for that as well. Remember, it will be my word against yours.'' He moved a little closer to her.

"I think my word would carry the greater weight.'' She edged into the kitchenette.

"A reporter looking to get her name in the news? Think of what a good lawyer could do with that in a courtroom.''

My god, he's going to hurt me. Too late she realized that he had backed her into a corner with no escape. Before she could think what to do, he was on her.

He tore at her clothes, slamming her hard against the wall. Zanita fought back with all her strength, screaming. LaLeche had been right about one other thing—she was no match for him physically. He had her at his mercy with ridiculous ease. Zanita sobbed, feeling utterly helpless against his aggression. *Tyber*, her heart called to him. *Tyber . . .*

LaLeche unzipped his pants, holding her captive with one powerful arm across her throat, blocking her air passage. She couldn't stop him. *Nothing was going to stop him.*

Later, she could never figure out what had caused her to blurt out what she did. At the last possible second, she screamed, "We have a file on you!''

LaLeche froze. He raked her with a contemptuous sneer. "What kind of file?''

Zanita was shaking uncontrollably, tears streaming down her face.

"Answer me, dammit.'' He grabbed a hank of her hair, slamming her head back hard into the wall. Little spots appeared before her eyes. Zanita willed herself not to pass out, afraid that if she did, she might not get the chance to wake up.

"An—an FBI file. They know all about you, LaLeche.

They've been after you for years. They'll find you. And when they do, you'll pay for what you've done to innocent, trusting people.''

LaLeche paused, thinking over her words. ''Did they trail me here, or was this investigation strictly your idea? Tell me or I'll end this here and now.'' The dire threat paralyzed Zanita.

He slapped her across the face, splitting her lip.

''It—it was my idea, but they—they know we have the file.''

''Then they probably haven't been trailing me. . . .'' A bead of sweat trickled down his forehead. ''They don't have anything on me, you know. Not a damn thing. Still . . . It's best I don't press my good fortune.'' He abruptly released her.

''Today's your lucky day, Zanita. It appears I must be on my way again.'' He strode quickly to the door and opened it, cautiously checking to see if the coast was clear. He turned back to her. ''I'll be seeing you . . . *sometime.*''

He was gone as quickly as he had come.

Zanita slumped down to the floor, clutching her stomach. The aftermath of shock would soon be setting in. A roil of nausea flipped her stomach. Her insides churned. She rushed to the bathroom, just making it.

She vomited repeatedly into the commode. When the spasms had passed, she automatically rinsed her mouth out and brushed her teeth, not even thinking about what she was doing. When she noticed a toothbrush in her hand, she couldn't remember how it had gotten there.

She sagged back against the wall. Her only coherent thought was: *Tyber.*

As soon as her wobbly legs could support her, she rushed out of the bathroom, grabbed her purse where it had been knocked to the floor, and ran out of the apartment as fast as she could.

She needed to—*had* to—reach Tyber. Somewhere in the back of her mind, she knew she wasn't thinking rationally.

She was probably in shock. But it didn't matter. Nothing mattered except reaching Tyber.

Somehow, she was in her car, driving to the mansion. Horrifying, disjointed thoughts raced across her mind. What if LaLeche had headed out to the mansion? What if he had already harmed them? These tortured thoughts hammered at her as she sped along the highway to the house, miraculously not stopped by a trooper for speeding.

Overlying everything was the gut-wrenching irrational fear, the unqualified *need* to see Tyber. To have him hold her. For him to rub her back and whisper in her ear in that special way he had, telling her not to worry, that everything would be all right.

Fumbling in her purse, she found the gate opener, letting herself onto the grounds. She turned into the curve of the drive, her tires squealing as the car braked to a stop. It was still rocking when she slammed the door, racing up the stairs and into the house.

Passing the parlor, she noted Hambone lying in the sun in front of the large picture window. She closed her eyes in relief, not stopping her frantic search. She headed toward the rear of the house and the kitchen. Before she could get there, the hall door swung open.

Tyber padded out of the kitchen in stockinged feet and jeans, a half-eaten brownie in one hand, a stack of computer sheets in the other. He didn't notice her right away because his attention was focused on the readouts in his hand.

He looked so completely *normal*, she had the absurd desire to cry.

When he realized that she was standing there, he stopped, staring at her in controlled silence. His raking glance did a swift survey of her torn clothes, her cut and swollen lip, the already purpling bruises.

"Where's Blooey?" she demanded in a quivering voice.

Tyber regarded her intently. "He's out in the far acreage planting spring bulbs. What happened to you?" His voice was evenly modulated steel.

Her bottom lip began to tremble. Suddenly she covered her face with her hands and sank to the floor, sobbing.

The computer papers and brownie fell unheeded to the floor. Instantly, Tyber was beside her, kneeling down, gathering her in his arms. "What is it? What is it, baby?" He rocked her in the security of his embrace.

"It–it was LaLeche." She sobbed.

Tyber went still. "What did he do?"

"He–he cornered me in my apartment. I don't know how he found me—he must have been watching me." The very idea brought tremors. Tyber rubbed her back, silently urging her to continue, dreading what he was about to hear.

"He said he wanted revenge . . . against both of us. He said he could—he could d-do whatever he wanted to me and there was nothing I could do about it." She clutched his soft flannel shirt in an iron grip. Above her bent head, Tyber closed his eyes in pain for what she had suffered.

"Are you hurt, baby? Let me take you to a hospital."

"No! I want to stay here with you! I don't want to go anywhere!" She seemed almost hysterical. Tyber tried to soothe her.

"I understand, sweetheart, but if he . . . hurt you, you need to go to the hospital."

"He didn't . . . get that far. I was so scared, Tyber. I told him we had a file on him. He stopped. I don't know why. Before he left, he told me he would come for me again. He—" She couldn't go on.

So LaLeche hadn't raped her as he had feared. Tyber sent a silent thank you heavenward. Silly, he knew, but faith showed up at the oddest times.

No, LaLeche didn't rape her, but he had scared her witless. She would carry the scars of this for the rest of her life. It would be a long time before her spunky confidence came back. She had lost a lot of her bright-eyed innocence today. And the bastard had physically hurt her, used violence against his baby. . . .

Tyber wanted to kill him.

261

"What if he comes here, Tyber? He threatened Blooey and Hambone—said he would poison the poor cat." Still clutching his shirt, her tear-streaked face beseeched him. Tugged at him. When he looked at her, he wanted to cry himself.

The bastard had really done a number on her.

He would pay. But not now. Now he needed to take care of her, reassure her as best he could.

"Don't be frightened, baby; you're safe here. I would never let anything happen to you." To reinforce his words, he pressed kisses tenderly against her eyes, her forehead, her cheeks. His tender ministrations opened up a flood of emotions in her, and she sobbed in great wracking spasms; she broke his heart.

He scooped her up in his arms and carried her upstairs to their bedroom. Afraid she would go into shock, he gently removed her clothes, placing her tenderly under the heavy quilts.

Knowing that his own body heat was the best remedy, he quickly shed his own clothes, getting under the covers and wrapping her to him.

"Don't cry. Don't cry. Don't cry." He rocked her in his arms. "You're safe. I won't let him touch you, I swear. I love you too much to let anything happen to you. Kiss me, Curls— that's right. Again. So sweet. You're so sweet."

"Hold m-me, Tyber."

"I'm holding you. See? I'm holding you right against me; there's nothing to be afraid of."

"You won't let him—" She shivered against him.

"No. Never." He held her tightly to him.

She put her arms around his neck, drawing him down to her. "Make love to me, Tyber, please. Erase his touch, his memory, his words. You won't let him hurt me?"

"Shh." He kissed her gently on the mouth, cognizant of her emotional and physical fragility.

Her lips clung to his in need, in passion, in reaffirmation of all that was good and decent in her life. This was Tyber, her safe haven.

He came over her, covering her with himself. A human

blanket of warmth and security.

His lips played with her ear. Lulling. Calming.

"What did I say to you?" he whispered.

"You–you said you loved me."

Tyber did not want her to think of anything but his words to her. He wanted her thoughts only on him; he wanted to eradicate the ugliness, the horror she had experienced. He inserted his leg between hers, opening her to him. "Tell me again, baby."

"You said you loved me—Tyber!" He entered her with one sure, even stroke.

"Yes, I love you," he breathed softly in her ear. Purposely, he moved in her, gently at first, his stroking actions, designed to be soothing, slowly became more powerful with each drive against her.

"Again," he insisted of her, wanting her to know him now, to feel him and never forget that he was the one.

She moaned against his shoulder. "You said you loved me."

His tongue swirled around her lobe; his hands slid down under her derriere to cup her hard against him. He rocked tight to her, locked deep inside.

His hand came up now to caress the side of her face, pressing it flush to his own so her lips were against his ear, and his against hers. In this intimate pose, he asked her the one and only thing he wanted to hear. His voice was a hot vibration against the inner folds.

"*Tell me*," he demanded breathlessly.

"I love you."

"*Yes*," he groaned. It was a deep, heart-felt sound that came from somewhere around his soul. He rubbed his cheek against hers. "Always. Always."

"I love you," she whimpered. "Oh God, Tyber, I love you."

"I know, baby. I know." His mouth covered her own, melding with it, fusing with it.

263

The culmination of their union came to them both at once, complete and everlasting. An ending. A beginning.

Tyber slipped quietly from beneath the blankets so as not to awaken Zanita.

She had fallen asleep in his arms shortly after they made love. The events of the day, the emotional roller-coaster she had experienced, and finally, this last physical act had taken their toll. Her energy resources depleted, she had fallen into an exhausted slumber.

Good. Sleep was the best healer.

He slipped his clothes back on, silently leaving the bedroom on stockinged feet. When he reached the foyer, he picked up the hall phone, punching in a set of memorized numbers. The call was answered promptly. Tyber did not waste time on preliminaries.

"Where is he?"

"Who?"

"Don't play games with me, Sean. I know you would have followed him when he left my house on Sunday. Now, *where is he*?"

"Why do you want to know?"

"He threatened Zanita. Scared her. Bad."

There was a brief pause, then, "He's renting a little cottage outside of Hill Town up on Blue Ridge Road. Yellow paint. White trim. Number 109." Tyber made to hang up, but Sean forestalled him. "Evans!"

"What?"

"Don't do anything stupid. I'll be right behind you. You'll have fifteen minutes."

"I owe you one, buddy. Thanks."

Tyber searched out Blooey, giving him an edited version of what had happened. Blooey was furious, threatening to take up arms himself and go after the scurvy toad.

Tyber calmed him down, asking him to check in on Zanita while he was out, instructing him not to wake her. Blooey knew exactly what Tyber was about. The Captain took care of his own. Aye, he was a good man to serve with.

"Ye don't have to worry none about me, Captain. I'll take the watch for ye. Go about yer business now."

The small house was dark except for the one light shining in the right front room.

Tyber debated the best way of gaining entrance, finally deciding that the simplest ways usually worked the best. He knocked on the front door first. He didn't really expect La-Leche to answer, so was taken off guard a little when he did.

LaLeche appeared faintly surprised to see Tyber Evans on his front stoop. He made to shut the door, but Tyber stopped him by shoving his way into the house. Gaining entrance, he slammed the door closed behind him.

"I want to talk to you, *Xavier*." Tyber's soft tone held a lethal intensity.

"Maybe some other time. As you can see, I'm a little busy right now." LaLeche ignored Tyber, busily emptying out a bureau and throwing the contents into a duffel bag.

Tyber ground his teeth together, resisting the urge to choke the life out of this scumbag. "I ought to just kill you, but I guess I'm going to have to be civilized and warn you first. Stay away from Zanita. If I ever see or hear of you coming near her again, I'll—"

LaLeche stopped packing. He turned and faced Tyber, a knowing smirk on his face. "You'll what? Don't jerk with me, *Doctor* Evans. For christsakes, you're a physicist."

"Sometimes," Tyber responded smoothly.

LaLeche regarded him in a new light. "Interesting. I'd love to stick around and discover all of your intriguing facets, but I really need to be going."

"I don't think so."

"Now there's where you're wrong, Doctor. Get out of my way." He made to push past him, but Tyber slammed him against the back of the door.

"You're going away all right, and for a long time, pal. But before you go, I intend to reach an understanding with you. I want you to forget all about Zanita. I want you to forget about ever coming near my lady or anything else of mine again. I want you to forget all about any twisted notion you have for revenge. And to make sure you do"—Tyber slammed his fist hard into LaLeche's groin—"a little something to remember me by."

LaLeche doubled over, clutching his middle. The man had a fist like iron. "You son of a bitch," he rasped.

"You don't know the half of it. If you think you're cute with special effects, you should see how adorable I can become with lethal substances."

"What do you mean?"

"I'm a regular MacGyver."

"What's that supposed to mean?" LaLeche tried to straighten up, gasping to regain his breath.

"If anything should ever happen to Zanita, or me for that matter, I'll make sure that certain *plans* are set into motion. For instance, have you ever seen a man suffering from radiation poisoning? It can be a slow, painful death. First your hair falls out; then your teeth. You bleed—"

"You're bluffing."

"No, I'm good at solving problems. Do yourself a favor—don't become one for me."

"Shit."

LaLeche believed him. Tyber shoved him roughly aside, almost causing him to fall to the floor. He threw the door open. With a last look conveying his deadly sincerity, Tyber quietly closed the door behind him.

As soon as he cleared the walkway, Sean and his men began surrounding the house.

Tyber got into his truck, closed his eyes, and exhaled deeply. He had been bluffing. But like any good pirate captain, he knew when to face an enemy down. Even when he didn't have any cannons on board. Regardless of what happened, LaLeche would never bother them again.

* * *

Zanita was still sleeping when he crawled back into bed with her.

She immediately turned toward him, burrowing into his warmth. He enfolded her in his embrace, rubbing the top of her head with his chin.

"Where were you?" she mumbled.

"Miss me?" She nodded sleepily against his chest. "I got a phone call. How are you feeling, baby?"

"A little sore, but otherwise okay." A small shudder coursed through her body with the recent memories of La-Leche.

"Are you sure?" He massaged her back.

"Yes, really. It was horrible, but the horror is already receding thanks to your fine treatment, Doc." She smiled against his skin.

Tyber let out a pent-up breath of relief. She was going to be okay. "He's been arrested."

"Was it on the news?"

"No." He didn't elaborate and Zanita didn't ask. "Extortion. A couple of women identified him by his picture. Said he seduced them under the name of Marvin Broconol, took photos, then blackmailed them by threatening to show the pictures to their wealthy husbands. Since one woman is divorced and the other is a widow, they were both very eager to nail the s.o.b. Several others have come forward with various complaints. All felonies. He'll be gone a long time, I imagine."

"The important thing is that his days of duping people in need are over. It's such a pity, really. Healing practices can be so beneficial. All it takes is one rotten apple—"

"In this case, the one rotten apple shouldn't spoil the bunch. I agree with you; there are many decent, good people out there trying to effect a change for the better with new methods. But keeping an open mind cuts both ways."

"Now that this is over, I guess . . ." Zanita hated to say this, but she didn't quite know how Tyber felt about her moving in with him on a permanent basis. Now that she had admitted her love to him, there was no more deceiving herself.

She knew exactly where she wanted to be. Forever.

But how would Tyber feel about it? Even though he had confessed his love to her, he still was a very private person. He might prefer to maintain his privacy. She twirled the hairs on his chest, gathering courage. "I'll be moving back to my apartment."

"I don't think so." The Captain's tongue darted playfully in her ear. She shivered in response.

"No?"

"No."

Was he sure? "But Tyber—"

"I have a new case for us to investigate." He didn't add that he had searched high and low the past weeks for something, *anything* that would pique her interest so she would stay with him.

Zanita smiled to herself. "Really? What is it?" She snuggled into his broad chest.

"There's a man who lives right here in Massachusetts, on Martha's Vineyard, who claims his tavern is haunted."

"So, he's a nutcake. So what?"

"So . . . several *reputable* sources agree with him."

"Hmm . . ."

"So . . . you can't possibly leave." He bent his head to honor the hollow above her collarbone with very talented lips. Preoccupied, Zanita patted Tyber's head, her mind already on the story. Or so it seemed.

"Tyber?" She asked absently.

"Mmm?" He buried his head in her neck, running his hot mouth creatively up the side of her throat.

"Will you marry me?"

He paused for an instant, going stock still.

"Yes."

He resumed his meanderings about her neck. *As if he hadn't just made a momentous, turning point-in-his-life decision.*

Zanita clutched a handful of his thick hair, pulling his head up. "How come you answered so fast?"

Behind half-closed lids, those beautiful light-blue eyes twinkled, a spark of exaltation mingled with rising passion. A lazy smile inched across his handsome face, curving his cheek. His expression made her distinctly apprehensive.

Just before he lowered his head to hers, he replied in that uniquely roguish way of his, "Did I ever explain to you about the speed of light? No? Well, baby, it goes something like this. . . ."

It was the quintessential Tyber answer. Zanita was to learn that night, and for the rest of her adventurous life with Doc Evans, that everything is simply a matter of perspective.

Except love.

Love, Tyber maintains, is positively absolute.

And he should know.

After all, the man is a genius.

JAYNE·ANN KRENTZ

writing as Jayne Taylor

WHIRLWIND COURTSHIP

Chapter One

It was six o'clock in the morning when Phoebe Hampton finally managed to stumble into a clearing in the Oregon woods and spot the cabin. She had been picking her way steadily along the bank of the stream for two hours, growing hungrier with each step. The promising fragrance of a wood fire had been assailing her sensitive, if rather ordinary-looking nose for the past fifteen minutes. It had driven her to feats of somewhat reckless abandon, such as sliding down an outcropping of boulders instead of going around them and nearly tromping through a patch of poison oak before spotting it. The last had made her wonder how much of the stuff she had plowed into in the first panicked flight during the night. Well, it couldn't be helped. She vowed to wash her hands before touching her face, however.

The face she was trying to protect from an unpleasant rash was a reasonable frame for the nose. Phoebe had always thought a little sadly that her face was rather ordinary and not at all the type which caused men to turn around for a second look. Still, Richard seemed content with it. She had no notion of how a beautifully lashed set of blue-green eyes which regarded the world with a lively intelligence set off her features to the more discerning. This lack of perception on her part was attributable to the fact that the rounded frames of her glasses got in the way whenever Phoebe happened to be looking in a mirror. No one had ever been successful in talking Phoebe out of wearing the glasses, however. She felt they added an important professional touch to her business wardrobe.

Years from now—Phoebe told herself encouragingly as a huge black Labrador who had been sitting on the porch of the cabin gave a yelp and bounded forward—she would look back on this weekend as the most thrilling of her life. The thought was gratifying to the spirit of adventure and romance Phoebe usually tried to keep firmly under control, but the practical side of her nature found it highly unfortunate that real adventure was composed of such a high degree of discomfort and fear.

The Lab trotted eagerly up to her and Phoebe leaned down to stroke his sleek head with a feeling of relief. The cheerful attitude of the advance greeting party gave her hope for an equally friendly welcome from the people in the cabin. Surely the owners of such a happy dog must be decent people. She gave a last pat to her new ally and then glanced up as the cabin door opened.

The man who lounged against the frame of the door regarded her without any of the dog's enthusiasm. In fact, he looked downright disgusted, Phoebe thought in surprise. Of course, it stood to reason that a man encountering a woman emerging from the forest at this hour might be hoping for something more in the line of delicate, svelte blonds rather than a brunette with a definite tendency toward *roundness*. But before she could open her mouth to begin what would only be an incredible explanation, her rescuing hero spoke.

"What the hell do you think you're doing? You can just turn right around and walk back to your car!"

It was too much. Phoebe was scratched, exhausted, hungry, and had barely survived a terrifying experience. She might not look like Venus rising from the waves but she certainly deserved better than this! Deliberately she pushed a lock of heavy, jungle cat brown hair which curved around her shoulders back behind an ear and glared at the man.

"I realize I'm probably not your type and I can assure you, you're not what I had hoped for either! Still, I need help and as you're the only one around, I'm going to have to impose on you. My name is Phoebe Hampton and I have just spent a miserable night in this forest, trying to follow the stream. Do you think you could bring yourself to spare me a cup of coffee and something to eat?" This last request contained a wistful note which Phoebe instantly regretted. But she really was very hungry. And tired. The black Lab, at least, responded to her with a concerned tongue which leaped out to caress her hand. The man, on the other hand, did not seem in the least impressed.

"If you're hungry, I imagine it's your own damn fault. You should have thought to pack some food with you. Or didn't my charming aunt . . ." he broke off, leaving Phoebe wondering how his aunt had entered the conversation. "Where did you park your car?" he continued impatiently, moving a little further out on the porch and leaning forward to plant two strong, competent-looking hands against the railing. Doing so brought him fully into the sunlight and revealed the brilliant red of his hair and bushy brows. Ice blue eyes ran speculatively over her figure in blue jeans and plaid shirt and Phoebe abruptly wished she had stayed on that last diet. But she had gotten so tired of broiled grapefruit and poached eggs!

"I didn't drive," she explained politely, "I was driven. Somewhere up there." Phoebe waved a hand which indicated the vague distance behind her. "Oh, I had a car but it broke down last night on the highway. I was on my way to the coast, you see," she added helpfully. "I had rented the car for the weekend on one of those special rates the rental companies give and when it died, I was so furious that I got out and started walking. When these two creeps in a pickup came along and offered to help, I was stupid enough to think they were just a couple of nice farm boys . . .'' Phoebe blinked back tears of frustration and fury. How could she have been so dumb? ''They turned off the highway shortly after picking me up and . . . and just kept driving. It seemed like hours!'' She took a steadying breath. ''I was taken to a cabin and as the situation was deteriorating rapidly I thought I'd best take the first opportunity of getting myself free.'' Phoebe swallowed as a dark memory momentarily clouded her clear sea eyes. No doubt about it, she decided, real, genuine fear was not a pleasant aspect of adventuring.

She noticed the pure disbelief in the red-headed man's icy eyes. Damn! Why couldn't she have stumbled on someone with a more, well, heroic nature? A tall, dark, handsome soul who would have instantly detected the state she was in, taken one look into her eyes with his own dark, intense gaze, and known she was telling the truth? This man didn't appear to have a gallant bone in his body. For some reason, a part of her brain noted that the body in question wasn't too far off the proper heroic mold. True, he was only about five inches taller than Phoebe, but the lean, strong lines of his build weren't softened at all by spare flesh. The observation was somewhat forced on her due to the fact that the man was dressed only in close fitting, faded jeans. A bare chest covered with curling red hairs tapered into a flat, hard stomach which paired with narrow hips. The proportions were fine, she admitted to herself. A couple of inches more height, black hair and steel grey eyes, and he would have been perfect. Well, in her situation she would just have to be grateful for whatever she got. It was obvious she wasn't his idea of perfection, either! But things could have been worse. The main job now was to convince him she needed help.

''I'm sure your fellow conspirator, Aunt Flo, has already told you I don't have a telephone up here. The absence of phones and electricity is one of the main attractions of the place,'' the man told her ruthlessly. ''Which means, of course, there's no way to verify your story short of driving back down the mountain which I do not intend to do until Monday morning!''

"But this is only Saturday!" Phoebe observed, surprised by this latest twist. The police should be notified as soon as possible, she knew.

"Correct. I am suitably impressed by your powers of observation but the innocently astonished look is somewhat overdone. Aunt Flo should have briefed you more thoroughly. Now suppose you tell me the truth and then hike back out to where you parked your car? You can report the failure to my aunt and that will be the end of the matter. I'm feeling reasonably tolerant this time."

"Tolerant?" Phoebe inquired cautiously, trying to grasp just who he appeared to think she was. Or had she stumbled onto a madman?

"I'm afraid I lost my temper the last time my aunt tried her matchmaking techniques. The girl wound up in tears and Flo didn't speak to me for a month. Now, unless you want to bring things to the same conclusion this time, I suggest you leave at once. Jinx! Come here!" he called to the dog who had taken up residence at Phoebe's feet. The black Lab glanced at him soulfully and remained where he was.

"Thanks for the vote of confidence, friend!" Phoebe smiled down at the dog who thumped his tail in return. "You'd give me a cup of coffee, wouldn't you?"

"That dog usually displays more common sense!" The man shrugged one shoulder disgustedly and turned to go back inside the cabin, calling back to her, "The hell with it! Come on in and I'll give you a cup before I send you packing!" Muttering something about being too damn softhearted, he vanished into the dark interior.

Phoebe hesitated a moment, her nimble mind logging the harsh, arrogant planes of her host's face, the cool blue eyes, and the forbidding tone of his voice. Not a particularly warm welcome, all in all. She was going to have her work cut out for her, she decided, convincing him first not to force her back into the woods and second that she needed a ride down the mountain to the nearest police station or sheriff's office. But then, wasn't she accustomed to handling men and getting what she wanted from them? At least, she admonished herself sadly, she was usually successful in the business world. The same could not honestly be said about her private life. Well, she would view this as a difficult business arrangement and take it from there. Straightening tired shoulders, Phoebe hurried forward with the dog at her heels. For a cup of hot coffee she felt she could tolerate a few insults. She had to get a foot in the door somewhere.

She climbed the two shaky steps onto the porch and peered into the cabin doorway. There was only one room. Windows set in the wooden walls let in a certain amount of sunlight which, in turn, illuminated the wooden floor with its threadbare rug in front of a stone fireplace. An old Salvation Army relic of a chair was placed to take advantage of the hearth on which was stacked a hefty pile of kindling and logs. A cot with a sleeping bag rolled neatly at the end occupied a side wall and a small wood stove completed the furnishings except for a few odds and ends which Phoebe didn't have time to examine. Definitely a bachelor retreat, she thought, moving toward the stove where the redheaded man was pouring out the coffee she would, at that moment, cheerfully have fought for. A pan of water resting on a table caught her eye.

"Do you mind if I wash my hands first?" she inquired politely. Taking his brusque nod as an invitation to proceed she quickly scrubbed her hands and dried them on a nearby dish towel—which was none too clean, she noticed. Well, with any luck, a commodity which she had not been favored with lately, the handwashing would get rid of some of the poison oak toxins.

"Thank you," Phoebe murmured with great feeling, reaching out to wrap her fingers around the chipped mug being handed to her. Long lashes dipped behind the dusty lenses of her glasses as she closed her eyes to inhale the aroma appreciatively. When she glanced up again it was to find the man perched on the table, studying her with a mixture of curiosity and wariness. Standing so close to him she was suddenly very aware of the naked, nicely tanned chest. No, the muscles didn't ripple and bulge across his shoulders, but there was a sensation of wiry strength in him which she couldn't help comparing with Richard. He wasn't as tall as Richard, who towered over her in the best romantic tradition. And, of course, he didn't have Richard's marvelous black hair and silvery-grey eyes, but there was something about this man . . .

"It got rather cold last night. Good thing you knew enough not to asphyxiate yourself by running the car heater too much while you waited to make your grand entrance," her host said heartlessly. "Come on, you can drink the coffee out on the porch. There's a table and a couple of chairs out there." Pouring himself a cup, he led the way toward the door. Phoebe followed obediently, cradling the mug carefully and casting longing glances at the ice chest standing in the corner.

"I know this sounds picky but do you have any canned milk?" she asked after taking an experimental sip of the thick brew.

"There's some in the cupboard over the stove," he told her grudgingly. He went on out to the porch and sat down somewhere just beyond her range of vision. Phoebe thought quickly. If she moved fast enough . . .

"I'll get it and be right out!" she called, moving purposefully toward the ice chest.

Inside lay a wealth of temptation. A carton of eggs, a package of bacon, bread, and much more were nestled there. It was too much. Phoebe told herself she was not going to starve in the midst of plenty simply because she had been unlucky enough to find an ungallant, ungracious hero!

"Have you had breakfast yet?" she raised her voice to inquire, hunting through a small cupboard for a frying pan.

"No, I'll eat after you're on your way," he yelled back firmly.

"You're going to have a long wait, pal," Phoebe whispered as she set about the business of preparing breakfast with her usual casual efficiency. Jinx sat watching expectantly.

"What's going on in here?" a harsh voice demanded a few minutes later and Phoebe glanced up to see the man's sleek shoulders blocking off the light in the doorway. The smell of frying bacon drifted tantalizingly across the room and out of the corner of her eye she saw his nose twitch in response.

"I'm not accustomed to wood stoves, but you seem to have a healthy fire going in there," Phoebe motioned to the pot-bellied iron stove. "And it looks as if you've got more than enough food to see you through until Monday so I decided to help myself. Out of the goodness of my heart," she concluded sweetly, "I decided to cook enough for two."

"The hell you did! Now listen to me, woman . . ."

"Phoebe. Phoebe Hampton," she corrected him idly, turning bacon with a fork. "I didn't catch your name?"

"That's because you know damn well what it is!" he thundered, regarding the delicious smelling breakfast with a curious combination of hunger and frustration.

The way to a man's heart, Phoebe thought grimly. When you couldn't knock 'em over with seductive green eyes, blond hair, and a delicate, sexy figure, you resorted to the practical approach. Feeding men well always seemed to put them in a better mood, she had learned.

"The only thing I know about you at this point is that you've got a scheming aunt and you are blessed with a typical male ego," Phoebe informed him, sipping her coffee and eyeing the bacon with a critical eye. Any time now she should be able to pop the eggs into the frying pan.

"Is that right? And what's wrong with my ego?" he demanded. "Just because I'm onto my aunt's crazy schemes to compromise me with a woman, doesn't mean I've got an abnormally inflated ego!"

"I didn't say it was abnormally inflated. Merely that it was typical of the male of the species. They're all inflated. Ask any woman!" Phoebe smiled at him condescendingly and slid the eggs neatly into the pan. Before he could comment further she said blithely, "But tell me more about this compromising business. I'll admit it has a lovely, romantic ring to it, but it just doesn't happen in this day and age!''

"I didn't say I would consider myself compromised," he replied vengefully, "only that my Aunt Flo thinks somehow she can force me to the altar that way. My poor aunt lives in a different world part of the time, if you haven't already guessed."

"A world in which a man might still feel duty-bound to do the honorable thing?'' Phoebe grinned, poking gently at an egg.

"Exactly. Comes from reading too many of those historical romances!"

Phoebe winced, thinking of the shelf full of such romances she had at home.

"On her previous attempts, she's usually involved unsuspecting, helpless little types who might really be hurt. I'll have to admit you're outside the normal style!"

"Ah!" Phoebe announced with dawning comprehension as she flipped bread over on the griddle and soaked it in real butter. None of the low cholesterol stuff for this man, she noted. "I see. I was supposed to be a misty-eyed little femme fatale! Well, I've always wanted to be, at least for a weekend. But one of the hard facts of life is that you're stuck with the hard facts of life. I'm dreadfully sorry to be such a disappointment but when you get back to . . . " She glanced at him inquiringly, "Portland?" At his grudging nod she continued. "When you get back there, you'll probably find the next candidate waiting in line, fragile and blond. Where does your aunt dig them up, I wonder?"

"The last one was a daughter of one of her bridge partners! The one before that was the niece of one of the members of her garden club! Where the hell did she find you, anyway?" He sounded genuinely interested. She must be markedly different from the norm, Phoebe thought with an inner grimace.

"Perhaps she decided it was time to switch to a new style for you. Poor man! What your life must be like! Even in this day and age it would take a firm resolve to go around seducing the relatives of your aunt's best friends and then refusing to marry them! I mean, the daughter of a bridge partner!''

''I didn't seduce them!'' He snapped in a very irritated tone. ''The type of female my aunt sees fit to pester me with is not the type I care for!''

''I see,'' Phoebe nodded wisely. ''You don't like fragile blonds. Perhaps you prefer redheads? You like looking like a matched set of dolls when you go out?''

''Oh, I like fragile blonds,'' he shot back, a gleam entering the piercing blue eyes momentarily. ''It's just that I prefer them a bit older and wiser than what Aunt Flo usually locates! Someone more your age, for example!''

''One who won't go crying to Aunt Flo and her mother when the affair is over?''

''Exactly!''

''Let's eat,'' Phoebe instructed firmly, dishing out the meal and handing him a plate which he accepted with a look of surprise. Picking up some knives and forks she led the way out onto the porch with the same confident manner she would have handled a room full of upper management.

''How old are you, precisely?'' the annoying man asked as he followed her. ''Twenty-six? Twenty-seven?''

''Twenty-seven,'' she informed him aloofly, seating herself. ''Old enough, as you say, to know better than to think a man like you would marry me to make an honest woman out of me!''

''Ouch! I think my aunt has a better opinion of my honor than you do!'' he groaned with a hint of a smile as he lowered his lean frame onto the chair beside her and hoisted a fork.

''I'm starving!'' Phoebe noted fervently, munching a piece of toast with delicate greed. Privately she was thinking that her companion must be around thirty-four or thirty-five. And he looked as if he'd lived every year of that estimate! Small crinkles at the corners of the blue eyes and laugh lines around the hard shape of his mouth gave evidence that he could enjoy the world at the same time that he challenged it.

''You do look a little on the undernourished side,'' he remarked with what Phoebe felt to be unnecessary snideness.

"Used to the skinny types, hmmm?" she smiled back sunnily, digging into her food with a passion engendered as much by a strange sense of hurt as by hunger. If he were a gentleman he would not have called attention to her figure. Before he could get in another such comment she went on quickly "Look, I realize you don't believe me but I truly don't know your name and it's difficult cooking breakfast for a man under such circumstances. Could you humor me?"

"I'm Harlan Garand, as if you weren't very well aware," he said, becoming a trifle more accommodating as he ate. It was understandable that a man might be a bit testy before breakfast, Phoebe decided. She had been right to feed him.

"Thank you. And what do you do for a living? I mean, when you're not running from teenage beauty queens?"

"I'm sure my aunt has filled you in on all the details!" he said unhelpfully.

Phoebe tried again. "Well, actually we were rather in a hurry and there were some vague areas . . ."

"What do you imagine I do?" he asked sarcastically. The mouth full of egg blunted the tone somewhat, however, and the blue eyes regarded her with a certain curiosity as if wondering how far she was prepared to carry the story.

Phoebe leaned back in her chair and studied him. It was necessary to keep some sort of conversation going, she realized. If she talked long enough she might be able to convince him of her plight. He really ought to put on a shirt, she thought absently. So much masculine flesh on display at this hour was disconcerting. However, it did give her a starting point. Feeling as if she deserved a spot of revenge for his comment on her own figure, she coolly allowed her gaze to travel the lean hard length of him.

"Perhaps you're an artist? One of those terribly intense creatures who ignore food while they're working?" Smiling benignly at his startled expression she continued enthusiastically. "Yes, a lean, hungry, artistic type whose dear aunt is worrying herself sick, wondering what will become of you if she doesn't find you a nice girl to settle down with. After all, you aren't getting any younger . . ." She broke off deliberately to survey the touches of grey barely noticeable at his temples and then went on. "Or maybe you're an airport control tower operator who sits hunched over a radar screen all day long, drinking tons of coffee, and living on tension and nerves. Then again you might be a tennis bum; traveling the world with the beautiful people and living on junk food. Yes, that might be it. Wasting your life away until your poor aunt has decided to make a last ditch effort to force you into a more conventional life style before you burn yourself out . . ."

"I do not," Harlan Garand announced wrathfully, "play tennis! Nor do I work in a control tower and I have never painted a stroke in my life since kindergarten! I get the point. It's obvious you find my masculine physique somewhat on the thin side but don't think that means I'm susceptible to a mothering approach! As it happens, I have a perfectly healthy appetite and I am quite capable of cooking for myself, as Aunt Flo is well aware. If her latest tactic is to fix me up with a little domestic type, she's way off base!"

He paused, gathering a deep, indignant breath. "Furthermore, it might interest you to know I am not considered unattractive by all members of the opposite sex."

Phoebe smiled kindly, sensing herself on safe territory suddenly. True, his tone of voice was rather intimidating, but she had pursued enough business strategies in high tension situations to know that the eyes were where the truth resided. And there was a definite gleam now in that blue gaze, even though the brows above it were bunched ferociously.

"Perhaps some of the scrawnier members of the female community might find you appealing, but . . ." Phoebe moved one hand in a languid, dismissing gesture as she let her words trail off meaningfully.

For an instant she wasn't altogether certain she had judged her man correctly. Just for a second she wondered if she had misread that flicker in the icy eyes and then Harlan gave a crack of appreciative laughter. It was, Phoebe decided, a pleasant sound and she grinned in response.

"All right," he finally chuckled. "We're even! Do you always get revenge?"

"You know what they say," Phoebe grinned, "don't get mad; get even!" She paused and then asked interestedly, "Tell me, why is your aunt so determined to marry you off?"

Harlan shrugged. "Didn't she tell you her fears about me never marrying and providing her with lots of grandchildren to spoil?" When Phoebe shook her head, he continued. "Well, after my mother died, Aunt Flo cared for me. She never married and I played a very important role in her life, I guess—the family she never had. As a result she's every bit as concerned about my future as a real mother would be. Perhaps more so."

"You do return her affection, don't you?"

"I love Aunt Flo dearly. But she's not going to dictate my love life!"

Phoebe nodded understandingly. "I know exactly how you feel!"

"You do?" This was said with a fair degree of skepticism.

Phoebe nodded vigorously. "Absolutely. I have a brother who went so far as to actually try and buy me a husband!"

Harlan stared. "What happened?" He appeared fascinated in spite of himself.

"Well, you have to understand that after our parents died, Steven and I naturally grew very close. He's a real brain, you know. Invents things. The royalties started coming in while he was in his early twenties. He's well into his second million, as far as I know. At any rate, he thought I should have the kind of man I've always dreamed of. Tall, dark and handsome. Steve also thought he should be from a good family, if you know what I mean. We had been born into ye olde middle class and he decided I should practice a little upward mobility."

Phoebe moved her hands expressively. "Well, he picked out a good candidate from among his friends on the golf course, brought him home, and I promptly fell head over heels in love.

I was twenty-five at the time,'' she added, wanting to explain her poor judgment.

"Go on," Harlan prompted. She couldn't tell whether or not he believed a word of what she was saying, but at least he didn't stop the conversation.

"That's about it. I had a whirlwind courtship and the next thing I knew found myself engaged. Unfortunately, three weeks before the wedding I discovered the real reason my tall, dark, and handsome fiance had done such an enthusiastic job of sweeping me off my feet!'' Phoebe's blue-green eyes clouded. "Steve had paid off his family's debts and gotten them back on their feet."

"A touching story," Harlan said mockingly.

"Better than the one you told me!" she pointed out spiritedly.

"Mine has the virtue of being true!"

"So is mine!"

"It's strange. With eyes like yours, I would have thought you would have had a very difficult time lying successfully," Harlan commented.

Abruptly Phoebe's lower lip threatened to tremble. She was so tired and this man was so obstinate. Unconsciously she rubbed the bridge of her nose in a little gesture of fatigue, closing her eyes to try to think of how best to approach him.

"Please, couldn't you bring yourself to at least let me stay here with you if you won't drive me down the mountain? I really don't have a car parked conveniently down the road. I wouldn't even know how to find the main highway from here! And it would be a very long walk out of these woods, even if I followed the trail, which I'm afraid to do. They might be looking for me."

"Who might be looking for you?" he pounced, obviously hoping to trap her.

"Those two punks who grabbed me yesterday," she said wearily. "I feel safe here with you and, although I think I'd survive another night on this mountain, I don't like the prospect at all!" It was true, she thought dimly, she did feel safe here. In spite of his ungentlemanly behavior there was a compelling aura of strength around this man. The added sense of protection provided by his large dog was not lost on Phoebe either. No, if he wouldn't drive her to the police, she had to make him let her stay until he was ready to leave on Monday morning. She couldn't face the thought of making her way down to civilization alone!

"You're going to stick by that crazy tale?" Harlan demanded irritably.

"I haven't got a better one and I'm too exhausted to think one up at the moment," Phoebe smiled apologetically.

He sighed. "I meant what I said, you know. I'm not leaving until the weekend is over." A frown knitted the heavy brows.

"I know. I can wait. Probably no one's even missed me yet. Ferd will start getting upset this evening. I told him I intended to be back Saturday night. And I told Richard I would see him Sunday night so he's not likely to come around until then. He won't really start to worry until Monday morning. I didn't have any other plans involving friends this weekend so no one's going to wonder about me. It's a shame to let the trail of those two punks get so cold, though. But maybe the police won't believe my story, either," she added, struck by the thought. Surely what the men in the truck had done constituted kidnapping and there would have been a rape charge involved if she hadn't freed herself when she did, but how would she ever prove it?

"It's not likely they'll listen to your tale if I'm the one who brings you back to Portland on Monday morning," Harlan agreed drily. "Who's Ferd?"

"An evil-tempered budgerigar who shares my apartment with me. Parakeet to you," Phoebe smiled wanly. "I got him on sale."

"Ferd the Bird?" A hint of a smile touched the hard mouth for an instant.

Phoebe nodded, thinking of how upset Ferd was going to be at having been left alone for the entire weekend. Luckily she had filled his seed and water dishes Friday morning. He wouldn't starve to death.

"And Richard?" Harlan pushed almost gently.

"You'll let me stay?" Phoebe asked eagerly, sensing that he was weakening.

"I didn't say that," he corrected quickly. "I intended to spend the weekend alone, without any females in the neighborhood. All I wanted to do was fish and maybe hike a bit. You're spoiling everything with this stupid trick. What did you do? Get someone to drop you off down at the main road and then hike in here so you would have the excuse of not having a car to take yourself back to Portland? And who is Richard, anyway?"

Phoebe sighed. "Richard is Richard Elton Chambers III. Sometimes known as merely the Third to me and my off-base sense of humor. You're the only one who knows that, by the way. I've always been careful to refer to him as Richard. Never Dick, of course," she added absently.

"Of course." Harlan nodded seriously and then glanced down at the dishes on the table in front of him. But not before Phoebe had seen the spark of humor moving deep in the blue eyes. "Are you going to offer to repay breakfast by washing the dishes?" he inquired, glancing up again.

"Some people would consider that having cooked it was sufficient payment," Phoebe noted.

"I'm feeling a little put upon at the moment," he retorted. "I think you ought to offer to wash them, too."

"Ah, well. No such thing as a free lunch, I suppose," Phoebe replied with what she privately considered a rather good-natured tone of voice. She was so tired! "Down at the stream, I take it?" she asked, getting painfully to her feet and stacking the plates and mugs.

Harlan nodded, watching her curiously, a ghost of a smile touching the corners of his firm mouth. "Sorry. No running water, either. Didn't my aunt brief you?" For some reason he followed her down to the bank, propping himself against a rock to watch the process. There was a hint of approval in his eyes when she rinsed the dishes away from the flowing water but he said nothing.

"Why won't Richard the Third be checking up on you until Sunday night?" Harlan suddenly asked as Phoebe dried her water-numbed fingers on the towel. She looked at him, surprised by the reintroduction of Richard as a topic of conversation.

"Sunday night I'm supposed to have thought the whole matter over and perhaps changed my mind." Phoebe arranged herself as comfortably as possible against a sun-warmed boulder and leaned her head back tiredly. A slight rasping sound made her lift a hand to her thick hair only to find a leaf embedded in it. Hateful man! She thought grimly. He could have mentioned the fact earlier!

"Forgive me for sounding somewhat dense. But what exactly is Richard hoping to hear from you?"

"I told him I'd let him know whether or not I'd changed my mind about not marrying him," Phoebe explained, closing her eyes. Richard seemed very far away now, both geographically and in her thoughts. Last night had given her several hours in which to fulfill her promise and think about her decision. After the initial fear of being found by her kidnappers had faded, there hadn't been much else to think about except where to place her feet as she made her way downhill following the stream. She hadn't dared try and find the main road. That would have made it too easy for her captors. So, she had spent the long difficult hours thinking about Richard.

"Well? Did you?" Harlan asked. Then he spoiled the human interest he was displaying by adding, "Or did you decide to wait and see how you made out with me, first?"

"Nope." Phoebe tried to summon up a little spirit. "I made up my mind before I even found your cabin! I'm going to give Richard the same answer that I gave him earlier. Of course, I will explain that I'm suitably aware of the honor he is offering and go on to say how I hope we can remain friends but that I just don't think we'd be very happy together."

"What will Richard say?" Harlan asked as if he couldn't resist.

Phoebe opened one eye to see him watching her intently. "He'll point out that I'm not getting any younger, that he can give me a very fashionable life-style, that he's really very fond of me . . ."

"Merely fond?"

"You don't know Richard," Phoebe told him wisely, closing her eye again. "A blazing love is not quite his style. Such a pity, too. He certainly looks the part."

"What part?"

"You know, the tall, dark, handsome, masterful type. The kind women always break their hearts over. Or would, if the type really existed outside of romantic novels." Phoebe wriggled a bit, settling herself more comfortably against the sun-warmed boulder. "But I imagine it's not altogether his fault. Richard was born with a position to uphold, you know."

"No, I didn't know. What position?" Humor was edging Harlan's voice again and Phoebe had the impression she was beginning to serve as a source of amusement for him. Well, it was one way of paying her way.

"The position of being the Third, naturally," she said clearly as if to a not-very-bright nine-year-old. "Haven't you ever met any fine, upstanding types who come from fine, upstanding families with just the proper amount of fine, upstanding money?" Phoebe frowned questioningly, opening her eyes briefly to peer at him through the lenses of her glasses.

"You look quite fierce when you do that," Harlan commented apropos of nothing as far as she could tell.

"Do what?" she asked blankly, frowning still more.

"Frown like that behind those glasses."

"Oh." She shut her eyes again. So tired! And her muscles ached.

"To get back to your question," Harlan's voice went on smoothly. "Yes, I have met a few people such as you describe . . ." There was a distinct pause. "The name Chambers is beginning to ring a distant bell." There was another pause

290

but Phoebe was too worn out to open her eyes to see his expression. "Are you trying to tell me you've decided you don't want the type of marriage Chambers is offering?"

"I'm one of those idiotic women who read too many romantic novels. Rather like your aunt, I guess," Phoebe explained, feeling herself succumbing rapidly to sleep. "We like to think that somewhere there is a tall, good-looking, wonderfully domineering man waiting to sweep us off our feet. Some women don't compromise. Your aunt may have been one. Personally, I'm giving myself three more years to find him. If he hasn't shown up by the time I'm thirty, I'll start looking at the Richard the Thirds of this world."

It was only as she felt herself going off completely that a stray thought flashed across her exhausted brain. She never had found out what Harlan Garand did for a living. She heard him move, heard him mutter something about how worn out she looked, and then she was asleep.

Chapter Two

When Phoebe awoke some time later it was to the combined prodding of a damp, inquisitive nose and a bracingly masculine voice. She was pleased with the level of alertness that allowed her to distinguish the fact that the nose and the voice each had different owners.

"Lunchtime. Going to sleep all day?" said the voice, obviously not intending to let her have the luxury of going back to sleep, even if she answered the question in the affirmative.

Phoebe opened her eyes, groped automatically for her glasses, and sat up as she pushed the frames in place. Funny, she didn't remember removing them but she must have because they were conveniently at hand beside her. The dog, who owned the wet nose, whined happily and licked her cheek affectionately. Somebody is glad to have me here, Phoebe thought, feeling pleased. She stroked the black fur and looked up at Harland Garand, wondering if he'd made up his mind about letting her stay the weekend.

"Are you waiting lunch for me?" she asked naively, blinking in the light of a sun which had reached its zenith and wondering if she dared ask the other, more crucial question.

"Not exactly," he explained kindly, stretching down a hand to help her rise. The other hand held fishing tackle and a basket. "I'm waiting for you to fix my lunch."

"I see." She peered toward the basket. "Fresh fish for me to fry?"

"Don't get sassy."

"That means you didn't have any luck." Phoebe smiled sympathetically.

"Right. So you're going to have to throw something together out of the ice chest. I wasn't in the proper frame of mind for good fishing," he added by way of excuse. "I have reached a decision, however. I can't figure out a way to make sure you get safely back to Portland if you really haven't got a car—not without ruining my entire weekend by driving you back. So you can stay. But if you're going to enjoy the accommodations, you can damn well pay the tab!"

Relief washed over Phoebe, reflecting itself in her blue-green eyes. His own narrowed in response. He was going to let her stay, she thought exultantly. This notion was immediately followed by a small cautionary voice.

"You mean I'll pay my way by doing the cooking and the dishwashing?" she hazarded, wanting to make certain they each understood the other.

"Are you volunteering any other services?" he countered, cocking one red brow.

"Not if it means digging a new pit for the outhouse!" she grinned.

"How about if it means warming my sleeping bag?" he asked interestedly, blue eyes glinting in the clear sunlight.

Phoebe flushed but pulled herself together quickly. He was only teasing her, of course. She manufactured a sigh of mock regret and fixed him with her most mournful expression.

"Isn't it a pity I'm not your type? Don't fret, though, I really am a pretty good cook!"

"A man alone in the wilderness can make certain adjustments," he pointed out. "It's true, I normally prefer the willowy blond types, but it gets awfully chilly around here when the sun goes down. You look as if you might be nice and . . . cuddly.'' Phoebe glimpsed the laughter in his eyes and refused to be intimidated. Yes, she could manage this man. He wasn't any different from most males. And she sensed no viciousness in him. She would be in no more danger of sharing his bed than she wished to be!

''I'm refusing for your own good, you know,'' she confided. ''Think of how you'll be able to face your aunt with a clear conscience knowing you didn't actually seduce me. Besides, think of me! Do I deserve to be ravished, only to be abandoned, a shattered husk of a woman, after we return to Portland and you go back to willowy blonds?'' Phoebe was struggling to contain her laughter and failing badly. ''I couldn't bear to have my heart so cruelly broken!'' She turned and started back toward the cabin, still chuckling. Jinx danced happily at her heels.

''You're absolutely right. I wouldn't want you to suffer from a broken heart caused by me, but I am considering the satisfaction of seeing you suffer from a well-tanned rear end!'' Harlan announced, striding up the steps beside her and holding open the door of the cabin with unconscious courtesy. At least Phoebe assumed it was unconscious. After all, it wasn't as if she were a welcomed guest! She grinned back at him, assessing his lean build and the height which wasn't so much greater than her own. What was he? Five-foot-ten or so? She stood five-foot-five inches herself.

''You'd have to catch me first, and even then I think the battle would be fairly equal! Some of this, er, roundness of mine is muscle, you know!'' she threatened lightly.

His blue eyes glinted again. ''Better keep in mind that you're still here only because I can't figure out a way to get rid of you! I expect a little more in the way of groveling appreciation.''

''I'll remember,'' Phoebe promised, running a hand through her tangled hair and watching as another leaf fell from it. ''I haven't had much experience groveling, you understand, though.''

"I'll be happy to instruct you," Harlan announced, taking a menacing step forward, eyes alight with devilment.

"Perhaps after lunch?'' she suggested, stepping backward quickly and holding out a hand placatingly. They might not be each other's preferred romantic types, she knew, but it was still better to keep things on a superficial, bantering level. Just to be on the safe side, physical contact should be avoided, Phoebe told herself, assessing the situation with all the skill she normally applied to managing her department at the large timber firm where she worked. She wasn't altogether certain about why he had changed his mind about letting her stay so quickly. She had been prepared for more discussion on the issue, but now that she'd won a partial victory, she didn't intend to lose control of the situation. Perhaps after lunch she might even reintroduce the idea of him driving her back to Portland. After all, if Harlan had given up the initial fight against letting her stay so readily . . .

"You think a bit of food will tame the savage beast again?'' he inquired.

"I thought it might be worth a try. I'm really not yet in my best fighting form.''

"I noticed you must have had a hard time of it walking in from the main road this morning. Why didn't you stick to the trail? You appear to have taken the scenic route!''

"I've told you, I didn't come from the main road. I followed the stream and there wasn't any trail!'' Phoebe responded briefly, turning away to sort through items in the ice chest. When she moved to the small table with her hands full of sandwich makings she noticed he had placed his fishing tackle neatly against the wall and was rummaging around in his overnight bag. An instant later he pulled out a shabby looking work shirt and slipped it on.

"It's going to be interesting to see if you stick by your kidnap story all weekend,'' he remarked, buttoning the shirt.

"Is that why you decided to let me stay? To see if you

could browbeat the truth out of me?'' Phoebe asked sweetly, slicing tomatoes.

"Well, I have to admit this is definitely a new approach from Aunt Flo. If she wanted to whet my curiosity, she's done it this time. But, to be honest, the main factor in my decision was the fact that you're old enough to know better than to get involved in a situation like this. People might be able to make life difficult for me if I drove back to town Monday morning with a child just out of her teens . . .''

"But they'll just look at me and say I should have had more sense, right?''

"Right!'' He sauntered over to the frayed arm of the old chair in front of the fireplace and settled down on it, watching as she prepared the sandwiches. "And in the meantime, it might not be so unhandy to have a cook and housekeeper around the place. I mean, it's not as if you're a guest I'll have to entertain.''

"I'm glad you're beginning to look on the positive side,'' Phoebe muttered drily. "Do you want mustard on your sandwich?''

"Would I have packed mustard if I didn't like it?'' he asked reasonably.

"Excellent point,'' she chuckled, spreading mustard liberally on both sandwiches. A more in-depth search of the ice chest produced a couple of apples and some cheese. "Good thing you packed a lot of food,'' she commented, putting the small repast together attractively on a platter and hoisting the whole thing expertly on one palm. Summers spent working as a waitress during her college years still paid occasional dividends, she reflected.

"It's your responsibility to ration the food through Monday morning,'' Harlan informed her, rising lazily to his feet. "Running out would really put me in a bad frame of mind.''

"I trust I don't have to make it go three ways?'' Phoebe asked, glancing at the tail-wagging Labrador who had levered himself to his feet to follow them out onto the porch.

"Jinx's food is in a sack in the closet,'' Harlan told her

helpfully, sitting down at the small table and reaching greedily for one of the handfilling sandwiches.

Phoebe didn't reply but settled back in her chair to enjoy the meal. It was so peaceful here within sight of the stream. Hard to believe that only last night she had been so frightened and cold and hungry. Idly she slipped a piece of cheese to Jinx who had settled himself near her under the table. Would the two so-called hunters be out looking for her? They had started drinking shortly after picking her up. Perhaps they had sobered enough by this morning to decide the safest thing to do would be to hightail it out of the area? Phoebe tried to put herself in their place. A couple of guys out for a weekend in the woods, complete with rifles and beer, had spotted a woman alone and decided to have some "fun." But their victim had escaped and by now they must realize there was a chance she could provide enough descriptive evidence to help the police apprehend them if she chose to. True, many potential rape victims would not want to get involved with the law, but they couldn't know for certain how Phoebe would react. One of them, at least, would be harboring a grudge. Phoebe had thrown a pan full of boiling water in his face before making her escape. She shuddered involuntarily. She could still hear his outraged scream of pain.

"What are you thinking?" Harlan's voice broke into her thoughts, sounding genuinely curious. Phoebe swung her intelligent gaze to meet his.

"About last night."

"You don't look too pleased. Not working out as planned, huh? I imagine it's because this is one of those schemes which looks a good deal better in the evening than it does in the cold light of day?" His lofty tones were laced with mock sympathy.

"Something like that," Phoebe agreed uninterestedly, too relaxed at the moment to work up any antagonism. That nap this morning had been precisely what she needed. How far had she walked last night? It had seemed safer to keep moving and she had allowed herself only one short rest period a couple of hours before dawn. But it had been so cold, rest had been impossible and after a short time she had pushed herself to her feet, knowing she had to get down the mountain. She wondered where she had read that advice about following a stream to find one's way off a mountain. Probably in one of the romantic adventures she read in such quantities. The thought made her smile slightly. They were good for something, after all, even if they did tend to fill one's fantasies with images of impossibly tall, masterful men who never seemed to exist in real life. But then, in all fairness, the fiery, spirited heroines probably didn't exist, either!

"Don't worry too much about it," Harlan said with sudden, surprising gentleness. It took Phoebe a moment to realize he was referring to the scheme he felt had been perpetrated on him. "I know how persuasive my aunt can be and I know how her mind works." He smiled at her. "I'm sure she made the whole thing sound quite reasonable. You seem like a sensible sort of woman, though. I'm rather amazed you let her talk you into it!"

Phoebe couldn't help herself. She burst out laughing, flinging up one hand as if to ward off his words. "Please don't talk to me about being sensible! It goes along with having wholesome looks and a secure job! I'm trying to enjoy the weekend!"

"I think you get a fair share of enjoyment out of life," Harlan noted, munching his apple and eyeing her thoughtfully. "You look like a basically happy sort of person. Is the Third a happy person, too?"

They were back to Richard again. Why was Harlan so interested?

"Yes, in his own way, I think he is," Phoebe answered quietly. "It's just that his way could never be mine. I know it's probably foolish of me, but I want more out of a romance than he can give me. And he needs a different sort of wife too."

"He's dull?"

"Terribly," she sighed.

"Why did you let matters get to the point where he was

asking you to marry him?'' Harlan asked, sounding disapproving.

Phoebe glanced at him quickly, wondering if he deserved an answer. Harlan Garand certainly had no right to judge her actions! Still, it was a point she had pondered herself.

''A good question,'' she told him at last. ''I'm not sure how things got as far as they did. I expect it was because it was a comfortable situation at first. I was new in town and Richard makes a very pleasant escort, except that he hasn't got much of a sense of humor. But there I go, being picky.''

''That's right. You forget the man has a position,'' Harlan admonished, the laughter dancing briefly in his blue eyes.

''True. Add to that the fact that I read far too many romance novels and it's plain to see the affair was doomed from the beginning,'' Phoebe smiled self-deprecatingly.

''So when my aunt and your mother proposed last night's little plan, it sounded rather exciting?'' Harlan suggested understandingly.

Phoebe laughed and shook her head ruefully. ''No fair trying to trap me! I'm having a hard enough time as it is keeping my version of events straight!''

''Keeps the conversation from dragging,'' Harlan pointed out rather more good-naturedly than Phoebe would have expected in the circumstances. ''What do you think Richard the Third will say when I deliver you on Monday morning?''

Phoebe shrugged unconcernedly. ''He hasn't got the right to say anything. I've already told him we're through . . .'' A sudden thought struck Phoebe's romantic side at that moment, however. ''But it would be interesting to know what he would say if he realized I'd spent the weekend with another man . . .'' Her voice trailed off distantly as she tried to conjure up a picture of Richard jealous.

''I know what I'd do if I were him,'' Harlan said with unexpected, soft menace.

''What?'' she asked curiously, fixing him with a direct, inquisitive look.

''If I considered you my property I would probably half kill the other man and make sure you were made fully aware of my feelings!'' The words were spoken so softly and with so much certainty that Phoebe started. ''You'd never stray again,'' he promised, blue eyes holding hers in a steel mesh.

''Good grief! You are a violent type, aren't you? I can assure you, the Third would never resort to such activity, though. It wouldn't be fitting for someone in his position, you see. A jealous rage would mean a *scene*. Richard doesn't get involved in *scenes*!'' Phoebe gave a little gurgle of laughter at the thought. ''Besides, I'm just not the type of woman men get that worked up over!'' she concluded ruefully.

''You're supposed to be spending this weekend rethinking his offer of marriage, Phoebe. If Chambers is any kind of man, you're playing with fire,'' Harlan warned her harshly and then added on a rough note, ''Do you sleep with him?''

''No!'' Phoebe was too flabbergasted at the unexpected question to give it the setdown it merited. The man certainly had an unholy nerve prying into her private life like this! Just because he was willing to tolerate her presence for a couple of days didn't mean there weren't limits! Belatedly, but with a strong feeling of righteous anger she told him, ''It's none of your business, but the relationship never progressed quite that far!''

''Then maybe he won't come after me with a gun,'' Harlan remarked, seeming to relax.

Phoebe stared. ''You never had any need to worry,'' she informed him tightly, unable to conceive that Harlan Garand had seriously begun to fear Richard Elton Chambers III.

''I don't think you know that much about men,'' he replied coolly.

''Perhaps not that much about your kind of man,'' she retorted scathingly. ''Is that how they settle things where you come from?''

Harlan grinned. A sharklike grin. ''I only know how to handle things in a similar situation. If I'd bedded you and asked you to marry me, I'd definitely consider you private property until matters between us were well and truly over. Perhaps longer! Certainly as long as you were 'rethinking' a proposal of marriage from me! I wouldn't tolerate lightly an incident like this weekend!''

Phoebe fought to control the breathless feeling which was building in her chest and cast about desperately for a way to bring the conversation back under her command. In a distant corner of her mind a tiny voice wondered what life would have been like if Richard had taken such an approach to women. But, then, if he had, she wouldn't have been one of the women he would have approached! Men like that preferred spirited, sensuous little blonds or redheads. Perhaps with alluring green eyes . . .

''But what if, like the Third, you had only asked me to marry you and hadn't quite got around to making love to me?'' she managed to counter, wondering why in the world she was asking such an incredibly provocative question! It wasn't like her at all!

''I can't see myself conducting such a restrained courtship.'' Harlan smiled more pleasantly now. Obviously his own imagination was at work, Phoebe thought grimly. Visions of a petite blond were apparently dancing in his brain. ''If I were in love, I would be making every effort to take full advantage of the situation!''

Phoebe took a deep, steadying breath. ''Well, all I can say is, you and Richard are two entirely different types of men and I may have been hasty in my initial decision to tell him I wouldn't marry him! He's beginning to seem quite civilized!''

''And dull,'' Harlan reminded her.

''And dull,'' Phoebe agreed with resignation. ''Still, a woman should consider the positive side of the matter, as Richard has not been at a loss to point out. I'm not likely at this advanced age to encounter a man who will become more impassioned about me and Richard *is* fond of me. If I could excite him to a slightly higher degree of feeling . . . you've given me an idea.'' Phoebe drifted into silence, soft eyes focusing somewhere in the middle distance while she considered the situation.

"What's the idea?" Harlan demanded with a foreboding expression. The red brows laced together threateningly.

"Maybe I should try inciting a bit of jealousy in Richard. If you're right and even a mild-tempered man would become upset over an escapade like this weekend . . . perhaps there are hidden depths to his nature that I'm not yet aware of although I strongly doubt it . . ."

"Phoebe, I don't like the way your mind is working at the moment. If you're seriously interested in the man, which doesn't appear likely from what you've said, I suggest you go down on your hands and knees and beg his forgiveness for the mess you've gotten yourself into! The last thing you should be worrying about is making him jealous! Why do women always want to play that stupid game? If you want him, go back to Portland, tell him you got involved in this crazy scheme solely to make him jealous, that nothing really happened between you and the other man, and you're desperately sorry . . ." Harlan bit off the end of the sentence, apparently having trouble picturing Phoebe in such a dramatic role. She didn't blame him; it was a bit hard to imagine herself on her knees in front of Richard. "Maybe, just maybe, he'll let you off lightly!" Harlan concluded.

"Would you in his spot?" Phoebe asked shrewdly, the rational, practical side of her nature wondering why in the world she was being driven to continue this strange conversation with a man she had known less than a day!

"I might trust you if I loved you and believed that nothing had happened, but I sure as hell wouldn't let you off very lightly. I'd take into consideration the fact that you'd done it on a foolish whim to make me jealous and proceed to give you a demonstration of what jealousy really is in a man! I'd want to make the point quite clear, you see, so you wouldn't be tempted to try it again!" Harlan quirked an eyebrow and met Phoebe's fascinated gaze with a level one of his own.

"Do you have a serious girlfriend?" she demanded breathlessly, sea eyes shining behind the lenses of her glasses as she contemplated him.

"I beg your pardon?" Harlan appeared a trifle nonplussed at the switch in topics.

"Do you have a girlfriend? I mean, one you really care about?" she persisted.

"There is no one floating around at the moment to whom I plan to propose marriage, which is what I think you have in mind," he told her dryly, eyes resting on her in a puzzled fashion. "Why?"

"Because you talk exactly like one of those marvelously domineering heroes in a romantic novel—the kind your aunt and I read. And I simply wondered if there was a woman in your life who was the recipient of all that masculine possessiveness and masterfulness," Phoebe explained impatiently, so well acquainted with the characteristics of such heroes that she forgot they might be unknown to her host.

"Are you planning to apply for the position?" he inquired politely, the blue gaze mirroring a combination of masculine confusion, humor, and a spark of indignation. He probably didn't appreciate the notion that he sounded like some character out of a novel, Phoebe decided with an inner grin.

"Good heavens, no!" she assured him honestly. "I'm well aware that neither of us is the other's ideal mate! But even if I were to find your characteristics in a tall, powerful type who could literally sweep me off my feet, I'd probably chicken out. All I'm asking is for someone whose temperament falls somewhere between Richard and yourself. A man with enough passion to be a bit possessive, but definitely not someone of whom I would have to be afraid. That would take all the fun out of the thing," she explained helpfully.

"I see. You think that any woman of mine would go in fear of me?" Harlan asked, obviously making a valiant effort to work through her obscure thinking.

"A woman with my nature and the physical characteristics of a petite blond—if that's not a contradiction in terms— would." Phoebe laughed. "You certainly do appear to have a violent streak in you that would require a brave and spirited woman to handle."

"You don't consider yourself brave and spirited?" Harlan asked deliberately.

Phoebe smiled, her soft eyes brimming with humor. She shook her head in a negative gesture. "Oh, no. Not in the least. At my size and age and in my work bravery and spirit aren't the qualities a woman cultivates, even if she thought she had the rudiments of them!"

"I see. What qualities do you cultivate?" Harlan asked, looking intrigued.

"Practicality," Phoebe told him firmly. "Efficiency, a cost-effective approach to business matters, and practicality. Also cooking."

"How does the cooking fit in with those other fine qualities?" Harlan demanded, grinning.

"Cooking is what I hope to use to capture my man when I finally do meet him," she informed him wisely and deemed it time to terminate this incredible conversation. "Would you mind if I took a bath?" she asked abruptly, rising to her feet and collecting the remains of lunch.

"You do have a way of changing the subject," Harlan remarked, not bothering to assist her. Instead he stretched his legs out in front of him and fondled Jinx's ears with absent affection.

"Comes from years of practice ending lengthy business meetings," she told him, moving toward the door to the cabin. "What about the bath?"

"Well, you can use the stream. It's warmed up a bit now. Still going to be cold, though. There's some soap on the small table beside the cot. Be sure to rinse off away from the water, though!"

"Spoken like a true, environmentally conscious Oregonian," Phoebe tossed back over her shoulder.

"You ex-Californians are just jealous," Harlan chuckled.

"How did you know I'm from California?" she called back, hunting for the soap near the cot.

"We Oregonians can spot 'em a mile away."

The afternoon passed very comfortably or at least, Phoebe thought, it became comfortable when she had finally warmed her body back to a normal temperature after bathing in the chilled mountain stream. Harlan returned to his fishing, well above the spot Phoebe had chosen for bathing. Locating a worn paperback copy of a science fiction thriller, Phoebe settled down beside Jinx who was reclining near Harlan in the classic pose of the contented dog. There was little conversation between the three but a sense of companionship crept quietly into the atmosphere and lingered. Phoebe glanced up at one point to watch Harlan land the first fish of the day and realized with a start that she hadn't even thought about the unfortunate events of the preceding night for at least an hour.

"Congratulations!" she called obligingly when Harlan held the flapping fish for approval. "Who's going to clean it?"

"I'm including that among the household chores," he informed her, a warning gleam lighting the blue gaze. He placed his catch carefully into the basket. "You remember. The ones you're doing as a means of paying for the weekend!"

"The last fish I cleaned was in high school biology and that was intended to be a dissection! No telling what would remain of your poor fish if I actually attempted to clean it!" Phoebe thought it unnecessary to add that the biology exercise had nearly made her physically ill.

"I'll teach you," he told her and went back to his fishing. Phoebe lifted one brow aloofly and returned to her book. She had no intention of being coerced into cleaning Harlan's fish. Cook them, yes. Clean them, no.

Two hours later Harlan announced there was a sufficient quantity of fish for the evening meal and began to pack the tackle. The reel safely stowed into the box along with the rest of the gear, he reached in and removed a large, efficient looking knife.

"Here you go," he informed Phoebe, handing it to her hilt first.

Phoebe's large eyes widened slightly behind the lenses of

305

the tortoiseshell frames as she stared first at the knife and then at the man holding it out to her. He had meant what he said!

"Harlan, I'm not going to clean those fish!" she announced with absolute finality. "It would make me sick!"

"Are you hungry?" he asked simply, ice eyes glittering in the late afternoon sunlight.

"Yes, but . . ."

"Then you can clean them."

"I don't know how!" she tried plaintively. Phoebe decided that for the sake of harmony she would prefer to avoid a direct challenge. Perhaps he would back down if she pleaded ignorance. He couldn't force her to clean them, of course, but she wanted his good will for the remainder of the weekend. Still, nothing could make her clean those slippery looking fish!

"I told you I would teach you." Harlan reached into the basket and pulled out one of the creatures. Before Phoebe could look away he had removed the head with a neat slice and proceeded to finish the job.

Jinx observed the operation with mild interest and Phoebe watched in sick fascination. In a couple of minutes Harlan passed the bloodied knife into her unresisting palm and pulled another fish out of the basket.

Desperately she turned the full force of a pleading, almost green gaze on him, unaware herself just how potent it was. He seemed proof against it, however, and directed her firmly to get to work. The fish lay poised on a rock in front of her and he guided the hand holding the knife to the proper position.

"No!" Phoebe snapped out the refusal, recovering from the sight of the first operation rapidly and getting a firm grip on herself. Anyone who knew her well would have recognized the uncompromising nature of her present tone. Many a man had backed down when she spoke in that voice in her work environment. It was cold, clear, and utterly final. Why, she wondered frantically, didn't Harlan seem to recognize it?

"Clean the fish, Phoebe, or so help me I'll do it with your hands under mine!" One hard, square hand reached out to close over hers as she held the knife limply in front of her. Deliberately he applied pressure and the blade began to sink into the scales squishily.

"It goes much more neatly if you do it with a quick, sharp blow," he told her grimly. "But we can saw our way through if you prefer."

"*No*," Phoebe repeated, disgusted at the panicked note which had found its way into her voice. "Please, Harlan . . ." Even as she begged him to release her hand she exerted her own not inconsiderable strength in an effort to free it. It didn't budge him. This was ridiculous, she thought lightheadedly. She surely ought to be able to handle a situation like this! But she couldn't manage to free herself and the blade sank steadily downward. For a long instant there was a sharp, intense, silent battle of wills and muscles, and then an awful crunch came from the head of the fish. It was the last straw. Phoebe surrendered.

"All right, Harlan. I'll do it! I promise! But please stop this ghastly sawing business. I can't stand it!" It was true, she could feel her stomach beginning to churn. Anything would be better than this slow butchering!

Harlan released her immediately, holding her stunned eyes with his own.

"Don't ever get the idea," he told her coolly, "that simply because you convinced me to let you stay the weekend, you can manage me! When I feel strongly enough about an issue, I always win. Now clean the fish!"

Without a word, Phoebe lowered her smoldering gaze to the fish, swung the knife in a short, violent arc, and began the process of getting dinner on the table. A cook, she reminded herself, shouldn't balk at this end of the business. It was only because she had been lucky enough to be born into an age of supermarkets that she hadn't had to learn the task earlier. With bracing thoughts such as these and by pretending that each thrust of the knife was somehow a way of working out her anger at Harlan, she made it through the basket of fish.

"Maybe next time you'll think twice about crashing a man's

fishing weekend," was the only comment Harlan made when the job was done.

Phoebe said nothing, but got shakily to her feet and walked over to the stream to thoroughly wash her hands. Thank God, she wasn't going to lose control over her stomach! After the first two fish it had elected to settle down, a fact for which she was exceedingly grateful.

"Was that why you made me do it?" she asked without looking at him. Her words were remarkably calm and cool now. Harlan couldn't know it but it was a tone she generally reserved for making difficult members of corporate upper management see the errors of their ways. An aloof, superior tone which said clearly she might have to do things their way, but it was obvious to any fool that it would be the wrong way.

"I think it's going to be the only revenge I'll get," Harlan explained quietly, coming up behind her as she knelt by the water. There was a pause and then he asked almost gently, "Was it really that bad?" There was a note of genuine concern in his voice now. Phoebe found it infinitely satisfying.

"Yes!" With a whirling movement she scooped a stream of icy water in his direction.

"Hey!" Harlan yelled as the water soaked his face and a fair amount of shirt front. He made a grab but Phoebe was already flying up the incline, releasing her tension in the laughter she left trailing behind. Jinx, not knowing the name of the new game, but willing to participate, raced madly along beside her, yelping joyously.

When Harlan appeared in the doorway several minutes later, Phoebe was busily engaged in mixing biscuit dough. She glanced across the room as his shadow fell over the wooden floor and was unable to contain a grin at the sight he made standing there in his soaked shirt, tackle box in one hand, and basket of fish in the other.

"You look as if you fell in," she told him sweetly, fingers busy in the dough. One glimpse of the laughing blue eyes had been enough to assure her that the crisis was over. He had accepted her revenge in good humor and she was relieved.

Harlan's eyes always told you exactly where you stood, she thought.

"Some man is going to have his hands very full keeping you under control," he remarked ruefully, striding through the room to pull a dry shirt out of his traveling bag. "I shall pity the poor guy. Even if he is a lot bigger than you!"

Phoebe chuckled. "I'm beginning to think I'll be better off with someone considerably smaller than me," she told him lightly.

"No, no, Phoebe," he corrected, flashing her his best shark smile as he buttoned the dry shirt. "You don't need someone who is too big or too small. You need someone who is exactly right for you."

Phoebe decided not to continue in the rather provocative direction the conversation was taking. She'd had enough for the moment. She needed time to recover from the surprising loss in the recent contest of wills between them. She had lost such battles with men before in the business world. Everyone lost there at one time or another. But she had never encountered a man who cared to enforce his mastery over her outside the corporate setting. The whole event had uncomfortable similarities to a conflict out of a romantic novel and Phoebe was rapidly coming to the conclusion that being mastered by a man was not all it was cracked up to be in the books she read—especially when the man didn't fit the proper physical image in the least and, furthermore, was extremely unlikely to fall head over heels in love with her!

Chapter Three

Harland built a pleasant, crackling fire after dinner and Jinx wandered over to stretch out in front of the fireplace on the thin rug. His master groped around in a bag and then produced an unexpected bottle of wine and a jar of popcorn with the air of a magician. Phoebe laughed with pleasure and the evening settled down enjoyably. She crouched in front of the fire, wielding the old-fashioned corn popper and dispensing the results to dog and man alike. Jinx, it seemed, had a passion for the stuff. When everyone except the dog had eaten a sufficient quantity, she reclined against the base of the chair Harlan was occupying and the three of them gazed quietly into the fire, each thinking their own thoughts. Phoebe had just finished a leisurely sip of wine when she suddenly became aware of the fact that Harlan's strong hand was toying very gently with her tangled hair. She froze.

"Phoebe?" he questioned softly, his hand moving slightly.

"Yes?" She didn't move or turn to look at him. Instead she launched into a private lecture to herself on the fact that it wasn't in the least flattering to have a man make overtures when one happened to be the only woman for miles around!

"Are you going to holler rape to my aunt on Monday morning just because I'm going to kiss you tonight?" Harlan asked in a low, husky voice. The fingers of his hand moved down to stroke the nape of her neck under the curving fall of dark hair.

Phoebe felt herself tremble. How was she going to handle this little twist, she wondered. After all, it certainly wasn't as if he were bowled over by her ravishing beauty or exquisite figure! Treat it lightly, she told herself. He surely wasn't laboring under a raging desire, she decided with a rueful smile, so he wasn't likely to get out of hand. In a brisk, bracing tone she chided,

"Of course, I'm not going to scream 'rape' because we both know full well you aren't going to rape me! And if you're honest with yourself and me you'll admit you really don't even want to kiss me! Just because you're miles from your usual supply of small blonds, don't sacrifice your principles, Harlan!" She turned her head a fraction to glance up at him, willing him to smile in response.

"Do you always go around telling men what they want and don't want?" he inquired interestedly, his hand still at her nape. She watched his eyes and something she saw there made her worry for the first time. They weren't smiling back at her. In fact, the intensity which had crept into the blue gaze was altogether new. It reminded her of the rough way he had lectured her earlier about trying to make Richard jealous. Had she misjudged him badly? Put herself back into danger in a desperate attempt to flee it? But she still saw no viciousness or brutality in him. If she was very careful . . .

"Only occasionally," she said as lightly as possible, attempting a small, friendly smile. He didn't smile back, but the blue eyes warmed a degree or two.

"Only occasionally," he repeated thoughtfully, moving his hand to catch her chin between thumb and forefinger and thereby trap her wary gaze.

"I think you're lying to me again," he noted, one russet

brow quirking upward. "But this time I can see the truth in your eyes. I think you've had a lot of practice telling men what to do, haven't you?" He didn't sound angry or upset by the knowledge, Phoebe thought. He seemed more amused now than anything else. Before she could respond he leaned down until his mouth was only inches above her own. "But you won't be giving me orders, even if you think they are for my own good! Not tonight. Not ever." He didn't raise his voice in the least but Phoebe heard the same implacability she had heard that afternoon when he had forced her to clean the fish.

Perhaps the easiest, least provocative move would be to simply give him a willing, lighthearted kiss, she thought as his head lowered further. He might be one of those men who felt challenged when a woman resisted. She hadn't personally encountered any, but they were supposed to be around somewhere! Most of the men she'd known simply drew back a little sulkily if a woman put her foot down and refused to get involved in an embrace—the drunk and vicious rapists of last night excluded! But Harlan bore no relation to them!

Wide-eyed, Phoebe felt her chin angled higher and his lips on hers. The caress began almost gently, searchingly, as if Harlan was merely curious and had decided to satisfy his mild interest in her.

For a frozen time Phoebe remained passive beneath the touch of his mouth, experiencing a strange curiosity herself. This man was so different from Richard! Then, very slowly she sensed a controlled demand begin to emanate from him, a demand that she respond. Before she could make up her flustered mind on how to deal with his increasing ardor, he suddenly broke off the kiss and lifted his head to study her flushed features in the firelight.

Without a word he removed her glasses and set them down on a small table beside the chair. Now what? Phoebe wondered, worried about the significance of the act more than she cared to admit. She had better move now to regain a measure of control over the situation! But as if sensing her determination, Harlan reached down, pulling her around to face him.

"Harlan!" she squeaked, startled to find herself kneeling between his blue-jeaned thighs. "Wait a minute, I . . ." But she wasn't allowed to finish her sentence. His mouth came down once again, this time on lips which had been open to protest and his tongue plunged urgently between them. Phoebe began to struggle in earnest. A kiss or two she would have been willing to forfeit, she told herself furiously, but Harlan had stepped too far out of bounds by this last action. Angrily she tried to free herself from the grip of his hands on her shoulders, twisting her head in an effort to evade his mouth. But he held her as if she were without any power at all.

"Relax," he soothed, his lips moving deliberately to her throat.

"Relax!" she yelped, outraged by the effort to cajole. "Things have gone far enough. Take your hands off me this minute!"

"We've barely begun," he pointed out with male logic, easing her backward onto the rug, disturbing Jinx who obligingly got to his feet and moved off to settle elsewhere. "Now hush and let yourself go. You'll enjoy it."

"Of all the arrogant, overbearing . . ." Phoebe got no further. An instant later she was flat on the rug, his lean weight cushioned by her full, gentle curves. My God, she thought irrationally, he weighs a ton! And she was grimly aware that he was making no effort to take any of his own weight on his elbows. Instead he was using it to anchor her firmly beneath him.

"Harlan! That's enough! I mean it . . ." Again her words were cut off, this time by his mouth as he covered hers. Now she was vividly aware that he had banked some of the earlier demand she had sensed in him. Instead there was an insistent, sensuous, prodding quality. It was as if he were determined to stoke the embers of her passion until it flamed into life and matched his own.

With a deliberate, blatantly male move of sexual aggression he forced his leg between hers. The feeling of utter female helplessness which surged through Phoebe at the action

313

swamped her and with a moan she began to respond to his warm, invading mouth. She felt the sheer masculine satisfaction in him at the small surrender and knew she had made a mistake. But it was too late to stop. She wanted to sample more of the passion which was beginning to flow through her veins like hot honey. Richard had never kissed her like this, she thought blindly. No one had ever kissed her quite like this! It made her feel womanly, warm, and wanted.

Dimly she felt Harlan's hands at the buttons of her shirt, but she couldn't bring herself to protest. She felt him undo first one, then another, and another until her rounded breasts were protected from him only by the thin lacy stuff of her bra which had its clasp in front. Would he discover that? she wondered dizzily. A second later she felt his fingers on it and then her breasts were free of any restriction as he deftly found the secret of the catch.

Harlan drew in his breath at the full softness of her, moving one hand to cup it gently, palming a nipple in a stroking, gentle fashion that made it harden.

"Ah, Phoebe, you're exactly what a man needs in these cold mountains!" he breathed, lowering his lips to the tip of a breast and taking it into his mouth. "So soft and inviting . . ."

A log broke in the fireplace, sending a shower of sparks up the chimney and momentarily throwing an added light into the room. Phoebe opened dazed sea-green eyes to meet the passion in Harlan's blue gaze and somewhere in her reeling mind a tiny voice finally managed to make itself heard. She must put a stop to this! Harlan cared nothing for her! He was only amusing himself on a cold night with the only woman around!

"Please," Phoebe begged, knowing now she had no power to force him to cease his lovemaking. "Please, Harlan. Don't go any farther. Let me go."

"Why?" he questioned almost absently, his attention on the small hollow of her throat. She sensed his thumb continuing to move on a nipple and almost groaned with the sheer excitement of it. But he didn't really care for her! She must remember that!

"Because—because you don't love me!" she blurted in a kind of despair.

That halted him. His heavy, sinewy frame went still and he raised his head to look down at her, the ice of his eyes reflecting an unfathomable expression.

"Do you demand that all your lovers be head over heels in love with you before you'll go to bed with them?" he finally asked roughly.

"Oh, Harlan! Is it so wrong for a woman to want a man to love her before she takes such a risk?" Phoebe pleaded gently.

"You're worried about getting pregnant?" he queried gently.

"Among other things," she smiled tremulously.

"What other things?" He sounded curious, she thought. But she also knew instinctively that the crisis was over. She could tell by the way the passion was fading from the blue eyes, replaced by a hint of humor and the curiosity she had noted. Unconsciously she breathed a small sigh of relief. He felt it and a tiny smile quirked the hard line of his mouth.

"I asked what else you were afraid of, Phoebe." he reminded her.

Feeling more relaxed now, she smiled up at him with a touch of sauciness.

"Oh, the usual things a woman is afraid of with a passionate man," she quipped, feeling once again in charge. Harlan wasn't going to force himself on her. As long as she stayed firm in her resolve, he wouldn't carry his lovemaking any farther.

"You're afraid of being hurt emotionally?" he suggested.

"Of course! Remember I told you earlier today that I couldn't bear to have my heart broken when we return to Portland and you go back to your blond beauties?" Phoebe's blue-green eyes sparkled now with laughter.

"Are you admitting that I already have that much power over you?" he countered.

The humor vanished instantly from Phoebe's face. Just

315

when you thought you had the man back in hand, he said something outrageous!

"You're twisting my words, Harlan," she said very firmly, surreptitiously attempting to close the front of her blouse. Without even remarking on the movement Harlan forbade it by the simple expedient of trapping both her hands under his as he leaned on his forearms above her.

"We both know you're not going to rape me, Harlan Garand, so why continue to tease me like this?" she said, trying to make herself sound rational and not the least flustered.

"We both know that? Tell me, Phoebe Hampton, how do *you* know I won't take you here and now?" he challenged, a distinct glint lighting the blue eyes.

For a long instant Phoebe stared at him, unblinking, and then she smiled again, ever so slightly.

"You'll stop," she announced with a serene certainty. "I'm very sure that you are not a really brutal man. I've told you this is as far as I want to take matters and you'll go along with it, even if you're upset with me. I trust you."

He held himself very still above her for a long moment, watching her face intently as if searching for something there which persisted in eluding him. Phoebe tried to read the flickers of emotion moving in the ice-blue depths and failed.

"You trust me, do you?" he repeated slowly, considering.

Phoebe nodded mutely, afraid to answer lest her words disturb the delicate balance of the situation. She must do nothing now to taunt or tease. Not if she wanted to avoid spending the rest of the night in his arms! And she did want to avoid that, didn't she? Phoebe refused to go into the question any more deeply just then. Right now the important thing was to regain the safe level of companionship she and Harlan had enjoyed earlier in the day. His lovemaking was far too dangerous for her peace of mind!

"It seems to me that we should be able to exchange trust for trust, don't you agree?" Harlan asked, almost conversationally, but the blue eyes never released her.

"What—what are you talking about?" Phoebe whispered nervously.

"If you can trust me, I should be able to trust you. Tell me the truth about how you got to the cabin today, Phoebe," he instructed suddenly forcefully.

"But, Harlan, I've told you the truth . . ." Phoebe began, feeling desperate.

"I don't understand it!" he muttered, abruptly rolling away from her and getting to his feet in a fluid motion. "How can you lie and look at me like that at the same time? I would have sworn . . ." He cut himself off and shook off the anger Phoebe had seen rising in his eyes.

She could only marvel at Harlan's abrupt mood shift as he strode toward the cot on the far side of the room. She fumbled with the buttons of her blouse as he undid the strings on the sleeping bag.

"With a little squeezing we can make this cot do for both of us," Harlan remarked, no sign of emotion in his tone now. "I intend to sleep on it, by the way. My recently demonstrated chivalry does not extend to surrendering the only bed in sight to you when there's no reason in the world we can't share it!" He tossed her his shark grin as he unrolled the bag.

Phoebe watched him cautiously. "That's all right. If you have any extra blankets, I'll take the rug here in front of the fireplace," she said in a studied, casual tone.

"Come now," he said bracingly, "I thought you trusted me!"

"Well, I do." Phoebe hesitated and then added in a very low voice, "Within reason."

He ignored the qualification. "It gets cold in these mountains at night and the floor isn't going to be particularly warm or comfortable," Harlan pointed out matter-of-factly.

"It's better than what I had last night," Phoebe remarked pertly, feeling pressured. She got stiffly to her feet, feeling almost dizzy from the activity.

"Yes. Last night." The words were bitten out in a short manner which clearly demonstrated his opinion of her tale.

"Why can't you tell me the truth about that, Phoebe?" He left the sleeping bag and moved to stand in front of her, one hand reaching out to lightly stroke the line of her jaw. "I'm no longer in the mood to strangle you as I was this morning. It will be safe to confess now," he coaxed.

"I thought you already knew the truth!" she quipped, making a production of finding her glasses and slipping them protectively into place.

"But I want to hear it from you," he insisted.

Phoebe sighed regretfully. "Let's dig out those extra blankets," she suggested grimly, turning away. Without a word he crossed the room to a storage closet and hauled out a variety of what looked like old wool military blankets. He helped her spread them out in front of the fireplace and then handed her a flashlight so she could make the necessary trip outside. Jinx went along to stand guard and Phoebe was grateful for the dog's presence. Being outdoors in the mountain darkness brought back unpleasant fears she had been able to ignore during the day.

The three occupants of the cabin settled down to sleep a short time later. Phoebe discovered within ten minutes that the floor was, indeed, going to prove uncomfortable as well as cold when the last of the fire died away, her practical voice added silently. She considered telling Harlan she was having second thoughts and was almost on the verge of saying something when his voice came from the far wall. It was laced with rueful amusement.

"Phoebe?"

"Yes?"

"There is just one thing I have to know."

"What's that, Harlan?"

"Do you have a lot of success at keeping your men in their proper place with that line?" She could sense his smile in the darkness.

"What line?" she inquired innocently.

"That one about trusting the poor guy. It doesn't leave him a lot of options, you know!"

318

Phoebe gave a muffled giggle. "I have always found it quite effective," she told him demurely, wishing privately there really had been a variety of men needing to be kept in place. Or perhaps just one particular man . . .

"So we all obediently back off, control our raging ardor, and try to live up to your ridiculous trust in our honor!" There was laughter in Harlan's words. "The Third's been buying this line for some time now, I take it, since you say you haven't slept with him?"

"I don't think Richard sees it as a 'line' exactly," Phoebe explained carefully, thinking of the few times he had actually attempted much of a pass. "He always seemed . . ." she broke off and tried again. "He didn't seem to mind . . ." Face it, she told herself sternly, Richard's lack of desire was one of the main reasons she had been unable to fall in love with the man!

"The Third is a fool. Come here, Phoebe." The laughter was gone from Harlan's voice now and in its place was a new, rough note of command.

"Why?" she demanded, startled.

"Because I've told you to. Come here, woman. Don't put me to the trouble of fetching you."

Phoebe lay frozen for a moment considering the change in the situation. Harlan sounded quite determined and she couldn't be at all certain whether or not he was teasing her. On the surface it didn't sound like it. The rather belated notion that she had pushed her luck too far occurred to Phoebe.

"Harlan . . ." She began carefully, not moving.

"Come here, Phoebe," he ordered softly. "I'm not going to tell you again."

She didn't doubt him. When he wished, thought Phoebe wryly as she unrolled herself from the blankets, Harlan Garand could assume command with an alarming authority. Unable to think of a clever way out of the tangle, she got to her feet. Deep down she kept telling herself that he wouldn't really force himself on her. But even as she reassured herself, a small voice asked if that was her real fear. Or was she afraid of wanting him to do exactly that?

319

She was still wearing the jeans and blouse in an attempt to keep warm. Now she wrapped one of the blankets around her and, clutching it tightly, trailed slowly over to stand beside the cot. In the dim light of the dying fire, Harland regarded her speculatively, blue eyes shadowed and mysterious. With an abrupt motion he flipped back the top of the down-filled bag. Phoebe saw he was sleeping in only his jockey shorts and she gulped, clinging more tightly to the blanket.

"Get in," he said almost tonelessly.

"Harlan, I . . ."

"I said, get in. But first take off your jeans. They'll be too uncomfortable to wear inside the bag."

A wave of panic washed over Phoebe as she stood there, shivering in her cold, bare feet. Harlan looked quite determined to enforce his order and she could see no effective way of fighting him. She was at his mercy, the mercy of the cold night, and the mercy of her own inner longing.

"Move, Phoebe. It's getting cold."

Phoebe's fingers went reluctantly to the button of her jeans and she stepped out of them under the shelter of the blanket. For once in her life she felt absolutely helpless to resist the will of a man and it was both frightening and exhilarating. Harlan watched her, never taking his eyes from her face. A moment later she slid down beside him, reveling in the warmth and fearing the worst. When his arm closed around her, his hand rested almost casually on the breasts she had freed earlier from the bra. Phoebe closed her eyes and waited for she knew not what.

"This is much better than the floor, isn't it?" he asked silkily.

"It's warmer," she agreed in a tiny voice as she lay curled into the heat of his body.

"And more comfortable?" he suggested coolly, daring her to disagree.

"Yes," she responded stiffly.

"You're wondering what happens next, aren't you?" he persisted wickedly.

"Yes." The words were barely a whisper.

"You," he informed her with a soft, mocking smile, "are just going to have to trust me!"

Sunlight, warm and cheery, wakened Phoebe on Sunday morning. She lay quietly for a moment, savoring the warmth of Harlan's unconscious embrace and then, very stealthily, unzipped the sleeping bag. The easiest thing to do, she decided, was to be up and dressed before her host awoke. She spent almost five whole minutes slipping the zipper down notch by notch and then began to slide with utmost caution until her toes were out from under the weight of Harlan's leg. Delicately she edged his arm upward, about to slip from beneath it when with a sleepy laugh Harlan came awake in a hurry, clasping her rounded body firmly and tucking her back into the warm bag. When she was safely settled against him again, he lifted himself on one elbow and leaned his head down to kiss her slowly and lazily, showing no consideration at all for the effects of his rasping morning beard against her soft skin. The blue eyes glittered with humor as he regarded his wide-eyed victim.

"You have an interesting knack of looking slightly astonished whenever things don't go the way you planned them," he chuckled. "It's a temptation to disrupt your schemes just to see that look. Do you normally get your own way in most things?"

"*Normally*," Phoebe stressed, struggling to a sitting position and fixing him with her severest frown, "There aren't that many people trying to get in my way!"

"Don't frown at me like that," he protested. "Didn't I behave myself last night and let you sleep in peace?"

"After terrifying me first!" she retorted waspishly, her eyes going to the tousled red hair.

"Didn't the Third ever terrify you just the least little bit?"

Phoebe's frown became even more severe as she scrambled around for her glasses. She had no idea why he kept mentioning Richard!

"Richard Elton Chambers III is, above all else, a gentle-

321

man!'' Phoebe informed Harlan in a haughty tone, looking down her nondescript nose. ''He wouldn't think of doing anything like that!''

''He doesn't know what he's been missing,'' Harlan remarked feelingly. ''You were perfectly fashioned for cuddling on a cold night, Phoebe Hampton.'' He grinned. ''All nice and round and warm and soft...'' He broke off, apparently amused by the rising tide of color in her face. ''As you said, the man must be very dull, indeed!''

Phoebe shrugged. ''I expect it comes from having the proper amount of money and the right background,'' she admitted, taking advantage of his relaxed grip to swing her legs over the edge of the cot and pull on her jeans quickly. She felt much more in control when she was fully dressed.

''You think dullness is an inherited characteristic of someone who is financially successful?'' Harlan asked interestedly from his position in the sleeping bag.

''Not necessarily. My brother is a self-made man and he's not dull in the least, although I may be somewhat prejudiced!'' Phoebe smiled thoughtfully, walking across the room to refold the blanket she had left in front of the fireplace. ''But maybe that's the difference.''

''What is?''

''Whether or not a person has made his money or been born into it.''

''The Third was born into his, I take it?''

Phoebe nodded. ''Oh yes. He's the third, remember.'' Phoebe stepped over to the door to open it for a pleading Jinx. ''Next time I get involved I think I shall make an effort to be sure he comes from a background more similar to my own. I would never have fit into Richard's world anyway. Still, I must admit, it was nice while it lasted!'' She thought briefly of how gorgeous Richard was in full evening dress. It was a definite shame the man's personality did not match his looks!

''Sounds to me as if you may have been guilty of using the poor man,'' Harlan announced. ''He must have been getting some feedback from you if he was inspired to offer marriage!''

Phoebe heard the disapproval in his voice and shook her head firmly.

"Never. I gave him no reason to think I was ever that attracted to him. To tell you the truth, I was as surprised as anyone when he asked me to marry him! Surely he must have known that something was missing from our relationship, pleasant though it was."

"Maybe he felt the spark of passion and restrained himself in the hopes you would someday return the feeling," Harlan suggested, climbing out of the sleeping bag unselfconsciously and stepping into his jeans. Phoebe glanced away hurriedly. When she looked in his direction again he was busy rolling the bag.

"No, I don't think one could say that the Third was motivated by any strong romantic impulses," she mused with a small smile. "What that man needs is an attractive ornament for a wife. Why he thought I'd suit the role is beyond me, although I must admit I was flattered!"

"You don't think you're the ornament type?" Harlan inquired, sounding intrigued as he pulled a clean shirt out of his traveling bag.

"Could I borrow an extra shirt if you have it?" Phoebe asked. "This one is beginning to itch!"

Without a word, Harlan tossed her an old work shirt which Phoebe deftly caught. "Thanks, I'll wash mine today and then I'll be able to give this one back to you!"

"You didn't answer my question," he pointed out.

"About being an ornament?" she sighed. "I would have thought it was obvious! Of course I'm not the type! I told you yesterday, I plan to use my cooking to catch my man!" She flashed him a grin and opened the door to follow Jinx outside, feeling that she had managed to put the peculiar relationship between Harlan and herself back on a safe, bantering basis.

Forty-five minutes later, neatly shaved and looking the picture of masculine vitality, Harlan polished off the last of his crisp bacon and complimented Phoebe on breakfast.

"I suppose," he added, chuckling, "I should be grateful I

haven't had to beat you to make you assume the traditional feminine role around the cabin!''

"I do have a sense of fair play, you know. I'm quite aware of the fact that I barged in on your weekend, that I'm eating your food, and have otherwise been a general nuisance," Phoebe smiled back. "I'm willing to try and repay some of the hospitality, no matter how reluctantly it may have been extended! What's on the agenda for this morning? Are you going to fish again?''

"I was going to suggest a hike down to the falls and back. It will work up an appetite for lunch. Besides, Jinx needs the exercise. He's going to get fat if you keep sneaking him scraps under the table like that!''

Phoebe withdrew her hand guiltily and then laughed. "A hike would be great," she agreed, getting to her feet to clear the table. "We'd better take advantage of the sunshine while we have it. This being Oregon, the rain could arrive at any moment," she added sweetly.

"That's simply a myth Oregonians tell Californians. It discourages them from emigrating," he informed her loftily.

The walk to the point in the stream where the rushing water cascaded whitely over a mighty outcropping took most of the morning, but it was worth it. Phoebe was thoroughly enjoying having the day in the woods and Harlan Garand all to herself. Common sense, of course, intervened from time to time reminding her that it wasn't going to last long, but Phoebe decided she would take advantage of the pleasant excitement which seemed to be associated with Harlan's presence. She would be careful, especially tonight, but the temptation to play with the fire of his personality was hard to resist. The sunlight slanted down through the trees, removing the morning chill, and lending a special clarity to the fresh mountain air. Reality would return soon enough.

Phoebe was in the midst of preparing a late luncheon after the return from the morning walk when Jinx began barking furiously. Harlan was outside collecting firewood for the coming evening. Jinx, who had been sitting in the open doorway

324

sunning himself suddenly leaped to his feet and crossed the porch at a dead run. Phoebe glanced at him as he disappeared and then went back to her salad making. The dog had probably sensed a deer and the hunter instinct in him had leaped to the fore.

Several minutes later the barking ceased abruptly and Phoebe grinned to herself. Poor Jinx. He'd probably lost the deer and would be back shortly, pretending nothing at all had happened.

But it wasn't Jinx who next appeared in the cabin doorway. It was Harlan, looking quite scruffy. His short red hair was awry and there was a good deal of dust on his jeans. He stood silently regarding Phoebe with a strange expression in his blue eyes, as if he hadn't seen her properly until now.

"What's wrong?" she asked, the faint trace of astonishment he had commented on earlier much in evidence as she peered at him questioningly through the lenses of her glasses.

"Is Jinx okay?" she prodded, facing him with one hand holding the knife she had been using to spread mustard.

"Jinx," said Harlan very distinctly, "is fine." He glanced back over his shoulder and then returned his level stare to meet her curious one. "Could you please," he said carefully, "run through your story of the Great Escape briefly?"

"Why?" Phoebe asked, floored by the unexpected request.

"Just the part about how you got away," he specified, ice eyes pinning her, demanding an answer.

"Well, one of them had gone outside to get more wood for the fire. They had freed me to prepare some dinner and I had a pot of water boiling on the stove. It was to be used to cook the noodles for one of those package dinners they had brought along. I had a sudden thought that I might not get a better chance and I just—just tossed the whole pot of water at the man who was supposed to be keeping an eye on me. He screamed. It was awful! I ran out the back door and into the woods. I kept going, listening for the sound of water. They tried to follow but I wasn't afraid of getting lost and they were, I guess. At any rate they gave up after a while. I knew I couldn't use the road but I had read somewhere that one could follow a stream off a mountain. Harlan, why are you asking me such a question now?''

''Because there is a gentleman outside who bears a strong resemblance to a boiled lobster asking for you . . .'' He broke off abruptly as Phoebe went very white very quickly. The knife in her hand dropped unheeded to the floor.

''Hey! Honey, it's okay! It's all under control, I promise you!'' Harlan leaped forward, the strange expression he had worn earlier giving way to a heartwarming concern. Phoebe managed a shaky smile.

''Sorry. It's only that I had almost put the whole mess out of my mind, telling myself I'd worry about it on Monday. I felt so safe here with you and Jinx . . .'' Phoebe wished she could keep her lower lip from trembling.

''You *are* safe,'' Harlan swore with great feeling, holding her firmly by the shoulders. ''Perfectly safe. I've got the guy tied up nice and tight. Jinx is standing guard. The way the man was sneaking up on the cabin he's lucky he hasn't suffered a good deal more than he already has! Neither Jinx nor I take kindly to shifty types!'' Harlan's tones were ruefully soothing as he held her close against his dusty shirt, one large hand gently stroking her thick, rich hair. ''When the fight was over and I asked him what the hell he thought he was doing he said something about looking for a 'friend,' a female friend, at that! I didn't mean to startle you so. I was trying to be cool about the whole thing, you see, because I'm in a position of having made a ghastly mistake and now I've got to figure out a way to apologize!''

Phoebe found herself chuckling into his shirt. ''You don't owe me anything in the way of apologies,'' she murmured. ''In the beginning, I thought it might be pleasant to have you find out the truth but you've more than made up for whatever you thought of me by providing me with one of the most interesting weekends I've had in a long time!'' Privately, Phoebe decided it was the best weekend of her entire life but the practical side of her nature warned her to keep things light. She *had* to keep things light!

"How can you say that?" Harlan groaned. "I made all those terrible accusations! No wonder you thought my ego was so damn inflated." He looked momentarily disgusted with himself and Phoebe found herself laughing.

"You gave me shelter and food when I needed them badly. I had the protection of you and your noble hound. I've learned how to clean fish and you topped everything off very pleasantly by making a pass which did wonders for my feminine ego. Then you capped even that by proving yourself a true gentleman and not taking advantage of me! Throw in the excitement of the initial kidnapping and the fact that you've caught one of the villains and what more could a woman ask for out of a weekend fling?" Phoebe stepped back in to the circle of his arms and blinked at him through glasses which had been tilted slightly askew.

Harlan shook his head uncomprehendingly. "Incredible," he mumbled to himself and then his old familiar grin flashed into place as he caught her chin between thumb and forefinger. "Treasure that one moment of my gentlemanly behavior last night, Phoebe," he advised. "I've made a couple of mistakes with you which I don't intend to repeat in the future! One of them was thinking you could lie to me. I should have known that with those eyes you could never hide the truth for long. No wonder I felt so confused every time I looked at you and asked for the real story!"

He paused, still looking down at her. "The second mistake was in letting you talk me out of making love to you last night. I won't repeat that one, either!"

Chapter Four

Phoebe's response to Harlan's words would not, she felt, have done her credit in front of her staff who held the view that she could handle almost any situation. He must be teasing, of course, but his words left her momentarily breathless and mute. Before she could gather the courage to ask him what he meant he was tugging her along behind him as he led the way outdoors.

"Come on and see if this joker looks familiar. We really are going to be in a fix if Jinx and I have cornered an innocent victim! Of course, now we've got a trespassing charge," Harlan remarked, holding her wrist in a firm grip.

Phoebe stared down at the infuriated man lying trussed on the ground. How could she have been so foolish as to get into a truck with such a creature? If she hadn't been so angry at the failure of the rental car and anxious to get to her destination she would have exercised more common sense! She had done a fair amount of damage with the hot water but remembering the fact that she had been in fear of being raped or even killed, she couldn't feel too sorry about it. Harlan idly fingered the small gun which Phoebe recognized with a shiver.

"Jinx found him hiding in the woods at the edge of the clearing. The guy was so frightened of the dog he forgot to use this." Harlan wrapped the weapon in a handkerchief and smiled unpleasantly. Phoebe prudently decided not to inquire into the cause of his humor.

"This is the man, all right—one of them. The other was bigger." Phoebe said quietly, looking away from the fury and hate in the kidnapper's face.

"So much for the remainder of my bachelor weekend in the mountains," Harlan noted absently, studying his captive. "We'd better get going. I've already done enough to impede justice by making it impossible for you to report the kidnapping, Phoebe. I don't want to add any other sins to my growing roster." He leaned down to pat an alert Jinx who was now all business as he stood guard over his victim. "Keep an eye on him, my friend, while Phoebe and I get packed." Harlan glanced at Phoebe. "Come on, honey, let's move." He suited action to words and headed toward the cabin.

Phoebe turned dutifully to follow and then stopped for one last speculative look at her former tormentor. It was a mistake. The small cruel eyes were fixed on her as if she were potential prey. For the first time, the man spoke, his voice sounding harsh and raspy, a sound she remembered so well from Friday night.

"Max is still free and clear," he snarled in a hoarse whisper. "He'll get you, you bitch! I swear it!"

"Care to repeat that to a police officer?" Phoebe asked spiritedly before turning firmly on her heel and moving quickly toward the porch. The thought of the other kidnapper running around loose wasn't a pleasant one but she told herself that if the one named Max had any common sense—and he had seemed the more intelligent of the two—he would be in the next state by now.

The ride back to Portland was accomplished in what Phoebe privately thought must have been record time. The captive was left to fend for himself in the rear of the vehicle with Jinx who growled every time the man moved. The fear of dogs seemed genuine and the sight of the big black Lab sitting so alertly beside him was all the intimidation needed to keep him quiet.

The encounter with the police went efficiently, much to Phoebe's amazement. She had half expected that no one would believe the outlandish story, but Harlan's presence seemed to lend her some credibility although he was right when he had remarked that the forces of the law were not going to look kindly upon his unwitting impeding of their work. One older, grizzled detective saw fit to give the younger man the sharp edge of his tongue in a scathing tone which Phoebe had a hunch was used indiscriminately on any who fell within his jurisdiction from mayors to bums. Harlan took the criticism with a properly sober expression and then spoiled the effect by saying,

"I'm sorry, sir, but the minute Phoebe walked into camp I ceased functioning in my normal rational manner." He glanced at a reddening Phoebe and grinned unrepentantly. The flush deepened as the detective turned to look her over appraisingly.

"And as for you, young woman, I should think you would have had more sense than to accept a ride on the highway like that! Don't you ever read the newspapers?"

"Yes, sir," Phoebe whispered guiltily, avoiding Harlan's eyes.

"Then you know that the proper procedure is to stay with the car, doors and windows locked, and wait for a passing highway patrol car!"

"Yes, sir," she whispered again. She didn't need to be lectured on the subject, Phoebe thought bitterly. It had been a stupid stunt and it had only been sheer luck she had come out of the situation unscathed. Of course, if she hadn't been so foolish she would never have met Harlan Garand and that experience had been worth a good deal . . .

With a certain fascination, Phoebe went through the routine of police work. She gave her statement in as much detail as possible, doing her best to describe the other hunter in the truck. The police seemed to agree with her private analysis that he would probably flee the state. Harlan listened attentively when this particular probability was discussed but volunteered no comment. Phoebe had the impression he wasn't altogether convinced.

Patiently they took her through every detail, digging out maps, and drawing circles on them in an effort to estimate how far she might have walked before stumbling onto Harlan's cabin.

"We'll start searching for the place where you were held this afternoon, Miss Hampton," she was told. The detective yelled instructions over his shoulder to have the sheriff's department contacted.

During the entire procedure Harlan never left her side and Phoebe found herself surprisingly grateful for the support. When they were at last excused, he escorted her back out to where the jeep had been illegally parked with Jinx inside and announced he would drive her home.

"The first thing I'm going to do is take a shower, a *hot* shower, and wash my hair!" Phoebe informed him, climbing into the seat and greeting the dog affectionately. "Not that I wasn't impressed by the novelty of bathing in a cold stream, but there is definitely something to be said for the amenities of civilization!"

She gave directions to her apartment building in downtown Portland and settled back as Harlan switched on the engine. He seemed unnaturally quiet during the drive to the charming older building which overlooked one of the city's numerous parks. She found herself chatting freely in an effort to cover the silence. It was necessary to do so because she had no intention of allowing the man to think she was in the least depressed about the imminent conclusion of the spectacular weekend. All too soon he was halting the vehicle in front of the familiar red brick building with its sunny bay windows. Summoning a bright smile and an appropriately casual remark, she turned in her seat to say goodbye to Harland and Jinx.

"I want both of you to know that I've had a very exciting weekend and I shall be happy to recommend the accommodations to the travel agency that booked them for me," she began cheerily.

"Good," Harlan grinned, climbing out of his side of the jeep and motioning Jinx to stay behind. "I thought for a moment there the primitive aspects might have put you off the place!"

"All part of the atmosphere," Phoebe said airily, thinking it was very polite of him to see her to the door.

"I'll have to see the landlady about the key. It was in my purse, which, as far as I know, is back at that cabin," she told him as she jumped out of the jeep to join him on the sidewalk.

"That will teach you to accept rides from strangers . . ."

"Please! I don't need any more lectures read to me on that subject!" Phoebe informed him with a trace of tartness. What did he and the police think she was? Stupid?

"And if you hadn't decided to take off by yourself to spend a day at the coast you wouldn't have been driving alone in the evening in the first place!" Harlan plowed on, warming to the topic as he took Phoebe's arm and guided her forcibly toward the neat little entrance of the apartment building.

"I had every right in the world to take off by myself Friday night," she interrupted, ruffled.

"It never would have happened if you'd belonged to me instead of the Third!" Harlan shot back with the air of a debater who has scored a major point.

"I don't belong to the Third! And what's that got to do with anything? I would still have the right to spend a weekend by myself, regardless of whom I happened to be dating!" Phoebe badly wished the conversation hadn't begun to deteriorate. It would have been so much nicer to have concluded things on a light note!

"Not if you belonged to me," he informed her loftily. "My woman would not have found herself free on a Friday night, you see. She wouldn't find herself free until the next morning.

Then, possibly, she might be allowed to go home and feed her bird!''

''Do you always force your dates to stay overnight?'' Phoebe snapped, feeling much flustered by the wickedly male expression he was directing down at her.

''Only the cuddly ones.''

''Harlan!''

Before Phoebe could continue to berate him for his teasing, he was drawing her to a halt in front of the door marked ''Manager.'' But as he lifted his hand to knock it was flung open to reveal an elderly lady in a stained painting smock who peered at them with snapping grey eyes.

''Phoebe! I thought I heard voices out here! Where have you been all weekend? You were supposed to be back Saturday. You know I like my tenants to alert me when they're planning on being away for an extended period . . .'' She broke off suddenly to frown up at Harlan.

''Who's this?'' she demanded, wiping her hands absently on the smock.

''Harlan, this is my landlady, Mrs. Morrison. She, uh, paints. Very well, too,'' Phoebe smiled at the thin woman, noting the streak of chromium yellow in the halo of curly white hair. ''This is Harlan Garand, Mrs. Morrison, a friend of mine.''

''Hmmm. Close friend?'' Mrs. Morrison inquired, eyeing Harlan shrewdly.

''Very close,'' Harlan supplied agreeably, saving Phoebe from having to answer. There was an instant's silence while each appraised the other and then he asked politely, ''Will I do?''

''You'll do.'' The woman turned her piercing gaze on Phoebe. ''I like him a hell of a lot better than the other one!'' she proclaimed as if it were the last word on the subject. Phoebe wished very badly the floor would open and allow her to descend into the basement.

''Mrs. Morrison!'' she begged, well aware of the amusement in Harlan's smile. ''How—how did you know I had been gone?'' she asked lamely, trying desperately to switch the subject.

"That damn bird of yours, of course. Started yelling Saturday afternoon and has kept it up off and on all day today. Could hear him clear out in the hallway, according to the Thompsons,'' Mrs. Morrison told her grimly.

"I'm very sorry,'' Phoebe began hurriedly. "I know Ferd gets a bit temperamental when I'm not around for long periods of time. I'll go right up to him,'' she edged away, reaching out to pluck at Harlan's sleeve. He remained standing where he was, giving a fair imitation of a rock.

"You're forgetting that you've lost your key,'' he reminded her gently.

"Oh, yes,'' Phoebe turned back to her landlady. "I've lost my purse and I wondered if you could get me another key? I could have it copied in the morning . . .''

"How did you lose your purse?'' came the predictable question.

"I'll tell you later, Mrs. Morrison. I really think I ought to be getting along to Ferd. He'll be in a frenzy!''

"True.'' The woman disappeared inside the apartment and returned a few minutes later with a key. "Here you go. Now, I'll want to hear what happened, later, understand?'' White brows lowered severely.

"Yes, Mrs. Morrison,'' Phoebe smiled in relief. "I'll tell you all about it, I promise!''

"All about it?'' Harlan inquired interestedly as they headed for the elevator.

"Well, I expect I'll have to expurgate certain portions,'' Phoebe admitted with a wry chuckle. "But I'm sure Mrs. Morrison's imagination will fill in the blanks!'' The elevator arrived and she hesitated before stepping inside. "There's no need to take me any farther,'' she said carefully, not wanting him to feel in the least *obligated*. "I appreciate everything you've done for me this weekend and I'll always be grateful to both you and Jinx for catching that awful man . . .'' Phoebe hurried into the elevator which showed signs of wanting to close. It was an older model and she had learned it was best not to argue with it. "Thanks again, Harlan. I had a very exciting time . . ." Phoebe stopped in midsentence as Harlan stepped into the elevator.

"There's really no need . . ." she began nervously.

"Hush, Phoebe. I'm going to come up to your apartment. We have things to discuss and besides, I want to meet Ferd." The amusement in his eyes confused her. Harlan was playing havoc with her nerves, she decided, in a way Richard had never succeeded in doing. She must be very careful, she told herself firmly. There could be no future for her with a man who much preferred the fragile blonds of the world. She knew instinctively she should protect herself as much as possible by ending things quickly. The silence which pervaded the elevator for the remainder of the trip to the fourth floor didn't appear to phase Harlan at all. He seemed quite at ease and when the door slid open in its creaky fashion, he took her key, checked the number, and started across the hall to the proper entrance.

"I'm curious to see what your place looks like," he told her as he twisted the knob and opened the door. "I have an inner vision of how you would decorate a home and I want to see how far off it is!"

"Oh. Well, I suppose . . ." Phoebe stopped as the sound of the opening door set off an incredible screech from within the apartment.

"Ferd!" She rushed inside, heading toward the cage hanging in a corner of the living room, the occupant of which was madly racing back and forth across a wooden perch while yelling at the top of his tiny lungs.

"Ferd, behave yourself! I'm home now and you've still got plenty of water and seed—so control your feelings or I won't let you outside the cage!"

Phoebe stood for a minute, eyeball to eyeball with the infuriated parakeet, and then stepped back as Ferd slunk away to the far side of his cage, mumbling evilly.

"I have to be firm with him. He knows I got him on sale

335

and can't return him to the pet shop!'' Phoebe explained as she straightened.

"He looks vicious," Harlan observed, walking across the hardwood floor with its brilliant throw rugs to examine the bird more closely.

"He is," Phoebe assured him, surveying the blue and white creature affectionately. One bright eye regarded her balefully and then it switched to the man beside her.

"Fee, fie, fo, fum," roared Ferd in his highpitched voice, "I smell the blood of an Oregonian!"

"Now, Ferd, remember what I said," Phoebe admonished him severely. "Do you want out of that cage or not?"

Ferd instantly leaped to the bar nearest his door and looked out expectantly, his attention completely refocused on an object a good deal more important than Harlan—freedom.

"Do you think it's safe to let him out?" Harlan asked apprehensively as Phoebe unlocked the cage and inserted a finger toward Ferd.

"You're bigger than he is," she pointed out as Ferd climbed regally aboard and allowed himself to be removed from his residence.

"Just make sure you keep him out of my way or I'll fetch Jinx to protect me," Harlan ordered, glancing around the room appreciatively, taking in the romantic wicker furniture and the multitude of hanging plants. A small smile crossed his face as he strolled over to the elegant fan chair and gingerly lowered himself into it.

"Don't worry, it wouldn't dare collapse beneath you," Phoebe assured him, allowing Ferd to transfer to her shoulder where he used his beak to tug ruthlessly at strands of hair. "Would you like a cup of tea or something?" she added, feeling somewhat at a loss as to how to handle him now that the man showed every sign of making himself at home on her territory.

"That would be nice. I'll fix it while you have your shower," Harlan replied easily, eyeing her disheveled appearance politely. "Then we'll go have a bite to eat at that pizza place I saw down the street. It's almost dinner time!''

The situation was getting a little out of hand, Phoebe thought anxiously.

"Harlan," she said delicately, "This is the night Richard is supposed to come by for his answer . . .''

"I remember." He may have remembered. He obviously didn't particularly care, she thought, beginning to grow irritated.

"Well, I don't think it would be very hospitable to have you here when he arrives," she clarified firmly. "Regardless of the answer I'm going to give him!''

"Don't worry about Richard, honey. I intend to make the matter very plain to him," Harlan said calmly.

"What matter?" Phoebe demanded forebodingly, frowning at him.

"What a pair!" Harland leaned back in the fantasy chair and eyed the two confronting him. "It's clear Jinx and I are going to have our work cut out for us!''

"Harlan, will you please explain what's going on? Why are you sticking around?" she asked bluntly.

"I'm sticking around to make sure you give the Third his answer," he smiled.

"I'm quite capable of giving it to him alone!''

"Apparently you aren't or you wouldn't be having to repeat it. If you'd been firm the first time, he wouldn't be coming by tonight to see if you've changed your mind, would he?" Harland asked reasonably, stretching his legs out in front of him as he eyed her growing annoyance. "What time was he due to receive his second set of walking papers, anyway?''

"Don't talk like that!" Phoebe bit out. "Richard is a very nice man who has done me a great honor by asking me to marry him. The least I can do is try and let him down as gently as possible. I certainly don't intend to be rude about the matter!" She glanced at the digital clock on the radio. "He'll be here at seven-thirty," she answered his question belatedly.

"That gives us an hour and a half to get a bite to eat. If you hurry the shower, we'll be back here in plenty of time.''

Phoebe stared at him, brow furrowed in concentration for a long moment. It was plain the man wasn't going to leave until he desired to do so. It would probably be safer to get him back outside the apartment. She might have a chance at keeping him from getting back in. Finally Phoebe nodded.

"All right," she agreed rather shortly, and turned to head down the hall to the bathroom, determinedly ignoring the suspiciously bland smile on Harlan's face as he watched her leave. The man was impossible! One minute she felt in danger of falling for him and the next he made her want to strike him with the nearest large object! She wondered forlornly if the little blonds had any better luck keeping him in line and in the next breath wished there weren't any little blonds at all in the picture!

The pizza was very good and Phoebe had a glass of the red wine that Harlan ordered to go with it but nothing could make her forget the upcoming interview with Richard Chambers. As the time wore on, she felt herself growing increasingly nervous which, in turn, only served to heighten her irritability. Disgustedly she told herself she wasn't behaving in her normal manner at all. Remaining largely oblivious to Harlan's deliberately casual conversation, Phoebe set her mind to work on the problem of getting rid of her escort before Richard arrived. Harlan showed every sign of carrying out his threat and attaching himself to her for the remainder of the evening. She couldn't fathom why he should want to do so, but there was no doubt about the awkwardness which was going to develop if she didn't detach him soon.

It was seven-fifteen by the time Harlan walked her back to the apartment door, having insisted on stopping by the jeep to give Jinx a brief break. Phoebe had no luck in convincing him to leave her at the elevator and when she fished her new key out of her pocket he immediately removed it from her hand and proceeded to open her door. Firmly she stepped just over the threshold and turned to face him, a polite office smile on her expressive mouth.

"Thank you very much for a pleasant evening and a most

338

interesting weekend . . ." she began formally.

"You must be mistaking me for the Third," he told her casually, taking a determined step forward. It had the effect of driving her back a pace. "Save your polite farewells for him. I don't intend to leave yet."

"Now, Harlan, it's getting late. Richard will be here any minute and the two of us have something very important to discuss, as you know full well. I should think a man of your intelligence would understand that this is not the sort of social conversation which will be improved by adding a third party!" she snapped waspishly, losing patience with the man filling her doorway.

"Don't worry, honey. I'll handle everything," Harlan said soothingly, forcing her back completely from the door and immediately following up his victory by moving into the room. "Have a seat while we wait for the Third. You know, I really like this place. It looks exactly as it should. Both sides of your nature are here. Lots of romance in the living room and possibly the bedroom . . ." He broke off to lift an inquiring eyebrow, inviting her to confirm his guess. When Phoebe simply glared, he continued, "And the practical streak is represented in your tidy little kitchen." He nodded as if congratulating himself on having analyzed her so well and then he grasped her wrist and pulled her along behind him toward the settee.

"Harlan, I've been very patient with you," Phoebe started wrathfully, trying with a total lack of success to free herself. "But now you're going too far! Please leave this instant! I won't have you here when Richard arrives and that's final!" She was tugged down alongside him on the pillows.

"Honey, you're going to have to learn that I don't always follow orders very well. I'm more accustomed to giving them, you see. So why don't you relax and we can wait for Richard in a more peaceful atmosphere."

"Stop talking to me as if I were a child! You have no right in this apartment and I refuse to tolerate your unwelcome presence one more minute . . ." Phoebe halted in midstride as the doorbell rang demandingly. She sat staring at Harlan with a stunned expression.

"He's early," she whispered helplessly, feeling the outrage seep out of her and a strong sensation of inevitability take over.

"I'll let him in," Harlan offered, getting to his feet.

"Harlan, no!"

But it was too late. Harlan was already at the door, throwing it open with a grand gesture as he greeted the startled Richard with a jovial smile. Only the ice in his eyes gave any indication that the smile was not altogether genuine, Phoebe thought grimly.

Tall, dark haired, and very good looking, Richard Elton Chambers III stood staring at the lean, redheaded man facing him. In the strained atmosphere Phoebe couldn't help but be aware of the differences in the two men. Richard was his usual elegant self, attired now in casual slacks and corduroy sport coat which had the effect of making Harlan's faded jeans and workshirt even more rough looking than they normally would have appeared. With his height, Richard always looked good, Phoebe thought, wishing mightily she could have fallen in love with the man. But seeing him next to Harlan she knew even more clearly than before that something important was missing in Richard's makeup—something very apparent in Harlan's. There was no question which of the two men dominated the scene. And Phoebe found herself resenting Harlan's easy self-assertion.

"I'm Harlan Garand and you don't need to introduce yourself," he was saying helpfully to the taller man, waving him casually into the room as if it were his apartment and not Phoebe's. "You're Richard Elton Chambers the Third. I'm pleased to meet you," he added with due politeness, holding out his hand which was reluctantly shaken by a confused looking Richard.

"I see. The name is familiar," Richard said with great civility, Phoebe thought. "You're a friend of Phoebe's?"

Harlan took in the full effect of the other man, running an

obviously perusing eye from the top of Richard's carefully styled hair to the tips of his expensive Italian leather loafers. Then he smiled and Phoebe, recognizing the smile instantly, unstuck herself from the settee and bounded forward in an attempt to forestall his next words. But she was too late. Much too late.

"You could say that," Harlan answered Richard's question. "We just spent the weekend together."

For an instant the only sound in the room was a furious little squeak from Phoebe. Then she found her tongue and rushed toward Richard, taking a grip on his arm and leading him into the living room.

"Don't listen to him! He's got a very strange sense of humor. What he means is, he gave me a lift out of the mountains after these two awful men gave me a lift on the highway and then kidnapped me! Oh, it's a long story . . ." she began desperately.

"Phoebe, what's going on here? Where have you been all weekend? I tried to call you this morning and there was no answer. Where did you run into this Mr., uh, Garand, anyway?"

Poor Richard, Phoebe groaned inwardly. He must be hopelessly confused.

"Sit down, Richard," she ordered gently. "I'll fix you a drink and explain the whole thing . . ." He would understand once she had a chance to outline the sequence of events logically. Richard was a very logical man. It was how he ran his company—logically.

"You tell him all about it, Phoebe," Harlan instructed from behind her. "I'll get the drink. You'll probably need one, too, I imagine."

"But you don't know where everything is . . ." she protested, turning to fix him with a furious expression.

"Now, honey, there's no point in trying to make Richard think we're not well acquainted. I'm sure he's grasping the situation in detail!" With that, Harlan disappeared in the direction of the kitchen and began opening cupboard doors energetically.

"Oh, Richard, I'm so sorry everything's so confused, but there is a reasonable explanation, I promise!"

"That man . . ." Richard began tenaciously.

"Yes, I know. He can be very annoying. The fact of the matter is, I owe him a debt of gratitude, though. I might still be trying to find my way down that mountain if I hadn't run into his cabin, you know. And that terrible hunter might have found me and done something drastic!"

"Okay, Phoebe. I can see you've been through an upsetting experience. Take it from the top and explain to me exactly what did happen."

Phoebe smiled, thankful for Richard's calm, understanding approach. She drew a deep breath, determined to get through as much of the story as possible before Harlan returned. She could hear the clink of glasses from the kitchen.

Concentrating totally on the good looking, if rather perplexed, man in front of her, she told Richard the story quickly and succinctly, glossing over the weekend she had spent with Harlan with the comment that she had stumbled into his camp and he had given her a ride back to Portland the next day. But Richard Elton Chambers III had not gotten to be Managing Director of the Portland branch of the family's timber firm on his looks alone.

"You arrived Saturday morning at the cabin and that man didn't bring you back until this afternoon?" he asked slowly.

"Well, you see, he didn't believe my story right away. It wasn't until that terrible man came creeping around, the one I threw the boiling water on, that Harlan realized I was telling the truth." Phoebe watched Richard with a hopeful expression.

"Phoebe, this is all a little hard to absorb . . ."

"Exactly my opinion on Saturday morning, Chambers," Harlan agreed genially, carrying a tray of drinks into the living room with the air of a gracious host. "You can see why I hesitated to take Phoebe at face value when she appeared on my doorstep at six o'clock in the morning with such a ridiculous tale! Of course, after I had gotten to know her better, much better, I realized she was telling the truth." He set the tray down on the glass-topped rattan coffee table and handed a glass to Richard.

"I would have trusted her at once!" Richard declared firmly. Phoebe smiled at him gratefully.

"You would?" Harlan asked with obvious interest. He glanced speculatively at Phoebe who wanted to yell at him abusively. "Oh, I agree she looks fairly harmless right now. But you should have seen her this weekend with her hair all tangled and her jeans a mess. She had lost a button off her blouse which gave her a very disreputable looking décolletage. All in all, she appeared quite abandoned on Saturday morning. If you'd been in my place you'd have wanted to see how much more abandoned she'd get by Saturday night. It's no wonder I waited a while to bring her home!"

"Harlan Garand! Will you shut up? I've had it with you!" Phoebe leaped to her feet, fists clenched at her sides, full bosom heaving.

"Garand?" Richard appeared to be making some connection in his mind. "Anything to do with the Garand freight forwarding firm?" He turned his grey glance on Harlan intently.

"Yes." Harlan's response was stiff, the mocking note gone completely from his voice as he switched his gaze from Phoebe to Richard. He plainly was not inviting any more inquiries into his job, she thought, sitting down.

"You know of him, Richard?" Phoebe asked, frowning at the taller man.

"Well, yes. I'm aware of the firm, at least. We've used it a number of times to make arrangements to ship to Hong Kong and other places in the East. It's a very successful one, I believe, with offices throughout the South Pacific . . ." His fine brow creased momentarily. "Didn't the old man die a couple of years ago? Are you John Garand's son?" he pursued.

Phoebe glanced at Harlan in time to see him respond with a short, swift inclination of his head. The icy eyes slanted a quick look at her as if to see how she was taking this news.

"A *very* successful firm?" she asked with unnatural gentleness.

"I do all right," he said briefly, sipping his drink and watching her over the rim of the glass.

Before she could follow through with her questions, Richard interrupted.

"Phoebe, I want to get something straight here. This man, who has a certain reputation, I might add now that I place him, says you spent the weekend with him." Richard took a breath and Phoebe knew what was coming next. What she didn't know was how to counter the implicit accusation.

"What I'm asking is, did he bother you in any way? You say you were escaping from two would-be rapists. Was there, in fact, a third who should be dealt with?" Richard drew himself impressively to his feet, turning to glare accusingly at Harlan. "I am not without influence in this town, Garand. If you've abused Phoebe in any manner, I shall see to it that those two kidnappers aren't the only ones to suffer the full weight of the law!"

"Richard, Mr. Garand gave me shelter and a couple of meals. Nothing more," Phoebe hastened to say clearly, thinking that Richard was behaving as if he were facing a board of directors. Instinctively she tried to soothe the stern expression from his handsome face.

"You're neglecting to mention the fact that we slept together," Harlan contributed with harsh bluntness.

"Phoebe!" Richard turned to face her. "Is that true? Did he force you . . ."

"No! Please, Richard, try to understand. It was very cold and there was only one sleeping bag . . ."

"You slept with him willingly?" Richard looked thunderstruck. "My God! What would your brother say! And here you were supposed to be considering my proposal of marriage! How could you even think of allowing yourself to be seduced? Especially if you had only barely escaped being raped a few hours before you met this man! Perhaps your original story

344

was not the whole truth? Perhaps you've thought up some wild story to explain Mr. Garand's presence . . .''

"My brother!" whispered Phoebe, thoroughly stunned. Suddenly Richard's lack of belief in her story no longer mattered at all. "What do you know about my brother?" A terrible suspicion began to crystallize.

Richard looked taken back by her barely voiced question. It was obvious he had hit his stride as the offended party and had no wish to give up the role to her. "I didn't mention the fact that I know your brother because he had warned me not to imply that he and I had ever had any business dealings . . ." he began stiffly.

"What business dealings?" Phoebe cried, leaping to her feet, a white fury burning deep in her breast.

"Your brother designs for us on occasion. He's helped us a great deal with some new pulp machinery. When he found out you were coming to Portland a few months ago to look for a job, he mentioned the fact to me. I instructed our personnel department to keep an eye out for your résumé. I was more than happy to do your brother a favor and give you a job, Phoebe. You've done excellent work for us and . . ."

"What about asking me to marry you?" Phoebe snarled. "Was that part of the favor you were doing for Steve?"

"Of course not! But after I had met you and gotten to know you, I realized that we'd make a good match. Your brother was frankly very pleased. He has already agreed to do some more work for us. You know he only works when he feels like it and we've been extremely lucky to have his cooperation . . ."

"Get out of here!" Phoebe hissed, enraged. Her glittering gaze encompassed both men. "I want you both out of this apartment or I swear to God I'll call the police!" She reached behind her, groped for a weapon, and felt her fingers close around a small dish which had served as an ornament on the end table. She hoisted it threateningly.

"Now, Phoebe," began Harlan, moving toward her even as Richard stepped back toward the door. "Calm down! Behave yourself! Do you want the whole apartment building to hear you?''

"Don't touch me!'' she warned, evading his grasp. "You're no better than he is! You gave me no idea who you really were or what you did! I thought you were a nice guy who *worked* for a living!'' She was being horribly unfair, knew it, and couldn't help herself. The feeling of being much abused was too strong to let her think rationally. "You never told me you owned a huge company and were rich! Like he is!'' She pointed an accusing finger at the hapless Richard who shrank back under it. "I asked you what you did for a living!''

"Phoebe, put down that dish and listen to me! You're acting like an obnoxious child . . .'' Harlan's hand whipped out, caught her wrist and removed the potential weapon. With equal efficiency, he grasped the other wrist and locked them together in a one-handed grip.

"You're totally irrational at the moment and it's only because you've had an exhausting weekend that I'm not going to turn you over my knee and beat some sense into you! Be grateful! The temptation is almost more than I can resist. Don't worry. Chambers and I are leaving. I think he's got the message that you don't intend to marry him. Now, try to get yourself under control. I'll call you tomorrow evening, understand?'' His hand tightened around her wrists as she struggled furiously.

"I hear you!'' Phoebe gritted. "Now get out of my apartment!''

Harlan held her an instant longer, seemed about to say something else, and then released her abruptly, striding toward the door where Richard hovered anxiously. A moment later, both men were gone and Phoebe was left alone with her hurt and anger.

She did something she hadn't done even after learning how her brother had sought to buy her a husband the first time. She cried. Ferd moved restlessly in his cage. His limited vocabulary didn't include words of comfort.

Chapter Five

"This is rather short notice, don't you think, Miss Hampton?" Melvin Waller peered disapprovingly at Phoebe as she sat stiffly on the other side of the desk.

"My reasons for giving only two weeks notice are personal, Mr. Waller," Phoebe replied aloofly. And I certainly don't intend to go into them with you, you old gossip, she thought feelingly. She gave her superior stare for stare and, as usual, won the small contest. There was no way in the world she could stay at Richard's company now. Not after all that had happened. When she had finally dried her eyes, doused her blotchy face in cold water, and fixed herself a small bite to eat last night she had known that leaving her job was the first step that must be taken to regain her pride.

"Miss Hampton, you hold an important position with Chambers Timber. A *management* position . . ." Waller began dubiously. "Your role in data management . . ."

"No one is indispensable, Mr. Waller. Lois can cover for me. She's been involved with the budget figures and the organization matrix. In fact, she would be an excellent candidate for my replacement."

"Chambers Timber may think twice about promoting another woman into management if they make a habit out of only working a few months and then giving notice!" Waller told her snidely.

"Then Chambers Timber had better be very careful if it decides to start discriminating. There are laws now, Mr. Waller. Furthermore, you know as well as I do that my work has been more than satisfactory. Lois Crompton has been with the firm for several years so no one can possibly say she's *flighty*. You would do well to consider her." Phoebe got to her feet. "If you will please see that those papers get to Personnel, I will begin organizing things for my departure." She turned with a small, highly professional smile and walked out of the office. Men!

Phoebe was careful to keep out of any corridors where Richard might be encountered and at noon she escaped to a downtown park to eat a lonely hotdog purchased from one of the many sidewalk vendors. It was overcast, but that seemed normal to Phoebe after having lived in Portland throughout the late winter and early spring. It fit her mood, she thought, indulging herself in another spate of self-pity which lasted until nearly one o'clock. At five minutes to the hour she pulled herself together with great determination and began to make plans for the future. It helped to itemize, categorize and organize, she thought with rueful humor. The logic of the situation came easily. It was the emotional side of the thing which was causing problems. She must, Phoebe told herself, avoid that aspect and choose a course which would cause her the least amount of problems.

The most important and immediate concern, now that she had handed in her resignation, was not to be at home that evening in the event Harlan actually followed through on his promise the night before and called. Of the two men she had thrown out of her apartment last night, Phoebe decided sadly, Harlan was the one who had managed to inflict the greatest degree of hurt—which was, when one stopped to consider, an idiotic state of affairs. She had been prepared never to see the man again and now that she had an excellent reason not to do so, it hurt. It wasn't that he had lied to her exactly, she thought during the bus ride home. He had simply misled her. She remembered with painful clarity the discussions on men from comfortable backgrounds and winced. From what Richard had implied last night, Harlan Garand came from just such a background! Which only made it all the more impossible that he should be genuinely interested in her, she told herself grimly. She had been a novelty, bursting in on his private weekend with a wild story and looking quite different from his normal preference in females and . . .

Why was she dwelling on the subject? Phoebe scolded herself as she opened the door into her snug little apartment. She wasn't being in the least sensible! One minute hating the man because he couldn't possibly be really attracted to her and the next telling herself she wouldn't want him to be!

The well-tailored white suit and snappy little sandals were relegated to the closet as Phoebe slipped into a comfortable western style shirt and denim slacks. She ran a brush through the thick mass of hair which framed the gentle roundness of her face and stared into the mirror with unusually strong feelings of self-dissatisfaction. Round! Everything about her seemed round! Round face, round hair, round figure . . . Well, she wasn't really fat, she reminded herself with a slight resurgence of spirit. It was just this slight tendency toward plumpness . . . The hell with it, she thought and left the apartment feeling generally annoyed with life. She even ignored Ferd's parting remarks.

There was plenty of daylight outside and she knew that this far north it would last until nearly nine o'clock. Phoebe started walking, not really caring where she was going—some vague notion of finding a place to eat guiding her steps. Several blocks down the street she found a natural foods restaurant and treated herself to a sunflower seed salad and a bowl of yogurt.

Feeling better for the act of self-denial dinner had represented, she continued on down to the theater district and idly read the marquees advertising films. She had never gone to a movie alone before but it was a way of killing the evening and she felt it would be good for her to practice a bit of assertiveness.

When she emerged from the movie house after sitting through two dull features and the cartoon it was after ten o'clock and dark. Going to the movies alone had proven to be a boring experience. It was the sort of activity that needed to be shared to be completely enjoyed, she realized dismally.

The walk home through dark streets didn't seem particularly attractive so she spent another twenty minutes waiting for a bus which finally deposited her two blocks from the apartment building. The shadowy park on one side and the forbidding doorways on the other gave Phoebe a strong impetus to hurry. Unbidden, memories of the kidnapping the previous Friday came back to trouble her. Why had she stayed out after dark? She should have timed the movie and left in the middle so as to be home before nine . . .

She didn't notice the dark figure detach itself from the side of her building and step forward until he loomed directly in front of her, blocking the path.

"I know this is going to sound depressingly like an irate husband interrogating his errant wife, but damn it! Where the hell have you been all evening?" Harlan's unmistakably rich voice came out of the darkness, conveying a high degree of impatience and irritation. In fact, Phoebe realized, he could be described as downright angry.

She glared at him, recovering from the awful start he had given her and snapped peevishly, "Why did you have to scare me to death like that? I nearly screamed!"

"Serves you right! One would think that any reasonably intelligent woman who had been kidnapped only a few days ago would be a little more cautious about being on city streets at night!" Harlan informed her righteously. "Come on, let's go inside. It's been raining off and on and I'm tired of trying to avoid it by standing under that little umbrella your landlady considers an awning!"

Phoebe glanced automatically at his damp hair, gleaming in the streetlight. He was wearing a suede jacket complete with lambswool lining and looked as though he could have just ridden off the range. It had the effect of making him seem more intimidating than ever. He had caught hold of one wrist and was dragging her along in his wake, heading for the front door.

"I do not recall inviting you into my apartment," Phoebe began haughtily as he pulled her down the entrance hall and stabbed the elevator button with a certain viciousness.

"No? I distinctly recall telling you I would be phoning this evening." He turned a menacing look on her. "When I got no answer by eight o'clock I invited myself on over. I thought you might be pulling a childish trick like refusing to answer the phone. When I got here I discovered you had pulled an even more infantile trick: You had disappeared for the evening! I've been waiting for over two hours, Phoebe Hampton, and I am not in a charitable mood. And to think I came over here with the best of intentions!" he concluded disgustedly.

"Really?" she inquired with deep scorn. "What intentions?" The elevator door opened to receive them as if doing the world a favor and Harlan yanked her inside.

"I had planned to offer you a job, of course," he informed her, looking down at her as if she were a little slow mentally.

"How did you know I was in the market for one?" she gritted, feeling abused and not at all sure how to retaliate.

"Didn't you hand in your resignation today? Where's your key?" Silently Phoebe dug it out and handed it to him. He pushed her through the elevator door and down the hall where he unlocked the door, prodded her inside, and closed it behind them. He tossed the key down onto a small table.

"Well? Didn't you?" he insisted, turning to face her.

"How did you know that?" she inquired icily, hands on the curve of her hips. She watched helplessly as he shrugged out of the heavy coat.

"I figured it would be the first action you took." He hung up the coat in her hall closet and started toward the living room. The wicker settee squeaked alarmingly as he threw himself down on it. "Pretty furniture, but I don't think it's going to wear well," he observed, calmly unfastening the top button of his shirt.

"Stop avoiding the issue and tell me how you knew I had resigned!"

Harlan sighed. "I thought you might have done so because it is exactly what I would have done in the circumstances." He regarded her levelly. "There, does that satisfy you?"

How could he know her so well, Phoebe thought furiously!

"The answer to your kind offer of a job is no! There! Does that satisfy you?" she retorted, seating herself angrily in the fan chair.

"I never made the offer. I merely pointed out that it had been in my mind to do so when I first arrived this evening. That was two cold, wet hours ago. I am no longer feeling magnanimous," he told her politely.

Phoebe shrugged with a great air of not caring and leaned back in the chair to eye him thoughtfully through narrowed lids. "Then why," she asked with equal politeness, "are you still hanging around?"

"The first reason is that I'm still waiting for an answer to my initial question," he responded coolly.

"The one about where I've been this evening?" she probed with great casualness.

"Precisely."

"You don't really expect me to tell you, do you?" Phoebe felt her self-confidence returning slowly. There were limits, even for people like Harlan Garand! He couldn't force her to tell him what he wanted to know and she was beginning to derive no small pleasure from being able to deny him something!

"I most certainly do," he contradicted. "I didn't spend the past two hours growing increasingly kindhearted."

"It's none of your business."

"Phoebe, either you tell me where you've been or I'll come over there and wring the information out of you. Don't play games with me!'' He didn't raise his voice but Phoebe suddenly knew he would do exactly as promised.

"I went out to eat and then I went to a film." She made no effort to keep the resentful tones out of her voice.

"Alone?"

"Yes! The last thing I wanted tonight was an escort!" she flared.

"Still mad at all men, huh?" He smiled slightly, lounging back into the pillows of the settee and regarding her with a superior, mocking expression which did nothing to endear him to her.

"I feel," she pointed out drily, "that I have justifiable cause."

"Phoebe, I don't care what you think of the Third. I know full well your heart isn't broken over him and your pride, which constitutes the only damaged part, will recover. But I want to get one thing straight between us: I never lied to you this weekend!" There was so much intensity in the last few words that Phoebe blinked in astonishment.

"There are different ways of lying," she remarked evenly.

"I'm aware of that fact."

"You misled me."

"I was functioning under the notion that you knew the whole truth about who I was and what I did for a living. I assumed you were playing some game and saw no reason to participate." Harlan watched her closely.

There was a long moment of silence while Phoebe struggled with the knowledge that she wasn't being totally fair.

"You could have told me who you were after you realized I wasn't lying to you," she finally said forcefully, foreseeing the probable end of the discussion and knowing she was only postponing the inevitable apology.

"Come on, honey!" Phoebe told herself to take no notice of the endearment. Harlan was just being casually cajoling. "What was I supposed to do? All I could think about after that creep showed up in the front yard was getting both of you to the police! I felt like an absolute idiot for having been so egotistical as to think you had followed me from Portland! Be realistic, Phoebe! At that point I had a great deal on my mind!''

Phoebe drew a deep breath, knowing she was beaten and knowing that accusing him of lying had only been a way of trying to protect herself. But she was an honest young woman and it would be impossible for her to maintain the defense much longer.

''All right, Harlan. I apologize for saying you lied to me. My only excuse is that I was rather upset last night. Your interference during my discussion with Richard did not predispose me to look kindly upon you!''

Harlan seemed to relax slightly as Phoebe made her ungracious apology. A small lift at the corners of his mouth told her he was satisfied. Having got what he came for, namely an apology, he would no doubt be taking his leave, Phoebe thought a trifle despondently. So? Wasn't that what she wanted?

''You've been kind enough to apologize to me,'' he commented mockingly, ''but don't think I'm going to return the favor for my 'interference' last night. I wanted Richard Elton Chambers III out of the way and decided to make certain you followed through on your plan to get rid of him . . .''

''What in the world has Richard ever done to you that you should feel so hostile?'' Phoebe interrupted bitterly.

''Nothing. I wanted to keep it that way.'' Harlan seemed uninterested in discussing the matter further. He paused, as if trying to decide how to phrase his next words.

''I mentioned at the cabin that I had made a couple of mistakes in dealing with you, Phoebe . . .''

''I don't think we should go into that any further,'' she said tonelessly.

''But I wish to have everything out in the open,'' he smiled almost gently. ''I realized Saturday night that something was quite wrong in my analysis of the reasons for your presence at the cabin but I couldn't quite bring myself to believe your outlandish story, either. As I said yesterday, now I know why

I was so confused. Your eyes are crystal clear, you know," he told her lightly. "In the future when I want to know whether or not you're telling me the truth all I will have to do is make you face me, eye to eye, and simply ask you. It's going to simplify my life considerably!"

The man seemed ridiculously pleased with himself, Phoebe thought, more annoyed than ever. What in the world did he mean by saying his life was going to be simplified?

"Mistake number two I mention again only to make it clear that I don't intend to allow you to control our romantic interludes as easily as you did Saturday night! It embarrasses me even to recall the way I backed off from the situation after you fed me that dumb line about trusting me!" Harlan grimaced ruefully.

Phoebe, knowing quite well there would probably never be another such interlude between the two of them, allowed herself a small, mischievous smile, eyes sparkling behind the lenses of her glasses.

"Come, Harlan, you wouldn't deny me my one successful gambit of the weekend, would you? Everything else certainly went your way! When I think of those awful fish!"

He grinned suddenly. "Enjoy your victory! Next time I will be the one making the decisions about where to stop!"

"Were there any other mistakes you forgot to mention?" Phoebe prompted smoothly, wanting very badly to get off the subject which implied a potential romance between them. Harlan was only teasing her now, she told herself.

"Yes, as a matter of fact, there was. I didn't mention it yesterday because I wanted to think about it. I also wanted a chance to check out the Third. The last mistake I made was in not telling you I intend to marry you, Phoebe." Harlan spoke simply, his eyes never leaving hers.

Phoebe, making a valiant effort to recover from the shock, stared at him blankly as if he had just announced he was from outer space. Making a strong attempt at rallying herself, she snapped briskly, "You surprise me! I didn't think you would allow yourself to be motivated by misguided notions of masculine honor. You made it perfectly clear at the cabin that you had no intention of being maneuvered into marriage!''

"I refuse to be maneuvered, but that doesn't mean I'm opposed to the whole idea! Phoebe, we got along famously this weekend, in spite of the fact that we were at cross-purposes part of the time. And I need a wife. Dear Aunt Flo is right about that, much as I hate to admit it. Garand Freight Forwarding has been in the family for three generations. It would be a shame to let it go into other hands. There are so few traditions left in this world. I'm thirty-five years old, tired of the singles scene, and tired of having a series of eligible young females paraded in front of me. I want someone I can trust completely, someone who doesn't care much about the social world, someone I can talk to, someone with a sense of humor, someone who's resourceful . . .''

"Brave, loyal and honest! Good grief, Harlan! Please stop or I shall have to get out my old Girl Scout uniform and reread the laws!'' Phoebe found herself suddenly convulsed in laughter.

"I am not accustomed to having women go off into gales of merriment at the thought of marriage to me . . .'' Harlan began a little roughly, getting abruptly to his feet and striding across the room to where she sat giggling. Determinedly he reached down and hauled her up beside him.

"Really? How many have you proposed to?'' Phoebe managed as the outright laughter subsided gradually into a series of chuckles. She had to treat Harlan and his proposal with the humor it deserved, she thought wildly. Otherwise she would probably cry!

"None,'' he admitted wryly. "You're the first woman I've thought seriously about marrying. I've been quite content with a bachelor existence until recently . . .''

"Until you got lucky and stumbled on an overgrown Girl Scout! Well, Harlan, don't worry. I'm sure the whole thing is only a temporary aberration brought on by feelings of guilt and the fact that you're probably a little sorry for me. In a few days you'll be happily back into the swing of things and the skinny little blonds will start looking very good again! You'll be extremely grateful to me for not taking advantage of your momentary weakness!''

Phoebe removed her glasses to wipe the tears of laughter and some other emotion which she refused to acknowledge from her eyes. ''Let me see,'' she began lightly, replacing the frames with an absent gesture. ''I shall have to find the proper wording for refusing your proposal. Perhaps I could use the phrases I was practicing for Richard and never got a chance to try due to an unwarranted interruption at the time! Harlan, I am duly aware of the honor you have extended to me in making me this offer of marriage, but I must regretfully decline . . .''

''Phoebe, my dear, I haven't made you an offer of marriage,'' Harlan interrupted to point out emphatically. There was a touch of answering humor now in the brilliant gaze he centered on her face and the firm mouth was twisted slightly at the corners.

''I beg your pardon!'' Phoebe began with a small grin. ''I seem to have misunderstood . . .''

''You did. I never asked you to marry me. I don't intend to ever ask you. That would be inviting the severest form of rejection, as you've just been at pains to demonstrate! My ego couldn't take it. No, honey, I'm *telling* you that we're going to be married. There, that's much simpler, isn't it? No room for arguments, jokes, scenes, etc.''

''Harlan, what's the matter with you?'' Phoebe demanded, laughter fading rapidly from her voice as she caught the determination in his. She peered up at him speculatively. ''It's not in character for someone like you to want to marry someone like me. If you're really looking for all those admirable characteristics I'm sure you'll find them in a woman from your own world. One who's small and blond in the bargain! I'm sure your aunt could help you locate a charming creature who will suit the role of Mrs. Harlan Garand to perfection!''

''What do you know of my world, Phoebe? There's a great

deal you don't know about me or what I want out of life, but you'll learn. I have great faith in your native intelligence!'' Harlan smiled almost gently, removed her glasses delicately and, placing them down carefully, pulled her close into a tight embrace.

Despite the gentleness of his voice, there was nothing soft about Harlan's kiss. It was as if he took up the lovemaking where he had left off on Saturday night, Phoebe thought frantically, feeling her response rise almost immediately to meet his. How could he demand and receive such instant reciprocation when her brain was clearly calling for caution from her body? Had she no self-control left at all when it came to this man? She must! Her future happiness depended on not surrendering completely, Phoebe lectured herself, even while her lips softened beneath his and her mouth opened to receive the warmth of him. His arms tightened as he felt her weakening and Harlan deliberately pursued his advantage.

Telling herself she could retreat and reestablish her barricades later, Phoebe surrendered to the onslaught. Even in his present mood of conquering, dominating male, Harlan's arms held more satisfaction than Phoebe had ever before known. For the first time in her life she was dealing with a man who was able and willing to use his strength and his sexual technique when words failed to get him what he wanted. The power of it was overwhelming.

Sensing her crumbling resistance, Harlan shifted his hold, letting strong hands mold her body against his until she was fully aware of the male need growing in him. His mouth left hers to nibble delicately at the tip of her ear and Phoebe found herself clinging helplessly to him, the only steady object in a room which had begun to whirl dangerously. The tighter she clung, the more Harlan consolidated his attack, taking advantage of every weakness, every tiny retreat, seeming to revel in each new surrender. It wasn't until Phoebe felt her feet leave the floor as Harlan swung her into his arms that she came back to some vague sense of reality.

''Harlan!'' she gasped, her head spinning as she was cradled against his chest. Dimly she was aware of the fact that he was striding down the hall to her bedroom apparently oblivious to the weight in his arms. The romantic side of her nature was thrusting fiercely to the fore, pointing out that he was treating her exactly as if she really were a tiny, fragile blond. The practical streak was at a loss to know how to stop him.

"Harlan, wait," she tried feebly.

"Quiet, sweetheart," he ordered softly, huskily, finding the door to her bedroom and entering as if he had every right. "I forgot to mention one other reason why I intend to marry you," he whispered, dumping her lightly on the bed and following immediately, sprawling across her bed with casual disregard. "I find you irresistible, my cuddly little Phoebe. You fill my hands so sweetly with your softness and I find I want more and more of you. As my intentions are quite honorable, I fail to see why I should bother trying to restrain myself! Besides," he grinned wickedly down at her, "I have the distinct impression I can make you do anything I want when you're in my arms. The temptation to exercise that kind of power is more than I can withstand!" He lowered his lips deliberately to the hollow of her throat. "And I have an urgent need to find out what you're like when you let yourself go completely, my Phoebe!" His hand moved along the curve of her hip, into the dip of her waist, and on up to rest beneath the heaviness of one breast. His thumb glided across the tip, exciting the nipple through the layers of fabric.

Phoebe closed her eyes, trying desperately to reason through a situation that was not at all reasonable. Harlan didn't, *couldn't* really want her—not as a wife, not forever! She was merely something new in his world. A woman who represented a change of pace, but not one of the type he admitted admiring! His mad proposal was born out of his feelings of guilt, she told herself. He must be given time to think, to reconsider. And he must do it before he had made love to her completely! She couldn't bear to have him change his mind afterward!

"Harlan, listen to me!" Phoebe begged, trying futilely to

twist out from under the length of his hard body. "You haven't done anything right tonight!" The last was uttered in a tone of outraged despair and it stopped him cold.

Harlan lifted his head and simply stared down at her. Phoebe returned the look, heart in her mouth.

"Would you mind explaining that last remark?" he inquired deliberately, not moving. One red brow crooked upward warningly.

Phoebe licked a dry lip, gathering her thoughts, trying to marshal them into arguments which would buy her what her physical strength never could—time.

"Harlan, I don't believe for a moment that you really mean to marry me."

"No?" There was a dangerous seasoning of steel in the deep voice.

"No," Phoebe responded with growing firmness. "I told you, I think you're acting out of some misguided idea that you owe me something. Or perhaps I'm different enough from your normal choice in women to intrigue you for a short time. But if you are the least bit serious, you owe me a lot more than what you've seen fit to give me tonight!"

"What the hell is that supposed to mean?" he growled, the hand on her breast tightening.

"It means that just because I don't happen to be beautiful and blond and thin, I don't want to be treated that way by the man who says he wants to marry me!" she whispered nervously. "Look at it from my point of view, Harlan," she begged. "You accost me on my way home tonight, inform me that you're going to marry me for all sorts of wholesome reasons, and then pick me up and carry me off to the bedroom— my *own* bedroom, I might add, as if you had every right in the world! Even you have to admit that's rushing things somewhat! A woman deserves more than that from a prospective husband!" Phoebe concluded feelingly.

"What more does she deserve?" Harlan asked menacingly.

"Some romance, for heaven's sake!" Phoebe was rapidly taking heart from her own words, her spirit surfacing as she realized how just her cause was. "I'll bet you never acted this way with any of your little blonds!"

"I never planned to marry any of them!" Harlan snapped, sounding mightily aggrieved. "I thought you were a woman of common sense! What do you want with all those dumb games?"

"That goes to show how little you know about me!" she shot back. "I want to be romanced! To be courted!"

"As I see it," Harlan continued in almost conversational tones, "I now have two options open. I can revert back to my recently interrupted attempt at seduction. Which attempt, I believe, would be entirely successful. On the other hand, I could try and convince you that I'm well aware of what I'm doing by marrying you."

Phoebe drew a careful breath. "There is," she said delicately, "another alternative you might consider."

"Which is?" he asked with mild interest.

"You could," she said softly, "court me."

"Court you?" he repeated, obviously surprised. "Phoebe, I told you at the cabin that I don't see myself as able to conduct a very restrained sort of courtship, which is probably the type you have in mind!"

"Harlan, all I want is a little time. Time for you to make certain of your feelings and time for me to understand mine. Is that too much to ask? I want to be certain there's really love between us!"

Harlan glared down at her for a long moment. Then he appeared to come to a decision. "I will," he announced with the attitude of one who is making a huge concession, "court you until the end of the Rose Festival." His expression dared her to throw out a counter offer.

"The Rose Festival ends somewhere in the middle of June, doesn't it?" Phoebe frowned, trying to recall the publicity she had seen on the annual event.

"It ends on the tenth of June. We'll be married no later than the eleventh," he stated uncompromisingly.

"But, Harlan! That's only three weeks away!" Phoebe wailed.

"Take your pick: Three days from now or three weeks from now."

"I promise to consider the offer very seriously over the next three weeks," Phoebe said with fake calm.

"Don't look too smug, Phoebe," he warned mockingly. "You've asked for a courtship and you'll get it. But it will be run by my rules!"

Chapter Six

The yellow roses were waiting outside her door the next morning. Phoebe discovered them as she prepared to leave for work. She immediately assumed the florist had made a delivery error and was about to take them down to the manager's office when she noticed the card addressed to herself. With a funny twinge of elation, she ripped it open and read the brief note inside. It was scrawled in a huge, lazy hand which she knew instantly belonged to Harlan. It read simply, "To match your bedspread." Wryly, Phoebe smiled and remembered once again how at home the man had made himself in her bedroom the previous evening. A further almost indecipherable line told her to be ready for dinner at seven. Typical arrogance, she told herself, inserting the card back into the envelope and carrying the flowers inside the apartment. He hadn't even signed the note! The assumption that there were no other men in her life who might be sending yellow roses was as annoying as it was accurate.

"Look at these, Ferd. Harlan's first effort at courtship. What do you think?" Phoebe extended the roses toward the cage and the bird eyed them thoughtfully for a moment and then pronounced his verdict:

"Fee, fie, fo, fum . . ."

"Yes, yes, I know," she interrupted him. "You smell the blood of an Oregonian. It's a pity we haven't had more time to work on your language lessons!"

At ten o'clock Phoebe received a phone call in her office from Richard's secretary. She was requested to appear in the managing director's office in fifteen minutes. Phoebe knew the curtness of the instruction was a little something extra added by Janice Taylor, the secretary. Poor Janice would have given her right arm to be dating Richard, Phoebe thought with a sigh. She wondered if she ought to drop a hint or two in the other girl's ear. She could have told the blond, for instance, that Richard needed someone more conservative looking for his wife. Someone who could project refined elegance, not a showgirl level of beauty. Phoebe had often wondered how she had qualified for Richard's consideration herself, feeling she fell far short of the elegant look or even the showgirl look! Well, now she knew. Was she never to be free of her brother's influence?

"Go right on in, Miss Hampton," Janice remarked coolly, not even bothering to glance up from her typing. Phoebe studied the California-look hairdo, the silk blouse opened one button too far and the slightly pouting cast of the artfully colored lips and almost said something. Then she changed her mind and walked into Richard's office without a word. She did not anticipate a pleasant interview.

Richard rose as soon as she entered the room and Phoebe smiled politely, taking the chair he indicated.

"Hello, Phoebe. Sorry to pull you away from your work but I felt we should talk. I, uh, understand from Personnel that you've handed in your resignation?" He spoke hesitantly, the grey eyes not quite focusing on her.

"That's right. I think it would be a bit awkward for me to stay on after what happened Sunday night, don't you?" Phoebe was amazed by the calm sound of her own voice.

"Phoebe, I wish you would reconsider. You've done an excellent job here and have become a valuable member of the staff in only a few months." He paused. "I also want you to know that I'm sorry for not believing your story about being kidnapped. I talked to the police this morning and have let my acquaintances on the force know how strongly I feel about them finding the other man who was in that truck . . ."

"Thank you, Richard," she said politely, "I'm sure they'll do their best. As for filling the position I'm vacating, well, perhaps there is someone else's sister looking for a job . . ." Instantly, Phoebe wished she hadn't been so blatantly rude. Richard didn't deserve that. He couldn't help the way he behaved. He was a product of his environment.

"Phoebe, please! As much as I value your brother's genius and his contribution to this company, that doesn't mean I would have given you a position of genuine responsibility unless you were properly qualified! One doesn't staff a firm of this size with incompetents just to please certain people!"

Phoebe winced. "Oh, Richard, let's not discuss this any more. The truth of the matter is, I wasn't going to marry you regardless, so the result is the same as far as our relationship goes . . ."

"No, it's not the same! I have my pride, too, you see. I want to make it clear that just as I wouldn't have hired you if I hadn't been impressed by your credentials in information and data management, I wouldn't have asked you to marry me if I hadn't thought you'd make a good wife! Please believe me. Your brother's intelligence and wealth would be an asset to any family in this day and age, but I wouldn't have married you just to obtain a closer connection with him! I truly wanted to marry you, Phoebe." He looked directly at her now, apparently intent on convincing her of the basic integrity of his intentions. "You . . . you're different," he added lamely.

"Different?" she queried, intrigued by this new, hesitant side of a man who had always seemed so logical, deliberate, and controlled.

"You're nice to be with. I can talk to you and you don't

365

expect me to . . . to carry out the playboy role, if you know what I mean.'' He looked away again, focusing his gaze out the window toward the snow covered peak of Mount Hood in the distance.

''I see.'' Phoebe smiled with a measure of understanding. ''I hadn't realized how you felt pressured by your image.''

''That's just it! With you I don't feel that way!'' Richard smiled ruefully. ''I can relax with you.''

''But I could never have fallen in love with you, Richard,'' she said gently.

''Why not? You seemed to enjoy going out with me.''

''Dating you was one thing. I did enjoy your company. Very much. But I don't think we would have been happy together for the rest of our lives. You need someone beautiful who won't mind mixing continuously in the crowd you move with. I'm not that woman, Richard.''

''You could have adapted, Phoebe . . .''

''I might have been able to adapt but I don't want to adapt. There's a huge difference. Now if you want to meet someone who has both the looks and the willingness to be your wife and the social ornament you need, I suggest you step out that door and introduce yourself to your secretary!''

''Janice!'' Richard looked stunned.

''She's head over heels in love with you, Richard. Didn't you ever guess?''

''No, I . . .''

''Oh, you might have to guide her along the ways of society, but I guarantee she'll be a willing learner! In fact, she'd make a career out of being your wife!''

''But Janice is beautiful! She'd expect so much . . .'' Richard faltered, realizing he'd made an unforgivable blunder.

''Whereas us homely types don't pressure a man unduly?'' Phoebe got to her feet with great dignity and even managed a distant smile. ''Goodbye, Richard.''

She swung through the door and pulled it closed with unnatural softness behind her. What had she ever seen in that man? For an instant she stood regarding the hurt look in Janice

Taylor's attractive brown eyes and then she stepped over to the desk and leaned down confidentially.

"He's all yours, Janice. Want some advice?"

"What are you talking about, Miss Hampton?" Janice's carefully made-up face was unable to hide the degree of surprise she was experiencing at this unexpected assault from the sedate Phoebe Hampton.

"I'm talking about buttoning that blouse," Phoebe reached over and did it for her before the other girl could react. "Go wash off some of that makeup. You scare him. And get that hair back out of your face. You'll need a more refined image to catch Richard. Remember, you have to sell yourself to his mother and sister as well! The last tip is, don't make him feel that he's expected to be a super stud. Let him do the talking. He loves to talk about himself!"

"Miss Hampton!" Janice looked fascinated.

"One more thing. Do you play tennis?"

Suddenly Janice Taylor grinned. "No, but I'm willing to learn!"

"Then you've got it made. I was never ready to make the supreme sacrifice. Not the athletic type, I guess. Which only goes to show that I wasn't really in love with the man, doesn't it?" Phoebe winked and walked out the door.

Harlan's unmistakable knock sounded on Phoebe's door at five minutes to seven that evening and she went to answer, having serious second thoughts about the whole matter but unable to think of a way out. It wasn't as if, she told herself, there was a great deal of choice in the matter. While she wasn't quite sure what he would have done if she hadn't been waiting for him, she knew Harlan well enough now to know there would have been inescapable reprisals. Besides, this strange whim of his had to end soon, she thought glumly. Why shouldn't she take advantage of the situation to enjoy the excitement of his company while she could? Or as long as she could keep him out of her bed, at any rate! That way, Phoebe knew with a strong sense of certainty, lay pain. She would never, ever be able to put Harlan Garand out of her mind if she once allowed him to possess her. And that's what making love with him would be, Phoebe thought. An act of possession on his part, an act of surrender on hers. Not a very modern approach to the subject!

"Good evening," she greeted him very properly, opening the door to reveal Harlan dressed in an evening jacket. At once she was very glad she had dressed for the occasion.

"You didn't mention where we would be dining so I hope this is suitable?" She indicated the soft, clinging green gown, its halter top displaying a tantalizing amount of smooth, erect back. Her hair had been brushed into a sleek cape which was parted in the middle and curled softly inward at the ends. Small evening sandals completed the outfit, together with a tiny gold bracelet.

"You look perfect," Harlan smiled, moving his elegantly covered shoulders through the door. "Soft and rounded and incredibly sexy!"

"Sexy?" Phoebe stared at him, astounded. It was not a term which had often been applied to her before!

"Yes. Sexy!" Without another word, he stepped toward her and planted a quick, proprietary kiss on her surprised lips. "The contrast between my Phoebe dressed like this and my Phoebe in jeans is delightful."

"Harlan, you're embarrassing me! If you're going to spend the evening talking like this . . ." Phoebe broke off, very flustered.

"I have lots of things to discuss tonight. After all, this is the first day of the courtship!"

"You're really going to go through with it?" she asked dubiously, one brow climbing over the top of the rounded frames of her glasses.

"Naturally. Did you get the flowers?" He glanced around the room, saw the yellow roses displayed prominently on the table by the window and looked enormously pleased with himself.

"They're lovely. Thank you very much," Phoebe smiled

politely, wanting to tease him about the sheer male ego he was exposing, but not quite daring.

He nodded. "Good. Let's go, then. Better bring a wrap; it could get chilly later."

"Yes, Harlan."

"That's what I like to hear," he told her approvingly, holding the door as she swept through, into the hallway.

"Enjoy it while you can. You won't hear such words very often!" she informed him with a regal lift to her chin. Phoebe ignored his chuckle.

The restaurant he had chosen was terribly romantic, she decided. Candlelight, snowy-white linen, silver and crystal, and an emphasis on French cooking. Phoebe glanced around as Harlan held her chair and smiled sweetly.

"Roses in the morning, candlelight and wine at night. Do you do a lot of courting, Harlan?" she inquired demurely, taking the seat which left her facing the stone wall—and Harlan. He obviously intended no distractions, she thought, realizing he knew quite well what he was doing when he seated her.

"No, darling, a lot of seduction," he informed her easily, settling into the large chair opposite her.

The tips of Phoebe's small ears burned as she felt the hovering maitre d' stifle a smile. "Harlan!" she snapped, brows coming together reprovingly.

"You asked for it, honey," he told her carelessly, accepting the wine list and the menu. "Now, I promised myself I'd try very hard tonight, so don't provoke me," he instructed as the man disappeared.

Phoebe sighed. "Yes, Harlan. I wouldn't want to put a strain on your good manners or your good intentions!"

"That's right. Now let's choose dinner so we can get on with tonight's discussion!"

"You've got the evening completely programmed?" she demanded, feeling her lips twitch in an effort to keep from smiling.

"I've got the next three weeks planned!" he informed her

grandly. "You wanted a courtship, you'll get it!"

What have I let myself in for, Phoebe wondered, unable to ignore the excitement and tension between herself and Harlan. The romance might come to a bad end, but at least it wasn't going to be as dull as it had been with Richard!

With the arrival of the first course and a bottle of California Sauvignon Blanc Harlan plunged into the topic of the evening.

"Courtship," he began impressively, "is supposed to be a time when two people discover the likes and dislikes of the other."

"You've been reading up on the subject?"

"I've wracked my brain trying to figure out a way of occupying the next several evenings other than making love to you. Discussing likes and dislikes seems an ideal beginning!"

"I see," Phoebe nearly choked on her salad.

"Now. Do you or don't you like children?"

"My own or someone else's?" Phoebe asked, beginning to get into the spirit of the thing.

"Don't be flippant," Harlan ordered, grinning. "We are discussing the heir to the Garand Freight Forwarding business!"

"If my husband was absolutely convinced he wanted a child or two and if he was certain in his own mind that he would make a good father, I would consider becoming a mother."

"Don't be so cautious, Phoebe! It's obvious you were born to be a mother!" Harlan proclaimed, refilling her wine glass.

"Is it? I have that maternal look?" she asked crisply, not very happy with his comment.

"You have a loving look," he corrected mildly, catching her eye and smiling blandly. "You are one of those women designed by nature to create a home."

"What makes you such an expert?"

"Instinct."

"Well, your instinct is wrong this time, Harlan. I enjoy my career and don't see myself tied to a kitchen sink!"

"Ah, that's where we differ! Now I picture you barefoot, pregnant and most definitely confined to the kitchen!"

"Harlan Garand! Quit teasing me or I'll take myself home right this minute!" Phoebe was torn between laughter and indignation. Laughter won.

"That's better," he nodded approvingly.

"I'll make a deal with you," Phoebe offered brightly. "You agree to split the child-caring duties and spend lots of time with your heirs and I'll agree to have one or two of the little darlings. Fair enough?"

"Sounds reasonable," he nodded. "Maybe we should go a step farther and split the breadwinning, too."

"I'll run half of Garand Freight Forwarding and you'll run the other half?" Phoebe suggested.

"I'm not saying I'll give up my position as president," he corrected, "but I expect we could find you a position somewhere in the firm."

"Sounds like a clear case of nepotism."

"What's the point of running your own company if you can't do as you wish?"

Phoebe laughed outright, the happy sound turning the heads of a few amused diners nearby.

"I'm not sure I like the idea of taking orders from you all day long!" she protested.

"But I'm so good at giving them!" he grinned back.

"I'll just bet you are! I still haven't forgotten those fish! No, I think I'll maintain a separate career."

"Independent little creature, aren't you? Did the Third know what he was letting himself in for when he asked you to marry him?" Harlan asked interestedly.

"Oh, I found out this morning what my real attraction was," Phoebe chuckled, beginning to relax with the second glass of wine.

"You saw Chambers today?" Harlan asked, some of the humor fading from his eyes. He watched her obliquely, waiting for her response.

"Yes, he'd just discovered I'd turned in my resignation and wanted to assure me that I didn't have to go to such lengths. He said that I had been an asset to the company and that his

371

offer of marriage had been genuine. Prompted by the fact that he could talk to me," Phoebe confided.

"Talk to you? What the hell did he mean by that?"

"I don't make him feel pressured into being a playboy type," Phoebe smiled.

"I see. Well, I don't think there's any more need for you to discuss your past relationship with the man, Phoebe. It's finished. I don't want you to get into a position where you start feeling sorry for him!" Harlan was all business now, lecturing her firmly across the table.

"Some of the romance is going out of my evening, Harlan," she noted drily.

"Is it? That's all right, courtship is also an opportunity for the male to assert his right as head of the new family!"

"Courtship," Phoebe pointed out determinedly, "is an opportunity for the female to change her mind and get out of a situation that doesn't look promising!"

"It's a time when said female had better practice a little feminine subservience or risk getting paddled in front of God and the maitre d'!"

"No more romance tonight?" Phoebe pouted. "How depressing! And I had such high hopes this morning after the roses arrived! But, I suppose it's typical for the male to resort to threats of physical violence when he can't get what he wants by intelligent argument . . ."

"I can get what I want any time I choose," Harlan told her with mocking menace, "by taking you to bed and we both know it. If you wish me to continue with the other aspects of courtship, such as flowers and conversation, you had better heed my wishes in such matters as Richard Elton Chambers III. To be blunt, I don't want you seeing him in anything other than a business sense!"

Phoebe burst out laughing. "Poor Harlan! You feel so self-sacrificing, don't you?"

"I consider I'm being extremely generous, yes," he agreed readily, his expression lightening as he studied her laughing face. "It's not every woman I'd go through a courtship for!"

Abruptly Harlan's gaze shifted to a point past her left shoulder.

"Friend of yours?" he asked and Phoebe turned to see Julie Chambers advancing on them. Beautiful, thin, blond, Julie. Phoebe could have wished for anyone else at that particular moment.

"Phoebe! How are you, dear? Richard told me what happened on Friday. How ghastly for you! Thank heavens you're all right. You must have been absolutely terrified!"

"I was, Julie," Phoebe acknowledged her with a polite smile, knowing now that she and Richard's sister could never have been friends. "But everything's all right now. The police have one of the characters, thanks to Harlan here, and it's probably only a matter of time before they pick up the other one. Your brother has instructed them to put forth their best efforts," she added with a touch of mockery. She turned in her seat and made introductions.

"How do you do, Miss Chambers," Harlan said calmly, eyeing the shimmering length of the attractive girl who seemed to preen under his regard.

"Harlan Spencer Garand? Of the Garand firm? I believe my brother has mentioned you . . ."

Phoebe watched the other woman's light blue eyes clash with Harlan's brilliant gaze and felt such a wave of jealousy that she had to exercise considerable self-control just to stay in her seat. Some primitive reaction was trying to drive her to her feet to confront this other woman who was so obviously what Harlan wanted. Or was what he'd want again after he'd gotten over his temporary interest in Phoebe!

"Won't you sit down, Miss Chambers?" Harlan invited cordially, apparently oblivious to the flash of pain Phoebe knew had crossed her face. What was the matter with her? Wasn't it better to let Harlan find out the truth about himself quickly rather than a couple of weeks from now?

"You and Phoebe are out celebrating the lucky escape?" Julie hazarded, glancing from one to the other. She knows, Phoebe thought. Those malicious little blue eyes see everything. And Richard has probably already told her . . .

"Phoebe and I are going to be married," Harlan corrected. "In a way, though, I suppose we ought to be celebrating her escape too. If she hadn't had the courage to free herself I would never have met her!" He smiled into Phoebe's eyes and she warmed instantly. He was being very kind, she thought.

"Married!" Julie turned toward Phoebe. "You and Richard are through, then? Permanently?" She seemed intently interested in Phoebe's answer. Probably relieved I'm freeing her brother for a more suitable marriage, Phoebe decided and nodded.

"I see." The other girl turned a cool gaze back to Harlan. "Exactly how did the two of you meet? It's all quite sudden, isn't it?"

"Well, just between the three of us," Harlan began in a suspiciously confiding tone, "there wasn't much choice. I mean, after all, Phoebe wound up spending the weekend with me, you know!"

"Harlan!" Phoebe's poor protest was lost in Julie's outright laughter.

"You mean you're marrying the girl because you've compromised her? Oh, Harlan! What a marvelous joke! Wait until I tell my date!" Julie nodded toward the far corner of the room where a man was seated alone, staring across at them. "This is great! Everyone's going to love the story!"

"Julie, please," Phoebe began, glaring at Harlan who simply smiled benignly.

"My compliments, Phoebe," Julie smiled falsely. "You got a much better catch than Richard would have been. I mean, everyone knows the Garand firm is a very successful one! I'm sure Harlan here is much wealthier than my brother! And to think you trapped him into marriage! It's the best story I've heard in ages!" She got to her feet, smiling down at Harlan. "Please excuse me now, I really can't keep this one to myself any longer!" She lifted perfectly manicured nails in a graceful gesture of farewell and moved off.

"Now we can return to our conversation in peace," Harlan announced contentedly, picking up his knife and engaging his steak in battle.

"Harlan Garand! How could you! Of all the mean, cruel, malicious things to do to a woman . . ." Phoebe began, barely able to speak with the intensity of her emotion.

"Cruel? I wasn't cruel to her!" Harlan protested, looking incredibly innocent.

"Not her! Me! The woman you claim you want to marry! How dare you embarrass me by telling her you're marrying me because I spent the weekend with you!"

"You're a fetching sight when you're angry, honey, but you aren't doing your digestion any good. Why don't you calm down and have another glass of wine? I got rid of her, didn't I?"

"No, thank you! I would prefer to go home!" She ignored his last comment.

"But I'm not ready to take you home. Simmer down and stop looking at me with that Ferd expression! I didn't bring any birdseed along. Or is that part of the courting ritual I don't know about?"

For a long moment Phoebe locked wills with him across the white linen tablecloth and then her sense of humor got the better of her.

"Harlan, you're absolutely impossible!" she groaned, reaching for her wine glass.

"I'm a good dancer, though," he told her brightly. "Finish your dinner and I'll show you!"

"How come," Phoebe inquired an hour later as Harlan led her back to the small table in the lounge, "we only dance the slow dances?"

"You forget. I'm an older man," he grinned down at her. "Besides, I'm only concerned with the dances which give me an excuse to hold you. You're such a pleasant armful, sweetheart!" He reached out and lifted her hand. "Tomorrow we should go shopping for a ring. I'll meet you on your lunch hour and we can go to the jeweler's . . ."

"Harlan . . ." Phoebe began worriedly. A ring would make the whole unbelievable situation too real. It might make everything hurt too much when it all ended!

"No arguments, honey. I'm anxious to get my mark of ownership on you. The old male ego at work, you understand."

Phoebe flushed.

"If I could, I'd be buying leg irons tomorrow and a matching slave collar," Harlan continued, pinning her beneath his glittering look.

"What's the matter?" Phoebe demanded, rallying her forces bravely to confront the very masculine expression he was wearing. "Don't you trust your own abilities to keep me where you want me?"

"Not entirely. At least, not yet." Harlan regarded her deliberately for a moment. "Once you're mine completely and I've wrung all the promises and words out of you that I want to hear, I'll feel more confident. This courtship . . ."

"You promised me the courtship," Phoebe broke in hurriedly, anxious to keep him from changing his mind. It was true, he hadn't actually guaranteed not to take her to bed during the next three weeks but she had the impression that they shared a certain understanding on the subject. It was a delicate tightrope that Phoebe was walking and she knew it. The seductive danger lay all around her and if she had any sense she'd run a hundred miles in the opposite direction. Somehow she couldn't bring herself to deny her own desire to bask in the magic of his attention as long as possible. But she must manage it without letting herself get too badly hurt. The experience of being courted by Harlan Spencer Garand was worth a certain amount of pain, but not the deluge which would be hers if she gave herself to him completely.

"You don't need to remind me of what I got talked into last night! I shouldn't have let you do it. I know I shouldn't!" Harlan sighed ruefully. "If I had any sense I would drive you home right now, take what is mine, and put an end to this nonsense!"

Phoebe smiled tremulously, aware of the danger in his present mood.

"Think how noble you're going to feel in the morning if you stick by your promise tonight!" she suggested hopefully.

"I'm going to feel like a fool in the morning," he corrected. "Let's dance!"

Later that night, Phoebe started toward her bedroom, her hands at work on the fastening of her gown as she moved. She was in the process of freeing herself from the bodice when she realized the bedroom window was wide open. It brought her to a halt. A strange feeling of something not being quite right coursed down her spine in a wave. That window had been closed when she left for the evening. Had someone entered her apartment? She remembered the convenient fire escape near the window. But what would anyone want . . .

Without another thought, Phoebe backed out of the room, clutching the front of the gown to her throat and raced to the door. Flinging it open she spotted Harlan instantly as he leaned casually against the wall waiting for the elevator.

"Phoebe! What's wrong!" he demanded, striding forward immediately and grasping her shoulders in a painful grip.

"I think," she began, breathing deeply in an effort to bring her emotions under control, "that someone has been in my apartment while we were out! Oh, Harlan, that awful little man said his friend Max would get me! Do you think . . . ?"

Chapter Seven

"You're absolutely certain that window was closed when we left this evening, honey?" Harlan asked for the third time as they stood in the living room trying to make sense out of the incident. A rapid tour of the small apartment had revealed nothing missing and if there had been any footprints on the fire escape the evening rain had washed them away.

"As sure as I can be, Harlan. I suppose there's a possibility I forgot to close it, but . . . ." Phoebe's voice trailed off thoughtfully. She knew she had closed that window!

"If only Ferd could talk," Harlan commented.

"Fee, fie, fo, fum," began Ferd obligingly, hopping from one perch to another, his beady eyes on the two humans.

"Shut up, Ferd," Phoebe said absently. She had refastened the gown and kicked off the sandals. Moving across to the fan chair she sat down and looked up at Harlan consideringly.

"I think we have to go on the assumption I was wrong," she began wearily. "We certainly can't call the police on such flimsy evidence!"

"Still, in the morning I think I'll give that detective we

378

spoke to a call and let him know what happened. Just in case. He can make what he wants to out of it.'' Harlan studied her silently for a moment and then stepped in front of her, leaning down to take one of her hands in his and tug Phoebe to her feet.

"Come on, honey. It's getting late and we both have to be at work in the morning."

"Good night again," Phoebe smiled. "And thanks for looking through the apartment with me. Sorry to have sounded so panicked a few minutes ago."

"I can't even imagine you in a real panic, Phoebe," he grinned. "But there's no reason for you to have to spend the evenings being nervous, either. Get some things together and I'll take you somewhere else to spend the night."

"There's no need for that," she protested quickly, a sudden suspicion forming in her mind.

"Of course, there's a need for it! I'm not going to leave you here alone and that's final! You'd lie awake all night wondering if somebody was going to come through that window! Even worse, I'd be worrying about the same thing! So come along now, there's a good girl, and get whatever you'll need for tomorrow . . .''

"Harlan, I'm not going with you!" Phoebe dug her toes into the rug beneath her feet and glared at him.

"Why not?" he inquired, lifting an eyebrow curiously. "Ah! Wait a second. You think I'm going to take you to my place, right?"

"Well?" she challenged. "Isn't that what you have in mind?"

"If it is?"

"Then you can forget it! You promised me a courtship!" Phoebe concluded on a wail.

"And you think that if I take you home with me you won't get your courtship?"

"I would probably," she said with grand dignity, "never see another yellow rose from you again!"

"Maybe you'd have something much better than roses," he suggested, blue eyes glinting.

"What could be better than yellow roses in the morning?" she retorted, trying to keep her words flippant. She would not go home with him tonight!

"How about me in the morning?" he asked curiously.

"It wouldn't be the same," she informed him, shaking her head firmly.

"I'm crushed. But that doesn't change matters. You're still not spending the night here."

"I won't spend it with you, either!"

"No, I concede defeat for tonight. I'm taking you to Aunt Flo's. There, does that satisfy you?"

"Your aunt's? But it's midnight! We can't go barging in on her at this hour! She doesn't even know me!" Phoebe said quickly, thinking of a poor, elderly soul being dragged out of her bed by an inconsiderate nephew and having a strange woman thrust on her.

"I told her all about you this morning. Called her from the office before I even looked at the mail my secretary had opened for me! She's dying to meet you and the drama of the whole thing tonight will charm her enormously. Now stop making difficulties and pack a nightie or whatever it is women pack when they go visiting. Don't forget your toothbrush!"

Phoebe surrendered. It was late, she was tired, and finding that window open had been an unnerving experience. She packed her nightie and a toothbrush and then walked back out into the living room where Harlan was thumbing idly through a magazine.

"Can I bring Ferd?" she asked. "He won't like being left alone overnight again so soon and there's no telling what sort of tantrum he might decide to throw."

"Bring Ferd, by all means. He'll get along famously with Aunt Flo. Did you pack something to wear into the office tomorrow?" Harlan indicated the small bag in Phoebe's hand.

She nodded. "Yes, but I'm not sure the situation is worth

all this, Harlan. I mean chances are I did leave that window open and . . ."

"I'm not going to have you fretting over it, honey," he announced, getting to his feet and tossing the magazine aside. "Get the bird and whatever he needs. I'll take your bag."

A few minutes later Phoebe found herself seated in the front seat of Harlan's Jaguar, Ferd's cage on her lap. She had put the cover over it, but the bird could be heard muttering to himself inside. It was obvious he didn't think very much of being hustled off in the middle of the night.

"I'm going to stop by my place and pick up Jinx and a few other items," Harlan informed her blandly as he put the car in gear and pulled neatly out of the parking slot in front of the apartment house.

"I see."

"Still think I'm going to drag you off to my bed and make wild, passionate love to you tonight?" he inquired interestedly, flashing her a slanting glance.

"Just concerned about losing my morning roses, as I mentioned earlier," she told him airily, wondering what it would be like to have him do exactly as he had suggested. What would one night of wild, passionate love with Harlan be worth? A lifetime of regret? A lifetime of memories? Phoebe fixed her gaze firmly out the window at the dark streets slipping past the luxurious Jag.

"My God! I can see I've spoiled you already! I shall have to place a permanent order for yellow roses with the florist!" Harlan drove out of the downtown area and began the climb into the nearby hills where the older and wealthier residential areas were to be found. She should have guessed, Phoebe told herself as she caught sight of some of the elegant homes slumbering in the light of streetlamps. Harlan didn't appear to be lacking materially.

Some time later he angled off the road onto a winding drive which led to a surprisingly modern-looking home nestled in among the firs. Phoebe surveyed the sleek lines of wood and glass appraisingly.

381

"Like it?" Harlan smiled, watching her face carefully.

"I suppose I was expecting something older in this neighborhood. It's lovely, Harlan. Did you have it specially built?" Phoebe glanced at him, wondering why he had an almost anxious look on his lean features. Was he really concerned that she should like his home?

"Yes, last year, in fact. After I had settled down to being a businessman at last."

"When did you take over your father's firm?" Phoebe asked, remembering something Richard had said on Sunday night about a John Garand.

"Two years ago," Harlan replied shortly.

"You don't sound as if it was your goal in life," Phoebe heard herself say gently, looking at him in the glow of the car's interior lighting system.

"It wasn't at the time. But strangely enough I've come to enjoy it. Being in charge has its advantages! I'm satisfied with my work and that's why I've started thinking about complying with family tradition and producing an heir." He grinned across at her.

"You're willing to force some other young man into the business on the grounds that he'll come to enjoy it, too?" Phoebe lifted one brow aloofly.

"Maybe we'll have a daughter who will turn out to be a natural business leader!"

Phoebe laughed at that. "And here I was thinking you were a born male chauvinist!"

"Only when it comes to my wife," he elaborated, turning in the car seat and resting one arm along the back. Phoebe found herself very aware of the silence, the warmth of the car, and the power of his presence. She clutched Ferd's cage tightly and waited.

"What is it exactly that you want from a wife?" she heard herself say very softly, almost breathlessly.

"I want a Phoebe Hampton who is so in love with me she won't worry about who I am or what I am. She'll be willing to have my children and, if necessary, she'll compromise all her fine thoughts on a career. She won't care if I have designs on her relationship to a brilliant and wealthy brother. She'll create a home for me, entertain my business friends as necessary but be happy to escape to the mountains or the sea, and clean the fish I catch. She'll have eyes only for me and never look at another tall, dark, and handsome man again in her life, having discovered that she much prefers a red-haired, blue-eyed man who will never have cause to suspect her loyalty . . .''

Phoebe stared at him, uncertain how to take the intensity of his tone and the grimness of his expression. For a moment she wavered on her own emotions and then the ever-present sense of humor came to her rescue. She deliberately controlled a giggle and fixed him with a gentle, understanding, worshipful look.

"You want a woman who would follow you barefoot wherever you chose to lead?" she suggested in dulcet tones, almost batting her long lashes at him, but managing to restrain herself.

"Exactly," he agreed, obviously pleased at her comprehension.

"That's funny," she went on cordially. "I would very much like to find a man who would do all those things for me! No wonder men like the idea of having a wife!"

Harlan lunged for her, but Phoebe was already grabbing at the door handle and twisting herself and the bird cage out of the car. The laughter rippled in her throat as she stepped quickly out of reach and stood looking down at him.

Harlan, having missed in his first attempt, moved more slowly across the leather seat and climbed out to stand beside her with a mockingly dangerous expression.

"You," he stated, "are sadly in need of a husband! Not many men, if they knew what they were getting into, would be willing to assume the responsibility! I'm certain the Third never realized how incorrigible you are or he would have dropped the notion of marrying you after the first date! You're lucky to have found someone like me, Phoebe Hampton, who will take charge of such a trying specimen of the modern, liberated woman and teach her a basic fact of life!''

''Which is?'' Phoebe demanded lightly, meeting the glitter of his eyes in the moonlight.

He stretched out a firm hand and rested it heavily on her shoulder, guiding her toward the house.

''Why, that she won't be truly happy until she's given herself, body and soul, to the right man!''

''My, you do have a fine opinion of yourself, don't you?'' Phoebe grinned admiringly.

''Let's just say I know what I want and I won't be satisfied until I get it.'' He halted in front of the door, hunting for the key. A moment later he twisted the knob and greeted Jinx who came bounding forth to meet them with a cheerful yelp.

''Easy, boy. Remember your friend, Phoebe?''

Phoebe stretched down a hand to pat the dog. At that moment Ferd, sensing a new presence on the other side of his cage cover, chirped warningly.

Jinx froze.

Phoebe lifted the cage a bit higher, just in case the hunting dog instincts in Jinx couldn't tell the difference between a parakeet and a pheasant.

''Jinx, this is a friend of mine,'' she began cautiously. ''Love me, love my bird . . .''

''Behave yourself, Jinx,'' Harlan began firmly. ''Ferd wouldn't even make a mouthful!''

''Harlan, darling! What's going on here?'' A new voice from the darkened living room made Phoebe glance away from the tableau of dog and bird. It was her turn to freeze.

''Cynthia!'' Harlan sounded genuinely startled, Phoebe decided. ''What the hell are you doing here?''

''Poor Harlan,'' Phoebe muttered at his side, watching the golden vision glide toward them in the moonlight which illuminated the room through an endless wall of windows. ''You must spend half your life asking women what the hell they're doing creeping up on you!''

He swiveled an angry glance down at her and then refocused his attention on the blond as she came to a halt in front of him and turned a green-eyed gaze up to him.

Phoebe felt herself turning very cold and came to the conclusion that spending the night in her own apartment would have been much more enjoyable, regardless of the questions raised by the open window. Why were there so many beautiful blonds in the world? Thin ones, at that! She absorbed the graceful picture the unknown Cynthia made dressed in a flowing garment of some slinky white material which draped beautifully over a perfectly carved, delicate figure.

"Waiting for you, naturally. I let myself in with the key you leave hidden outside. Remember showing me the spot? Jinx knows me and he certainly doesn't mind, do you, boy?" Cynthia turned an amused glance toward the dog but Jinx was still poised, transfixed, in front of an equally transfixed Phoebe. Only Ferd seemed able to react and he was beginning to sound agitated over the change in his routine.

"I smell the blood of an Oregonian!" he chirped with great ferocity in his tiny voice. Jinx quivered.

"Who's this, darling? Aren't you going to introduce me?" Cynthia stepped closer to Harlan and rested a delicate hand on his sleeve. The action seemed to bring him out of the trance he'd been in for the past several seconds.

"Cynthia, this is Phoebe Hampton. Phoebe, this is Cynthia Prescott. All right, the introductions are over. Kindly explain what you're doing inside my home, Cynthia." Harlan began to take charge again, reaching out to snap on a light switch, and flicking a warning look at Phoebe who had begun edging toward the door, bird cage held high. Jinx moved forward a fraction of an inch to follow.

"Stand still, Phoebe," Harlan growled. "You're not going anywhere. Cynthia?" he prompted firmly, confronting her as she stood looking helpless and beautiful, green eyes wide with innocent surprise.

"Harlan? What's wrong? You know I often spend the night here! I got back into town earlier than I expected so I thought I'd come on over and say hello."

"Did you? Well, as you can see, I'm otherwise occupied this evening so I suggest you take yourself off," Harlan replied coolly, not bothering to confirm or deny Cynthia's statement that she frequently spent the night. Phoebe decided glumly that meant it was probably true.

"But, darling!" Cynthia began in a throaty, pleading voice. "I've been longing to see you. You're the reason I came back early from Hawaii. I've thought over the things we said to each other before I left and I realize I made a mistake . . ."

"Cynthia, I'm not going to stand here discussing the matter with you tonight! It's late and I've got other plans. Please leave before I lose my temper completely and throw you out!"

Harlan's voice sounded altogether harsher and more determined than it had when he had confronted her in the cabin clearing and told her to leave, Phoebe thought wonderingly. If what Cynthia was implying was true, then she, Phoebe, had come into Harlan's life just after he'd been through a lover's quarrel. Perhaps he'd been put off beautiful blonds temporarily and that was the reason Phoebe had appealed for a time? She clutched her bird cage and stared at the other woman, wondering how to salvage her own pride. The thought was immediately followed by the depressing idea that her pride might not be the most important part of her needing to be saved. Her heart was unexpectedly in much greater danger.

"Oh, darling, are you still upset with me? You know how quickly I lose my temper and say things I don't really mean! I don't blame you for trying to teach me a lesson by seeing someone else but now that I'm back, ready to apologize, you can . . ." Her words jerked to a halt as Harlan grabbed hold of the slender hand which had been touching his arm and hauled Cynthia ruthlessly toward the door.

"Out!"

The green eyes filled with lovely, unshed tears, making the woman look like a drowned flower, Phoebe thought unhappily, remembering how her own face turned blotchy and red when she cried.

Harlan had Cynthia through the door and Phoebe heard him

demanding to know where the woman had parked her car. There was a soft response which Phoebe couldn't catch and then the couple disappeared down the drive. Phoebe continued staring after them until a tiny movement by Jinx broke her paralysis.

"Traitor!" she hissed at the dog who favored her with a brief glance before returning his attention to the covered cage. "How could you let another woman in here? What kind of a watch dog are you, anyway?" Phoebe stepped back. "No, you can't have Ferd. He's about the only friend I have left in this world!"

Phoebe glanced out the open door toward the Jaguar, wondering if Harlan had taken the keys out of the ignition. Probably. She wasn't altogether sure she could drive it successfully enough to back it down the drive anyway. She turned to set Ferd's cage down on a nearby table and went to sit primly in a large overstuffed chair. She let her gaze wander around the room, taking in the plush green carpet, the modern, comfortable furniture and the incredible view of the city through the expanse of windows. There was a deck leading off the living room, a number of interesting, framed wall hangings which appeared to be Asian in design, and a sophisticated stereo system. A pleasant, subtly done room, Phoebe decided, and automatically wondered if the beautiful Cynthia had helped in the design.

What did Harlan want with a woman like that, anyway? Of course, she *was* beautiful but couldn't he see the cold, calculating look in those green eyes? Probably not. Men were notoriously short-sighted when it came to lovely creatures like that. Phoebe wondered what they had quarreled over which had sent Cynthia off in a huff to Hawaii. Marriage? How long had the woman been Harlan's mistress? Phoebe jumped as the front door closed and Harlan strode loudly into the room.

Phoebe looked up at him as he came to a halt in front of her, hands on his hips. The hard set of his mouth and eyes did not invite questions, she thought.

"On the subject of Cynthia, I will make only one comment

387

and that is that she and I are through. You're not to concern yourself with her, Phoebe. Is that understood?" Harlan regarded her forcefully, blue eyes hooded.

"You have lipstick on your cheek, Harlan," she said gently.

"Damn it to hell! Women!" Harlan turned on his well-shod heel and disappeared down a hall, presumably in search of a bathroom mirror.

Phoebe was still sitting in the overstuffed chair when he returned, a small overnight bag in one hand, the lipstick gone.

"Shall we be going? Come on, Jinx!" Harlan snapped his fingers but whether it was to secure the obedience of herself or the dog, Phoebe wasn't certain. Without a word she removed Ferd's cage from the table and followed Jinx out the door behind Harlan. Harlan stuffed everyone into the Jag and then climbed into the driver's seat with an economy of motion which amply demonstrated his current mood. With a muted roar, the car was backed efficiently down the drive and back onto the curving road.

Phoebe said nothing as they climbed a couple more miles into the hills and Harlan made no effort to start a conversation, either. He brought the vehicle to a halt in another drive, this one surrounded by a massive lawn and perfectly trimmed hedges. He slammed out of the car. Before Phoebe could struggle out of her side of the car with Ferd, he had her door opened and was reaching in to take the cage.

Phoebe stood gazing up at the beautiful old Victorian home in front of her with admiration. It was totally different in style from Harlan's house and carried the elegant patina of age.

"My grandfather had it built," Harlan broke the self-imposed silence to inform her, indicating the old house with a nod.

"The family mansion?" Phoebe asked calmly. "The one where two generations of Garands have been born and raised?" She could be cool, too, damn it!

"Yes, but not where the next will be raised!"

"Cynthia doesn't like this place?" Phoebe could have bitten her tongue out for the catty words, but it was too late.

"I don't like the place!" he snapped, handing her the bird cage. He led the way toward the imposing front door and set a heavy finger on the door bell. Almost immediately a light went on in an upstairs window. A few seconds later it was thrust open and a handsome woman in her sixties stared down at them.

"Harlan Garand! You look like you're leading a parade! What's going on?" a firm voice demanded.

Phoebe felt her humor momentarily come alive again at the thought of the picture they made standing on Aunt Flo's doorstep. Harlan, followed by a woman in an evening gown holding a cage, followed by a large, black dog.

"I'm bringing my future wife home to meet the family! What else would I be doing here at this hour of the night, Flo?" Harlan grinned up at the woman. "Aren't you going to let us in?"

"I'd do better to switch on a tape recorder and have you repeat those words!" The window slammed shut and a light was turned on inside the hall a short time later. In another moment the door was flung wide and a tall, striking woman, her grey hair in wild disarray, stood there examining Harlan and his entourage with eager, blue eyes—the same blue as Harlan's, Phoebe thought.

"So this is Phoebe? Come in, come in, my dear! You can't have any idea how anxious I've been to meet you! Ever since Harlan called this morning to tell me about his weekend I've been beside myself with impatience! I must admit, however, that you chose a strange time to bring her around, Harlan!"

"There's been another small adventure, Flo," Harlan told her, pushing Phoebe ahead of him, into the hall. "When I brought Phoebe home tonight, her bedroom window was open. She's fairly sure she left it closed and since that other kidnapper is still loose, I thought it would be a good idea to have her spend the next few days elsewhere!"

"The next few days!" Phoebe gasped. "I thought you meant I'd only spend the night here!" She turned at once to her hostess. "Please, Miss Garand, I have no intention of imposing on you for any longer than this evening! I had no idea Harlan meant me to stay for a few days!"

"Call me Flo, Phoebe, and of course you'll stay! Just as long as Harlan thinks it's necessary! I see we're going to have Jinx to protect us, too. That was nice of you, Harlan . . ."

"You're going to have Jinx and me too!" he corrected, leaning forward to give his aunt a kiss on the cheek. "I considered taking Phoebe to my house but she's talked me into this crazy idea of a courtship and she's afraid that once I have her safely tucked into my bed the yellow roses and candlelight dinners will cease!"

"Harlan!" Phoebe protested furiously. "How dare you talk like that! Don't you have any conscience at all? Doesn't it bother you in the least to embarrass me in front of your aunt?" The nerve of the man!

"Don't worry about it, Phoebe!" Florence Garand chuckled delightedly. "I've known him a lot longer than you have and tried for a number of years to control him. I assure you, it's hopeless! Do tell me all about this evening, Phoebe. You're certain you left your window shut?" As she spoke Harlan's aunt was leading the way up a carved staircase, its treads covered in a rich plum colored rug.

"Well, as certain as I can be. Of course, there's always the possibility I simply forgot and left it open. Normally I wouldn't have thought twice about it, but the weekend made me a tad nervous!" Phoebe confided, following the woman with Ferd's cage. Harlan brought up the rear, carrying the overnight bags.

"A tad! Good grief, my dear! From what Harlan told me, you went through enough to drive a sensible person to a nervous breakdown!"

"Well, perhaps a fit of the vapors," Phoebe temporized, thinking that the house was made for fainting heroines, perhaps not slightly plump, sensible heroines in glasses, though.

"I think you were amazingly brave about the whole thing! Plus, you managed to free yourself too! And then having to contend with Harlan on top of everything else!" Flo hesitated beside a door in the upstairs hall and pushed it open. "Will this do for tonight? It's already made up. If you find another bedroom you prefer tomorrow we can always have it prepared."

"This is lovely, Flo," Phoebe smiled appreciatively as she glanced around at the huge four-poster bed, flowered wall paper and fluffy white rug. "I shall feel like a Victorian lady tonight!" She walked into the room happily.

"She looks a bit like a lady from the last century, doesn't she, Aunt Flo?" Harlan interrupted, lounging in the doorway behind them. "I mean she's not skinny and hard looking like most modern women!"

"Harlan, I'm not in a mood to be teased about my figure tonight!" Phoebe warned, whirling to confront his lazy grin. She wouldn't mention Cynthia in front of his aunt and he probably knew it, but that didn't mean she had forgotten! She turned her back on him and set down Ferd's cage.

"Harlan, she's right! Stop teasing her. It's late and the poor girl's been through enough. You know where your room is. Why don't you take yourself and your dog off and go to bed? I'll take care of Phoebe!" Flo ordered.

"Yes, ma'am. Good night, Flo. Good night, Phoebe." Harlan stepped forward, dropping a dutiful kiss on the cheek of each woman and did as ordered. Jinx, with a last wistful glance at the bird cage, followed.

"I admire the way you handle him," Phoebe said fervently, sinking down onto the thick bed.

"It comes with experience. Don't worry, you'll soon get the hang of it." Florence smiled kindly, a definite twinkle in the bright blue eyes. "Yes, you look as if you'll do very well for Harlan. He needs a real woman. To think of all the time I've wasted trying to find one for him and then he ups and discovers his own! So much for matchmaking!" Flo turned back toward the door.

"There's a connecting bath through that door and my room's at the end of the hall if you need anything. There will be a woman arriving at six o'clock to fix breakfast and take care of some of the chores. Harlan said you work so I imagine you'll want to eat early? Six-thirty all right?''

"Yes, thank you," Phoebe smiled gratefully. "You've been very kind, Flo."

"Nonsense! I'm delighted to have you here! I'll catch up on the details tomorrow but for now you'd better get some sleep!" She was gone in a swirl of pink housecoat.

Phoebe looked over at Ferd's cage and after a bit got up to go across and remove the cover.

"Well, Ferd, what do you think?" she asked softly, opening the door to his cage and inserting her finger. Ferd stepped aboard, eyeing her thoughtfully as he rode the finger outside.

"Fee, fie, fo, fum," he finally announced as if it were the last word on the subject.

"Succinct and to the point," Phoebe commented. "But I was hoping for sympathy, not common sense. Back you go! It's time you were asleep, anyway!"

Breakfast the next morning was an informal affair served in a sunny old-fashioned nook the Victorian architect had specifically designed for the first meal of the day. When Phoebe descended the stairs promptly at six-thirty, dressed in the neat suit she had packed the night before, it was to find her hostess already seated and reading the morning paper.

"Phoebe! Good morning! How did you sleep?"

"Perfectly, Flo. How about you? I hope our midnight arrival didn't upset your rest too much?" Phoebe took a chair and reached enthusiastically for the silver coffee pot. There was real cream, too!

"Best night's sleep I've had since Harlan announced he was going to build his own home!" Flo grinned.

Phoebe looked at her sharply, wondering where Harlan was. He was supposed to drive her to work this morning . . .

"Why did you sleep well that time?" she asked. "Had he been getting underfoot around the house?"

"Oh, no. I was happy to have him with me after he returned. He'd been living in the Far East, managing one of the offices Garand has there. When my brother died, he did his duty and returned to Portland. But I knew he didn't want to leave Hong Kong and he didn't exactly welcome the idea of the increased responsibility of running the whole operation. That was two years ago. It took him a year to adjust and decide to keep the business. For a time, I was sure he might sell the whole thing to an outsider! When he came home one day and said he planned to build on a nice lot a couple of miles from here, I realized he was staying.''

''I gather the feeling of family tradition has caught up with him,'' Phoebe agreed drily. ''He's even talking about an heir!''

''I'm so glad! He's shown no interest whatsoever in the women he's met during the past two years. Heaven knows, I did my best to find a suitable wife for him but he got furious every time! I guess he's one of those men who has to come to terms with things in his own style. I have the impression he did a much better job of selecting a companion that I was doing.''

''Thank you, but it isn't exactly settled yet, Flo. I mean, you know how Harlan is, always plowing into things, determined to have it all his way. We've only known each other since Saturday morning and I'm not at all sure . . .''

''Not at all sure you want to wait until after the Rose Festival to get married? Why didn't you say so, sweetheart? I'll be happy to advance the date! How about this Friday?'' Harlan swooped through the door, a bunch of yellow roses in one hand, and Jinx romping at his heels. His hair was still damp from the shower, red tendrils curling at the back, and he appeared amazingly fresh. He planted a husbandly kiss on her startled lips.

''Harlan, you know perfectly well I didn't mean that! I was explaining to your aunt how we hardly know each other . . .'' Phoebe's words were cut off as the wet roses were thrust into her surprised grasp.

''Mind the thorns, honey. Have you got a vase for these, Flo?''

''I've got rose vases stored all over this house. You know

that! Just a second and I'll dig one out!'' Florence disappeared in the direction of the kitchen.

"Harlan! I do wish you wouldn't give your aunt the definite idea that we're going to be married! She'll be so disappointed if it doesn't work out!'' Phoebe scolded, frowning at him as he took a seat across from her. He thrust a coffee cup in her direction and she found herself automatically pouring his morning coffee like any good wife. Irritated, she set the silver pot down heavily and glared at him.

"Don't look at me like that, honey! A wife is supposed to be sweet and loving and full of cheer at this hour of the morning! Besides, what are you mad about? You got your roses, didn't you? Fresh from Flo's garden. You'll have to see it, Phoebe! It's magnificent. Growing roses is a major hobby here in Portland, you know! People here take it quite seriously . . .''

"I'm aware of Portland's interest in roses, Harlan. We're discussing something else entirely . . .'' Phoebe was forced to cease her lecture as Harlan's aunt appeared, carrying a magnificent crystal vase filled with water.

"Thank you, Flo,'' she smiled, carefully setting the gorgeous roses into the crystal. "Ummm. They're beautiful!'' Phoebe took a moment to inhale the fragrance, the curve of her hair swinging forward as she leaned over them.

"Eat your breakfast, Phoebe. I want to get to work early. Don't forget I'm picking you up at noon so we can select a ring!'' Harlan ordered, pouring cream over his cereal and helping himself to the toast. He smiled at his aunt.

"I haven't had a chance to tell you, but Phoebe is a terrific cook. In fact, that was how she convinced me to let her stay on Saturday morning. I was all set to hustle her back down the mountain but before I knew what was happening she was feeding me!''

Flo laughed. "The surest way to a man's heart. There's always a grain of truth in those old sayings! I expect it's instinct for a man to look with favor on a woman who can cook! Just as it's instinct for a woman to be drawn toward a strong, dominant man!''

Phoebe gagged on a bit of cereal and choked embarrassingly until Harlan's hand landed with a thud in the middle of her back. Then she managed to regain her composure.

"Phoebe isn't accustomed to the idea of having a man around to keep her in line," he explained kindly to his aunt. "She's been used to giving the orders and she's got a little adjusting to do!"

"Give me one good reason why a woman should be attracted to a domineering male except in a romantic novel!" Phoebe demanded grimly, casting a decided glare at Harlan.

"You read those too? I'm so glad. We'll have to go through our collections and compare!" Flo enthused. "But the reason why women love such men is quite obvious, isn't it? A man who shows he can take care of himself and exerts some control over his environment is a man who can care for and protect a woman and her children too. It's a survival characteristic, if you ask me!"

"You see, Phoebe? No need to fight an instinct," Harlan chimed in teasingly.

"There is never an excuse for bullying someone else!" Phoebe fought back, feeling outnumbered but determined not to surrender easily.

"Does Harlan bully you?" Flo asked with great curiosity, staring at her nephew as if she hadn't seen him before.

"Horribly! I'll have you know he even made me clean his fish after he caught them!"

"Simple division of labor principle!" Harlan defended himself. "Anyway, she deserved it for crashing my weekend!"

Flo's laughter halted the battle and she sobered only after a great effort. "You two are great together! That settles it! Seeing you face each other over the breakfast table has removed any doubt I might have had. We'll have the engagement party this Saturday night!"

Chapter Eight

"Harlan, what are we going to do? We've got to stop your aunt before she goes ahead and plans an engagement party!" Phoebe groaned as the Jag was brought to a halt in front of her company's towering downtown office building. She had been remonstrating futilely with the man at the wheel ever since they had left the house and had gotten precisely nowhere.

"Why? We're going to be married, so I don't see why we shouldn't have the party." Harlan switched off the ignition and leaned over to pull her against him. "Stop worrying! It will be a small affair—especially with such little notice. Aunt Flo won't overwhelm you with strangers, if that's what's concerning you, honey." He paused. "That reminds me, we must phone your brother."

"You know damn well what's concerning me!"

"Now don't go getting upset with small things . . ."

"Small things! You think Cynthia Prescott is a *small* thing?" Phoebe felt her voice rise into a higher register and was helpless to keep it from happening. Visions of the golden Cynthia had haunted her dreams during the night and the other woman's beauty was as fresh in Phoebe's mind this morning as it had been last night in the moonlight.

"I told you to forget Cynthia!"

"I'm finding that rather difficult! My God, Harlan! It was obvious she felt quite at home in your house last night!" Phoebe blazed.

"So? I make no apologies for my past. It should be meaningless to you just as yours is meaningless to me. It's the present and the future we're concerned with and don't you forget it!" With that, Harlan yanked her tightly against his chest and crushed her furious lips beneath his mouth, holding her with both hands in a grip that Phoebe knew was going to leave bruises.

Phoebe struggled desperately for a long, painful moment and then gave up in despair. How could she fight him when he held her so closely? His kiss, his arms—when she was experiencing them—were the only things that mattered in the whole world. It was depressing to be so much in the power of a man, she told herself. It was also exciting and exhilarating beyond words. She felt herself relax as Harlan's mouth took hers fiercely.

"Damn!" he muttered thickly against her lips, "But I wish we were anywhere else but here on a city street at seven-thirty in the morning! I'd show you how pointless it is to fight me, Phoebe honey. You want me as much as I want you! Why don't you do us both a favor and admit it?" His hands moved, shaping her waist beneath the jacket of her suit and then sliding along the softness of her blouse to the fullness of her breast.

"Harlan!" she managed to beg. "Someone will see us!"

"So?"

"This is Portland! Things aren't done that way here!"

He sighed. "All right. But don't think you can keep putting me off. I can tell you right now you're going to wind up in my bed before the next three weeks are over!" He set her away from him with an air of determination. "I'll be back at noon. See that you're waiting here on the front steps!"

Phoebe removed herself from the car, feeling weak and shaky. She didn't trust herself to speak, so she slammed the Jag's heavy door and turned to march up the steps of the office building. It was only as she glanced back over her shoulder to make sure Harlan had driven off that she saw Richard standing on the sidewalk below, staring at her. It was too much. She couldn't face another male just then. Phoebe fled through the revolving doors and into the elevator.

An hour later Phoebe glanced up from a monthly report she was writing to answer the phone.

"Phoebe Hampton? This is Cynthia Prescott. We met last night." The saccharin sweet tones made Phoebe's skin crawl. What a morning this was developing into, she thought dismally.

"Yes, Miss Prescott? What can I do for you?" she said in her most businesslike voice, trying to imply she was being rudely interrupted.

"I thought you deserved an explanation for that small scene last night. I mean, I know I'd very much want to know what was going on in a similar situation!" A throaty little chuckle followed. The woman to woman approach, thought Phoebe grimly.

"Harlan explained what little needed explaining, thank you," she said firmly.

"Oh, no need to be coy about it, Phoebe. We both know a man couldn't begin to give an adequate explanation of that sort of thing—especially as infuriated a man as Harlan was last night. He's really something in a temper, isn't he? But perhaps you haven't known him long enough to learn his various moods?"

"What is it you want, Miss Prescott?" Phoebe pressed coldly.

"Just to give you a word of warning, my dear. I've been acquainted with Harlan for a lot longer than you have and we've been through a good deal together, including a number of lovers' quarrels. I admit this last one was my fault, what with refusing to marry him as soon as he wished, but he'll come around. He always does. It might be hard on you, though, if he used you to take revenge against me. That's why I'm calling. Don't let him talk you into doing anything drastic while he's upset with me. As soon as he recovers his temper he'll want me back and it would be a shame if you got hurt in the process!"

Phoebe couldn't believe it! She had heard of women who threatened other women over a man but she'd never been in such a position before in her life! Desperately she tried to think how to deal with this awful person on the other end of the line. At that moment several years of business experience came to her aid. One fought fire with fire.

"It's very thoughtful of you to warn me, Miss Prescott," Phoebe began coolly. "But I happen to know Harlan is a man who takes what he wants. If he'd wanted you badly enough as his wife, you would have been married to him by now. Please don't concern yourself over my welfare. I can handle him and you both. Don't forget, I'm the one who stayed behind last night. The woman in possession, Miss Prescott, is the woman with the advantage. Don't bother calling again!" Phoebe hung up the phone carefully. Where had Cynthia gotten her number, she wondered.

She was still mulling that one over when twelve o'clock arrived and she reluctantly headed toward the elevator. Harlan wouldn't appreciate being kept waiting. Visions of him storming into the building in quest of her made Phoebe move more quickly.

The Jag was double-parked directly in front of the building. It was typical of Harlan to pull a stunt like that in the height of midday traffic!

"I was just about to come and find you," he announced, leaning across the seat to open the door.

"That thought had occurred to me!" she responded feelingly, slipping into the soft leather.

"Good. You're learning," he grinned and pulled into traffic with casual disregard for other drivers. Or at least it appeared casual but Phoebe was willing to bet he knew exactly what he was doing!

"Harlan, don't you think we should wait a while for the ring?" Phoebe tried one last time. "We've still got three weeks to go and so much could happen in that length of time!" Such as my meeting a few more Cynthias, she added to herself.

"I told you, honey, I want my ring on your finger. I'm not prepared to risk losing a good cook like you!" He seemed absolutely determined to be cheerful and enthusiastic, Phoebe thought resentfully.

A few minutes later he had parked the Jag in a downtown garage and was hurrying her along the sidewalk toward a prosperous looking jewelry store.

"Come in, Mr. Garand! We've been expecting you!" a sturdy gentleman in a refined suit greeted them as soon as they were inside the door. "Right this way. I've done my best to prepare a fine selection for your perusal. I do hope you'll find something you like!" Beaming his confidence in his wares, the man led them toward a private table and indicated they should be seated in the plush chairs. Wordlessly, Phoebe watched as several velvet lined trays were spread before her.

"Harlan," she finally whispered frantically, feeling the walls closing in quickly. "Let's talk about this some more . . ."

"Choose, Phoebe, my dear, or I'll do it for you!"

She looked up into his face and saw there what she had seen the day he had forced her to clean the fish. She had learned her lesson that day. In this mood, there was nothing for it but to comply.

"All right, Harlan," she agreed forlornly, gazing down at the glittering array before her.

Rings were held out for her approval and she dutifully tried them on, nodding her appreciation in an effort not to offend the jeweler. He had every right to be proud of the rings he was displaying. It wasn't his fault she was having trouble working up genuine interest.

Time passed and she began to get nervous. Harlan was determined that she make a selection before leaving. Finally, in desperation, she picked up a small gold ring set with an emerald. It didn't seem as flashy as its neighbors and Phoebe decided it was somewhat like her in that respect.

"Perfect. It matches your eyes when you're upset and yelling at me!" Harlan grinned. He took it from her limp hand and gave it into the jeweler's keeping. "You'll have it sized for us? We're having an engagement party on Saturday night and it would be great to have it by then . . ."

"Of course. You can pick it up tomorrow in fact, Mr. Garand," the jeweler nodded, smiling happily.

"That will be great. Come on, Phoebe. There's still time for a short lunch if we hurry. I'll take care of the purchase when I pick it up tomorrow, all right, Mr. Bernard?"

"That will be fine."

That afternoon at five o'clock, Harlan was again waiting for her in front of her building. Phoebe descended the steps reluctantly and got into the Jag with an air of resignation.

"Stop sulking, honey. I've told Aunt Flo we won't be home for dinner. I'll drive by your apartment so you can change and we'll go out to eat."

"More candlelight and wine?"

"The best I can find. There's one other item on the agenda. We're going to call your brother. He'll want to be at his sister's engagement party."

Her brother's startled exclamation over the phone line half an hour later was sufficiently loud to reach Harlan who was standing several feet away.

"I know it's rather sudden, Steve, but I promise to tell you the whole story when you get here . . ." Phoebe began cautiously.

"Is he there?" Steve Hampton demanded.

"Well, yes, as a matter of fact, he is. We're going out to dinner . . ."

"Put him on the line!"

Without a word Phoebe handed the phone to Harlan who accepted it willingly enough.

"How do you do, Steve?" he began cheerfully. "Before you get upset about the fact that I'm marrying your sister, let me answer a few of your questions before you have a chance to ask. One, I am quite able to financially support Phoebe. Two, the family line is very good. Garands have been in Portland for a century. That's a long time on the West Coast, you know. And three, I can handle Phoebe! What?" Harlan listened for a moment and then a slow smile began to shape the line of his mouth. "Yes, I agree with you. Number three is the most important item on the list! If you recognize that, I think we'll discover that we think alike on important issues!" Harlan perched himself on the phone table and threw Phoebe a look which said clearly that what was coming next was strictly man-to-man talk. With a disgusted word, she turned and walked out of the room, leaving the two most important men in her life alone to get to know each other over the telephone.

The pattern for the rest of the week was established. Harlan drove Phoebe to work every morning and fetched her at night. He greeted her with yellow roses over the breakfast table daily and kept her out late at night dancing. By Friday morning Phoebe was a nervous wreck. Her brother was due to arrive Saturday morning and she had yet to make hotel reservations for him as he had stated firmly he did not wish to stay at Flo's. She hadn't argued with him, although it would have been nice to have him close. She knew he always preferred to stay in a hotel when he visited. He had an ingrained fear of imposing on people, he claimed, but Phoebe privately thought her brother simply liked having the freedom of a hotel atmosphere. He was a man who liked his own company. And in his line of work, privacy was a valuable commodity. It gave him the opportunity for creative thinking which was so important.

"Too many late nights for this girl, Harlan," Flo opined across the breakfast table Friday morning. "You're wearing her out!" She eyed Phoebe assessingly.

"I'm wearing her down!" Harlan corrected unrepentantly. "Here, Phoebe, have some more coffee. You do look a little slow moving this morning!"

"Thank you and may I say you're looking quite well yourself?" she muttered.

"Stop teasing her, Harlan," Flo said seriously. "If you don't want it to appear as if you've taken to beating her, I suggest you bring her home early tonight and let the poor thing get some sleep!"

"Oh, all right. But it will probably be a mistake. Haven't you noticed how much more obedient she's been when she's tired?" Harlan inquired of his aunt as he spread jam on his toast.

"What are you going to wear tomorrow night, Phoebe?" Florence demanded in a determined effort to change the subject.

"Frankly, I haven't given it a moment's thought!" Phoebe responded crushingly.

"Well, don't you worry about it. Tomorrow morning we'll get rid of His Highness here and go shopping. Pam has everything well in hand for the party, as usual and there'll be no need for us to do anything but appear tomorrow night!"

True to her word, Flo took Phoebe shopping Saturday morning to several very small, very elegant boutiques she had not yet discovered herself. When she got a look at the price tags, Phoebe decided it was just as well she hadn't. But at last a gently draped gown in colors of the sea was located, much to Flo's satisfaction.

"The color of your eyes, my dear. It's gorgeous!"

Steve Hampton arrived shortly before noon and Harlan took Phoebe to the airport to meet him. She had a moment's worry as the tall man with the dark brown hair and the almost-green eyes so much like her own walked toward them from the ramp. She took an uncertain step forward, meeting her brother's demanding gaze unflinchingly. Then she was hugging him affectionately as he smiled over the top of her head at the red-haired man behind her.

"I only hope," Steve told Harlan, shaking hands cordially, "that you know what you're getting yourself into!"

"At least I won't ever be bored!" Harlan grinned.

"Well, little sister, so you did your own matchmaking this time!" Steve smiled down at Phoebe as the three of them moved toward the luggage claim area. "I have to admit I couldn't have fixed you up better myself! This one doesn't even need to have the family finances straightened out!"

"Steve!" Phoebe gasped, mortified. And then, seeing that Harlan didn't appear to be offended she demanded, "How did you know? You only have Harlan's word that he can support me!"

"Don't be ridiculous, Phoebe," Harlan chuckled. "Your brother has spent the time since our phone call having me thoroughly checked out, haven't you, Steve?"

"Of course," Steve agreed readily. "Wouldn't you have done the same?"

Harlan nodded. "Naturally."

Phoebe looked from one to the other suspiciously. "Are you two serious? You would sic private detectives on each other before you would let him marry into the family?" Their answering nods of confirmation told her all she needed to know.

"Men!" she groaned, not for the first time.

Phoebe descended the carved staircase at eight o'clock, as ordered by Flo, to find Harlan waiting for her at the bottom. She paused a few steps from the last stair, filling herself with the sight of the lean, utterly masculine length of him. The evening jacket fitted him to perfection and the whiteness of it contrasted with the rich red of his hair gleaming in the light of the hall chandelier. Dark slacks and shoes polished to an elegant gloss combined with the silk of his shirt to lend him an understated tone of quiet elegance. He looked, Phoebe thought abruptly, tall, red haired, and handsome—every woman's dream.

Harlan watched her come slowly down the last few steps without saying a word, brilliant eyes going over her from head to foot in an almost hungry glance.

"You are perfect," he said in a low, husky voice, reaching out to take her hand. "And you're mine."

Phoebe stared at him wordlessly, trying desperately to read the depth of his feelings in the hard planes of his face.

"Oh, Harlan. Are you sure? Really sure?"

He smiled. "Positive." And then he put a hand into a jacket pocket and removed a small case. A jeweler's case.

"My ring," Phoebe murmured, fascinated as he opened the small object and removed the delicate emerald. He slid it easily onto her finger and then raised her hand lightly to his lips.

There was an attitude of finality about the procedure as if the act of placing his ring on her finger sealed them together. Phoebe trembled with the overpowering sensation of being told in no uncertain manner that she was his. Her eyes met his and he leaned forward to touch her lips lightly with his own.

"My own, cuddly Phoebe!" he smiled wickedly into her wide eyes.

"And I can cook, too," she breathed, groping for a response which wouldn't sound as if she had lost her composure completely.

"What more could a man ask?"

"All right, you two, time to stop admiring each other and prepare to greet your guests. I hear a car now," Flo instructed, coming into the hall from the living room. She was followed by a smiling Steve whose expression widened into a grin as he caught sight of his sister's face.

After that Phoebe lost track of time. She obediently greeted guests, relying on the experience she'd had with people to get her over difficult moments. She stood and chatted in small groups, answering questions easily, skipping lightly over the ones which threatened to pry too deeply into her association with Harlan. Either Flo or Harlan stayed by her side for the first hour, making sure she was comfortable with their friends and parrying the questions with her. When one was with her, the other was with her brother, who quickly found himself in

405

an interested circle of men demanding to know about patents, and royalties and licensing.

Phoebe had just caught a glimpse of Steve's head in the crowd and was thinking of gravitating in his direction when she was stopped by a voice at her elbow.

"I understand you only recently met Harlan?" an elderly dowager queried pointedly.

"Harlan is the type of man who sweeps a woman off her feet," Phoebe smiled blandly, not bothering to elaborate on the exact time of the meeting or the location.

"Someone told me you ran into each other in the mountains over the weekend?" the woman persisted, her diamond earrings flashing heavily in the elegantly lit room.

"What else could I do but marry the girl after an incident like that?" Harlan chuckled, coming up behind Phoebe and planting a tiny kiss on her shoulder. The warmth in his eyes and the very proprietary little caress was not lost on his listeners who smiled in response.

Around ten o'clock Phoebe managed to escape to the refreshment table. Her appetite, which had deserted her at dinner, returned in full force now that the first crucial hours of the party were behind her. She was studying the relative merits of shrimp canapés and small salmon sandwiches when a deep voice spoke behind her.

"Stick with the salmon sandwiches. The shrimp things are okay but not nearly as good."

"Thanks for the advice!" Phoebe chuckled, helping herself to a delicate sandwich and turning to face the voice. The movement of her head brought her eyes to the level of a handsome silk tie. She had to look at lot further to meet the steel grey eyes. Very tall, very dark, and very handsome, she thought calmly. The sight failed to move her at all. Nothing could now compete with red hair and blue eyes.

"I'm Phoebe Hampton," she smiled cheerfully.

"The guest of honor, of course. I arrived late and missed the introductions. I'm Matt Wentworth. Harlan and I know each other from business associations. How about some more of the champagne punch? I was just about to refill my own glass.''

"That would be marvelous." Phoebe held out her glass obligingly and watched as he filled it carefully.

"Have you and Harlan set a date yet?" he inquired pleasantly.

"No. I mean, it's still a little up in the air. He's talking about some time after the Rose Festival . . ." Phoebe said politely. She couldn't very well say that Harlan had set more of a deadline than a date!

"That sounds like Harlan. Once he makes up his mind, not much can stand in his way! You looked very thoughtful as I came up behind you a moment ago. You must be glad to get a small break from the throng out there!" He motioned toward the noise of the party in the next room.

"Actually, I was just thinking that I've been so busy this week I haven't even seen a newspaper! I was wondering how the market was doing. Very unromantic thoughts, I assure you!"

"You own some stock?" he pursued, sounding interested.

"I've been getting my feet wet for the past couple of years. Every so often I terrify myself and do something rash like buy an off-the-wall computer stock and then I get cold feet for a while, waiting to see what happens! I've been pretty lucky, though. My broker is excellent and I've done some studying on the subject."

"Keeping up with inflation, at least?"

"Better than that, on the whole." Phoebe smiled modestly.

"I knew it! I'm talking to a wizard! If you're doing better than keeping pace with inflation, I want to hear more!"

"Sorry, no tips! I have the feeling that as soon as I encourage someone to buy into the stocks I'm holding, the entire thing will collapse under me!"

"A healthy superstition. At least tell me the areas you're into?" he begged, beautifully white teeth revealed in an engaging smile.

407

"Well, energy companies have been doing well for me. Some electronics . . ."

"Tell me more. Would you mind if we moved out onto the terrace? It's getting warm in here." Without waiting for her agreement Matt Wentworth took her arm in a casual grip and guided her gently toward the open doors at the end of the room.

Phoebe, after a small hesitation, decided she was glad to have someone to talk to who wanted to discuss a subject other than her forthcoming marriage. She went with him willingly.

She was deep into a friendly argument about the future of the aerospace industry when a familiar, throaty laugh sounded from the other side of the hedge in the direction of Flo's rose garden. Cynthia Prescott. Phoebe broke off her comment on a company engaged in building a new space shuttle to frown uncertainly.

"Something wrong, Phoebe?" Matt smiled curiously down at her.

"Nothing. Just thought I heard someone I know." She launched determinedly back into her subject, wondering when the other woman had arrived. But the laughter floated toward them again and this time when Phoebe glanced out toward the garden she saw a flash of movement. A woman in a long gown and a man in a white evening jacket. Harlan! She knew it was Harlan and he was with Cynthia. The wave of despair which swept over her in that moment was almost more than she could bear. He couldn't do this to her! Not at the engagement party he had insisted on holding!

"I think it's time we went back indoors, Matt," Phoebe said, the enthusiasm and interest drained from her voice.

The laughter trilled yet again and Matt glanced across the hedge. "I see Cynthia is up to her old tricks," he said softly. "Is her presence in the garden the reason for your sudden desire to go back to the party?"

"I don't think . . ."

"Come now. Going to give up so easily? I've known Miss Prescott for some time and I can guarantee you she won't respond to subtlety. If you want her out of your life, you're going to have to throw her out, I'm afraid!''

Don't get mad; get even. Phoebe lifted her head proudly. She caught Matt Wentworth's expectant, encouraging look and smiled shakily. The adrenaline began flowing through her, the way it did when she decided to challenge a superior at work. Matt was right. Some people didn't understand subtlety at all. Harlan might or might not be to blame but Cynthia Prescott would never be blameless.

''Perhaps a short walk through the garden before we return, Matt?'' Phoebe felt her smile firm. That woman was no good for Harlan! Even if he had changed his mind about Phoebe, Cynthia was not the one he should think of using to replace her! Probably couldn't even cook! And she dreaded to think what kind of mother Cynthia would make!

''An excellent idea.'' Matt took her arm and they stepped off the terrace together, moving toward the path which led down through the rose garden and on to the stone goldfish pond—the path that would bring them face to face with Cynthia and Harlan.

The husky, sexy sound of Cynthia's voice became clearer now and Phoebe could hear Harlan's deeper tones occasionally. He wasn't laughing with her, Phoebe decided and wondered again which of the two was to blame for the jaunt into the rose garden. Matt guided her firmly around the last hedge and there on a bench sat Harlan and Cynthia. The other woman's floating gown seemed to have draped itself over the darkness of Harlan's slacks and her arm was in the act of moving up to his shoulder when she spotted Phoebe and Matt. She looked briefly startled and then the cat look came into the green eyes, visible in the moonlight, probably because, like a cat's, they shone in the dark, Phoebe thought grimly. She determined to get in the first word. Ignoring Harlan, who was staring first at her and then at Matt with an expression of growing annoyance, Phoebe smiled her best business smile.

''Cynthia, darling! I've been looking all over for you, haven't I, Matt?'' Phoebe moved forward quickly, leaning down to grasp the other woman's arm and help her to her feet. Cynthia resisted but she was smaller than Phoebe and, as Phoebe had often pointed out, some of the roundness was muscle. In a second she had Cynthia on her feet and was forcing her down the path toward the pond.

"Phoebe!" Harlan's voice came urgently behind her. "Where are you going?"

"Cynthia and I are going to have a little girl-to-girl chat. You know how it is. We have so much in common and so far we simply haven't found the time to discuss things thoroughly. I believe Matt wanted to speak to you, so this will be a perfect opportunity for all of us!" With a deadly sweet smile, Phoebe continued toward the pond, Cynthia's arm twisted in a painful grip.

"It's all right, Harlan," Matt said quietly behind them. "Phoebe won't come to any harm out here in the garden and I'm sure those two are dying to talk to each other. You know women!"

"I know Phoebe!" Harlan snapped. "She always gets her revenge . . ."

An instant later the voices of the men had faded so that the words could no longer be clearly distinguished. Phoebe pushed Cynthia through a row of bushes and brought her to a halt beside the pond.

"You want to talk to me, Phoebe Hampton? I'll talk! I'll tell you right now you don't stand a chance of holding Harlan! Who do you think you are, anyway? I've known him for years and he wants me! Can't you understand that? You may have had one flaming weekend up in the mountains but that was only because he was lonely and bored without me! He's a man and he's not above using a convenient woman! You may have put pressure on him through that crazy aunt of his but in the end he won't marry you, I promise! He's going to marry me!"

"Oh, shut up, Cynthia! Be honest with yourself! If Harlan had wanted you for a wife, you would have been married by now as I told you the other day on the phone. By the way, how did you find out where I worked? Just idle curiosity on my part, you realize. But it's been puzzling me.''

"A friend told me." Cynthia glared at her.

"A friend?" Phoebe applied a bit more pressure to the arm she was holding.

"Julie Chambers, if you must know! Let go of my arm!"

"I didn't realize you knew Julie. I should have. You're two of a kind. Well, that's really the only matter I was curious about. The rest of our little discussion concerns Harlan. You will leave him alone, Miss Prescott, or I will personally see to it that you suffer some very severe consequences. The first of said consequences being a mild dip in the pond!" Before the lovely blond could grasp her intention, Phoebe stuck a foot around her ankle, pushed gently, and watched with great satisfaction as Cynthia fell backward into the pond, scattering lily pads, splashing water and no doubt terrifying the fish. She only got out half a startled screech before she landed ignominiously on her backside.

"Phoebe!" Harlan hurried through the rose bushes, Matt following more sedately at his heels. "What the hell have you done with Cynthia?" He halted, frowning severely down at her and then turning to look at the furious blond struggling out of the pond. Phoebe could have sworn his lips twitched and he had to control a grin.

"Harlan, that woman is a menace! She threw me in here! I could have been badly hurt!" Cynthia's husky voice rose to a distinct screech as she looked down at the sopping gown. "Just look at me! Damn you, Phoebe Hampton . . ."

"What a pity, Miss Prescott. Too bad you slipped. But these stones here around the pond can be very tricky. You'll have to rush right home and change before you catch your death of cold!"

"I'll be happy to see you to your car, Cynthia." Matt stepped around Harlan and took hold of the frustrated woman's arm. "You really are quite damp, aren't you? We'd better hurry!"

"But . . ." began Cynthia helplessly, turning for a last glare at Phoebe before being hustled off by Matt Wentworth.

411

"Quiet, Cynthia, or the entire party will hear you and come running to see what happened. It's going to be a little difficult to explain, isn't it?" Matt counseled helpfully as the two disappeared up the path toward the far side of the house. A long, tense silence settled over the garden as Phoebe was left alone with Harlan. She continued staring in the direction her rival had gone, the cool anger she had been experiencing beginning to disappear as quickly as it had come.

"Well, Phoebe Hampton, you're living up to your reputation, aren't you?" Harlan's tones were unfathomable. Was he furious?

"That woman irritates me," Phoebe defended herself in a small voice.

"Apparently. Do you intend to spend the rest of our life throwing every woman who talks to me into a fish pond?" Phoebe didn't dare look at him. She knew one red brow would be climbing warningly.

"Only the skinny blond ones," Phoebe managed with an effort at flippancy.

"I see. Just how did you happen to be in the garden with Matt, anyway?"

"I was . . . was talking to him on the terrace and we heard . . ."

"In other words you were having a private conversation with one of your favorite masculine types. I believe Matt would probably qualify as tall, dark, and good looking?" Harlan's voice had a distinctly unpleasant edge to it now.

"We were having an extremely casual conversation on the stock market, if you must know! He certainly wasn't draped all over me as Cynthia was with you!"

"Cynthia was in the process of saying goodbye!"

"The hell she was! I've been getting nothing but warnings from her all week on how she was going to get you back!" Phoebe whirled, the soft skirts of her gown swirling around her ankles, and faced Harlan.

"I think we had better discuss the situation after the party, don't you?" Harlan said coldly, stepping forward to take her arm in a firm grasp. "We have guests to whom we should be paying attention! I will tell you now, however, that I don't want to see you out for any more moonlight strolls with Matt Wentworth or anyone else, for that matter! If you had stayed indoors like a proper hostess, none of this would have occurred!"

"You mean it's better for you if I don't know what's going on behind my back?" Phoebe turned a fulminating look up at him.

"I mean there's less likelihood of misinterpretation if you aren't out wandering around where you shouldn't be!" he snapped.

"Oh! You're being horribly unfair, Harlan!"

"I am a little upset over having had a longtime friend of mine tossed into a fish pond! And about finding my future wife on a moonlight ramble with Matt Wentworth! If that constitutes being unfair, then, yes, I'm unfair! That doesn't change matters, however! You're going to learn to behave yourself, Phoebe, if it takes me the rest of my life to teach you!"

Before she could say another word in her own defense, they were crossing the terrace and Phoebe was being thrust back through the open doors into the living room. The sudden necessity of facing a great many smilingly curious guests forced her to exert her self-control, but she managed.

Phoebe wasn't at all certain how she got through the rest of the evening. It took every ounce of willpower and stamina she possessed. She would never afterward be able to say exactly what she discussed that night, but no one seemed to have any inkling of what she was going through. She was accepted graciously into the Garand social world and Florence Garand beamed as if a great triumph had been accomplished.

"Phoebe, you were marvelous!" Flo enthused after everyone, including Steve, had left. "Mr. Cornwall and Hugh Ripley both made a point of telling me you have a real head on your shoulders! They said you were going to be a fine asset to the Garand family. And Bertha Hargate said she thought you were the most charming creature she's met in a long time.

413

I'm telling you I received nothing but praise all evening long. So did Harlan! I kept hearing the men say how lucky he was!''

"Did anyone get Cynthia Prescott's opinion?" Phoebe asked sadly, watching Harlan come toward them from seeing off the final departure.

"That woman? I didn't even invite her!" Flo said in surprise.

"She was here. I threw her into the fish pond," Phoebe stated. Better get the whole truth out in the open.

Florence stared at her for a second and then burst out laughing. "I couldn't have greeted her better myself! The fish pond is exactly where she belonged!"

"Regardless of your opinions on the woman, I won't have Phoebe making a practice out of assaulting anyone she happens to take a dislike to!" Harlan announced determinedly.

"Don't worry, I won't bother any more of your old friends!" Phoebe got out. "You can spend as much time disappearing into gardens with them as you want! Now, if you will both excuse me, I'm going to bed! Good night, Flo. Thank you for a very lovely party!" With a dignified flounce, Phoebe lifted her chin and moved toward the staircase.

"Phoebe, I'm not finished talking to you!" Harlan called warningly, but he was cut off by Flo's quiet comment which Phoebe couldn't hear.

Phoebe sailed up the staircase, down the hall, and into her room—only to collapse on the huge bed as soon as the door was safely shut behind her. Ferd chirped curiously from beneath his cage cover.

"Never mind, Ferd. It's a long story and I don't feel like going into it at the moment," she told him, depressed. What was she to do? Blindly, Phoebe stared down at the glowing emerald on her finger. She couldn't tolerate life with Harlan if he was going to humiliate her as he had this evening, Phoebe told herself resolutely. The way he had allowed that woman to . . . to curl herself over him! It was disgraceful! But, then, they were old friends, weren't they? How many other old friends did Harlan have hanging around? How many other women knew where he hid the key to his home? Face it, Phoebe girl, she lectured herself grimly. You've fallen in love with a man who's every woman's dream. And every woman was going to want him! How could she, Phoebe Hampton, hope to hold him in the face of serious competition?

Phoebe got slowly to her feet and began changing her clothes. She had her bag packed and Ferd ready to travel. She was waiting in the darkness of her room when Harlan's footsteps sounded outside her door. She held her breath, waiting to see if he would pause and knock or move on to his own room.

He hesitated. She could almost feel him lift a hand to knock and then he moved off determinedly down the hall. Phoebe sat waiting, rubbing the palms of her damp hands on the material of her jeans. She needed to get out of this house tonight. Needed to think. She would go back to her own apartment.

An hour passed and finally Phoebe decided it was safe to depart. Checking to make certain the note she had left for Flo was in place on the dresser, she opened the door carefully, having a little difficulty hanging onto Ferd's cage and the small suitcase at the same time. Soundlessly she moved out into the hall and began descending the stairs. A dark shape came forward to meet her as she stepped off the last stair tread.

"Quiet, Jinx! You'll wake everyone! That's a good dog. No, you can't say farewell to Ferd! Sit!" she hissed and was gratified as the well-trained animal obediently sat, ears cocked alertly as she hurried toward the front door. An instant later she was outside in the cool night air. It was going to be a nippy walk down the hill, Phoebe decided, thinking she would dig the sweater out of the suitcase as soon as she was out of sight of the house.

She started walking. At least it was downhill, she told herself with a small attempt at humor. She seemed to spend a lot of time hiking these days—surprising since she had never considered herself particularly athletic!

A car or two trundled by. Phoebe stepped into the bushes when they did so, not wanting to have to deal with offers of

Jayne Taylor

a ride from strangers. Several minutes passed and then another car's engine growled behind her. Clutching Ferd's cage carefully, she eyed the terrain at the side of the road, preparing to step behind a convenient tree or hedge. But this car was traveling awfully fast . . .

Before she could find suitable shelter the vehicle roared into sight around a curve in the road. Harlan's Jaguar! The brilliant headlights fell directly on her as she stood helplessly holding the cage and her bag. Then the car was brought to a screeching halt beside her, pebbles spitting evilly out from under the tires. Instantly the driver's door slammed and Harlan was out of the car and moving toward her. She had time only to grasp that he had dressed rather hurriedly in jeans and a familiar looking workshirt and then he was on her, all outraged male.

"Where the hell do you think you're going at this time of night?" he bit out furiously, grabbing the bag out of her unresisting hand and yanking Phoebe toward him. The commotion set Ferd to grumbling as he struggled to keep his perch inside the cage. Life had been difficult for him lately.

"I'm going home! I want to do some thinking, Harlan!"

"You're home when you're with me! Haven't you learned that yet? Get in the car! I'll take you *home*!" he snarled.

"I want to go back to my own apartment!" Phoebe protested, struggling uselessly against his painful grip. "Not to your aunt's place!"

"I told you I would take you home, Phoebe, not to Aunt Flo's. It's about time we celebrated our engagement properly! I've finally learned my lesson, woman! I should have known better than to let you talk me out of making love to you Saturday night. But to compound the error by letting you talk me into this ridiculous courtship was inexcusable! Tonight you won't begin to have enough words to talk yourself out of where you belong! In my bed!"

Chapter Nine

Harlan was right about one thing, Phoebe thought wryly as she sat huddled in the corner of the car with Ferd's cage on her lap. She definitely did not have enough words tonight! Her few pitiful efforts at reasoning with him failed utterly as they collided with the atmosphere of stony determination which permeated the vehicle.

"How . . . how did you know I had left?" she tried finally.

"Jinx came to my door whining. When I got up to see what was wrong I found you were gone," Harlan responded shortly.

"That wretched dog! He just wants Ferd back!" Phoebe bit her lip in frustrated anger.

"He had the sense to know I'd want you back, too!" Harlan informed her coolly.

"Where are we going?" Phoebe demanded suddenly, realizing they had turned off the main road.

"Home. I told you."

"But this is the road to your house!" Phoebe muttered nervously.

"That's what I said. Home."

"Harlan, I'm not going to your place! I refuse! I thought you were taking me back to my apartment . . ."

"Shut up, Phoebe."

"You can't kidnap me like this! I won't stand for it!" she blazed.

"Calm down, honey. You're getting yourself all worked up . . ."

"You bet I am! I won't be taken to your home and *raped*!"

"You'd rather I raped you at your place?" He inquired laconically.

"No! I mean, I don't intend to let you . . ."

"You're not going to have anything to say in the matter except to tell me how much you love me!" he interrupted unfeelingly.

"Never!" she vowed between clenched teeth, wishing she dared throw open the car door and leap to freedom. But the Jag was moving too fast. She would only succeed in seriously hurting herself.

"Harlan, please! Can't we talk this over? This is a serious step and . . ."

"Talking with you has only made things more difficult," he told her as he swung the Jag into the drive and switched off the engine. "I'm going to try another technique tonight. Stop looking at me as if your world was coming to an end, for God's sake!" He opened his door with a violent movement and climbed out rapidly, coming around to her side of the car at once.

"Here, give me that bird." He reached into the car and plucked the cage off her lap. "Out you get, Phoebe."

Without a word, Phoebe stepped out of the car as if she were walking on eggs. Numbly she allowed herself to be led to the front door of Harlan's home and pushed gently inside.

"The bedroom is down that hall, Phoebe," he prodded as she came to a halt just over the threshold. Harlan set Ferd's cage down, ignoring the indignant chirp from within and turned to lock the door behind him.

"If you think I'm going to go meekly down that hall and

418

wait for you in bed, you've got another thought coming!'' Phoebe finally found the courage to snap, spinning to face him.

He secured the door and stepped toward her purposefully. Phoebe immediately moved backward in a futile gesture of self-defense. But he was much too swift and an instant later she was swung high into his arms.

''Put me down!'' she stormed, scrambling helplessly with her hands, trying to dislodge his grip. But the blue eyes flamed down on her and she recognized the desire burning there. It made her weak and stirred her own blood.

''Harlan . . .''

Not bothering to reply to the poignant note in her voice, he strode down the hall as if she were weightless, kicked open the door to his bedroom with one booted foot and carried her inside. Setting her on her feet, he pulled her into his arms and covered her shocked mouth with his own. His arms closed around her like steel bands, holding her firmly in place for his kiss.

''Don't fight me, sweetheart!'' he ground against her teeth. ''I know you want me, too. It's going to be all right, I swear it!'' His lips became gentle as she surrendered involuntarily to the power of his embrace. It wasn't fair, Phoebe thought wildly. She shouldn't allow him so much control, so much dominance over her emotions! She struggled for words, words which had kept him from making love to her fully on previous occasions, but even as she tried to think, Phoebe knew it would be hopeless. He was in a new and different mood this time. Unswervable, determined, driven by a thirst for her which she could feel in the pounding of his heart and the fierceness of his hold.

His very need of her was seductive. Phoebe felt a totally feminine response that knew no logic, only a desire to satisfy his hunger for her. Dimly she felt her arms move up to encircle his neck and his strong hands instantly took advantage of her unprotected breasts, moving around to cup them, stroke them, claim them.

''My woman,'' Harlan breathed. ''My Phoebe.'' His fingers

went to work on the buttons of her shirt, halting now and then as they progressed downward to touch and smooth the skin of her upper breasts and then of her waist.

"Harlan!" she breathed. "Please be sure! Oh, please, please be sure! I couldn't stand it if you changed your mind in the morning!"

"Change my mind! When all I've been able to think about all week is how much I want you? I don't think I could ever get my fill of you! So soft and so womanly . . ." His words were lost as he buried his face in the thickness of her shining hair, found the tip of an ear, and then trailed down her throat in a slow, sensuous movement which made Phoebe shiver in expectation.

Phoebe felt herself lifted once more and settled gently in the middle of the bed. She watched him, sea eyes glowing with her love as he peeled off his shirt and stepped out of the jeans. Then the lean, hard body was beside her and he was reaching out to anchor her closely against the length of him.

Outside the massed windows and far down the hill the lights of Portland gleamed. In the moonlit room Phoebe looked up into Harlan's tense face and automatically lifted a hand to smooth the lines around his mouth.

"Phoebe?" he whispered, capturing her fingers in a tight hold and pressing them against his cheek. "You do love me, don't you? I want to hear you say it. I know it, but I want to hear it!"

"How do you know it, Harlan Garand?" She smiled gently. "What makes you so very sure?"

His grin flashed briefly in the dark and he hugged her closer. "Because you're so strong, honey. Much too strong to ever let yourself be bullied by a man if you didn't love him!"

"You admit it!" she groaned. "You admit you've been running me ragged? Ordering me about, telling me I'm going to marry you regardless of how I felt about it? Of all the nerve!"

"You deserved it. You turned my whole world upside down and now I'm going to do the same to yours!" He removed the tortoiseshell glasses, setting them on a stand beside the wide bed and then slowly and deliberately unfastened her bra, letting the fullness of her tumble into his hand.

Harlan lowered his mouth to the tips of her breasts, tugging gently at the nipples until they hardened in desire. His hand slid into the valley of her waist and up the curve of her hip. Then his fingers slid inside the waistband of her jeans and moved down to the clasp.

Phoebe moaned as he slipped off the remainder of her clothing, leaving her naked in his arms. Slowly, insistently, lingeringly his fingers stroked her smooth skin from her breasts to the dampening, secret place between her thighs until at last her legs parted for him.

"Tell me how you want me, Phoebe," he muttered huskily. "Tell me that you love me!"

"You said you knew," she protested in a small whimper, some small part of her mind unwilling to make the final surrender.

"Tell me!" he growled, his fingers tracing circles along the exquisitely sensitive skin of her inner thigh.

Phoebe gasped and buried her face in the hardness of his shoulder. She knew then that Harlan wouldn't take her unless she told him she wanted him. As aroused as he was tonight, there would be no rape. Just as she had known there was no brutality in him that first night. She could stop him now if she wished. All she had to say was no and mean it.

"I love you, Harlan. I want to belong to you completely!" The words were whispered into the sleek muscle of his shoulder and she felt it tense in response.

"You will, Phoebe," he swore. "You will!"

She felt him move, lifting himself, turning her so that she was beneath him, and then lowering the full weight of his body on her. The hard muscles of his thighs found a place between the satiny smoothness of her legs, making Phoebe feel deliciously defenseless. She wrapped eager arms around his chest, clasping him to her with an urgency that made him groan aloud his male need. Delighted with this response, she began to work her fingers down the length of his back. His breath came more quickly and she felt a tremor go through him.

"Come to me, Phoebe," he husked. "Give yourself to me, my darling."

"Yes, Harlan. I'm yours!" she responded in a tiny, quivering voice.

Suddenly his hardness was pressing fiercely between her legs, demanding admittance to the sweet, dark, hot place inside her and she could no more have denied him than she could have forbidden the earth to turn. She belonged to him and knew it completely, in every part of her, as he took her with the full force of his passion.

"I love you," she breathed as he forced her to move with him, respond to him fully.

"Phoebe, my darling, my own sweet darling!" His hands held her so tightly as if afraid even in that moment of total possession she would flee him.

Phoebe's desire flared to meet his and together they ascended the heights, hovered in an enchanted realm, and then leaped into space, finding for an instant the white heat of a sun before tumbling slowly, slowly back to earth.

For a long time after their descent, Harlan remained where he was, covering her soft, rounded body with his. He held her tightly, his lips pressed against the hollow of her shoulder. Gradually he seemed to regain his breath and his heart slowed to its normal strong, steady beat.

"You must promise me that you'll never, ever run from me again, Phoebe," he ordered heavily.

Phoebe smiled, gazing up at the beamed ceiling and feeling incredibly lighthearted.

"Oh, I don't know if I want to promise anything so rash, Harlan. Look where running away got me this time!"

"Phoebe!" There was no humor in his voice and she realized hers had been misplaced. He was in no mood for jokes, it appeared. Instantly she sobered.

"Yes, Harlan," she murmured obediently. "I swear I won't ever run away again."

"My God, woman! Don't let me ever hear you joke about it! Do you know how I suffered tonight when I found that damn note on your dresser? I could cheerfully have throttled you!"

"Instead you made love to me! Much more pleasant!" she smiled dreamily up at him as he raised his head to meet her eyes.

"When I saw you standing beside the road, holding that bird cage in one hand and the suitcase in the other, and looking so forlorn, I didn't know whether to read you the riot act or hold you in my arms and let you cry."

"So you chose to yell at me!"

"I did not yell at you! I thought I was very restrained, under the circumstances!"

"You call threatening to rape me being restrained?" she chuckled, kneading the column of his neck with the tips of her fingers.

His mouth softened and the corners lifted slightly. "I only knew I had to have you. After you pushed Cynthia into the fish pond and I realized for certain that you loved me, I could hardly wait for the party to be over. I fully intended to come to your room tonight and make you tell me what you felt for me."

"You were going to make love to me right there in your aunt's house?" Phoebe exclaimed, shocked.

"I know, I know, that's not the way things are done in Portland. But, yes, I intended to do exactly that! Then you took yourself so grandly up the staircase I decided to wait until you were in a better mood!"

"If you hadn't spent so much time bawling me out for pushing Cynthia in the pond I would never have gotten into a bad mood! What did you mean you realized for certain that I loved you after that . . . that incident?" Phoebe demanded.

"I know you too well, little one. You had to be in the grip of a raging jealousy to do something that outlandish!"

"I was not jealous!" Phoebe protested proudly. "It's just

that she was altogether wrong for you and I didn't want her hanging around!''

''Wrong for me? And what's right for me, sweetheart?'' he teased.

''You need someone who will be a good mother for your heirs, someone who has a head for business so you can discuss your work intelligently with her, someone who can cook . . .''

''And someone who fits me perfectly in bed? I agree. Couldn't have phrased it better myself!'' Harlan slipped off her, nestling her against him and leaning over to drop a husbandly kiss on her forehead. ''My wonderfully cuddly Phoebe! You're going to make nights up at the cabin much more enjoyable than they used to be!''

''Harlan,'' she began cautiously. ''You don't think I'm, well, too *rounded*, do you? I mean, for you I would even diet!''

''Don't you dare,'' he chuckled. ''I'll tell you if you start getting too plump! You're beautifully shaped, Phoebe, my dear. Nice, full curves a man can feel moving against him when you're caught up in passion! I always knew there was something missing with those skinny, scrawny blonds!''

Phoebe giggled sleepily.

''How about you, Phoebe?'' Harlan went on thoughtfully. ''Ready to abandon the tall, dark, and handsome types forever?''

''It's strange but I never realized how attractive red-headed, blue-eyed, masterful types were before! I'm a convert, believe me!''

''Good. Now go to sleep, Phoebe, my love. You can cook me breakfast in the morning,'' he told her with satisfaction.

''Wait a minute! What about your aunt! When she wakes up and finds us gone, she'll worry.'' Phoebe roused herself abruptly with thoughts of Aunt Flo searching madly through the house for them.

''No, she won't. I woke her up and told her I was off to find you,'' Harlan informed her, stifling a yawn. ''I let her know we wouldn't be back tonight.''

"Harlan! What will she think!"

"That we're celebrating our engagement. What else?"

The sound of rain woke Phoebe the next morning. She snuggled closer to Harlan's warmth and remembered the way he had awakened her again and again during the night as if his passion for her could only be temporarily satisfied. He had brought her to a wonderful new awareness of the power of her own body, she thought with pure, female delight. He seemed captivated by her, delighting in her response to him as if she made him experience his own maleness to the full. She loved him and he obviously wanted her. She would have his children, yell at him occasionally, cook for him, love him, and once in a great while condescend to clean his fish. Soon he would tell her how much he loved her!

"What are you thinking, honey, lying there like a tabby cat?" Harlan inquired lazily, coming awake to run his hand down her spine.

Phoebe stretched contentedly beneath the caress. "I was thinking how typical."

"What's typical?"

"It's raining, of course. Typical of Oregon."

"I've explained it's just a myth . . ."

"Take a look outside the window!" she mocked.

"Strange, I can't bring myself to look at anything except you!" Harlan laughed and hauled her close.

"I thought you wanted me to cook your breakfast!"

"When I'm hungry for food, I'll let you know. Right now I'm hungering for something else!"

Breakfast eventually got cooked. Phoebe, feeling great after a morning shower, found the kitchen a cook's dream.

"If I didn't know better, I'd say you had it built just for me," she told Harlan, setting a stack of feather hot cakes in front of him.

"Maybe I did," he smiled. "I built this place with the idea of making it a home, not a bachelor pad. That means that somewhere in the back of my mind was the idea of finding a wife, not a mistress. That reminds me," he added, setting down the morning paper to drop great chunks of butter on the hot cakes, "I'd better see about making arrangements for the wedding. I don't want you getting any ideas about enjoying the easy life of a kept woman!"

"Does that mean I get to go back to my own apartment for the remainder of my courtship?" Phoebe paused, "Which reminds me . . ."

"I know, I know. You didn't get your yellow roses this morning! I was wondering when you were going to remember."

"I knew once I let you have your way with me, my lovely courtship would come to an end!" Phoebe muttered, reaching into Ferd's cage to unclip his water dish.

"*I* knew that as soon as I had my wicked way with you, I could relax and start enjoying the good life of a pampered husband!" he grinned, watching as she filled the dish and replaced it in the cage. Ferd appeared to be content, for the moment. He mumbled occasionally to himself but other than that made no move to interfere in the conversation.

"About your apartment, Phoebe," he began in a more serious tone, munching thoughtfully on a bite of hot cake.

"Yes?" she asked idly, sitting down to eat her own breakfast.

"You'd better let Mrs. Morrison or whatever her name is know that you're moving out as of today."

"Today? But Harlan! We're not married yet and I have so much stuff to pack . . ."

"We'll be married as soon as I can get it arranged. In the meantime, I want you here with me."

"I don't know . . ." she temporized. "I'd be more comfortable in my own place until we really are married and it's awkward being a full-time houseguest at your aunt's . . ."

"You'll move in with me as of tonight," he stated firmly.

"Harlan," she began, equally firmly, confronting him across the breakfast table. "I would prefer to stay in my own place!"

"You'll do as I say, Phoebe. That kidnapper is still at large and I'm not having you in that apartment alone. That's final.''

He surged to his feet and stretched out a hand to yank her up beside him.

"But, Harlan!" Phoebe began in a broken protest that was cut off by his ruthless mouth.

"You taste of honey and butter," he told her. "I'm going to take you back to bed and taste every inch of your soft body. And you're going to tell me over and over again how much you love me. You won't be able to help yourself!" He scooped her into his arms and carried her down the hall to the bedroom.

Chapter Ten

Harlan at her side, Phoebe turned in her notice to Mrs. Morrison that afternoon.

"It will take me a few days to clear everything out," she explained quickly as her landlady eyed Harlan interestedly. Harlan returned the look with a wickedly bland one of his own.

"Moving in with him are you?" Mrs. Morrison demanded, waving a paint brush in Harlan's direction. "Don't blame you. Would have done the same thing myself!"

"We're going to be married, Mrs. Morrison," Phoebe said with great dignity, holding up her engagement ring. The emerald flashed in the sunlight. The morning rain had obligingly ceased around noon.

"I knew it all along. Knew it the day he brought you home," Mrs. Morrison nodded craftily, reminding Phoebe rather forcibly of Ferd in his more self-important moments. "Then when he up and took you off to stay with his aunt I realized it would only be a matter of time before he figured out a way to get you under his own roof!"

"You were so right, Mrs. Morrison," Harlan confirmed cheerfully. "Phoebe took a bit of coaxing, but she's finally realized what she wants!" He slanted a shark grin in Phoebe's direction, a grin which widened as the flush deepened in her face.

"You take good care of her, young man!" Mrs. Morrison admonished firmly. "For all her airs of being a modern young businesswoman, she's still very much a woman!"

"I'm not likely to forget it," Harlan promised. "Or let her forget it!"

"Harlan, I have a great deal of packing to do!" Phoebe interrupted the embarrassing discussion desperately. "It's getting late and your aunt is expecting us for dinner. We're due to see my brother off in a couple of hours . . ."

"I'm coming, honey. Just wanted to reassure Mrs. Morrison here, you know . . ." With a deep chuckle he followed her firm little back toward the elevator.

Phoebe selected a car full of items that afternoon, sighing as she took a last look around the apartment.

"There's still so much stuff in here! We'll never be able to move it with just the Jag. What shall I do with all this furniture?"

"You could have a yard sale," Harlan suggested. "But save the fan chair. I've grown rather fond of it."

They carted boxes and clothes into Harlan's house until it was time to leave for Aunt Flo's. Harlan had obligingly and with a great show of enthusiasm emptied out several drawers, cleared a space in the closet, and given her a bath to herself.

"We'll shower together naturally, but you can keep the rest of your female things in here," he told her, throwing open a door to reveal a plushly carpeted and mirrored room. Phoebe ignored his comment on showering and glanced around with pleasure.

"You're quite sure you didn't build this place as a bachelor pad? You really intended all this for a mere wife?" she queried innocently.

"A properly gilded cage," Harlan smiled, but the look in

his eyes was suddenly intense and Phoebe found herself feeling flustered.

"I suppose we ought to get ready to go to your aunt's," she suggested quickly, turning to move back into the bedroom.

"I suppose so."

Flo greeted them at the door, Jinx at her heels, with a look of such pleasure that Phoebe, who had been somewhat nervous over the encounter, relaxed immediately. She had been rather relieved when her brother had announced that as long as he was in the vicinity, he was taking a flight up to Seattle to settle some business with an aerospace firm. He had left on the special hotel bus to the airport that afternoon, promising to be back for the wedding. Phoebe was saved the difficulty of explaining her move in with Harlan. True, it was a modern age but brothers still tended to behave like brothers!

"Something tells me this is going to be one of history's shorter engagements!" Flo laughed, bending forward to kiss Phoebe lightly on the cheek. "Have you set the date, Harlan?"

"I'll make a few calls tomorrow, but I think Wednesday will work out fine. Steve says he'll be back by then," he answered complacently.

"Wednesday!" Phoebe squeaked involuntarily.

"Any problems with Wednesday?" Harlan asked smoothly, flicking an amused glance over her.

"No. No, I guess not," she smiled tremulously.

"Enjoy the sensation of being rushed off your feet, Phoebe," Flo advised wisely. "I'm certainly getting a kick out of watching it happen! I consider it one of my greater accomplishments in life that Harlan turned out exactly like one of the heroes in a romantic novel!"

"Except for the red hair and blue eyes," Phoebe pointed out smugly.

"Which only makes the achievement all the greater! Look at the handicap I was working with!" Flo laughed and led the way toward the living room. "Come along, Harlan, you can pour me a drink."

"Yes, ma'am," he agreed with mock obedience, leaving Phoebe to follow with Jinx.

"As for you, you idiot dog," she hissed, glaring down at the tail-wagging animal. "Don't try to kid me that what you did last night was for my own good! I know it's Ferd you're after!"

Jinx whined his innocence, dark eyes gazing up at her pleadingly. With a wry chuckle, Phoebe reached down and stroked his silky ears. "Why is it I don't seem to be able to hold my own around you and your master?" she groaned.

Harlan insisted on leaving relatively early, claiming he and Phoebe both had to get to work the next morning. Phoebe shook her head sadly at the door, turning to say good night to her hostess.

"You see how things have changed already, Flo? No more late nights dancing, no more yellow roses in the morning . . ."

"Nag, nag, nag," Harlan grumbled. "Come on, Phoebe. You, too, Jinx. It's time you went home. I'm sure Ferd missed your company." He bundled dog and woman into the Jag, leaning down to drop a quick kiss on Phoebe's nose before he shut the door. "Good night, Flo," he called. "I'll let you know the exact time of the wedding when I get everything settled tomorrow. Probably be around noon."

Jinx stood in the backseat of the Jaguar on the ride home, hanging his head over the front between Harlan and Phoebe.

"Are we going to take Jinx and Ferd with us on the honeymoon?" Phoebe asked laughingly as she scratched the dog's ears.

"That depends on where we go, I imagine. Can you leave the company early?"

"You mean, before Friday? I expect so. I've got everything in pretty good shape and it looks like the woman who has been my assistant will get my job, so the daily routine should flow fairly smoothly," Phoebe said thoughtfully. "Yes, I could leave on Wednesday. Can you?"

"I told you, one of the advantages of owning your own firm is getting to do what you want!"

"I'm impressed! Maybe I should look into setting up my own business when we return from the honeymoon instead of simply looking for another job!" Phoebe smiled.

"You want to return to work?" Harlan asked a bit distantly.

"Oh, yes!"

"Well, we can talk about it on the honeymoon. Where would you like to go?" Harlan swung the car into the drive and shut off the engine with a swift, easy motion. Phoebe climbed out, not waiting for him to open her door.

Jinx bounded over the seat and onto the gravel beside Phoebe.

"Anywhere I don't have to clean fish will be fine with me!" she told Harlan firmly.

"And here I was thinking I could work in another fishing trip this week!" he groaned, turning the key in the lock and opening the door to let Phoebe enter ahead of him.

Phoebe was on the verge of letting him know what she thought of the idea when the glint of moonlight on metal a few feet inside the darkened hall made her freeze. In the same instant Jinx growled a warning, sounding uncertain about dealing with a stranger who had already made himself at home in the house.

"Keep that damn dog under control or I'll kill him. I swear I'll kill him!" snarled a voice Phoebe recognized with a plunging sense of despair. The voice sounded vastly more dangerous than it had on Friday night because of the fear imbedded in it tonight. A scared man was an irrational man.

"Jinx! Down!" Harlan's voice was deadly quiet. The dog subsided alertly at his master's feet.

"The mysterious Max, I presume," Harlan continued calmly, moving unobtrusively to a point beside Phoebe and a fraction of an inch in front.

"Stand right where you are!" the slender, ugly man dressed in a black tee shirt and dark pants snapped, swinging the barrel of an equally ugly gun around wildly.

"We thought you'd be in another state by now," she whispered, sensing the tension in the man and dog beside her. Like a board meeting, she told herself crazily. Everyone so tense you could feel it! You had to get people talking. It was the only way to ease the atmosphere!

"I couldn't leave with you running around loose, now could I?" Max demanded in a high-pitched voice. "You had to be a fool and go to the cops! And we hadn't even done anything!"

"Not done anything!" Phoebe gasped in amazement.

"We just wanted to have a little fun," Max whined, sounding aggrieved. "But you spoiled everything! Threw that boiling water on Frank and then running away like that! I got to thinking about it later. I realized that with my brother in jail . . ."

"Your brother!" Phoebe interrupted again, surprised.

"Oh, yes, you bitch, I know you had him arrested! He, poor fool, had to have his revenge and look what it got him! But I won't be so dumb!" Max announced proudly. "No, I'm going to get even with you for what you did to him and cover myself at the same time!"

"It was you who left Phoebe's window open Monday night?" Harlan asked almost gently. "You must have taken the truck and fled for a time before you decided to come back for Phoebe . . ."

"I finally found the bitch from the address in her purse," Max explained impatiently, sounding more nervous by the second. He'd probably never done anything quite this dramatic before and was trying to work himself up to it. "But she was gone when I went to get her that night. When I came back later she still wasn't there. I didn't find out until the two of you showed up this afternoon that she'd moved in with you! I was beginning to think I'd wasted my time keeping an eye on the apartment house!"

Max suddenly reached out and grabbed Phoebe against him, locking an arm around her throat and motioning Harlan back with the gun. "Come on, both of you. I want to get this over with . . ."

"What are you planning? A short drive up into the hills?"

433

Harlan inquired coolly. "The police will find out, you know. They're tracing your brother's background now. Sooner or later they'll start wondering about you. You'd be better off taking your chances by leaving the country. Phoebe and I will give you twenty-four hours before going to the police. Time enough to catch a plane to South America . . ."

"Oh, no you don't! I wouldn't trust you for a second. You took Frank right to the cops, didn't you?" Max pointed out with totally valid logic. He began edging Phoebe toward the door.

Phoebe's whole focus of attention now was on Harlan. Harlan who was as taut as a coiled spring. She knew he was and yet he looked as if being threatened with murder was an everyday event! His eyes were on hers, she could feel him willing her to read his mind. Her feet dragged as Max pushed and prodded her in an arc around Harlan and Jinx toward the door.

In the dimly lit room Phoebe struggled desperately to understand the message from Harlan's brilliant eyes. He flicked a quick glance down to the gun in Max's hand and back and then she knew. She was going to have to do something, anything to throw her attacker off guard for a crucial second. She was the only one close enough to act! Deliberately she let her body go slightly limp. Not enough to make the man think she was actively resisting, only that she was terrified and finding it hard to move. Which wasn't far from the truth, Phoebe thought grimly.

"Here, you! Stop stalling! We've got a lot to do tonight!" Max's voice carried impatience. He was in the process of deciding how to angle both of them through the partially opened door and still keep an eye on Harlan. When he dragged her over the threshold she would have a small chance . . .

Max's body shifted a fraction. His arm at her throat didn't budge but he was having to move down a step with Phoebe held against him. It was now or never, she decided, and with every ounce of the muscled and non-muscled roundness she possessed she threw herself backward against him.

There was a shout as Max felt himself toppling backward

with Phoebe on top. She felt a blazing pain at the side of her head as his gun swept against her temple. But it was an automatic effort to regain his balance that brought Max's arm with the gun in its fist toward her head. The weapon discharged near her ear, deafening Phoebe but the bullet flashed away harmlessly, unaimed.

Phoebe was vaguely aware of Jinx's sleek black body hurtling past her, toward Max's throat as she rolled painfully to one side. A split second later, Harlan was joining the fray and in a matter of moments it was all over.

Dazedly, Phoebe struggled to a sitting position, one hand going to the side of her head instinctively to see if there was any blood. He must have caught her with the grip of the pistol, she decided blearily. Didn't that usually knock a person unconscious? Certainly it did in all the books she had read. Eyes burning, she watched the world spin, saw Harlan climb to his feet beside the still body of Max, and realized he was speaking to her. Phoebe tried a small smile, thinking how tall he seemed in the moonlight, towering over her as she sat there on the ground. Would she throw up first from the nausea or faint from the pain? It was going to be close . . .

Phoebe fainted at Harlan's feet in the best romantic tradition.

When Phoebe awakened her first impression was that it had snowed. But it was almost summer! Rain at this time of the year in Portland, yes. Snow never! It took a few minutes before the unrelieved vista of white resolved into hangings, walls, cabinets, and bustling figures. Even they were dressed in white, Phoebe realized . . . a hospital emergency room.

"Harlan?" she whispered, turning her head gingerly. But there was no blinding slash of pain at the movement. Only a dull ache.

"What the hell do you mean, she's all right! How can she be all right when she's unconscious?" Harlan's raging voice could be heard above the clatter and the sound of an incoming ambulance. "Why don't you do something!"

"Harlan?" Phoebe said in a more normal tone. "Stop yell-

ing at the poor man, for heaven's sake! I'm okay.'' She finally
spotted him as he turned a startled face in her direction and
then he was covering the space between them in long strides.

"Phoebe! Oh, my God! I've been so worried! I didn't know
what had happened to you! All of a sudden you were just
lying there so still and I felt so damn helpless! Don't ever,
ever do that to me again! Do you understand? Promise me!''

"Yes, Harlan," Phoebe said demurely, trying hard not to
laugh at the intensity of his orders. "Whatever you say.''

"Oh, sweetheart,'' he reached down to place the rough
palms of his hands on either side of her face, the harshness of
his voice fading into a husky broken sound. "I love you so
much. Please, tell me again that you're truly all right!''

"I'm fine, darling,'' Phoebe smiled up at him, catching hold
of his wrist and tugging his hand toward her lips so that she
could kiss it gently. "I'm just fine.''

Wednesday afternoon, following a simple ceremony, Harlan
stuffed Phoebe into the jeep alongside Jinx. He dragged Ferd's
cage off the back, handed it to his aunt and the box of seed
to Steve Hampton, and then loped around to climb into the
driver's side of the vehicle.

"You two enjoy yourselves and don't worry about Ferd the
Bird! He and I get along very well together! And I've got
several days' worth of sightseeing lined up for Steve here,
along with some charming young ladies I know!''

Harlan groaned beside Phoebe. "Poor man. Be very careful,
pal, I've met some of those 'charming young ladies.' You'll
find yourself in the same boat I'm in, if you're not cautious!''

"Sorry about the fix you've gotten yourself into?'' Steve
grinned.

"Nope. But I'm a firm believer in finding my own women.
Don't let Flo coerce you!''

"Fee, fie, fo fum . . .'' interrupted Ferd in a threatening
tone, his beady eye on Jinx who stared back balefully from
the rear of the jeep.

"It will be good for Jinx to get some rest from this creature,'' Flo remarked, chuckling down at the bird. "He's got

that dog buffaloed!'' Harlan twisted the key in the ignition and with a last wave at his aunt and Steve wheeled the jeep out of the drive and onto the main road.

''Jinx may need some rest,'' he informed Phoebe with a flashing grin, ''but I hope you've already had all the relaxation you need! I'm intending to enjoy my first and only honeymoon to the fullest extent!''

Phoebe flushed and laughed happily. ''Just because you haven't been able to lay a hand on me since Max clobbered my poor head . . .''

''That doctor and his instructions to let you rest!'' Harlan grumbled good-humoredly. ''Talk about trying a man's patience!''

''You made an excellent nurse,'' she assured him, reaching over to pat Jinx affectionately.

''Right down to the chicken soup. Even if it was out of a can! When I think of how many times you climbed those stairs at your aunt's . . .''

''Believe me, I would much rather have been taking care of you in our own home but Flo made such a production out of having you stay with her where she could keep an eye on you and then there was your brother . . .''

''I didn't think Steve was going to be wholeheartedly in favor of having me move in with you before the wedding!'' Phoebe smiled.

''That wasn't the problem,'' Harlan told her.

''No?''

''No, I explained our relationship . . .''

''Good heavens! And Steve didn't belt you one?'' Phoebe asked in disbelief.

''Of course not. He merely explained that if I didn't show up for the wedding on Wednesday, I might as well never show my face around Portland again!'' Harlan explained with a ready grin. ''As I was saying, Steve thought you'd be better off at Aunt Flo's too with a woman to keep tabs on you. As I was clearly outvoted I decided it was easier to climb stairs!'' He laughed and then glanced across at her, the expression on his lean features sobering for a moment. "I love you so much, little Phoebe. Believe me?"

"Yes. I'm not sure it would matter anyway. I love you enough for both of us." Phoebe smiled at him.

"I could kick myself for not telling you how I really felt the night I made love to you. But I swore that when I found you that evening I'd make you realize that you were mine. I was selfish enough and . . ."

"Egotistical enough?" she suggested with a tiny grin.

"And egotistical enough to want to hear you tell me you loved me and that you were mine before I let you know how I felt about you. I guess it was because of something you said at the cabin that first time . . ."

"About wanting a man to be head over heels in love first?"

"Yes. I wanted you to want me with no reservations. Even without the assurance that I loved you!" Harlan gave a small exclamation of self-disgust. "Forgive me, sweetheart?"

"This is my wedding day. I'd forgive you just about anything! And I do love you, darling." Phoebe felt the happiness rise inside her. "I could almost bring myself to forgive those two creeps who picked me up on the road that Friday night!"

"Don't get carried away! Besides, even if you decided not to press charges, the police have enough on them to keep them out of our hair for quite a while. A real pair of bunglers and social misfits if ever there was one!"

"Harlan," Phoebe smiled softly, the teasing gone now from her voice. "I don't really want to manipulate and control you. Do you believe me? Do you trust me?"

"I love you, Phoebe. I'll love you and trust you for the rest of my life," he said, his tone becoming serious to match hers. "Whatever one of us does for the other will be from love, not as a result of manipulation. Agreed?"

"How about cleaning fish?" Phoebe hedged, sea eyes sparkling.

"Well, of course, that's another matter entirely . . ."

Futuristic Romance

Star-Crossed

Saranne Dawson

Bestselling Author Of *Crystal Enchantment*

Rowena is a master artisan, a weaver of enchanted tapestries that whisper of past glories. Yet not even magic can help her foresee that she will be sent to assassinate an enemy leader. Her duty is clear—until the seductive beauty falls under the spell of the man she must kill.

His reputation says that he is a warmongering barbarian. But Zachary MacTavesh prefers conquering damsels' hearts over pillaging fallen cities. One look at Rowena tells him to gird his loins and prepare for the battle of his life. And if he has his way, his stunningly passionate rival will reign victorious as the mistress of his heart.

_51982-8 $4.99 US/$5.99 CAN

Dorchester Publishing Co., Inc.
65 Commerce Road
Stamford, CT 06902

Please add $1.75 for shipping and handling for the first book and $.50 for each book thereafter. NY, NYC, PA and CT residents, please add appropriate sales tax. No cash, stamps, or C.O.D.s. All orders shipped within 6 weeks via postal service book rate. Canadian orders require $2.00 extra postage and must be paid in U.S. dollars through a U.S. banking facility.

Name _____

Address _____

City _____ State _____ Zip _____

I have enclosed $_____in payment for the checked book(s).

Payment <u>must</u> accompany all orders.□ Please send a free catalog.

Futuristic Romance

WARRIOR Moon

MARILYN JORDAN

"A gripping tale of forbidden love and cunning betrayal!"

—Nancy Cane, Bestselling Author Of *Keeper Of The Rings*

Dedicated to upholding the ancient ways of her race, Phada is loath to mix with the men of her world—especially the hard-muscled brutes who protect her homeland. Yet despite her resolve, the young Keeper can't understand her burning attraction for virile and courageous Sarak. Although he is nothing more than a servant, he leaves her breathless with the stirrings of an emotion that can only be passion. But on a perilous quest to save her people from utter destruction, Phada must trust her very life to Sarak. And if she isn't careful, she'll find love, devotion, and ecstasy without end beneath a warrior moon.

_52083-4 $5.50 US/$7.50 CAN

WINTER ROSES

LYNDA TRENT

WRITING AS
DANIELLE TRENT

Bestselling Author Of More Than 10 Million Books In Print!

Although an antique-store owner and a skydiving football player have little hope of discovering a common bond, recently widowed Haley Roberts finds herself recklessly attracted to Pete Thatcher. But love proves logically impossible with a man whose perilous profession and fear-inspiring pastime strike terror into Haley's soul. Once before, Haley lost someone dear to sport and adventure. Does she dare put her heart at risk again?

_52075-3 $4.99 US/$6.99 CAN

LORI COPELAND

AUTHOR OF MORE THAN 6 MILLION BOOKS IN PRINT!
TWO COMPLETE ROMANCE NOVELS— IN ONE HEART-STOPPING VOLUME!

A Love Of Our Own. Abby King has plenty of advice when it comes to Lee MacNair's love life. Can she help it if Lee needs it? But soon the sizzling signals between them become impossible to ignore, and Lee seems to know exactly what he wants—Abby!
And in the same passion-filled volume...
Passion's Folly. Conservative Ellie Millstein knows it is a mistake to buy the luxury yacht with office heartthrob T.J. Templeton. It's strictly business, however, until Florida's sultry summer days lead to sweet seduction. Soon, Ellie and T.J. are headed for the rocks— unless true love can bail them out.

__52032-X $4.99 US/$5.99 CAN

When Lightning Strikes. Although Fritzi Taylor has always wanted a water bed, she never imagines that it will come equipped with someone to keep her warm! But she is swept away by rugged salesman Ryan Majors, who demands she seize the day and choose between love and the well-ordered life he thinks she's lived for too long.
And in the same breathtaking volume...
Tale Of Love. Hilary Brookfield's trip to North Carolina is supposed to be a time to mend her broken heart. But then she meets Garth Redmond and finds solace in his strong arms. Could this be the love of a lifetime she's been searching for?

__52040-0 $4.99 US/$5.99 CAN

Dorchester Publishing Co., Inc.
65 Commerce Road
Stamford, CT 06902

Please add $1.75 for shipping and handling for the first book and $.50 for each book thereafter. NY, NYC, PA and CT residents, please add appropriate sales tax. No cash, stamps, or C.O.D.s. All orders shipped within 6 weeks via postal service book rate. Canadian orders require $2.00 extra postage and must be paid in U.S. dollars through a U.S. banking facility.

Name _____
Address _____
City _____ State _____ Zip _____
I have enclosed $_____ in payment for the checked book(s).
Payment <u>must</u> accompany all orders.☐ Please send a free catalog.